A Tribe of Dragons and Dreamers

A Trial of Kingdoms Book 2

Sherry Leclerc

Ternias Publishing

Dedication

To my boys. Thank you for being my rocks and for sharing my love of story.

"I was just sleepwalking through my life, letting things happen, playing the part. But never really living, never really appreciating those around me.

Until you . . .You woke me up . . . With you, I've finally found my passion." -Dreyken

STERRENVAR
Northern Mountains
North
The Dark Lake
Darkwood
CF
NG
BF
Division Wood
EF
Fair Harbor
BF
GG
WG
Clearview
WF
EF
Sacred Forest
Fairwood
WF
Hope Bay
SG
DF
Dragonburn Mountains
Southwood

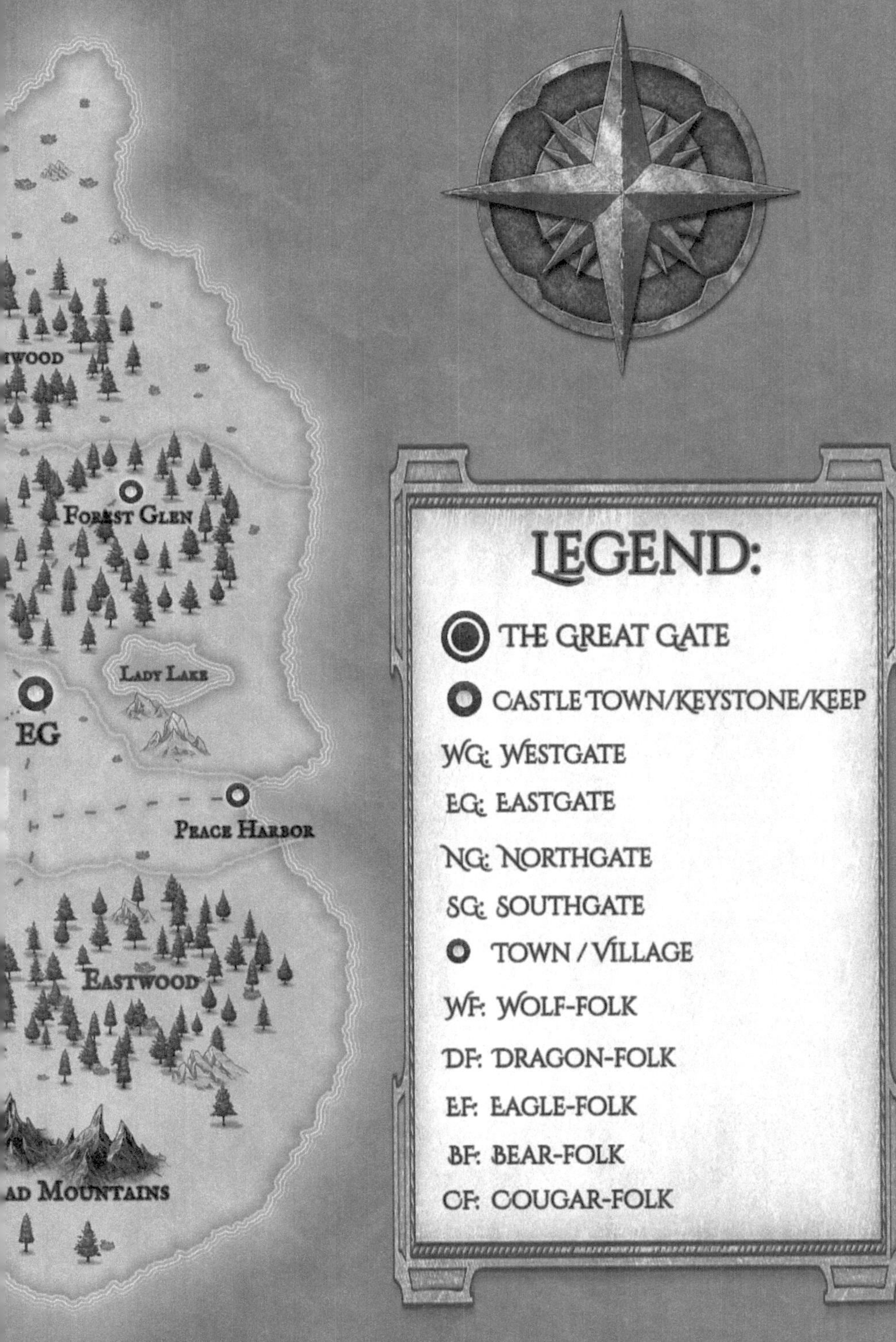

WOOD
FOREST GLEN
LADY LAKE
EG
PEACE HARBOR
EASTWOOD
AD MOUNTAINS

LEGEND:
THE GREAT GATE
CASTLE TOWN/KEYSTONE/KEEP
WG: WESTGATE
EG: EASTGATE
NG: NORTHGATE
SG: SOUTHGATE
TOWN / VILLAGE
WF: WOLF-FOLK
DF: DRAGON-FOLK
EF: EAGLE-FOLK
BF: BEAR-FOLK
CF: COUGAR-FOLK

Contents

CHAPTER ONE

Approach & Entry

Prolonged exposure to heat and sun while exerting yourself made for a long and miserable way to die.

Talwyn had been traveling on foot all day and the area between the Sacred Forest and the Dragonburn Mountains was bare wilderness. There was nothing to shield her from the sun that beat down mercilessly, getting hotter and more intense as the day wore on. Several hours after leaving the cover of the forest, the heat exhaustion and dehydration were making her dizzy and clumsy. She tripped over rocks and her feet slipped into pits in the ground where lichens, moss, and low, scrubby vegetation kept them hidden.

When she'd first left the shelter of the forest and saw the stretch of almost-bare land before her, she'd marveled at the terrain here. The landscape was peppered with hundreds of boulders of varying shapes and sizes that looked as if they didn't belong. How did they get here in such a random formation? It was as if they had been rained down from the sky, and there was a particular beauty in this wonder the Universe had created.

After many hours of traveling with no protection or water, it felt ironic that she'd thought this land lovely such a short time ago.

Raising her hand to her brow to shield her eyes from the blinding glare, she looked up at the landscape ahead of her. How much longer would she have to travel before she reached the Dragonburn Mountains? Would she even make it there? How long had it been since she last had food and water?

She couldn't give up, though. Her mission was too important and there was too much at stake. The fate of Southgate and, eventually, Sterrenvar, would be determined by her success or failure.

The future of the Stone Dragons themselves depended on her success, but the tricky part would be convincing them of that fact. Before she needed to worry about that, though, she needed to get to them first. Alive.

Talwyn was about a two hundred paces from the base of the tallest peak of the mountain range when she collapsed to the ground. She lay face down and motionless near the foot of the mountain for what felt like hours.

When the sun was going down and the air beginning to cool a little, she finally heard the whoosh of great wings descend upon her. She breathed out a sigh of relief. She had doubted they would come for her and, for a while there, she'd been convinced she would have to sneak in during the night.

The sound of the wingbeats drew nearer, and she felt the extra current in the air. It was gentle at first, then pressed down upon her more firmly as the dragon got closer. She could hear dirt and rocks scatter in the currents of air all around her.

Finally, without landing completely, the magnificent beast wrapped a clawed foot around her torso. Then she was weightless, her limbs hanging down, limp and lifeless, as they ascended into the air.

Dreyken carefully placed the woman facedown on the ground. It was tricky to release her from his curved talons while also not allowing her to drop hard upon the rocky ledge. Once she was secure, he quickly shifted back to human form so he could fit through the tunnels.

He looked down at the female, and the first thing he saw was the mass of red hair. He had noticed it when he went to collect her, but he hadn't really had time to get a good look. Now, as it covered her features and flowed down over her back to her waist, he could see it was the redder side of auburn. He'd never seen a such a shade before and quite liked the color.

Kneeling beside her, he cupped the back of her head, grabbed her at the hip, and rolled her toward him onto her back so she was face up. Her thick hair partially covered her face, so he brushed it away with a light touch, and when he did, his breath caught.

Though her features were not those typically considered beautiful by the males of his kind, he was immediately taken with her. She had a delicately proportioned and slightly upturned nose. Her lips were full and a deep pink color. Her cheekbones and chin were finely sculpted and flawless, the fair skin there spattered with freckles. As he let his gaze travel a little farther down, her vest enabled him to see that her shoulders were also freckled.

He shook his head. What in the Universe was wrong with him? How could these things be what caught his attention? He did not know who she was or what her purpose was in coming here, and she was lying on the ground, unconscious, after he'd just rescued her from death. He should be worried about her health, not about this sudden, unexpected attraction. How was it possible to be taken with someone so quickly?

"The mate-bond is very rare, but for those who have experienced it, they say it hit suddenly and powerfully, like being struck by lightning."

The memory of a snippet of conversation with his mother from many, many years ago came unbidden. He shook his head. He'd never believed in such things, of course. However, under the circumstances, that explanation was more palatable than the idea that he was some feral animal, barely able to control his urges.

Refocusing his attention on her health, he used the back of his hand to feel her forehead, cheeks, and neck. Her skin was hot and dry. This was not a good sign. It had cooled off some as the sun went down, but the nearest settlement was at least a day and a half away—depending on the people the traveler came from. That meant she had likely been walking in the sweltering heat for some time. And it had been unseasonably hot of late.

Luckily, they were currently at an altitude that made the air cooler and he'd laid her on the cool stone, so that should help.

Wanting to learn more about who and what she was, he let his eyes travel over her, searching for clues. She was clad in a leather vest that laced up the front and supple leather pants that laced up both sides. There were gaps in these garments where the sides did not quite come together, leaving a small amount of her pale skin visible to him through the leather laces. She also wore leather boots that came to just below her knees. She was lean and well-muscled.

Her clothing and fit form suggested she was a warrior. But she was not carrying any weapons that he could see. There were no packs or provisions near where he'd found her either. Why would someone travel all the way out here so poorly prepared?

She was also so tall that this stood out to him. To his knowledge, it was very rare for human women to be this tall.

But maybe she wasn't human at all.

A gust of wind blew through, sending the female's hair across her face again and raising gooseflesh on her exposed skin. This brought him back to his task, and bending to scoop her up, he carried her inside.

He cradled her close as he wandered through the corridors, carrying her to the section where they kept unwelcome visitors and those who broke their laws. It was far from the main area where his people lived and socialized, and this section went mostly unused since they rarely had visitors or lawbreakers. He laid her down on a stone ledge carved into the wall. It was covered in animal fur, and he hoped it would be comfortable enough for her.

He left her there for a few minutes while he went to fetch some supplies. When he returned, he placed a basin of water and a cloth on a ledge next to her. He also placed a cup of drinking water and a large piece of bread in the alcove above her bed, in case she was hungry or thirsty when she awoke.

He dunked the cloth into the water, then took it out again and squeezed out the excess. He placed the cool cloth on her forehead for a few moments before sweeping it gently down over her face. His primary goal was to cool her down, but this also removed the dust and grime, making her pale skin and freckles stand out even more. He continued wiping over her arms, hands, neck, and the exposed area of her chest, returning the cloth to the water from time to time to freshen it.

Dreyken leaned his face down close to hers, taking her in for a moment. Then he whispered, "I am sorry about this, but until I find out more about you, I cannot leave you free to wander through the tunnels. Good night and pleasant dreams."

Talwyn tried to fight the urge to peek at the male as he turned to leave, but she lost her internal battle. She lifted her lids slightly, just enough to glimpse him as he walked away. He was still nude after shifting, and she figured he probably thought there was no point in dressing quickly since she was 'unconscious.' He had thick, wavy, golden-blond hair that just touched his shoulders. It almost seemed to shimmer in the light of the few candles that lit the space. His shoulders and back were broad and well-muscled, and he had thick, muscular legs.

"Get ahold of yourself," she whispered to herself. "If he wasn't so attractive, you would have found his earlier behavior unnerving."

The male's coloring, build, and gait were familiar to her. It only took a moment for recognition to strike. She knew him from her dream-visions. This was the Dragon lord.

All the visions she'd had where she'd seen him came from others' perspectives, and never from anyone too close to him. This, coupled with the reactions they obviously had to one another, worried her. A lot. It meant they would become close one day unless she could do something to change that.

It would have been easier for her if he had been heartless and disgusting since she could never again allow herself to get close to someone in that way. As she had learned from experience, it left you vulnerable to having your heart and soul ripped apart. And she could not allow that to happen again.

Talwyn listened to the sound of the male's feet as he moved farther and farther away. When she could no longer hear him, she continued to lie still, taking in the muffled sounds, foreign smells, and the feel of the surrounding air. A seer's senses were second only to those of animal-folk. The air was damp and cool, but not uncomfortably so. It smelled a little dank but still clean and earthy. Listening carefully, she could hear sounds of life off in the distance. She could tell from the way the noise echoed that it was traveling down a tunnel from some distance away.

She continued to wait until the sounds of life died down, then she cracked her eyes open to look around her. As she took in the stone room, she noticed that the only furniture was carved out of large rocks. In the middle of the room, there was a bench. On the wall straight in from the door, which was made of thick metal bars, was another bed-sized alcove carved into the stone wall that also had furs laid on top. A thick, tall candle burned in an alcove chiseled into the rock on the other side of the room. Several smaller candles stood on various ledges that jutted out here and there along the cave walls.

Well, no need to worry about a prisoner lighting the place on fire, so why not have a candle or two?

She also noticed that both her bunk and the other one had smaller alcoves carved into the wall next to them. In her alcove, her host had left a cup of water and a piece of bread. She left these alone for the time being, however, not wanting to let her captor know she was awake just yet.

Talwyn sat up and threw her legs over the side of her bed, then she stood and tiptoed across the room and blew out all but one candle. Seers were not considered true Folk since they could only change their coloring, skin condition, and temperature, and their spirits weren't aligned with any animal. However, they had exceptional night vision, as most shifter species did. She would have little problem finding her way in the dark.

Moving over to the barred door, Talwyn crouched down and pulled a long, flat, narrow metal object from the inside of her left boot. She first tested the door by pushing firmly but slowly to minimize any noise. As expected, it was locked. Reaching through the bars, she inserted the metal instrument into the keyhole and turned it a little. The lock clicked open almost immediately.

Moving slowly and silently, Talwyn opened the bars and closed them behind her. She moved to the stone walls to her left. As she walked down the wide tunnel to explore, she ran her hand along the walls in an up and down sweeping motion. Inconsistencies in the stone might show a hidden door or some other hiding place.

After some time, she came upon a division in the tunnel. Since she already had her hand on the left wall, Talwyn took the left fork. After around the same distance again as from her chamber to the split, the passageway curved sharply to the right. Light spilled in from the opening at the end, but thanks to the sharp curve, she stayed hidden in the darkness.

Talwyn moved as close as she could to the tunnel exit, then she leaned out slightly, just enough to look. On the other side, she could see a large open space. It had several long stone tables spaced out across the area, as well as several benches and wooden chairs.

She could not see all the way to the right from her position, but she could see the end of the cavern to her left. There, she saw four other openings, which likely led to other tunnels such as the one she was currently hiding in. Thanks to her dream-visions, she knew where at least one of them led.

Suddenly, Talwyn heard voices approaching from the tunnel immediately to her left. Two women appeared and made their way to a stone bench perhaps twenty paces in front of her. They were speaking quietly, just above a whisper, but Talwyn could hear them clearly.

"The deadline is almost upon us," the black-haired woman said. "He will have no choice but to decide soon."

"We should go to the council and suggest they put more pressure on him," the female with the brown hair responded. "We should stress that our species needs bolstering. That he needs an heir."

"There are several attractive and willing females among us who would make a fitting queen and mother to the heir. I don't understand why the decision seems to be so difficult for him."

"Maybe he has taken a liking to more than one female," said Brownie.

"He is our leader, and an amazing specimen of a male," Blackie responded. "That's a lot of male for one female to handle. Maybe the females would be willing to share," she said with a chuckle.

The other female giggled. "Maybe we'll get lucky and he will choose us."

"Maybe we can think of a way to make that happen."

Talwyn rolled her eyes. She had listened to enough of this insipid conversation. Maybe the dragon lord wanted to marry for love and not just for duty. Then again, he'd probably be better off this way. It wouldn't be so hard on him if anything were to happen to his mate.

She shook her head. Stupid, morbid thoughts.

Talwyn turned until her left hand was on the opposite wall. Then, making the same sweeping motions as before, she made her way back to her cell. She remembered the Dragon lord as he walked out of here earlier. Those females were right about one thing—he was quite a specimen of a male.

Why, oh why, did he have to be so attractive? She'd found out when she peeked at him he was in extremely good physical form. He was not what she had expected of the chieftain of the Dragon-folk.

She shook her head. There was no point in worrying about their reactions to one another. The entire realm was in danger, and she had a very short time to convince the Stone Dragon Clan to help their cause. Once she left here, she would head to Southgate to help protect their keystone from the demonkin. Then, even if she was successful, she would head to the Great Gate.

She hoped against hope that if the keystones remained untouched, there would be no need to bring an army to protect the Great Gate. However, she and her fellow champions had foreseen that the possibility of a battle at the Gate was very high.

So she needed to win the Dragon-folks' trust. She needed them to come together with the others in the realm to protect their world. And she suspected convincing them that this would be in their best interest as well would prove very difficult.

Her time was limited. There was no time to consider romance, even if she wanted it.

CHAPTER TWO

Histories

Last night, after the strange woman's arrival, Dreyken found himself almost incapable of sleep. He tossed and turned, picturing her in his mind. He still marveled at how drawn he had felt toward her, even though he hadn't spoken a word to her yet.

Aside from how beautiful she was, he had noticed many other small things that led him to believe she was the kind of female he had been looking for. For example, when he was sponging along her arms and down to her hands to cool her off, he had felt callouses, which could be caused by manual labor or physical training. He also noticed that her nails were kept short but neat, which also supported that thought.

She had obviously seen her fair share of battles as well; there was a barely visible scar on her forehead, traveling from her hairline diagonally across her right eyebrow. He had also felt several small scars along her arms.

After some time, he'd drifted off to sleep, only to awaken a couple of hours later to dreams of her. Her face, her long, fiery hair, and her strong and fit form seemed to call to him, even in sleep. He sat up in bed, wondering if her personality would match her appearance or if he would end up disappointed. For the start of a plan was brewing in his mind, and he hoped against hope that the universe had sent her here to help him with his problem.

There's no use sitting here wondering about it, he thought. He needed to go see her.

As he made his way toward the cell, his excitement and anxiety ramped up in equal measure. This was not like him. He was the calm and steady leader of the Stone Dragons, the only clan of Dragon-folk remaining in the realm. But, of course, it was his station that put him in the predicament he recently found himself in.

When he reached the cell door, he paused before entering. The young woman was not only awake, she was practicing some kind of martial art, at times moving in slow and controlled patterns and at other times striking and punching with quick, forceful, and precise actions.

He was enthralled by the way she carried her body. Her movements flowed as she spun and leaped. It was beautiful and awe-inspiring, and proved that she was a warrior, just as he'd suspected.

Dreyken watched until she finished and bowed low. Then he entered the cell.

"I was watching from the doorway." He kept his voice low and friendly.

"I know." The female's expression was impassive and impossible to read.

"I hope you don't mind. It was mesmerizing. Beautiful. *You* are beautiful."

"Thank you." Her answer was simple and her tone polite, but he could have sworn he'd seen a hint of a flush that disappeared as quickly as it had appeared.

He considered her undoubtedly intentional unemotional response. She was studying him as much as he was her.

Dreyken's advisors on the Elder Council had been pushing him lately to choose a mate. However, none of the females in their clan had captured his attention the way this woman had. The unmated females in the clan would love to have a kind word or a compliment from him, but he felt none of them were truly interested in getting to know him. Those he had attempted to spend time with were too busy trying to impress upon him all the ways they would make a suitable mate for the leader of the clan.

Since Dragon-folk lived for many centuries, he hoped to find a loyal companion, a partner to share his life and his thoughts with. If he was lucky, it would be someone to share his heart with as well. He was not interested in simply choosing a mate who was well-suited for the position. He wished to find a mate he could love, and who would love him in return. It would be even better if he felt passionate about his mate, and she him. He did not even want to imagine living out the rest of his life in a partnering that was any less.

So far, this female before him was the first in a long time to stir any kind of physical or emotional response in him, and she wasn't even Dragon-folk. He knew almost nothing about her.

This was a situation that he would rectify right away.

Dreyken walked over to the wall opposite the woman and lit the candle. He didn't really need the light. He was a Folk, with naturally sharp senses. Aside from that, his people had lived underneath the Dragonburn Mountains for hundreds of years. They rarely left here ever since the dragons were slaughtered by the humans and demonkin almost four centuries ago. All his people could see well enough in the dark.

He didn't need the light, but he wanted it. He wanted to see her in full color, no feature dulled by the lack of light, and the one candle that flickered low on the shelf next to her bed was not quite enough. When he turned to face her, she was sitting on the bed, leaning forward with her heels at the edge, her arms over her knees, and her head down. He took a couple of steps closer, and finally, she lifted her head and looked at him.

Dreyken sucked in a sharp breath as he stared into a set of beautiful green eyes. She'd been unconscious yesterday, so he hadn't seen the color. They were the color of moss, only more vibrant. They reminded him of the rare, warm spring days he'd spent playing outside as a child.

His people did not go outside very often. When they did, they went by a schedule—especially those who could fly—so that there were never enough of them outside at one time to draw attention. Children started to shift during adolescence. Before that, they were sometimes permitted to play in the forest in the uninhabited area that lay between the mountains and the southern coast of Sterrenvar. It was those happier times, when he'd run between the trees, through lush undergrowth, and over moss-covered rocks, that those mesmerizing eyes now called to mind.

He let his gaze travel across her face, taking in every detail. She was even more breathtaking than he remembered.

Realizing he'd just been standing there staring at her, he shook his head. "I apologize for having to lock you in this cell, but I'm sure you can understand the need for caution and safety." He waited a moment, but she did not respond. She just continued to look at him.

"I hope you found the bread and water I left to be passable. I did not want to give you anything too rich for fear it would make you ill."

The impassive stare continued. Was she trying to unnerve him? Was she uncomfortable? Or was she simply rude? That would be disappointing.

"If you are feeling up to it, I can bring you more enjoyable fare." She nodded slightly. *Ah, progress!*

"I will go to get us some food. I hope that when I return, we can get to know a little more about each other over a nice meal." He turned and left the way he had come.

It was time for the morning meal, and the food was already being prepared down below. So, even though it was a good distance away, it didn't take long for Dreyken to return to the cell carrying a tray laden with food. He took two plates from the tray and filled them with meat and fruit. Moving to the only other bunk other than the woman's, he placed the plates in the middle and sat to one side. He gestured to the other side. "Please, come sit. Let's get to know each other a little."

Thankfully, she did as requested. "My name is Dreyken."

She nodded her head respectfully. Not just rude, then. He mentally sighed with relief.

"I'm Talwyn Survalor. You can just call me Talwyn."

"A beautiful name for a beautiful creature." He smiled at her but received no response to his compliment. "I am very interested in learning how you found yourself unconscious at the bottom of our mountain."

"The answer to that is simple, yet complicated." She looked down, and Dreyken thought her cheeks colored a little. "The brief response is, I found myself there because I came looking for you."

"I see." That was an interesting and unexpected response. "You are not human, are you?"

"No, I'm not."

"If you came here looking for us, I assume you know who we are."

"You are the Stone Dragons, the last of the Dragon-folk who stayed on this shore after all the true dragons were mercilessly exterminated."

Dreyken nodded his head thoughtfully. "It seems you know much about my people, yet I know nothing of yours. It would seem only fair that you tell me what people you come from as well."

Talwyn met his eyes. "I am a seer."

Dreyken's brow jumped in surprise at this revelation. "A seer? I thought the seers had been hunted down three hundred years ago."

"Like your people had been a century before that?" One side of Talwyn's mouth lifted slightly.

"Hmmm...I see your point."

"How did you know about that if you've been in self-imposed exile here all this time?" She tilted her head and looked at him through narrowed eyes.

Dreyken gave a sweeping gesture around him. "We seldom leave here, but we try to check on things from time to time. We would not want to be taken by surprise again, after all."

He paused for a moment as he considered their situations. "Well, it seems we have something in common. It wasn't too long after our dragons were killed off, and our clan numbers reduced, that the humans and demonkin turned their attention to your kind. My people had assumed that the seers had gone the way of our dragons."

"Yes, most others thought so as well, and we allowed them to think that way for a long time, keeping to ourselves when we could and sticking to the shadows when we couldn't."

"Now I am even more interested in finding out why you are here. Please, Talwyn, tell me."

Talwyn looked at him with a serious expression. "I am here to help you, and to ask for your help."

"I am sure you could help me," Dreyken said to himself in a low, whispered voice. "A seer. I could make that work."

Talwyn had no problem hearing his muttered words. She knew exactly what he meant, since she'd had visions of things that were to pass here in the mountain and had overheard those two females talking. But she pushed aside any reaction to his words. There were more important things to take care of first.

"Please." Dreyken spoke louder this time. "Tell me how you think you can help me and what it is you want from me."

"Before I do that, I need to tell you the story."

"The story?"

"The story of why any of us need help to begin with. And it is linked to our common history. I will recite it to you as it has been told to me." She shifted her body so she was facing him more fully and met his gaze with her own.

"All the different peoples of the realm are aware of the War of Fifty Years, as I am sure yours is." Dreyken nodded his agreement. "However, until recently, only the Elders, Sorcerers of the Light, and Gate Kings knew what caused this war. I mean, what truly was at the root, and what came to pass because of it." Talwyn glanced at Dreyken. He was watching her with rapt attention.

"In the center of our realm, there are ley lines that spread out and come back together. They are roughly shaped like this." She pushed the plate of food backward to make room and traced the shape of a diamond on the rock surface between them with her index finger. "From each axis, more ley lines spread inward until they meet in the middle. These ley lines surge with magical energy. Any sorcerer, at any ley line, and at any point along the lines, can use this energy to bolster their magical abilities. Where the lines join at the axes, their abilities are even stronger. In the center, which we call the Source, they all meet. There, the magical energy is so strong that many sorcerers have been destroyed trying to access it."

She looked up at him and met his gaze. "A few millennia ago, there was a powerful sorcerer who called himself Azedel. He had dedicated his life to learning how to use this source of magic to gain power and dominion over all the peoples of the realm. He discovered that when the stars and planets align in a certain configuration, it causes an interesting effect on the Source. The magical energy found at this hub is usually powerful, but unstable. During the alignment, it becomes focused and stable enough to access without the user being destroyed. But it is also so much stronger during this time."

Dreyken nodded thoughtfully. "My people have some knowledge of this. It is in our histories. However, they do not contain all the details you are giving."

"Azedel used the surge of magical energy at the Source to open a gate to another realm—a demon realm. He hoped to create and lead an army of demons, which he would use to help destroy our realm's leaders and to subjugate our peoples. His plan seemed to work for a time.

"Some of the evil beings Azedel brought over then turned on him as well. The chaos this caused created an opportunity for the Sorcerers of the Light to combine their power, sweep in, and push many of the demons back through the gate. It is believed that, during this Battle of the Gate, Azedel was destroyed. The Sorcerers of the Light then closed the gate and locked it with magic. Once closed, it could not be reopened until the stars and planets align again, stabilizing the power of the Source enough to use. None of the sorcerers of that time, as formidable as they were, had the power or knowledge to destroy the gate."

"Has no one discovered how to destroy the gate in the years since?" Dreyken's voice was laced with concern and his brow was furrowed. Talwyn's hopes were bolstered by his obvious interest.

"There are theories, but there've been no opportunities to test them out. They all involve the power surge from the Great Alignment, and that only happens once every three-thousand years.

"It's been estimated that there were a couple of hundred demons left stranded here in Sterrenvar. They began breeding with some human inhabitants of the Northern Mountains. The demonkin are not native to our realm. They are descendants of the demons left trapped behind. These creatures thought that if they banded together, they would be powerful enough to continue Azedel's plans for domination of the realm."

"How do you know that?"

Talwyn shrugged. "Dream-visions mostly. But we also like to keep informed by staying in the background and watching and listening.

"The part of this history that has been passed down through the years since," she said, "in one form or another, tells of how these demons gathered supporters from some of the realm's peoples by playing on greed and using manipulation. There were many who saw these machinations for what they were and resisted. The result was a war of many battles, and many deaths, that lasted fifty years before the forces of good were finally successful in pushing back these would-be subjugators. The demonkin now occupy an area up in the Northern Mountains and beyond, way up north, where the land is harsh and unforgiving. And there they remained. Until recently."

Talwyn looked at Dreyken again. His brows were still furrowed, but he looked more suspicious now. She suspected he was starting to understand where the story was leading.

"For years, my people have been getting visions of an evil that has been covertly trying to insinuate its way throughout the realm. At first, we thought it was just the demonkin trying to get the humans under their power. Now we know it is more than that. Almost all the humans have been affected in some way or other. The evil creeps in subtly, pretending to be friend, all the while manipulating their thoughts and hearts, playing on their fears and insecurities, using their greed against them."

Dreyken stood and paced. He seemed agitated, and she wanted to ask him what he was thinking. But she needed to finish first.

"For years, my people have been working behind the scenes, trying to cut off this evil influence when possible, and learning as much as we can."

Talwyn again paused briefly before continuing with the most recent developments. She watched Dreyken carefully, looking for signs of his reaction while at the same time trying to impart the significance of what she was saying.

"Several months back, more information came to us. It strongly suggested these same evil forces had begun the fear-mongering that led to the near extinction of the seer people. Since this has come to our attention, our people have been receiving more and more visions of war and violence. We believe they were trying to rid the world of seers so that they could keep the element of surprise on their side. And of course, our natural abilities would also make us a formidable enemy.

"We think this may also be why the dragons and Dragon-folk were targeted a century before. They wanted to get rid of their strongest opposition."

Dreyken paused in his stride and she could see the anger that burned in his eyes at this information but feared it may not be for the reason she hoped. She needed to make him understand what was at stake.

"Your people have always been a powerful force, Dreyken, strictly on the side of good. The demonkin would have had to take both of our species out of the picture for their plans to get anywhere. Putting almost a century between the attacks just made it harder to see the link between them."

Dreyken stood frozen near the middle of the room. He seemed caught up in his own thoughts.

Talwyn looked down at the floor, and sadness tinged her voice when she spoke again. "These are events my people should have foreseen with more clarity. So much needless death could have been prevented."

Dreyken finally turned to look at her. He must have recognized the pain in her expression because he reached to hold her hand. She gave his hand a squeeze in thanks.

"Since we could not clearly see what happened before or during those events, our Elders believe there must have been a powerful sorcerer blocking our visions. It is the only explanation that we can see."

"Well, that is all history now. We can't change it. We can only do the best we can in the present."

"But that's just it, Dreyken." Talwyn allowed the urgency she felt to seep out in her voice. "It is *not* history. It was only the beginning." Talwyn squeezed Dreyken's hand and locked her gaze with his, trying once again to emphasize the importance of what she was about to tell him. "It was centuries of preparation by this sorcerer—and whoever he has working for him—for what is coming soon. Some even surmise there is a cult of Azedel's followers behind everything since the timings are so spread out."

Dreyken sat next to her again, still not letting go of her hand. He looked worried.

Talwyn continued. "When the Sorcerers of the Light defeated Azedel and his demons, they knew they had to protect against such a thing happening again. So they created four keystones, each imbued with strong, positive magical energy, and placed them at the four axes of the ley lines. They inhibit any dark magic from getting through and interrupt the flow from the Source. They do not stop the stream of magic completely. Rather, the intent was to create an obstacle, or deterrent. It's like narrowing a channel so that less water moves through at any time. Except in this case, it's magic instead of water.

"As you know, there are four major kingdoms in our realm: Northgate, Eastgate, Southgate, and Westgate. Each of these kingdoms was founded on an axis of the ley lines. The castles are found in the center of their towns, which are surrounded by high stone walls. They have highly trained elite guards watching for danger. In the very center of each castle, there are heavily fortified, magically shielded keeps, and within each keep there is a keystone."

Dreyken glanced over at her. "So Sterrenvar is safe as long as we have the keystones, then?"

She gave him a wry smile. "Theoretically."

Talwyn sighed heavily. "Since the creation of the keystones, the seer people have appointed four guardians. Under us are trainees who are preparing to take our places should we fail in our duties. Each guardian is entrusted with watching over one of the gate towns and its keystone. We travel far and wide as well, watching and listening to discern any threat to the well-being of the realm, any hints of this evil returning. But our primary responsibility is protecting the keystones. If any of us should fail, or if the danger is significant enough, we will band together to protect the Great Gate, which was built directly over the Source."

"Aren't the Sorcerers of the Light also responsible for the magical protections placed over the Sacred Forest?" Dreyken's voice was curious and thoughtful.

"They are."

"Then, how is it that a group of sorcerers who were strong enough to create these keystones and place a system of protective enchantments over an entire forest couldn't also destroy the gate?"

Talwyn flashed him a small smile. "I asked that same question when I was first learning the histories. Again, I am not a sorceress, so I don't know exactly how it works. But, from what I've been told, it is much easier for sorcerers to create things than to destroy something previously made. Especially if it was made by another sorcerer."

Dreyken nodded slowly, and Talwyn gave him a moment to think before continuing.

"The most worrisome part is that the visions showing war and the subjugation of the humans have significantly increased recently, when the Great Alignment is so close. In a little more than a month from now, the stars and planets will once again be aligned as they were three millennia ago. Those with less-than-noble intentions could use the power of the Source if they can get to it. I'm sure you can guess what that means."

Dreyken's expression suddenly changed, and he looked cold. "I'm sure I could." Dreyken sounded almost dismissive. His tone was a harsh contrast to the concern Talwyn had seen in his eyes just a moment ago. "This is all very interesting and informative, but what is it you want from us?" Talwyn moved to free her hand from his, but he held tight.

"If you wish to ask that we get involved, to fight in this battle, I am afraid you are out of luck." His voice became more and more agitated as he went on. "After we lost so many people and the dragons went extinct, my people decided we would no longer involve ourselves in the affairs of humankind. It only brings trouble and sorrow. We protected the humans, traded with them, befriended them. Some of our people even lived among them. And what did it get us? *Slaughtered!* At the hands of the humans! They betrayed us! They do not deserve our help now. I would have thought your people would feel the same way, given they tried to do the same to you!" He was almost yelling by the time he got to the end of his brief speech.

Talwyn shook off Dreyken's hand and walked to the middle of the room. Standing with her back to him, she shared her personal story for the first time in a very long time.

"I was only eight years old when the humans and demonkin attacked." Her voice quavered with emotion. "Not much more than an infant by my people's standards. My parents refused to take up weapons against the humans. They said that the humans were being manipulated like puppets on strings. That they were a young people, easily controlled by those more powerful than themselves. Many of the seer people felt the same way as my parents. And why wouldn't they? They could all see the truth in their visions.

"So when our homes were attacked, instead of taking up the sword against them, some tried reasoning with them. When that didn't work, many of us fled. My mother grabbed my sister and me and took off, intending to hide us in the woods. Seers can run faster than most Folk species, but there was utter chaos as people ran in every direction, and our attackers were coming at us from all sides. And there among our human attackers, disguised to look just like them, were the faster and stronger demonkin. Of course, we knew what they were and what they had done, but the humans couldn't see past their illusions.

"My mother found a hollow under a rock, and she placed me in it. She hid the opening with branches and stones. That's where I was when my family was slaughtered. My mother and my sister. My sister had only twenty-eight years behind her. She had barely begun her adolescence. My father had gone to a human village a few days before to try for diplomacy, but he never returned. They probably killed him there before coming for us.

"I still dream about that day." Her body shook, and she tried to rein in her emotions, but it was in vain. "I can hear their screams, smell the blood. . . I can see it pooling just within sight of my hiding place."

Dreyken walked over to where Talwyn stood with her back to him. He grabbed her shoulder gently and turned her to face him. She didn't bother to wipe the tears that trailed down her cheek.

"I don't understand." Dreyken's voice was quieter now, but still agitated. "I *can't* understand why you would ask for help protecting them when *this* is your own experience with them. Why would you be willing to help them yourself when you have seen the destruction they can cause? Why, in the fiery heat of dragons' breath, would you want to protect the humans' lives when they took your own family's?"

"Because they were right!" Talwyn yelled. Dreyken leaned back and his mouth gaped at the force of her emotion. But her next words were barely more than a whisper. "My parents were right. But—they were also wrong.

"They were right because the humans were being used as tools. They were manipulated by an evil being who stayed hidden in the shadows as he preyed upon their fears, their greed, their insecurities, their naivety. He did this to them until he had forged the perfect weapon for himself. So who should we demand retribution from? The sword, or he who wields it? The sword does not ask to be used in this way."

Dreyken was watching her, giving her his full attention.

Her voice became fierce once again. "But they were wrong as well, because you can learn to defend against a weapon without having to destroy it. You can block a sword's strike, and the sword can remain whole. So by refusing to fight back, to even take up weapons in any capacity, they were allowing themselves to be cut down, their lives cut short because of their passivity.

"So, here I am." She held her arms wide in demonstration. "A seer guardian, because I believe the humans should never have become unwitting murderers, treated as if their lives are worth nothing more than to be used however 'greater beings' see fit. Their souls should not have to suffer condemnation, never to be returned to the Universe, because of the greed of those more powerful than them questing for even more power.

"Because of this, I watch vigilantly, in order to ensure this does not happen again. But I also fight and take up arms because I believe my people should *never* have to lie down and perish because we are unwilling to defend against an enemy's sword."

Dreyken ran his hands up and down Talwyn's upper arms before resting them on her shoulders. Her body shivered under his touch, but she sensed he was trying to comfort her, so she didn't pull away. When he spoke again, his voice was quiet, but firm. "Those are all very noble sentiments, Talwyn. I understand and appreciate where you are coming from. But that does not change the fact that my people are still angry and bitter over what happened. We took an incredible hit to our numbers, and losing the dragons made many of my people feel it is not worth it. That we should stay hidden and keep out of the drama that takes place outside our mountain. We can try making them see your point of view, but you should not pin your hopes on them agreeing."

"You are the dragon lord, Dreyken. Why would it not be you who decides?"

He squinted at her questioningly. "I never said I was the dragon lord. How did you—"

"How did I know?" Instead of answering, she lifted her eyebrows and looked at him pointedly.

"Right," he said, shaking his head. "Forget I asked. I may be the dragon lord, but I am not a dictator. I try to rule in a fair manner. If I were to just set down an ordinance telling them they *must* help rather than allowing them to weigh in—well, our numbers are not what they once were. I do not want to cause a rift in what's left of my clan."

"I can understand that, and I believe that willingness to listen to the people is a noble trait for a leader to have. But there is still another important detail that you and your people need to know."

"And that is?"

"You are going to be pulled into this war, whether or not you like it."

Dreyken stepped back and eyed her suspiciously before Talwyn held up her hands in defense. "It isn't me or any other seer you need to be worried about. In fact, this is one way I am here to help you."

"How is that?"

"As I told you, my people receive much of our information through dream-visions. One of my dream-visions showed demonkin being sent out to search for any remaining Dragon-folk."

"They are looking for us? Why?"

"I'm uncertain of the reason, as the Dark Sorcerer seems to be adept at blocking himself from us and gives orders to his underlings without explanations. I would guess, though, that it's because you could pose a significant threat.

"The good news is, by what we've Seen, we don't believe they're actually certain you are here. The bad news is that the possibility of you being discovered seems quite high."

"Possibility? You mean you don't know for sure?"

"No, not for certain." Talwyn sighed. "The past and the present, when we see them, are set, since the decisions have already been made and the actions completed or currently occurring. The future still depends on choices yet to be made or those that still have time to change. So until those final decisions are made, there are a number of possible outcomes."

Dreyken paused for a moment, nodding his head thoughtfully. "I will think about it," he finally said before turning and heading toward the cell door.

"Don't think too long," she called after him, and he paused. "Remember that this sorcerer is using more powerful tools than just humans. And whether or not you believe it, Dreyken, they are coming for us—for all of us."

CHAPTER THREE

Exploration

Talwyn stayed in her cell for the rest of the day, just waiting for night to fall so she could sneak outside under the cover of darkness.

To pass the time while she waited, she sometimes exercised and at other times meditated. In times like these, she wished her people had to sleep more often than every few diels, since there wasn't much else to do in the meantime. She was still wide-awake and alert when she finally noticed that the sounds of life were echoing down the tunnels less and less frequently.

Talwyn had always felt comforted under the cover of the forest, and less secure with the open air above her. The cover provided by a cave was different, however. The forest was a living, breathing thing where, at any time, there were many places to hide or to sit and watch, whether it be high in the branches of the trees hidden in the foliage, or low to the ground hidden among the plants and bushes. And there was always fresh air and the sounds and smells of life all around.

Talwyn always enjoyed being able to glimpse the sky through the treetops from the safety of the forest. She enjoyed the blue skies of a clear day or watching the moon and the stars on a clear night. She even enjoyed watching the clouds move and travel overhead or listening to the pattering of raindrops that fell through the leaves on a rainy day.

The Sacred Forest was not a typical forest. It was a magical place where the temperature was never too hot or too cold, where storms and fierce weather did not encroach. The forest needed water to survive, just as all living beings did. So, there were cloudy days and rainfalls, which her people enjoyed as much as the sunny days. Talwyn had always loved the fresh, clean scent of the forest after a rainfall and watching the trees and plants become fully alive and vibrant after a good drink.

Caves, however, made her uneasy. Seers usually adapted well in any situation and, after three centuries, she had long gotten past her crippling fear of holes in the ground and snug spaces. Yet there remained an unease related to the memory of when, as a small child, she'd been hidden for hours, surrounded by rock and stones.

Yes, caves provided shelter and concealment, but they were unyielding, and one could easily find oneself backed into a corner and trapped. Hiding spots were much more limited than they were in the forest, especially if someone came upon you suddenly.

Caves were hard, cold, and immovable.

"Huh." If her heart had been more like these cave walls, she could have been saved much pain.

Talwyn took another close look at the stone walls and ceiling of her temporary dwelling. She noted the many cracks, crevices, nooks, and ledges throughout. Maybe hiding wouldn't be so difficult after all.

Still, there was no breeze making the leaves chatter, no wind blowing her hair back until it danced wildly behind her. Therefore, tonight's first excursion would be back up to the ledge Dreyken had landed on when he first brought her here. Not only would she get some much-needed air and openness around her, but she could also look at the moon and compare its phase to the one she had seen in her vision of the attack. This would give her a better idea of how much time they had.

She unlocked the cell door the same way she had the night before. As she walked out of the tunnel and onto the ledge, she took a deep, cleansing breath and was thankful for the fresh outdoor air. Even though it was nighttime, the moon and the stars shone down brightly, illuminating the landscape. So she stayed in the shadowed areas, just in case the Dragon-folk had watchers.

She sat cross-legged on the cool stone and looked up to examine the sky. She was contemplating the relative positions of the stars and the moon, comparing it to what she remembered in her dream-vision, when she was distracted by the sound of wingbeats. From rather large wings, by the sounds of the whooshing off to her left. She stood and made her way over to the edge.

Looking down, she saw the enormous form of a dragon. Shifted Dragon-folk were much smaller than most veritable dragons, but they could still be double the size of a horse, depending on the physical size and strength of their human forms. The one flying a short distance below her ledge was on the larger side. At first glance, it looked like a shadow moving in the moonlight, as it was dark in color. Observing for a while longer, she saw its scales were a dark gray or black, and shiny in spots. She could see the moonlight glinting off its scales from time to time. Its coloring reminded her of a smooth, black stone with a metallic sheen that her people worked with from time to time. It was beautiful to behold.

The dragon was flying along off the south side of the mountain at an altitude below the lower peaks. These mountains were probably one or one-and-a-half days' walk from the southern shore of Sterrenvar, and there were no other villages in between this side of the mountain range and the ocean. Close to the foothills of the southern side of the mountains, there were some forested areas, some more sparse vegetation, and a few different species of wild animals.

Very smart. This was a great way for them to stretch their wings and hunt without drawing attention to themselves. Did they go by a schedule? It would be much harder to be inconspicuous if they were out in large numbers.

The dragon flew in ever-widening circles below her. After a few minutes, it suddenly dove to the earth at a great speed. It took the beast very little time to dispatch its kill and fly upward again to the height it had been flying at before. She carefully leaned out so she could see the dragon approach the mountainside below her and to her left. She couldn't see it as it landed with its prey, but she knew there were other entrances that led into these tunnels and caves. From what she had seen in previous visions and the dragon's relative position when it re-entered the mountain, she could make a very good guess about where she could find its landing spot.

Talwyn moved away from the edge and made her way back to the cave entrance. She quickly and silently walked back down the tunnel, past her cell, and to that turn at the end where she had stood hidden the previous night. Before stepping out into the dull light of the torches—set at regular intervals along the stone walls—she quickly changed her hair and skin coloring to match the black-haired Dragon-folk woman she had seen here previously.

She did not think she would run into anyone here tonight, but she had been taken by surprise before. Humans had a habit of changing their minds on a whim, where the seers only received visions when they slept or were in a state of deep meditation. She hoped that the Dragon-folk would be less fickle, but she did not want to take anything for granted, just in case.

She looked across to the throne, which was on the other side of the room and a little to her right, and toward the tunnel just behind it. Then she looked to her left, to the three entrances at the narrow end of the oblong room. Hearing nothing and sensing no movement, she walked across the room to the last tunnel, the one farthest away from her.

She'd had many visions about this mountain, and she knew the other two passages led to living quarters, branching out as they traveled downward. But this third one led to a cavern with its own ledge outside, on the southern slope of the mountain. It seemed to be where the Stone Dragons launched from when heading out to hunt in the area between the mountains and the sea. The tunnel also had chambers off to each side that held clothing and foodstuffs until they were needed. There was also an armory, with weapons and armor that undoubtedly hadn't seen use since the battle that sent the Stone Dragons into hiding here.

There were also a couple of surprises down this way that the Stone Dragons themselves didn't know about. Things she herself knew about through visions, yes, but mostly from seer metallurgist Anwyl Govan. The Dragon-folk would learn about them soon enough, though.

She crept through the tunnel until she came to the opening to the cave where she figured the way outside likely lay. It was more a doorway, really, as the stone had been widened to fit the large frames of the Dragon-folk males and smoothed out. She paused and pressed herself to the wall next to the doorway, listening for voices.

She heard two males talking about the kill and saying a prayer over the body of the prey, thanking it for its sacrifice to the people. Then she could hear them working tools to gut, skin, and clean the animal. She wanted to wait as they labored so she could see who the hematite-colored dragon was, and maybe gather some information at the same time.

She looked around to find a hiding spot where she wouldn't be seen when they exited the room. The tunnel was wide enough for two or three Folk to walk through side by side, and half again as tall as the dragon lord himself.

She looked up and scanned the rough stone walls and ceiling. She stopped when she found the perfect spot. A few paces above her head, there was a little alcove that looked as though it would fit her frame if she were lying down or crouching low. It was opposite the doorway, but not directly across. It was probably three feet to the left of the cave opening. Using cracks and ledges in the rock, she quickly climbed up and lay along the uneven stone ledge of the narrow alcove. It wasn't overly comfortable, but it would be fine while she waited for something to be said or something to happen.

It was an unfamiliar male voice that first spoke. "So, I hear you are being pressured by the council to choose a mate, my old friend."

"Unfortunately, yes." This voice she recognized, and she suddenly knew that he was the black dragon with the shining scales.

As bright as the sun in human form and dark as night in dragon form. Fitting. In the brief time she'd known Dreyken and the few conversations she'd had with him, she had gotten the sense that there was another side to him he was not quite ready to show her.

Only fair, since the same was true for her.

"Drarcio told me he overheard Sukia and Ninhré speaking about it." The male chuckled. "Apparently, they both would like the job. They might even be willing to share their duties."

Had this Drarcio overheard the same conversation Talwyn had, or did the women speak of it so often that it was well known in the mountain? Maybe they wanted people to overhear so word would get back to the dragon lord.

Instead of answering his companion, Dreyken growled at him. His friend guffawed.

Dreyken snarled at the male. "Just for that, Adrio, for having fun at your lord's expense, you can finish cleaning my kill by yourself."

Adrio laughed again as Dreyken stalked out of the room. Talwyn figured they must be close for him to get away with teasing his leader in such a manner.

Talwyn kept to her hiding spot until the sound of Dreyken's footfalls died out. She listened for a short time before deciding that Adrio, who was now humming a tune as he worked, would not be exiting anytime soon. So she hopped from her ledge on silent feet and glanced toward the doorway again before leaving. She could see herself becoming friends with this Adrio character.

Dreyken strode toward Talwyn's cell. Realizing how fast he was walking, he slowed to a casual gait, trying not to show his eagerness to see her. After all, he was Lord of the Dragons, coveted by the females in his clan. This seer female should be grateful for his attentions.

At least, that's what he told himself to calm his nervousness at the thought of seeing her again.

Dreyken arrived at the cell door, unlocked it, and walked inside. When he did not immediately see Talwyn, he turned in a slow circle until he was facing the door again, but she was nowhere to be seen. Just as he could feel his anger boil and a growl rising in his throat, something hit his shoulder and bounced off to land on the floor in front of him. It was a small stone.

He turned to look behind himself just as another stone came toward him from across the room, at a downward angle. He caught it just before it struck. When he looked up, he saw Talwyn perched where the wall of the cave curved into the high ceiling. She was balancing herself on two small outcroppings of rock that jutted from the wall.

"What are you doing up there?"

"Picking apples." Talwyn grinned and looked at him expectantly. It was a little amusing, but two could play this teasing game, so he continued his annoyed stare.

She sighed and jumped down, landing nimbly on her feet about nine paces below where she had been. "So few appreciate a sarcastic sense of humor these days." She shook her head slowly. "You've left me locked in a cave for days with nothing to do. Any person would climb the walls in such a situation." She flashed him another amused smirk. She was in a joking mood today, it seemed.

Dreyken tried to keep the stern expression on his face, but he knew he wouldn't be able to hide the mirth in his eyes. His friends had told him many times that his eyes always gave him away. Finally, he couldn't hold it anymore and the corner of his mouth lifted, unbidden. "Sorry, but I have to protect my people. Staying hidden has kept us safe for centuries."

"So have you decided yet whether I have come to help or to harm?"

He hesitated for a moment, weighing his words carefully. "I believe you when you say that you are here to help. The question is whether we really need that help, and if it is worth the cost of showing ourselves to the world again. We've had peace for almost four hundred years because people have stopped believing we exist."

"Yet, you know as well as I do, Dreyken, perhaps better, that there are those among your people who are tired of hiding here beneath this mountain. Who wish for more freedom. You are dragons! You are not meant to spend your lives hiding in the dark, but to spread your wings and fly! To feel the sun on your scales! Tell me, Lord Dragon, where is your joy?"

Dreyken stared at Talwyn in fascination as she gave her short, impassioned speech. She was a beautiful, strange, and thoughtful creature. It was possible that she was speaking of freedom for his people simply to appeal to his sensibilities and advance her own agenda. However, while he was certain that was part of it, for some inexplicable reason, he believed she was genuinely thinking of his people as well. Just what had she seen in her visions to make her believe this would be best for his people?

"There are those among my people who feel that way, who wish we could live freely again," he said. "However, as leader, I must think about what is good for the whole. If we get involved in this conflict, we are bound to lose more of our people. It would be unavoidable."

"What if I were to promise I won't try to influence your people one way or the other or try to cause any trouble between you? Would you allow me to address them? Allow them to vote as a clan, or to each decide for themselves if they want to help. I will keep my thoughts to myself as much as possible. Well, and to you. To the others, I will only present the dangers heading this way and what my purpose is in coming here, such as I have already told you."

Dreyken nodded quietly, looking at the floor. Talwyn stepped toward him, and when he raised his eyes to her, she was half a pace away. His breath quickened and his heart beat a little faster.

She looked into his eyes with a soft, almost sad gaze, and her voice was barely more than a whisper. "I understand why you want to hide your people; believe me, I do. With my people's history, with my own personal history—"

Her voice grew rough with these words, and Dreyken raised his hand to cup her cheek, stroking his thumb across her cheekbone. Why did it bother him so to see her upset when he'd just met her recently? Without seeming to think about what she was doing, Talwyn placed her hand on top of his and leaned into his touch. His heart now beat so hard he was certain she must hear it.

She cleared her throat, but it was still thick with emotion when she spoke again. "We seers have found ourselves pulled into this conflict by whatever power sends us our visions. But we never doubted for a moment that we would get involved this time around. Never doubted we would protect those innocents who are now being threatened, even if their ancestors had once been wielded against us. We are protectors. Guardians. It is what we were created to do, even if we didn't fully accept that role for ourselves until after tragedy struck."

She gently squeezed his hand underneath her own. She held his gaze, and her expression was earnest. "What are you meant for, Lord Dreyken?"

I was meant for you. Dragon scales! Where had that thought come from? His heart now raced, and he took a deep breath as inconspicuously as he could to calm himself.

Not wanting to give his reaction away, he stood silently, looking into her eyes. He knew that wasn't what she was asking, so why was it the first response his mind—or was it his heart—came up with? After a moment, he dropped his hand and took a step back.

This seemed like a good time to change the subject, before he did or said something unbecoming of the Lord of the Stone Dragons. He cleared his throat and took another deep breath to get his urges under control.

"I came here to tell you I thought about what you said, and I've called for the council and my advisors to gather this afternoon. I will introduce you and you can present your case to them."

"Thank you." Talwyn gave him a warm, genuine smile that lit up her face, and he was enthralled. He could possibly be persuaded to do whatever she wanted to get her smiles. It was probably good that he wasn't the only one involved in the decision making. He needed to stay clear-headed, but it was proving more difficult than he would have expected.

"I will come to escort you to the meeting when it is time."

With that, he turned and walked out of her chamber, leaving the cell door open behind him.

CHAPTER FOUR

The Lord & The Council

Dreyken dressed himself in the finely decorated and tailored leather clothing he wore for official business. He preferred his fighting leathers, but knew they were not always appropriate for someone of his station.

He remembered a time before everyone learned his face, when he could wander freely around his city under the mountain. Dressed like everyone else, he could speak to others just as any other normal citizen. He had done it so often he had even come to make a group of friends. Great friends—or so he'd thought. For years, they had spent all their free time together, sneaking around, exploring all the hidden areas of the caverns, teasing the young females.

Until he entered his adolescence and shifted for the first time.

It was then that his father decided it was time he introduced his heir to the clan as their future leader. Though they all knew of him, none had been given the opportunity to put the face with the name before. This custom of hiding the identity of the future dragon lord was one of his people's ways of protecting them until they were old enough to protect themselves.

His father had him dress in his fine clothing that day. Luckily, among the Stone Dragons, what they considered their finer clothes was still comfortable and practical. However, they were made by the finest clothiers in the clan and were adorned with gemstones and metal decorations. They would occasionally even be dyed to stand out from the clothes everyone else wore.

That was how he had dressed on the day his father had him stand at the upper landing of the hewn stairway that led down to the center of the city under the mountain. In his big, booming voice, amplified even more by the echoes in the cavernous space, his father made the announcement to all those in attendance.

"I present to you my son, Dreyken, your future dragon lord!"

From that day forward, most of his friends, and even the girl he had liked, treated him differently. Some of them were upset that he had not told them what he was to them. Some of them just seemed to stop looking at him as their friend, instead seeing and addressing him as their future leader.

All except for Drarcio and Adrio, who continued to treat him as they always had. They even continued the teasing and the mocking, and he was grateful for it. The three of them were never anything but their true selves around each other, and this was why they were now his first and his second, respectively.

His reminiscing was interrupted by a throat clearing behind him. He turned around to see Talwyn standing in his doorway. One side of her mouth was tilted up in a smirk.

"Well, Your Dragonship, are you ready to go to our meeting?"

Dreyken smiled at her words. Having just been thinking about Drarcio and Adrio, he realized one likely reason behind the ease he felt with her. She was not afraid to tease him, like with all the little plays on his title, and she spoke to him without pretense. Her playfulness, sarcastic as it was, reminded him of how his two best friends interacted with him.

Then a thought suddenly occurred to him, and he looked at her quizzically. "How did you know where my chambers are?"

"I know *many* things, my friend." She smiled coyly and quirked an eyebrow at him.

"Just how far do your gifts extend?"

"That's my little secret. But you'll get a better idea soon."

He noticed something was different about her, and he furrowed his brows. "Is your hair wet?"

"Of course! You can't expect me to go to a meeting with your council without cleaning up first."

"How did you know where to go?"

Talwyn simply raised her brow at him, as if to say, *do I really need to repeat myself?* Then she smirked. "I really shouldn't have had to figure it out by myself, though. A good host would have shown me where the amenities are."

"Wait. You had time to search out one of the pools or underground rivers in the short time since I left you?"

She lifted her eyes and her shoulders at the same time, as if she was shrugging with both. "Well, that may not have been the first time I've been out exploring."

The first time he'd left the door unlocked was the last time he'd visited her. He was sure of it. He shook his head at her. "Did I even need to bother locking the cell door?"

Talwyn pressed her lips together, tilted her head to the side, and narrowed her eyes. "Hmmm. . . I suppose it protected me from being attacked by a wild beast in the middle of the night."

Dreyken's mind suddenly, without his bidding, flashed to an image of himself as the wild beast attacking her in the night—in an entirely good way. His breathing and heart rate sped up--this was becoming a common occurrence around her, it would seem.

Talwyn jumped a little, then stared at him wide-eyed with a blush on her cheeks. Were his thoughts written all over his expression again, or had the same ones jumped to her mind once she realized what she'd said?

After an intense moment of staring at each other, Talwyn cleared her throat. "Come. Let's head to the meeting." He thought he heard her mutter something about self-preservation, but he couldn't be sure.

Dreyken led the way out of his chambers and through the tunnel that led to a narrow opening behind the throne hewn from rock. It was on one side of the large, open area of the room. He placed his hand on Talwyn's arm to stop her just before they entered. "Let me do the talking at the beginning. I will tell them why you are here, and then you can fill in any gaps."

Talwyn simply nodded in response.

Drarcio and Adrio were already standing on either side of the throne when Dreyken and Talwyn walked around from the back. Dreyken took his seat, and Talwyn moved next to, and slightly in front of, Adrio, who was now acting as a royal guard and councilor. His friend started at Talwyn's sudden appearance, but once he had a moment to look at her, a slow, mischievous smile bloomed on his face.

"Well, hello, beautiful. Where did you come from?"

"Now is not the time for flirting, Adrio. We are here on official business." Dreyken's voice showed some annoyance, and he worried his friend would recognize it for what it really was—jealousy. Talwyn didn't seem the type to care about his status, and Adrio was a good-looking male. And an accomplished flirt.

Dreyken would have to speak to his friend later and make his intentions clear. It might be early for that, but it was better to deal with it sooner rather than later to avoid any hard feelings in the future.

Adrio continued looking at Talwyn with that same suggestive smile—luckily, she ignored him—until the council elders approached and stood in front of Dreyken. Then his annoying friend finally moved his gaze forward.

Dreyken stood and moved to the front of the dais his throne sat upon.

Allow me to introduce our Council of the Elders: Herdrix, Airgan, Skyran, Andes, Usun, and Ildros." Dreyken indicated them in turn as he gave their names and they each gave a nod of greeting.

Dreyken was glad when Talwyn looked each council member in the eye as his name was given and bowed slightly to them once the introductions were complete. This show of respect might make her talk with them run a little more smoothly. He was already certain that not every council member would regard her presence positively.

"Welcome, Council of the Elders. I would like to introduce to you Talwyn, an emissary from the Sacred Forest."

The older man that Dreyken had introduced as Airgan spoke up. "An emissary from the Sacred Forest, you say? How did she find us? How did she get in here?"

"She came to the mountain looking for us. I found her passed out from exhaustion at the foot of the mountain and brought her inside."

Talwyn felt a brief stab of guilt at that comment, but quickly pushed it away so it wouldn't show in her expression. There may be a time when she'd tell him she'd been using her inner-sight to fake the symptoms of a heat-related illness, but that was a topic for another day.

"Why is she here? What does she want?" Airgan's tone was rude and demanding. It made Talwyn's hackles rise. First, how dare he speak to his clan leader like that? Second, how dare he talk about her as if she was not standing right in front of him?

With the patience and skill she'd worked hard for over the centuries, she kept her voice calm when she spoke.

"You know, I am standing right here. You can address me directly." She gave him a polite smile.

Adrio let out a choked cough, which Talwyn figured was actually a suppressed laugh. Dreyken let out a low growl of annoyance. She didn't know if it was aimed at Airgan, her, or Adrio, but she hoped it was Airgan. Dreyken should not allow his clan members to speak to him in that manner, even if they were an Elder Council member.

Airgan looked at her in surprise, but Talwyn continued speaking, calmly and politely, before he could give any other reaction. "I realize the Stone Dragons have been separated from the rest of the realm for a long time and are probably not accustomed to receiving guests. However, where I come from, one does not talk about another who is present as if the person is not there. It would be considered rude. But please, forgive me if your customs differ." She gave him one of her sweetest smiles.

Airgan looked at Talwyn with narrowed eyes, and his lips pressed together tightly as if he were holding back an angry retort. He glanced at Dreyken and seemed to reconsider. He bowed his head to her. "Of course. My apologies. As you said, it has been a long time since we've received visitors."

Talwyn nodded to him to show her acceptance of his apology. Then she addressed his questions. "I am here to tell you of a danger that has been stalking the realm for some time now. Whether or not you know it, our realm is on the brink of war. As for what I want, I want to help you prepare for what is coming, and to ask you to help the people of the realm in return."

"And why is it, exactly, that you believe we need your help?" This question came from the council Elder Dreyken had introduced as Ildros.

"As one of your own was a Sorcerer of the Light during the Battle of the Gate three thousand years ago, I believe you are already familiar with the histories?" She raised her eyebrows to prompt a response. The Elders nodded, and Skyran said, "We are."

"Your people were then hunted down, your numbers severely cut, and the dragons gone to extinction not four hundred years ago."

"And this is why our people are staying hidden, keeping apart from the realm's dramas. Our people have suffered enough!" Airgan retorted.

"I agree with Airgan," Ildros said. "We need to stay out of any new fighting."

"Please, allow me my say before you give a final decision." Talwyn hoped her agitation wasn't too obvious in her voice. *You're trying to convince them to join our forces. Don't do anything that could ruin my chances,* she chided herself.

"Do you not see the link I am pointing out to you here? These events, though centuries apart, are not isolated. Do you think it's a coincidence that the seer people were also targeted not a century after your people? Or that the demonkin are gathering again just a month before the stars will be in the proper alignment to make the Great Gate useable again?"

"It could very well be coincidence indeed!" Airgan tossed back. "You are talking about events that occurred randomly over the space of three thousand years."

"And you believe it is just a coincidence that both the dragon shifters and the seers were targeted during this period? We are the two races that would be the greatest threats to any power who would try to use the gate again."

"There is no proof to say otherwise!"

Talwyn suddenly covered her eyes with her hands and stood still, as if she were frozen.

Dreyken's concerned voice sounded from behind her. "What's going on? What's wrong?" he asked.

"Shh! You cannot talk to me. I can't see you, so you don't exist."

"That's a bit childish, don't you think?"

She dropped her hands, her eyes flashing fire at Dreyken, then Airgan. "Exactly! We cannot see the air we breathe, yet we know it's there because we live. We cannot see the scent of blossoms on the wind, yet we can delight in their perfume. We may not see the sun on a cloudy day, but the light fights its way through, nonetheless.

"You may not see the threat, but that doesn't mean the threat does not exist. My people have seen it! It would be naïve of you and your people to not prepare for the coming threat before it is upon you. You are a long-lived race! I am surprised to see such short-sightedness from you."

"And who are you to be giving us this advice?" Airgan asked. "How do we know you are telling us the truth? How do we know you are not a demonkin in disguise, trying to draw us out of hiding?"

Talwyn shook her head, disappointed. "You are elders. You surely know that you can tell if someone is a demonkin through touch. Their shape-shifting is a visual illusion only, so we can still *feel* the truth of what lies beneath. You know this, do you not?"

"We do," Ildros agreed.

"Then you can simply ask your dragon lord if I am as I appear to be."

All six sets of eyes, eight if you counted Dreyken's guards, turned to look at him. Dreyken cleared his throat, his eyes wide, hoping they didn't get the wrong idea.

"She had injuries, and I treated them, that is all. But, yes, she is as she appears."

"That still does not tell us who you are and if you can be trusted." This statement came from another elder—the one called Herdrix. His voice was challenging but, unlike Airgan, he did not sound hostile.

Talwyn was a little frustrated by their lack of trust. However, she understood it. Their people had been attacked as hers had, and they did not have the gift of Sight, which would help them know friend from foe. So she answered his questions.

"I am Talwyn Survalor, seer guardian of the keystone at Southgate." There were a couple of sharp intakes of breath, but she knew that most of those present would have already guessed she was a seer from their interactions thus far.

"Before you ask me for proof of my identity and my nature, I will offer it to you."

Dreyken raised a brow, and the elders looked at her with curiosity.

"I am not the first seer you have met."

"What do you mean?" Airgan asked.

"Many years ago, your previous dragon lord gave permission to a metallurgist to mine galanite from underneath these mountains. He was told to stay to the east and to not disturb your home or your people. In return, this metallurgist promised to never talk about what he saw here. Over time, he gained your people's trust and trained a couple of Stone Dragon apprentices, who are your current metallurgists."

There were some grumblings in the group, and the elders were looking at each other with astonished expressions. She needed to ease their minds before they assumed some sort of treachery. "He did not tell me these things or break your trust. These are things I learned from my dream-visions.

"In return for your dragon lord's hospitality," Talwyn continued, "he created things for your people. Decorations to adorn your clothes and your homes, structures to reinforce your tunnels and caves, even some weapons and armor. These last are seldom used, however. The metallurgist, as you may know, is called Aleyn Whitesteel."

The others continued to listen intently to her story as she went on. "Aleyn is a seer, and the best blacksmith and metallurgist our people have ever seen. He was one of the many seers who learned about the coming attack on your people through dream-visions."

Again, there were more grumblings as those present absorbed what she said. She gave them a few moments to work through what they had learned before clearing her throat to get their attention again.

"If you want physical proof outside of my knowing these things, Aleyn has left you some gifts. It will take some time to get there and back, but I will take Lord Dreyken to them."

There was a pause as the others considered what she had said. Then Airgan spoke again. "I do not think that would be prudent, my Lord Dragon. We still can't be sure she can be trusted."

Andes spoke up, saying, "I believe her."

Usun added, "As do I."

Talwyn gave a mental sigh of relief to have at least some support in the Elder Council. "Thank you for your trust in me."

"This is our dragon lord on the line here. Should we be taking chances?" Airgan asked.

"Let Adrio and Drarcio go with them," Andes suggested. "Unless, of course, you are worried that one lone female could take on three male Stone Dragons and be victorious?"

Airgan huffed a little at that, but to disagree would be an insult to the capabilities of the dragon lord and his two closest friends and protectors. Talwyn doubted he'd want to take it that far.

"I guess that would be acceptable." Then he turned to Dreyken. "That is, if you agree, of course, My Lord?"

Dreyken stepped up next to her to address the council, which Talwyn hoped was a show of support for her.

"I agree," he said. "We will meet again tomorrow, and I will inform you of what I have learned." He turned to Talwyn and swept his hand in front of them. "Lead the way."

CHAPTER FIVE

Follow the Seer

Surprised that she knew where she was going, Dreyken followed as Talwyn took the lead with confidence, heading down the tunnel to the right. Of course, as she was a seer, she probably did know the way.

He followed Talwyn through the dark tunnel, Adrio and Drarcio at his heels. They walked past the cavern leading to the southern launch toward the area where they stored their weapons and armor before Talwyn spoke.

"So, what is Airgan's problem? Does he have a dragon egg hidden in some orifice somewhere, irritating him constantly?"

Drarcio and Adrio both burst out laughing while Dreyken pressed his lips tight, trying to look stern and reprimanding. He couldn't hold out for long, though, and he let out a chuckle as well.

It was Adrio who answered. "Well, all I know is he has been beside himself lately, trying to force our dragon lord here to pick a mate. More specifically, to pick Airgan's niece as his mate. Maybe he was put out that his quest has been delayed."

Dreyken shot Adrio a warning look to get him to stop talking. Adrio just grinned at him. Sometimes he wanted to throttle his trouble-making friend.

"Why are they trying so hard to get you mated off?" Talwyn sounded genuinely confused.

Dreyken took a deep breath, then let the air out on a sigh. He moved up beside her to answer her question, knowing he would have to tell her eventually, anyway. At least, he would if he wanted to move forward with his plan—the plan he'd started formulating the first time he saw her face.

"In our clan," Dreyken began, "dragon lords typically take a mate by their two hundred and fiftieth year. In a little more than a month, I will reach my three hundred and fiftieth year."

"He's such an old man, just not necessarily in age," Adrio teased.

"I don't understand," Talwyn said. "Your people are almost as long-lived as seers. You haven't even reached half your expected life span. So what's the rush?"

"In our clan, the sooner a dragon lord produces an heir, the better. It wouldn't do for the dragon lord to meet his end somehow, for example, and not have an heir to take his place," Dreyken said.

"Wow, your people are kind of morbid." Talwyn grinned at him and jabbed him in the ribs with her elbow.

Dreyken smiled at her. This was the type of interaction he had missed once his father declared him as future heir all those years ago. He was grateful he had Adrio and Drarcio, of course. However, after a couple of hundred years with only the same two people interacting with him freely, it was such a breath of fresh air to find the same thing with another. It was even more satisfying to find it in a female he was interested in romantically.

"So, what's the problem?" Talwyn asked. "Why not just choose a mate?"

Dreyken felt a little. . . unsettled. . . about the matter-of-fact way she asked that question. He would have preferred to see a little emotion, maybe a flash of jealousy, considering how he already felt about her.

"Dreyken is a romantic," Drarcio offered.

"He wants to mate out of love, not duty." Adrio's voice suggested disgust, and he screwed up his face. But Dreyken noticed the mischievous glint in his eyes.

"While that is true, it is not the only reason." Dreyken looked at Talwyn as he spoke. "Before the events of four hundred years ago, our numbers and life spans meant it would eventually become more and more difficult to mate with someone that wasn't at least distantly related to you. Then, four hundred years ago, my people's numbers were reduced even more, and we have all been living in our village under the mountain together since, never interacting with outsiders."

"I see." Talwyn nodded knowingly.

Did she? Dreyken continued his explanation, wanting her to truly understand. "I've been told stories by some of the older Stone Dragons which show that, in the past, before the attacks, our people were open to mating with other peoples. It was even encouraged. Most often, the offspring could shift to dragon form after their adolescence, since our genetics are so strong. So the mates and children usually stayed with our clan. The elders of the time, and my grandmother in particular, seemed to think that mating with those outside our own kind made for stronger offspring."

Talwyn nodded her head in understanding.

"Now, with my people living their lives hidden under a mountain, shunning other peoples, we no longer have that opportunity."

"Dreyken wants us to consider going out into the realm to find mates if we cannot find our mates within the clan," Drarcio supplied. "Of course, this is also convenient for him since he has not connected with any of the females here."

"I've said it before, and it bears repeating, six hundred years or more is a long time to commit to if you do not truly love your mate."

"You are *such* a romantic." Adrio fluttered his eyelashes, and Dreyken gave him a friendly shove.

"If you ask me, Airgan's real problem is power; he always wants more of it." Drarcio's voice was thoughtful and concerned. "He is one of the strongest advocates *against* our people heading out into the realm to look for mates. Now he is trying to push Dreyken into mating one of his own family. All he cares about is keeping our people under the control of the council, and of politically maneuvering himself to hold more sway with the Dragon lord." He looked at Dreyken with eyebrows raised. "I just hope our dragon lord is too smart to fall for his schemes."

Talwyn stopped outside the entrance of the room that housed all their food supplies, effectively ending their conversation. Dreyken looked at her curiously. Why would she bring them here? He glanced at Drarcio and Adrio, who were looking back at him with questioning expressions he guessed would match his own.

Talwyn grabbed an oiled torch from a wall sconce and laid it on the floor. Striking two stones together, she quickly and efficiently lit the torch. She placed it back in the holder, then went over to a stack of large, heavy sacks. Talwyn moved the sacks away from the wall and then firmly pushed in a section of stone that jutted out slightly. It must have been a lever of some sort because, two paces above head-level, a large stone moved in and to the side, revealing a short, narrow passage.

Dreyken gaped at the opening. Another glance at his two best friends confirmed they were gaping, too. The three of them had spent their youths exploring all the tunnels, crevices, and caverns under the mountain. Or so they thought. But they had never found this.

"So, you really are a seer, huh?" Drarcio's voice was low and full of awe.

Talwyn looked at him over her shoulder and raised an eyebrow. "Were you doing a chore list in your head or something when we had that conversation in the throne room?"

"Well, no. I mean, it's obvious you know things that even we do not know." Drarcio gestured to the hidden passageway. "It's just that, I don't know. I always thought that seers were calmer. More patient. More—diplomatic." His cheeks reddened, as if he were embarrassed. "At least, our histories seem to suggest that."

Talwyn turned to face Drarcio. She tilted her head to the side as she regarded him, narrowing her eyes and tapping her forefinger on her chin as if she were deep in thought.

"Oh, yes." She pointed at him. "I see what you mean. Kind of like how all dragons are hot-headed." Drarcio opened his mouth to speak, but she didn't give him the chance. "Well, yes. I tried to get everyone in my village to sign a decree that would change our collective name to see-*er* rather than *see-erz*—you know, to show that we're all the same—but nobody wanted to sign it for some reason." Then she turned her back to him and pushed the sacks back against the wall, hiding the lever once again.

Dreyken dipped his head to hide his smile and tried not to laugh at her response.

Despite her sarcastic retort, Talwyn knew what Drarcio meant, and it was true that most of her people were the way he described. Truth was, she could easily be that person as well—calm and stoic like Seer Elder Berinon or her friend Maelona. But she had built this sarcastic façade around herself like armor years ago to keep others from getting too close. Maybe she would one day be ready to take the chance and open up again.

Today was not that day.

Talwyn approached the wall directly below the tunnel and looked up. "Well, boys, I hope you're not claustrophobic. The space looks plenty big to accommodate my frame, but with your massive dragon shifter girths, you may find it snug."

Talwyn swiftly scaled the short span of wall to the tunnel opening. When she reached the passageway, she turned back to the others. She reached down for the torch, and Drarcio handed it up to her.

"Come on. It isn't high. It can't be more than a vertical pace or two for your tall frames."

She disappeared into the passage and waited just inside for the others to follow. She heard the males squabbling below.

"There has to be a ladder around here somewhere," she heard Drarcio's deep voice say.

"Come on, you big oaf," Adrio chided. "Don't be a coward."

"If you're so good with it, you go first."

"Fine. I will." Judging by the how long she heard scrambling sounds before he appeared behind her, it took Adrio a little longer than it had taken her to find suitable hand- and footholds. But he was up and into the passage before long. Dreyken followed on his heels, and then Drarcio finally scaled the wall after them.

Talwyn was advancing on her feet, though she was crouched low. Glancing behind her, she noticed that the three men were forced to move forward on their hands and knees. She barely stifled the laugh that bubbled up at the sight of the three enormous males crawling around like babes who haven't yet learned to walk.

Now and then, she heard them squabbling at each other about who made what dust and dirt fall on them.

They continued like this, traveling uncomfortably through the tight passage for a couple of hundred paces. Finally, the passageway ended, and they all jumped down, one after another, onto a stone floor a couple of paces below.

Talwyn turned back toward the wall next to the passageway. She reached up high and pressed another hidden lever. The sound of stone-on-stone echoed down the tunnel as the door slid back into place at the other end.

They now found themselves in a tall and narrow tunnel. It was large enough for them to walk through at full height, single file.

They traveled for about fifty yards before there was a fork in the tunnel. Without hesitating, Talwyn took the fork to the left. They then continued down this tunnel for another few hundred yards before coming to a three-way split. Talwyn took the central passage and continued on, with the three Dragon-folk men following behind her.

This new passageway angled steadily downward for another few hundred paces. Then it turned sharply and became a little steeper. After some time, Talwyn extinguished the torch and placed it in a holder on the wall.

"What is that light up ahead?" Dreyken had noticed the opening that showed a dim glow beyond.

"What, you want me to tell you and spoil the surprise?" Talwyn grinned at him. "Trust me, you don't want me to ruin it for you."

As Adrio, Drarcio, and Dreyken stepped through the tunnel exit behind Talwyn, they froze and stared in awe. They had entered a cavern large enough that the three of them could change forms and fly around if they wanted to. And every surface—the walls, the ceiling, the stalactites and stalagmites—all glowed an iridescent blue-green color. Shallow water covered the floor of the cavern, and the dots of light from all around reflected in its surface.

Drarcio let out a low whistle. "Wow!"

Adrio gaped at the beautiful sight before asking, "What is this? Why are the walls and ceiling glowing?"

"Bugs. More specifically, glow-worms." Talwyn had seen this before in her dream-visions, but the reality was so much more vibrant. She was just as awed as the males seemed to be. "I didn't even know what to call them until I asked around to see if any others from my village had seen anything like them before."

"It's amazing." Adrio's voice was low and dreamlike.

Then Drarcio asked, "Why didn't we know about this place? Why are there no places like it in our city?"

Talwyn was spinning around slowly, taking in the sights. "You see what wonders you can miss if you fear venturing out and exploring?"

"Beautiful." Dreyken's whisper came from close behind her. When she turned to look in his direction, she noticed he was not looking at the mysterious lights all around them. Rather, his gaze was locked on her.

The lights reflected and played off his features—he must be reacting to the light play on her, as well. She hoped the light was dim enough to hide her blush.

She cleared her throat and turned her attention back to the cavern walls.

"This place is almost completely closed off from the tunnels and caverns of your city," she said. "The only way between the two, from the inside, anyway, is the passage we just took."

"But how did that passageway come to be there if my people didn't do it or even know about it?" Dreyken asked. "And as dragon lord, I am sure I would have heard about it if we did."

Talwyn didn't bother to tear her gaze away from the ceiling. "Aleyn."

Dreyken made a noise that sounded like a worried hum. Talwyn dropped her eyes from the sight above and locked her gaze with his.

"He would never betray your people." Her voice was low and earnest. "Your father was right to have trusted him. Aleyn worried about the Stone Dragons. He saw hints of what was to come, and he foresaw that many of you would refuse to believe you are vulnerable to such an extent. Because of this, you would not be as prepared as he would like you to be. So, he left you gifts.

"If you go to your weapons storage, you'll see there are more items in there than before, and of much better quality. He couldn't put too much in there before it was time. He knew no one went in there very often, but he did not want to take a chance."

"Why all the secrecy?" Drarcio asked. "Why did he feel the need to sneak around and leave us gifts? Why not approach us openly? We may have even provided him with aid."

Talwyn shook her head. "You know, I asked him something similar once. He said his visions showed him this way was best. He didn't explain it any further than that." She looked at Dreyken. "If I were you, though, I'd keep alert. It might mean that not all is as well in your clan as you think."

Dreyken looked at her questioningly. "Where is Aleyn now? Since we already knew him, why did he not come here himself? Not that I'm not glad you are the one who came. I am extremely glad about that." His two friends chuckled at his awkward words, but he ignored them. "I am just trying to figure out the reasoning."

"Aleyn has much to deal with at the moment. The last time he was here, a couple of months ago, he brought galanite back with him, as he has done every time he visited. He has been using it to create or infuse weapons and armor. Given what is coming our way, he has been very busy trying to ensure that our allies have as much protection and as many weapons as he has time to prepare. He has apprentices that help him, but he still does much of the work himself. His plan is to head to the Great Gate when everyone gathers and bring his creations to those who need them most."

"If the sorcerer behind all this believes that both of our peoples are a danger to him and he is coming here for us, won't he come for the seers as well?" Dreyken sounded genuinely concerned about her people, and it warmed Talwyn.

"I'm sure they've already been trying. We've learned from our past, though. This time, we are better prepared. Inside the Sacred Forest, we are magically shielded. Plus, our previous sorcerer put more protection spells on our village. If those two things weren't enough, its physical location is hard to find. It is located inside the Valley of Sight, which has interesting rock formations and plenty of trees that make it difficult to spot until you are almost right upon it.

"If they find our village despite all that, it won't really matter. Most of my people have recently scattered. Looking for information. Looking for allies. Preparing for any eventuality. But we will all meet together again at the Great Gate before the Great Alignment. We are hoping to have many other groups standing by our side to protect the realm, and our freedom, by then." She looked pointedly, almost beseechingly, at Dreyken as she said this.

"I know what you are getting at," he said, "but there are many among our people who will believe that this is not our fight and that we should not get involved."

Drarcio huffed behind him. "Many cowards, you mean. Those who are too influenced by the council. By Airgan and his cronies."

"I know your opinion on this matter, Drarcio, but I have to think of the good of the whole."

Talwyn looked at Dreyken with a frown. "The whole of your people, you mean, not the whole of Sterrenvar. It appears the Dragon-folk have spent so long underground hiding from the rest of the world that you have forgotten there is an entire world out there, despite your mating plans. Which, by the way, are still all about you. There is a larger realm that you are part of. No matter how long or how effectively you have hidden in the past, you cannot avoid the trouble that is coming. Many of my people have foreseen this. It is why I'm here."

Adrio cleared his throat and feigned a great interest in something on the ceiling. "For the record, I agree with Drarcio and Talwyn."

"What? Would you have me ignore the opinions of my people on the matter? I never wanted to lead my people in the same way the rulers of the past have. I have always wanted the clan to know that I would listen to the collective voice and not just dictate without a care as to their thoughts and feelings."

"How many of these opinions have you gotten firsthand as opposed to secondhand, through the council members?" Talwyn's voice was hard and her expression stony. "Let's face it, Dreyken, many of your people were born inside your mountain fortress and have never seen the outside world. Those who are old enough to have seen it have probably forgotten."

Her voice became lower, more intimate. "What about you, Your Lordship? Have you been outside of these stone walls, other than to hunt to the south while staying shielded by the mountains? Have you walked through the trees of the Sacred Forest as the leaves danced and sighed in the wind? Have you swum in the lakes of cool, fresh water that can be found all throughout our land? Fished in its rivers and at its shores? Have you ever just lay in a meadow, surrounded by wildflowers, breathing in their sweet scent as you look up at the clouds passing overhead?"

"You paint a pretty picture there, but it isn't realistic." Dreyken sighed, and it sounded resigned.

Talwyn stepped forward, standing so close in front of him she had to tilt her chin up to look into his eyes. She seemed to get through to him easier like this.

"No, what isn't realistic is you thinking that your people do not have a moral obligation to not just sit by as the evils of the world tear Sterrenvar apart. What isn't realistic is you and your people thinking you can sit here and ignore it all and, in the end, remain unaffected, untouched by the darkness. It will come for your people too, Dreyken, if you choose not to take a stand against it."

Adrio spoke quietly as he stepped forward to stand behind Talwyn. "She is right, Dreyken. You know she is. Deep down, you know it. You have been listening to the council for too long. It's time you started thinking for yourself, doing what you know is right, not what you think they want you to do." Drarcio stayed silent but nodded his agreement.

Dreyken huffed out a humorless chuckle and looked down at his feet. "You know, no others besides you two, and now Talwyn, would ever dare speak to me in this manner. To question my decisions." He shook his head. "Yet how can I feel angry with you when this blunt honesty is exactly why my two childhood friends are now my two most trusted advisors?

"However, you do not know, not really, the full extent of the pressure I feel daily. My every decision, my every move, has to be passed or dissected by the Council of the Elders. Then they debate on whatever issue is in question and push me to agree to whatever they think is best.

"It's my fault, of course, that it has gotten so bad." Dreyken shook his head at the situation. "I never wanted to be leader of the clan. I was still young when my father passed, making me dragon lord by birthright. So in the beginning, I was more than happy to let the council make all the actual decisions. Now it has become a bad habit, and they expect me to continue bending to their will. Anytime I push back, they do their best to make life very uncomfortable for me."

Drarcio stepped in front of Dreyken and looked him in the eye. "You know Adrio and I will always have your back. We were there when your father died. We know what the state of things was after his passing. But that was a long time ago, my friend." He placed a hand on Dreyken's shoulder. "Perhaps it is time you took your power back."

Talwyn watched Dreyken carefully as they spoke. He might just need something to shake him from the stupor he'd been in all these years. The beginning of a plan formed in her mind as she began walking again. "Come. There is still some distance to go yet."

CHAPTER SIX

Finding the Fire

Despite the recent heavy conversation, Dreyken could not help but continue to look around in awe as they traversed the cavern. The worms' glow lit up the large space and reflected off the water that covered most of the floor. They traveled across the room on a narrow ledge that was a few inches above the level of the water. The *plop-plop* of water echoing off the stone walls and the soft shuffling of their feet as they moved were the only sounds until they reached the other side.

Once they arrived at the opposite wall, Talwyn paused and looked up, and Drarcio swallowed loudly and shifted nervously on his feet.

Adrio looked at his friend with a smirk. "I never realized you were afraid of heights, Drarcio."

Drarcio sputtered and glared at Adrio. "I am not afraid of heights. The idea is preposterous. I am a Dragon-folk and I fly out to hunt regularly. I just can't help but feel that creatures of my size and mass are not meant to dangle from tiny hand- and footholds in the rock."

Dreyken watched as Talwyn climbed the slippery cavern wall and disappeared about twenty paces above them. One after the other, he, Adrio, and Drarcio made their way up after her and followed her into another tunnel. Thankfully, that tunnel was also dimly lit with glow worms that hung from the ceiling in places. Here, they did not cover every surface as they did in the cavern, but it was enough to cast a low light. This time, the passageway was tall enough for Dreyken and his two friends to stand in, but they had to walk single file.

The tunnel seemed to be level and only went on for about fifty paces before ending abruptly. Dreyken watched Talwyn look out into the black expanse before her. As she did so, she absentmindedly removed a piece of leather from her belt and wound it around her hand. When she got to the end of the strip of leather, she tucked in the end and went back to her belt for another strip. Dreyken now noticed that these were pieces of leather that had been wrapped around her belt in a decorative pattern.

"Do you always wear clothes that can be taken apart and used for other things?"

"I usually carry many things that could be useful." She wrapped the second strip of leather around her other hand. "I didn't think you would have taken me in as willingly if you found me fully armed, though."

"Probably not." Despite his answer, Dreyken thought about his reaction to her when he first saw her, and he knew he probably would have. But he would have stripped her of her weapons first.

"I left my pack and weapons hidden just this side of the Sacred Forest," she said. "I took only things that were inconspicuous or that I had foreseen I would need."

Talwyn grabbed a rock that jutted out from the wall to steady herself, then leaned out, reaching for something outside and to the right of the end of the tunnel. "In this case, I also knew better things awaited me here."

When she leaned back in, Dreyken noticed she was holding a heavy rope, which she uncoiled and let drop into the abyss below. It was then that he noticed it was firmly attached to a large metal loop embedded in the stone wall next to the tunnel opening.

He shook his head. It was unbelievable that all of this existed beside and underneath their mountain home, but they'd been completely unaware of it. Not only that, but an outsider who shouldn't know anything about their mountain was their guide to all the hidden places.

Talwyn grabbed the rope and swung her body out, passing the braided length underneath her thighs as she did so. This way, he realized, she could descend quickly but stop herself from hitting the ground too hard. Watching how she gripped the rope with her hands to control her descent, it became clear to Dreyken why she had wrapped her hands in leather.

Adrio and Drarcio had been standing quietly behind Dreyken in the narrow passageway, looking on and listening. As Dreyken had watched and spoken with Talwyn, he had almost forgotten they were there. So he jumped a little when Drarcio spoke up behind him.

"If you aren't going to make her yours," Drarcio said, "then step aside and let me make her mine."

Dreyken emitted a low and menacing growl at Drarcio's words. Drarcio held up his hands defensively. "I'm just saying. A female like that probably only comes along once in a lifetime, and given how long we live, that is saying something."

Adrio clapped Drarcio on the back, laughing. "Yes, and you could use all the help you can get landing a mate."

"Like you are doing any better," Drarcio muttered.

"Good point. Maybe she would prefer me. We should ask her." Adrio grinned mischievously.

Dreyken knew they were trying to get another reaction from him. They were succeeding, and he was annoyed they could read him so easily. So he turned away from them and watched Talwyn descend.

As soon as she reached the bottom, Dreyken grabbed the rope and followed. Adrio went next, then Drarcio. None of the men descended as gracefully as Talwyn had. At the bottom, they looked around at another vast space, though not as large as the one with the glowworms. It was also drier and darker than that other cavern. Though they could see around them with their shifter sight, Talwyn found a torch and lit it so they could see in more detail.

Dreyken was stunned by what he saw. He turned a slow circle to take it all in, noticing peripherally that his friends were doing the same. It was like a treasure hoard, only instead of gold and jewels, there were weapons and armor. Dreyken could not decide where to start and, guessing by the looks on his friends' faces, they couldn't either.

"There has to be hundreds of weapons in here," Adrio muttered.

Talwyn strode directly to one corner of the room. She released a sigh of contentment as she wrapped her hand around a magnificently crafted bow.

"Oh, Aleyn, you master of metals, you."

Talwyn turned to look at Dreyken, Drarcio, and Adrio again. "You and your people have no idea of the marvel of nature you have been sitting on top of here in your mountain lair." She held her new bow high in display. It glinted dully in the torchlight.

She looked around a little, then grabbed a short sword from a rack and handed it to Dreyken. "Here, try this."

Dreyken took the sword from Talwyn. He balanced it in his hand before slicing it through the air a couple of times. "This is magnificently crafted, but it is so light."

"Indeed, it is. That means it is less of a burden to carry over long distances. However, it also means you cannot rely on the weight of the weapon to do your work for you. Don't let its light weight fool you, though. The metal is extremely strong."

Adrio and Drarcio stepped forward to pick up some weapons. Adrio's expression was awed as he tested the heft of a mace. "What kind of metal is this?"

"It is called galanite," Talwyn answered.

Dreyken looked around at the abundance of weaponry and then looked at Talwyn. "And this is the metal Aleyn mined from under our mountain?"

Talwyn nodded. "It was discovered by one of the nomadic human tribes that still returns to the eastern end of the mountain range each winter. According to Aleyn, he had known of it for a couple of hundred years before he first came here to seek permission to mine it."

"Aleyn did all this himself?"

Talwyn sat on one of the small stone benches that dotted the room. "Well, he had help from the human nomads when they were in the area. They helped mine the raw materials and prepare them for use. There are more caverns and tools of the trade from here to the eastern tip. However, most of the craftsmanship you see around you here is Aleyn's handiwork."

"Impressive," Drarcio said.

"What does he expect us to do with all this?" Dreyken looked back up to the tunnel they'd entered through.

"Use it to fight, of course."

He looked at her with a wry smile and shook his head. "I mean, how are we supposed to get all of this back to the clan?" He pointed up to the entrance high above.

"That's the beauty of galanite. As I mentioned, it is incredibly light, yet also extremely strong. This makes it easier to transport and less tiring to wear or wield." Talwyn turned to take in all three of the males, then smiled at them. "You will carry some of it back to your storeroom, back the way we came." Adrio and Drarcio groaned. "Aleyn himself has been transporting some of his work back to our own village gradually."

Talwyn turned to meet Dreyken's gaze with an earnest expression. "As for the rest, Aleyn is betting on you. He believes you will make the right choice. So he hopes your clan will take what it needs and bring the rest to the field of battle for any allies who are lacking."

She turned her back to the men to collect a few items but continued her explanation. "There are some things he specifically left for me. I need to be prepared for the coming attack on your mountain, as you all should be."

Dreyken, Adrio, and Darcio watched Talwyn as she found a pack and placed a hauberk and coif made of fine galanite links inside. Turning to look at the males over her shoulder, she said, "Well, don't just stand there. Look around for armor and weapons suitable for yourselves and your top warriors. There are cloths over there for wrapping them in and heavy canvas bags for carrying them." She gestured toward the back wall. "Remember not to load each bag too much, as they need to fit through the passageways with us."

Then she went back to what she was doing. Dreyken noticed she found gauntlets and greaves and placed these next to the pack against the wall. Then she took the bow she had been admiring earlier and placed it against the pack, along with a quiver of arrows. Finally, she found a couple of knives of galanite, which she switched out with the ones she apparently had hidden in her boots.

Dreyken pointed to her feet. "So, you've been armed all this time?"

She looked at him and grinned. "It's lucky for you I'm trustworthy. But you should probably check unannounced visitors more carefully in the future."

Once she was done, she looked at them with a thoughtful expression on her face. "Adrio, Darcio, do you think you can handle things here for a bit? There is one more thing I must show Lord Dreyken. For his eyes only."

Dreyken looked at Talwyn quizzically.

"Oh, sure, sure, no problem," Adrio responded with a grin, glancing over to catch Drarcio's gaze. He was also grinning.

Talwyn raised an eyebrow at them. "Load up the bags and bring them to the far side of the glowing cavern. We should be back in time to help move them from there."

Adrio looked up to the tunnel opening and back at Talwyn. "How do you propose we get them up there?"

"You'll figure it out." With that, she turned on her heel and walked to the far wall. Moving into a shadowed alcove in the rock, she disappeared. Dreyken moved closer and saw a narrow opening that had been hidden by darkness and a section of jutting rock.

Dreyken shook his head. He was supposed to be the leader in this mountain, yet he'd been sitting on these secrets he likely would never have discovered if not for Talwyn.

"Well, why are you still standing here?" Drarcio asked. Dreyken shook himself and headed off after Talwyn.

The entrance was little more than a narrow crevice in the rock. Dreyken had to turn his body sideways to fit inside, then had to side-shuffle for a few paces until the tunnel widened enough for him to walk through normally. He again followed Talwyn through a maze of tunnels.

Talwyn paused before a fork in the tunnel. Dreyken wondered if she was trying to figure out which way to go. As he approached from behind, he breathed in deeply. He noticed the scent of fresh air from the tunnel to the left and—

Suddenly, Talwyn turned and grabbed him by his shirt and pushed him roughly against the cool stone wall behind him. Dreyken looked at her in shock—eyes wide, mouth open. Before he could even wonder what she was doing, her mouth crashed roughly into his. It took him a moment to catch up. However, feeling her lips move against his, her body pressed firmly to his, unlocked something inside of him.

Feeling the beast within him awaken, Dreyken pulled back slightly, releasing a growl from somewhere deep inside. He moved quickly across the narrow space, taking Talwyn with him and pinning her to the opposite wall. He lifted her, and she wrapped her legs around his waist.

Digging her hands into his hair, Talwyn met his eyes and spoke in a breathy voice that intimated her arousal. "There it is. There's your passion. I knew you had it in you."

Before he could contemplate her meaning, her lips were on his again. Dreyken parted Talwyn's lips with his own, then slipped his tongue inside, meeting hers in a sensual dance.

Dreyken felt as though he were going out of his mind with lust, and he pressed his body more firmly against hers as they explored each other's mouths. His arms were wrapped tightly around her. Feeling as though he would burst into flames if he didn't get to feel her skin, he slid one hand under her vest at the waist. As he'd imagined, it was silky-smooth and hot, and he wanted more. Just as he moved his hand higher, Talwyn tightened her grip on his hair and pulled his head back, breaking their kiss. She put her forehead to his, effectively holding him back from kissing her again while keeping them connected.

He'd dreamed of this, and now it was Talwyn who had acted first. He hoped that meant she felt the same for him as he did for her.

They were both panting hard, out of breath, trying to regain some semblance of control.

"Breathe." Talwyn's voice was low and shaky. Dreyken didn't know if she was talking to him or to herself, but it seemed like good advice, so he took a few deep, calming breaths. They were still pressed tightly together, so he could feel when she did the same.

As their breathing and heart rates returned to normal, Dreyken reluctantly took a step back so Talwyn could return her feet to the floor. He still had his arms wrapped loosely around her, not ready to give up all contact just yet.

"Does this mean you will consider becoming my mate?" He could hear the longing in his own voice. He hoped she didn't take it as a sign of weakness that his desperation for her was so evident.

"Let's not get ahead of ourselves." She smiled while gently pushing him backward. "You barely know me."

"I have been taken with you since the moment I first laid eyes on you. When I saw you for the first time, I finally felt hopeful that maybe I would not be forced to spend my life with a mate I do not love."

"This could be infatuation—and maybe physical desire. You have not known me long enough to know if you would be happy spending the next four or five hundred years with me." She took a deep breath, and her voice was gentle and steady when she continued. "Besides, so far you seem unwilling to consider leaving this lair of yours, and my duties and responsibilities lie beyond these stone walls."

These were not the kinds of things he was hoping to hear from her after such a passionate moment, but he had to admit that she had some valid points. So he would not argue right now, but he would contemplate solutions, and he wouldn't give up until he found one. After all, her answer wasn't "no." She'd merely voiced her concerns.

Talwyn turned and headed for the tunnel to the right. After a moment, he followed her.

A short time later, Dreyken could feel the tunnel descend. As they continued, Talwyn slowed her pace a little, so she was walking beside him.

"Tell me something, Dreyken."

"Anything."

"You are obviously a man capable of much fire and passion. So why is it you seem to be just walking blindly through life, letting others lead when that should be your place?"

Talwyn spoke softly as she said this, and Dreyken could tell she was genuinely curious, so he thought about it for a moment before answering.

"As a child, all I wanted was to have genuine friends—people who weren't afraid to treat me like everyone else. People who would be honest with me and appreciate me for who I am inside. The life of a leader is not one I would have chosen for myself. You never know when someone is being genuine with you or when they're just treating you a certain way because of who you are."

"And yet, this is the role you were born to."

Dreyken nodded, his expression now solemn. "Yes. I wish I could have had a couple of hundred more years before I had to take on the role of Dragon lord. I had assumed I would have more time, so I was not prepared when it happened."

"What happened to your parents, if you don't mind me asking? I assume they are both gone, since the leadership would have passed down to the surviving mate."

Dreyken glanced at her. "My parents were already older when I was conceived. It wasn't too long after my people came into hiding here." Dreyken huffed out a sad breath and looked at Talwyn. "I had an older brother who I never met. He was killed during the attacks on our people."

"I am very sorry to hear that," Talwyn replied. Dreyken knew she was sincere, having lost her family as well. So he nodded and gave her a small, sad smile. "I assume, then, that the dragon shifters are like my people and do not conceive very often?"

Dreyken nodded his agreement, feeling inexplicably sad about that fact. "As I mentioned to you before, even though Dragon-folk live almost as long as your people, it is expected for the dragon lords to conceive an heir as soon as possible. Especially since it takes some time in most cases. Hence the pressure I have been under lately. My parents lost their first heir, so even though they were older, they tried for another heir. And here I am." He lifted his arms slightly in demonstration.

"Dragon-folk births are always difficult and dangerous for the mother, no matter what the age. My mother, being past what one would expect for bearing young, had a hard time. She died in childbirth."

Talwyn said nothing, but she reached out and grabbed his hand, offering her warmth and support. He turned his hand over and linked their fingers together.

Dreyken took a deep breath. "My father died of an illness maybe fifty years ago."

"Is it common among your people to contract illnesses?" Talwyn would likely know that for many other species of shifters, it was not common at all.

"Not for young, healthy Dragon-folk. But it happens with older dragons from time to time. My father was one of the unlucky few."

"So how is it that your Elder Council ended up taking control in your stead? Our histories suggest such councils were meant to advise and support only."

"That is my fault, I'm afraid." Not for the first time, Dreyken felt a stab of shame and regret. "Like I said, I never wanted the role, and I never imagined my father falling ill so suddenly. I always assumed he would live to nine hundred years or more, then die from old age. I was not mentally prepared." The memory saddened him. "The Council of the Elders worked closely with my father before his death and, in my grief, I just let them continue making the decisions. They consult with me, of course, but in the beginning, I just ended up deferring to them, and that ended up becoming a hard habit to break, it seems."

"I don't want to step on any toes..." Talwyn shook her head, and her voice was harder when she continued. "Actually, I don't really care if I step on toes. I think it's time you took your power back."

"Power was never something I wanted."

Talwyn turned and pointed at him. "And that is exactly why you are the best dragon for the position."

"I didn't abandon our people or anything." He suddenly felt the need to defend his actions. "The elders knew how my father ran things, and I am sure the whole realm knows that Dragon-folk always endeavor to make the right decision."

"Yes, Dragon-folk have been known to be strictly on the side of good. Yet there are a few things you have to remember. First, there are always exceptions to every rule. There could be a few clan members who are more focused on what is best for themselves as opposed to the whole. You've already seen that with Airgan pressuring you to choose his niece.

"Even more importantly, Dreyken, your people have been through a lot. They deserve to have a leader who is passionate about leading them. Who is determined to give them a bright future."

"That has never been me."

"Yet it could be and should be you." Talwyn's tone was earnest, and Dreyken knew she believed what she said. "Your council seems mired in the rules of the past four hundred years, unwilling and afraid to waver in the least. But don't you think it's time, Dreyken, to give your people the leader they deserve? Don't you think it's time to think about bringing them back out into the world and demanding your place in it?"

Dreyken made a half-hearted, scoffing noise. "That all sounds great, but it is not very realistic."

"That's just it, Dreyken." Talwyn sounded frustrated with him now. "How do you know if it's realistic or not? When was the last time you were out in the world?"

Aside from hunting, hidden in the shadows of the mountain, Dreyken had never been out in the world. He had been born in these caverns, under this mountain. The farthest north of the Dragonburn Mountains he had been was when he rescued Talwyn at the foothills. So, instead of answering the question, he stayed silent.

Talwyn looked into Dreyken's eyes and held his gaze. "I am a seer, Dreyken. Not one hundred years after your people were nearly exterminated, mine almost were as well. We didn't know it back when your people and the dragons were targeted, but when we were attacked, we discovered the humans were being manipulated.

"So many people were killed because of our decision to not get involved, before we were targeted ourselves. Well, except for a few of our warriors who decided for themselves to get involved."

"Like Owyn Axedrifter." Dreyken had heard many stories about the fierce seer warrior. "My father told me of how he and a few of his seer friends aided us when we were being attacked."

Talwyn nodded. "Yes. Like Owyn Axedrifter. He was also one of the few who fought back when our own people were attacked. Many of my people chose not to fight because the humans were being wielded like weapons, blind to what was happening behind the scenes. Now there are fewer of us, and we are safely hidden in the Sacred Forest.

"We could attempt to stay hidden and let the humans fend for themselves, or we could learn from the mistakes of the past and realize that no clan in the realm will come out of this unscathed. Thankfully, my people have chosen to act this time around. What will yours do?" Talwyn paused for a moment.

"We both know you are capable of great passion," she added with a smirk. "Now you just have to find your passion for leading your people."

They were now in front of another three-way divide in the tunnel. Talwyn paused before choosing a direction and turned to face Dreyken. He was quiet, mulling over her words. After a moment, Talwyn spoke again.

"I am not saying it will be easy. Your people, and especially the Council of the Elders, are used to doing things a certain way. You are bound to have those among you who resist change. But your people, Dreyken, and all of Sterrenvar, are worth fighting for, and they are depending on you."

Dreyken stood silently before her, nodding thoughtfully. He had a lot to consider but, whatever happened, he had the feeling that he and his people would never be the same.

She lifted her chin to point to the tunnels before them. "There is still some distance to go, but this is the last division. The reason we've been having this conversation on the way here is that I need to know you accept your role as Dragon lord before I show you the rest of the way and what lies at the end. This is very important, Dreyken. It is something that can change your people's future. This is for the Dragon lord's eyes only."

Dreyken's brows lifted in surprise. He had no idea what she wanted to reveal to him, but it must have been very important if she was asking him to affirm his place with his people before she showed him.

"So what do you say, Dreyken? Am I showing you what lies at the end of the tunnel?"

Dreyken took a deep breath and made one of the most important decisions of his life.

"Lead the way."

"Very good." Talwyn gifted him with a bright smile and reached over to give his hand a squeeze. "Before we go, however, I have to stress to you that this has to stay a secret until the coming war has ended. If word were to get out about what is down here when the enemy still has its legions sneaking about, it could be disastrous. Do you understand?"

"Yes, of course."

"Good. Then follow me."

They headed down the center tunnel. The dark, dank passageway continued descending at a moderate slope. After a short time, the drip of water running off the walls and ceilings could once again be heard. Then the passageway turned to the left as the way got a little steeper.

"Is it just me, or is it getting warmer?" Dreyken asked.

Talwyn nodded. "There are some naturally occurring underground hot springs near to here, and some steam vents as well."

Dreyken shook his head. He didn't know whether he should be impressed or ashamed that an outsider knew so much more about what lie under his mountain than he did.

"This seems like a complicated maze of tunnels, and we've been traveling some distance," Dreyken observed. "Did you really see all of this in your visions?"

"I have had dream-visions of most of these caverns and tunnels many times. Any details I wasn't sure about, I asked Aleyn to fill in for me. Now I know the way by heart."

Curious about how her visions worked, he asked, "How do you know what to look for in your visions?"

"We don't." Talwyn looked at him. "We don't have the ability to see what, where, or when we want. Some people might say our visions are random. My people, however, believe that the universe sends us visions of where and when our help is needed the most. The universe directs us where we can do the most good, and it is our responsibility to do what we can to help."

Talwyn let out a small, sarcastic laugh. "Of course, until we were attacked three hundred years ago, we pretty much let the other species of the realm fend for themselves. The only times we got involved was if there was a danger to the keystones or the entire realm. We believed in not interfering with others' fates. Funny how the attempted genocide of our entire people changed our elders' minds about that. We learned the hard way that what happens to one affects the whole." She looked at him with a sad, sincere smile. "I wish they could have changed that viewpoint about a hundred years before they did."

If it could have turned the tide for his people, then he wished they would have, too. But the past was past, and there wasn't anything that could change it now.

Talwyn stopped walking at a dead-end in the tunnel.

"So now what? Did we take the wrong tunnel?" Dreyken looked around them in confusion.

Instead of answering, Talwyn placed her hand on the wall, pushing on a small outcropping of rock. A door-sized section of the stone wall pulled back slowly and slid open with a grinding noise.

Talwyn stepped to the side and allowed Dreyken to enter the chamber first. She walked in behind him, found a torch, and lit it.

As Dreyken's eyes swept the room, it took him a moment to register what he was seeing. His mouth dropped open. He walked to the center of the room and turned in a slow circle to take it all in.

His heart was pounding. Could it be? How could they have been sitting on top of such a treasure for centuries and never have even the faintest inkling about it?

He was shocked. He was elated. He was everything, all at once.

Could it really be?

"Am I seeing what I think I'm seeing?" It felt like his entire being was filled with wonder and hope.

"You are," Talwyn replied.

"This could change our future."

He walked slowly around the room. He let his hand run gently across the surfaces of what looked like oval-shaped rocks as he moved along.

"I can feel them." His voice was quiet, but his heartbeat pounded loud in his ears. "I was born after the dragons were killed off, so I have never seen one before. My dragon can feel the pull." He was awestruck.

Rocks had been piled at intervals around the room, and at the top of each pile there were two or three large, egg-shaped stones. At least, they would look like stones to those who didn't know better. But Dreyken knew what he was seeing.

Dragon eggs.

CHAPTER SEVEN

Dreams, Nightmares, & Visions

Talwyn and Dreyken made their way back to the cavern where Aleyn's weapon and armor creations were housed. When they arrived, Adrio and Drarcio were lifting the last of the large canvas bags loaded with items up to the tunnel entrance. They were using a pulley system they had fashioned from ropes.

"Well, look at you two," Talwyn said, smiling. "Looks like you figured it out on your own."

"We live on a mountain." Drarcio continued to pull the rope as he spoke. "It's not our first time having to maneuver loads." He grinned over his shoulder at Talwyn and Dreyken. "And what about you two? Was your little foray. . . productive?"

"Wouldn't you like to know?" Talwyn grinned at him.

Dreyken cleared his throat and changed the subject. "Let's finish up here and head back."

Talwyn pressed her lips together, trying to hold back her laugh. It was actually quite endearing to see the Dragon lord shy and flustered. But the humor and ensuing awkwardness also helped to change the topic and kept Drarcio from asking more questions.

The bag was now just a couple of feet from the top, and Talwyn and Dreyken watched the two large males as they hoisted it the rest of the way. Talwyn grabbed the items she had placed by the wall for herself as Dreyken went to help release the extra ropes used for the pulleys. Talwyn, Dreyken, and Drarcio climbed up the rope to where Adrio now waited.

Talwyn glanced down. The remaining pieces of equipment were nothing but darker shadows in the dark space, but there were still five or six times as much as what they were hauling today. Whether that was enough depended on how many Dragon-folk took up arms in the coming battles. But, either way, it was better than the scant, neglected equipment currently housed in their armory.

They retraced their path to the glowing cavern to begin the arduous trek back.

As they walked, Dreyken was quiet and contemplative. Not surprising, really. His mind was undoubtedly full of the implications of what she had shown him, so she left him to his thoughts.

When they returned to the tunnel just outside the food storage room, they each arranged a load so they could push it through the narrow space ahead of them.

"I don't know if the armory is large enough to hold everything," Drarcio said. "We may have to use another room as well."

Talwyn was certain they would. The first time she'd seen the space hewn into the rock that they'd set aside for weapons, armor, and equipment, she'd been surprised at its meager dimensions.

"I understand from the histories that the Dragon-folk had never been a warring race, and that is commendable. But you have to at least be prepared to defend yourselves."

Dreyken nodded thoughtfully. "I think we've become too complacent during our self-inflicted exile. We will need to change that."

It was late when they made their way out of the passageway and into the main throne room, where the meeting had been held much earlier in the day. Talwyn still carried the items Aleyn had crafted for her. The three Dragon-folk men had each chosen weapons and armor for themselves and were carrying these as well. The rest they had left in the storage rooms carved into the rock in the south tunnel. They were all tired from today's work, so Adrio and Drarcio took their leave and headed straight to the tunnel leading to their quarters.

Talwyn turned to walk to the tunnel that led to her cell, and Dreyken followed. "I know my way back, you know." She flashed him a small smile.

"I know." He reached out and took her hand in his. Talwyn was startled at first, but, after a moment of hesitation, she wrapped her fingers around his.

They walked for a few moments in silence before Dreyken spoke again. "Perhaps I should find you a proper room instead of a holding cell." He gave Talwyn an apologetic smile.

"My room is just fine. It has everything I need."

"Including some things you don't. Like doors with iron bars and a lock."

Talwyn gave a little chuckle. "Well, they're good for making sure no one sneaks up on me while I'm sleeping."

Dreyken gave her a sideways glance, shook his head, and laughed. "You really are quite a woman."

"I hope you mean that in a good way."

"Oh, I do."

"Also, up here I am closer to you." She squeezed his hand and gave him a small smile. "And not surrounded by Dragon-folk who may or may not appreciate me being here."

"All valid points."

"I would like for you to show me around, though."

He nodded. "I think I can arrange that."

"I have to ask, why are your rooms up here and not below with the others?"

He smiled at her. "Actually, I do have rooms below. They're quite opulent compared to most other rooms. Ostentatious, even. I prefer the simpler style of the rooms up here. I'm sure you've noticed they're attached to the throne room by a tunnel."

She nodded. "Of course."

"They are meant to be a space to prepare for meetings and events, or to take a rest from official duties. But sometimes I like to spend time up here just to relax as well, especially at night when everyone is below and it is quiet."

"Aren't you worried it will create a distance between you and your people if you are keeping yourself apart?"

The half-smile he gave her then was sheepish. A hint of a blush colored his cheeks.

"Okay, confession time. I haven't spent as many nights up here in one stretch as I have since your arrival."

"And that's another question I have. Why the Dragon lord? Why are your chambers up here so close to any prisoners you might be holding?"

"I'm sure you noticed the other rooms that were in the tunnel leading between my rooms and the jail area?"

She nodded.

"Those are rooms meant for my personal guard. Drarcio and Adrio. Technically, I should have summoned them up here the night you arrived."

"Why didn't you?"

He looked over at her with narrowed eyes and pursed lips. "I guess it was because you were a lone woman, suffering from exposure, and I didn't think you were much of a threat."

She tipped her chin down, lifted her eyebrows, and peered up at him from under her lashes.

Dreyken laughed. "Yes, well, I admit now that it was a poor assessment on my part, considering how crafty you've proven yourself to be since. But in my defense, that wasn't the only reason."

She stared at him, waiting for further explanation, until he finally cleared his throat.

"I'm not sure how to put it. I had this feeling. I guess you could call it a gut instinct. I believed we were meant to... meet, and I believed I could trust you."

"Well, at least you took the precaution of locking me up."

He smirked. "That would have made no difference if you wanted to get out, would it?"

Talwyn chuckled. "You have me there."

"I'll have to keep that in mind for the next time I rescue a seemingly helpless woman and bring her back to the mountain. I'll be sure to alert Adrio and Drarcio right away."

Talwyn laughed.

After a moment, Dreyken's countenance grew serious again.

"Are you sure it's the best plan to keep what you showed me to ourselves? What if something were to happen to both of us during the upcoming battles? Keeping this a secret might be good for protecting the eggs from getting into the enemy's hands." His voice was barely more than a whisper, though there was no one else close by. "However, it would also mean the secret would die with us if we were killed in battle."

Talwyn slowed her stride and looked at Dreyken. "As long as there is even one seer alive, your secret will not be lost. There is only a slight chance that it would be discovered if we lose at the Great Gate, but if it is, you can be sure the enemy will not leave the eggs intact."

"Realistically, do you think there will ever be a time when it will be safe to hatch the eggs and bring the dragons back?"

Talwyn paused thoughtfully for a moment. "Our visions have shown that if we are victorious, there will be a period of relative peace afterward. Relations between the realm's different peoples will be better than ever before. Not perfect, of course. But better. I think it will be safe then."

She smiled as the picture formed in her mind.

"Can you imagine it, Dreyken? A world where there is peace between all the peoples of Sterrenvar. Where those of certain species do not have to hide to keep themselves safe. Where the skies can once again be dotted with the majestic forms of flying dragons and Dragon-folk, day or night." She looked at him, her gaze hopeful. "Isn't that a world worth fighting for?"

He turned to her and gave her a small smile, his expression wistful. It was as though he pictured it as well and he longed for it, but he was afraid to put too much hope in it. "It is worth fighting for, Talwyn. I just hope everything works out that way."

Talwyn was a little disappointed when they reached her cell door. She turned to enter, but Dreyken gave a tug on her hand, pulling her to him. He looked into her eyes, and Talwyn's breath caught with the emotions she saw in his gaze. He cupped her cheek, stroking her cheekbone with this thumb, then he slowly leaned in and kissed her.

This kiss differed from the one they had shared in the tunnel. Where their first kiss had been hot and passionate, this one was warm and filled with emotion. The closeness of it was almost too much for Talwyn to bear after her past heartaches, so she pulled back after only a moment.

Dreyken let his gaze travel over her face, as if he were memorizing the shape and planes of it. Then, without speaking, he inclined his head to her and turned to walk down the corridor to his chambers.

Talwyn entered her cell and sat on the bed. She felt both excitement and dread at everything that happened between herself and Dreyken today. She was both exhilarated and drained. These were emotions she would have never guessed could coexist, and she tried to reconcile them for a moment before shaking her head at herself.

She could not allow herself to focus on that right now. There were more pressing matters to deal with.

She knew she needed to sleep tonight. The demonkin attack would soon be upon them, so she had to open herself up to visions. The more information she had, the better. However, she was also dreading sleep, as when dream-visions ended, a seer's own dreams began. She had been having nightmares long enough to know that after opening herself up today more than she had in more than half a century, tonight would be a tough night.

That night, Dreyken was pulled—unwillingly—from a very pleasant dream about the woman he was more taken with by the day. At first, he wasn't sure what had awakened him, so he lay still in the darkness, listening. It was only a short moment later when he heard it: the sound of someone screaming. There was only one person close enough for him to hear like this. He jumped up and ran down the passageway to Talwyn's cell.

When he got there, the barred door was locked. He could see Talwyn lying on her bed, writhing, as she sobbed, "No! Stop! Elis! No!"

Dreyken shook the bars hard, but they would not open. "Talwyn! Wake up! Wake up!" he yelled.

Talwyn bolted upright in her bed. She glanced at him briefly before bringing her knees up and leaning forward, wrapping her arms around her legs. Her entire body shook.

"Talwyn, unlock the door," Dreyken demanded. She kept her head hanging over her knees as she continued to sob. "Unlock the door!" he demanded more loudly. When she made no move to comply, he shook the heavy bars again in frustration. The dragon in him demanded that he get to her—that he protect her at all costs. These cells were made to resist a dragon's strength, though. So, heart racing, he took off back down the passageway to his chambers to get the key.

By the time he'd returned, she had calmed a little. Though her shoulders still shook, it was not as heavily as before. As he unlocked and opened the door, he could hear that she was taking deep breaths to regain control of her emotions. He went straight to her and sat next to her on her bed. Gathering her in his arms, he stroked her hair soothingly.

"Are you okay?" he asked when she seemed calm enough to speak.

She nodded. "It was just a dream."

"Is that really all it was?" His voice was gentle and coaxing.

She shook her head.

"Tell me," he gently requested. When she said nothing, he asked, "Who is Elis?"

There was a long pause. Dreyken had started to think she wouldn't tell him when she finally responded.

"Elisedd." She took a shuddering breath. "He was my mate."

Dreyken immediately stiffened, his hand pausing its caress of her hair. He felt a surprising jolt of jealousy, but it quickly faded as her use of the word *was* registered. Remembering how his strong, fiery warrior was reduced to screams and tears, remembering the fear that he heard in her voice, his next reaction was anger.

"How did he hurt you?" Dreyken's voice was low. He barely contained a growl.

When she didn't immediately answer, he did growl. "What did he do?"

"He died."

In that moment, all the jealousy and anger faded away, replaced by sympathy and sorrow. "I am so sorry, my heart. So very sorry."

He realized then what she had lived through. She had lost her parents and sister when she was just a babe. He was familiar with the pain of losing family, as he had experienced that as well. However, he couldn't imagine the added pain of losing one's mate and life-partner. So he continued to sit with her, comforting her as best he could.

He understood now why she resisted, even ignored their attraction at first. Why she still held back. After so much loss, the thought of opening up to someone and making herself vulnerable again must be utterly crippling.

At that moment, he decided he would do his best to always be there for her. To be her rock. To show her that time spent with loved ones is always worth experiencing, even if it ends in loss.

After some time, Talwyn calmed. Just when Dreyken thought she was going to be okay, her eyes widened in alarm, as if she'd just remembered something disturbing.

"Dreyken." Her voice was hushed and strained.

"What is it?"

"I had a vision. Before my dream, I had a vision." Her voice was rising in urgency.

"Stay calm, my love. Whatever it is, we will deal with it." He stroked her hair again, but then she turned to the side to face him, leaning away from his hand as she moved.

"The attack, Dreyken. The demonkin will attack two nights from now. I was wrong before. They are not just looking to cut your numbers again. They want your sorceress."

"Our sorceress?" Dreyken was confused and a little alarmed. "How do they know about our sorceress? How would they have that kind of information when we have been hidden from the outside world for four hundred years?"

"That's an excellent question."

"Athnie was born here. She is still very young. She would not have been known by outsiders who knew us before."

"I wondered that myself, but it's a question I could not see the answer to." She paused in thought for a moment. "As far as I can guess, there would only be a few possibilities. The dark sorcerer could have his own way of seeing, like a more deliberate version of what we seers do. Or, since some demonkin can change their appearance to mimic anyone, it's possible that they have been sneaking about, pretending to be Dragon-folk and gathering information."

"Those are very disturbing possibilities." Dreyken tensed with concern.

"And they aren't the most disturbing. Perhaps the most worrying alternative is that there is someone here, on the inside, who has been passing along information."

"I can't believe that." Dreyken stood and paced. "We are a small-enough community that I know everyone under the mountain, at least to some degree. I can't think of one person who would betray our people like that."

"What about Airgan?"

Dreyken knew why she suspected him. The older man had not exactly been welcoming, or even reasonable, where Talwyn was concerned. "Airgan is a lot of things: stubborn, stuck in his ways, maybe even power-hungry. But a traitor to his people? I cannot believe that. Besides, how would they even have gotten to him?"

"It wouldn't be the first time they used their illusions to infiltrate a group. In any case, we are just looking at possibilities. Without more information, we are just guessing. At times like these, I wish my kind really could see whatever we wanted."

They were both silent for a few minutes as they each mulled over their thoughts. Then Dreyken spoke again.

"I don't understand why they would want our sorceress. She is young and unpracticed. She hasn't even shifted yet."

"How old is she?"

"Twenty-six," Dreyken replied.

Dreyken knew Talwyn would know what this meant. Though there were slight variations between Folk species, if you compared her to a human girl, her physical development would be that of a fourteen- or fifteen-year-old.

"I didn't see what their reasoning is." Talwyn's expression was thoughtful, as if she was trying to puzzle it out. "I just know you'll need to protect her. If she hasn't shifted yet, that means she would not have the claws, teeth, and scales of an adult Dragon-folk to protect herself. Add to this the fact that she is not fully grown and her powers have not yet fully manifested, and she is very vulnerable."

Dreyken thought this over for a moment. "Okay. We will gather the dragon protectors in the morning. We will set up a protection detail for our sorceress and create a defensive plan."

Talwyn calmed some at his words. "Please request that she be present when we meet. I'm still not getting clear information, so I will have some questions for her."

"Of course. In the meantime, you've had a rough night." He took her hand in his and stroked his thumb soothingly across the back. "Try to get a couple more hours of rest."

"And you need to keep an eye out for any suspicious behaviors among your people. Look for anything out of place or out of character."

"I will, Talwyn. I promise. Now rest."

Dreyken laid her back on her bed. Instead of leaving, however, he lay down beside her and wrapped her up in his embrace. Talwyn relaxed into his warmth.

"Do you have nightmares often?" he asked her.

"Just every time I sleep."

"That must be difficult for you."

"It is." She sighed and stared up at the rock ceiling. "For years, I tried to go as long as I could before allowing myself to sleep. But when I decided to train to be a champion, I had to stop doing that. After all, what good are seer champions who don't give themselves a chance to see?"

Dreyken didn't respond. He just started stroking her hair again. Within a short amount of time, she drifted off to sleep.

Talwyn could sense a presence next to her before she opened her eyes.

This is where her warrior instincts would normally kick in and she'd take the intruder out before they even realized she was awake. Except, almost as soon as the presence registered, so did a familiar warm, earthy scent.

Eyes still closed, she said, "You aren't watching me sleep, are you?" She opened one eye and looked at him. He was sitting at the edge of the fur covered rock shelf she was sleeping on, next to her hips.

He tilted his head to the side. "I'm not watching you so much as I'm waiting for you to awaken."

"And waiting for me to awaken requires you to hover over me like this?" She pushed herself up to sit.

"It doesn't require it, no. But I brought you some food." He gestured to the stone bench in the center of the space, where a tray of dried meats and fruit sat.

"Well, thank you. That was thoughtful of you."

He stood and went to fetch the tray. Talwyn sat up, and when Dreyken returned, he placed the tray between them. He picked up a piece of fruit and took a bite. She started with a piece of dried meat.

"I thought I would show you my quarters under the mountain today."

She quickly swallowed her bite of food. "Really? That would be great. I think my dream-visions have shown me just about every hidden place there is, but I've only had the briefest glimpses of your actual community."

"After your vision last night, I lay awake thinking. I figure this will be a good way to spread the word quickly while allowing you to get a feel for the space. It will also be good if at least some of our citizens come to recognize your face as a friend to the Stone Dragons. I won't be able to show you everything today, of course. Since your visions show the attack happening so soon, that has to be our priority."

Since she was now chewing, she nodded her head.

Once they'd finished eating, they headed down the tunnel she'd explored on her first night. Like that time, they emerged at the eastern end of the throne room. Instead of heading to the tunnels to the right like they did the day before, this time they headed to the tunnel furthest to the left.

For some time, the seemingly deserted passageway continued steeply down... and down... and down.

They eventually came to a fork, and they took the tunnel to the right.

"This leads to the upper living areas," Dreyken said. Soon afterward, she could hear the sounds of voices echoing along the stone corridor, but they didn't sound close.

More tunnels branched off the main one as they traveled, but there were some personal living spaces off the main tunnel as well. This was made evident by the wooden doors fitted into the entrances at intervals along the corridor. One door open as they approached, and the woman stopped in the doorway when she saw Dreyken.

She bowed deeply. "My Lord."

"Good morning, Asa. I hope your family is faring well."

The woman straightened and smiled at him. "Yes, they are very well." She glanced at Talwyn and her eyes went wide.

"Asa, this is a guest of mine, Talwyn." Talwyn bowed her head to the woman.

"A guest? We haven't had one of those in . . . centuries. Welcome Talwyn."

The woman's words were warm, but her smile was tight and didn't reach her eyes. Talwyn couldn't fault her for feeling concerned, given how hard the Stone Dragons worked to keep themselves hidden for the past few centuries. Having a stranger just show up unannounced must definitely seem strange, and maybe even suspicious.

"Talwyn brings us some very important news. It will be shared with all the citizens once I've had time to consult with the protectors."

After taking their leave, they continued on until Dreyken stopped at the last door on the right, just before the next fork. Dreyken knocked and, without pausing, let himself in.

"Adrio, Drarcio, wake up," he bellowed.

Dreyken calling both names, indicating the two shared a room, surprised her—but only briefly. Almost as swiftly as the surprise hit came the realization that it made perfect sense for them.

Talwyn took in the room. It was larger than her cell, but furnished essentially in the same way. There was a stone table in the center of the space with a wooden bench on one side and two large wooden chairs on the other. Foodstuffs, dishes, and other items were stored in alcoves hewn into the stone walls. The fundamental difference between this space and her cell was that there were decorative and personal items here and there. They filled the space more completely and gave it a welcoming feel.

At the back of the space, there was a divider made of a wooden frame with panels of heavy cloth. There were paintings on the panels. Talwyn stepped forward to get a closer look. There were depictions of mountains with dragons circling above, flying free. Was there an artisan in the village who painted the cloth, or was Adrio or Drarcio the artist?

Talwyn was so engrossed in the images that she jumped when the panels suddenly folded to the side.

"What's going on?" Adrio asked. "You rarely come here looking for us."

He strode forward in leather pants and nothing else. Drarcio, in similar attire, followed right behind.

"Sit," Drarcio said, pointing to the chairs. Once she and Dreyken were settled, with Adrio sitting across from them, Drarcio went to an alcove, looked into a metal pot, then breathed on the outside. A short time later, steam wafted into the air.

Talwyn pointed at it past Adrio's shoulder. "So, you don't just breathe fire? You can do, what, some kind of hot breath?"

"The older and more practiced among us can," Drarcio said as he returned to the table, balancing four clay cups between his two hands. He placed them on the table and distributed one to each of them.

"And can those older and more practiced people also breathe fire in their human forms as well?"

"For the most part, yes," Adrio said.

Talwyn looked into the cup, then lifted it and sniffed. "Nettle tea?"

Drarcio nodded. "Yes. I like to have a cup when I wake up in the morning."

She took a sip of the hot liquid. "Um. It's good."

"So, what brings you here this morning?" Adrio asked.

"Talwyn had a vision last night," Dreyken said. All three sets of eyes turned to her. So she told them about what she'd seen concerning the danger to their sorceress and the demonkin attack, including that the signs point to it happening two evenings from now.

"I would like you two to help spread word among the protectors," Dreyken said. "Tell them to gather in the throne room this afternoon."

Drarcio nodded. "Of course."

"There's one more thing. Assign two of the best protectors to watch over Athnie." Dreyken glanced at her. "Our sorceress."

It was only then that Talwyn realized this was the first time she heard their sorceress's name.

When they finished discussing what needed to happen next, Dreyken led Talwyn out of the room.

"I have something to show you," Dreyken said.

At the fork just past Adrio and Drarcio's quarters, Dreyken led Talwyn down the tunnel to the right. Like everywhere else, torches dotted the walls at intervals, lighting the space. Here, however, there were no more doorways or tunnels along the way, until they got to the very end.

There, a wide wooden door with ornate carvings and symbols Talwyn was only vaguely familiar with, stood in front of them.

Dreyken pushed the door open with one hand and reached out to take her hand with the other. "These are my rooms down here."

He led her inside and closed the door behind them. The area they entered was much more refined than the other areas they'd visited. It was wide and spacious, with a high ceiling. The floor was level and polished. Many seating areas abundant with plush furs occupied the space. Time had been taken to make the stone ceiling and walls uniform and smooth, except for the places where alcoves were carved into them. There was at least that in common with everywhere else. But there were many of these alcoves here, some of which housed sculptures of metal or stone that were decorated with precious gems.

"I would have been happy to live in the same kind of rooms as everyone else," Dreyken said. His voice was shy, almost apologetic. Talwyn looked over to see he was rubbing the back of his neck. "These were my parents' quarters before me."

She nodded. "I understand." And she did. From what she'd learned of him since her arrival, she could see that the simpler rooms behind the throne room fit him better. Also, this large space must feel lonely and empty with just one person living here. It would be even more so for Dreyken if there were reminders of his family around.

"What I wanted to show you is this way."

Still holding her hand in his, he led her through another doorway and into a room just as opulent as the one before. But this time, there were curtains closing off one end of the room, and that's where he headed.

He pulled back a curtain and lifted it so she could walk through, then followed behind her. When he dropped the curtain again, it cut off the light from the many torches on the inside. There was only one lit on this side of the curtain, but as Talwyn looked ahead into the darkness, she noticed small, almost indiscernible flickers of light.

She walked slowly in that direction and stopped when she realized there was a drop-off a few paces ahead. This was clear because she could see a dark open space and then more flickering light across the way. When she neared the edge, she realized those dots of light were more torches on what looked to be a balcony that circled an enormous, circular, open space.

The Dragon lord's quarters were like the crown on the top of their community. There were levels upon levels of these circular balconies below them, all lit up with torches. Stone rails served as safety barriers. At intervals along each level, there were platforms open to the inner space, like the one she stood on now. She watched as, a few levels below, a Dragon-folk shifted and launched himself off of one of these platforms. He flew in a spiral pattern, landing on another stone platform a few more levels below.

And he wasn't the only Dragon-folk traveling this way. There were perhaps a dozen others of various colors and sizes taking off and landing, making it a quick hop from one level to another.

Talwyn sensed Dreyken move up beside her. "So this is how your people stretch their wings."

"We do have scheduled times to fly outside, but since it's much more visible, the times we can be outside are quite restricted." He pointed across the open space and down a couple of levels. "If you can see it from here, we have some levels that serve as marketplaces, where vendors can sell their wares and offer various foodstuffs."

"Where do you get your food?" she asked.

"We hunt and forage to the south of the mountain. There are also a couple of low mountain valleys where it is possible to grow certain crops. We are close enough to the southern coast that we often head there to fish. And there are plenty of springs and underground rivers to provide us with water."

He pointed to the lower levels. "There are more living quarters below, as well. And it's difficult to see from here, but the open space at the bottom is often used for gatherings, games, and entertainment."

She didn't doubt there was plenty of space down there to hold many activities at once. Unless they involved flying, of course, as that made a long distance seem much shorter. Like flying from level to level instead of walking.

"I would love to just wander around and explore down there." She looked at Dreyken. "I know we're pressed for time right now, but when the coming dangers are past, will you show me around?"

He smiled at her. "It would be my pleasure."

She looked down again, trying to see what was happening on the levels below. The area was so wide that she could see what was happening where the walls curved closer to their location, but it was very difficult to pick out any details across the way.

"Wow, this is... this is just amazing." She shook her head. "It's incredible what you've all built down here."

Peripherally, she saw Dreyken shift to face her. She tore her gaze away from the village life that carried on below her and turned to look at him.

"You can see why some of my people might be reluctant to leave here and venture back out into the wider world. Yes, we have limitations and restrictions, but it's comfortable and livable, and it's what we've grown accustomed to."

"You've become complacent."

He tipped his head one way, then the other. "In a manner of speaking."

She took a deep breath and blew it out slowly. "I would not be here disturbing you, asking you to turn your lives upside down, if I didn't already know what's coming.

"I don't know how the Dark Sorcerer found out about your people and where to find you, but he did. So, I don't regret coming here and disrupting your world. I'm glad I could warn you because, now that you know what's coming for you, you'll at least have time to prepare. And that gives you a fighting chance."

CHAPTER EIGHT

Warnings, Warhorns, & Weapons

With just over a day left before the demonkin attack, Talwyn and Dreyken had no time to spare.

After leaving Dreyken's royal quarters, they headed straight back the way they'd come. Dreyken stayed in the throne room to make sure everything was ready for the coming meeting. Talwyn headed back up to the ledge closest to her cell. She hadn't seen any exit higher than that, and she needed a high vantage point so she could double check for things she'd seen in her vision to ensure she had the timeline right. She also noted where the sentries were posted to see if any changes had to be made to prepare for the attack.

When she was done, she headed back to the throne room. She found Dreyken sitting on his ornate but uncomfortable-looking throne. Adrio and Drarcio stood on either side of him, and a young, adolescent female stood at the bottom of the dais. Talwyn recognized the girl from her vision and knew she was the sorceress.

As Talwyn approached the throne, Dreyken stood and made introductions. "I present to you Seer Guardian Talwyn Survalor. Talwyn, this is our sorceress, Athnie."

They bowed their heads to one another. The girl looked unsure and maybe a little scared, which was to be expected. Talwyn stayed next to her instead of mounting the dais to join Dreyken.

"The protectors will arrive shortly. I thought we should have some time to speak with Athnie first," Dreyken said.

Talwyn nodded her approval and turned to the young sorceress. "Athnie, has Lord Dreyken informed you of why I asked to see you here today?"

"Yes. He said that I'm in danger. That demonkin are going to attack and try to take me away." The girl trembled as she spoke, and her voice quavered. However, she also lifted her chin and met Talwyn's eyes.

Hmm. She is brave, willing to meet her fears head-on.

"They don't intend to harm you, from what I could see." Talwyn hoped this information would help calm the girl some. "However, they want you for some reason that I haven't been able to discern. Would you have any idea why? Have you been practicing any magic that might have drawn the attention of someone watching for those kinds of things?"

"No, I don't think so." Athnie shook her head. "The most powerful thing I have done so far is a fireball, but I've only been able to do small ones. They hardly even leave a black mark on the wall when I throw them."

Why would a dark sorcerer want an unpracticed, pre-manifestation sorceress?

"For now," Talwyn told her, "until we figure this out, keep close to your protectors. Do you understand?"

"Yes, of course. I will."

Talwyn placed a reassuring hand on the young female's shoulder and gave it a small squeeze.

Just then, the protectors started to filter into the room. Some of them nodded to Talwyn and some bowed, but none of them seemed surprised she was there. Talwyn mounted the steps and stood beside the dragon lord.

Dreyken leaned close to Talwyn and spoke in a low voice. "Adrio and Drarcio have already given them the reason for your presence here and informed them of the coming attack."

"Thank you, Lord Dragon." Talwyn met his eyes and gave him a grateful nod. Then she returned her attention forward to address all those present.

"Thank you all for coming. You now know of the coming demonkin attack." Those gathered answered in the affirmative or gave a nod. "For a long time before my people were attacked, we seers used our abilities only to look for and respond to threats directly related to us, or to warn the gate kings of danger. Whatever we saw about outside individuals or groups, we did nothing about. The seer elders of the time had reasoned that we should not interfere in any other group's free will, or their fate. It is for this reason that, except for a few of our warriors, we did not act when the dragons were attacked four-hundred years ago."

The many protectors in the room had been listening silently and respectfully to this point. Now there were several murmuring voices around the room.

"Don't worry, though." Talwyn spoke a little louder to be heard over the din. When they quieted, she continued. "We were punished for our mistakes. For our short-sightedness." She huffed and shook her head. "I am uncertain how much you know, since you were already here in the mountains by then, but not quite a hundred years after what happened to your people, the humans attacked the seers. My people. Many of us were slaughtered, including my family."

She paused, looked at the floor, and gathered her thoughts. And her emotions. After a moment, she continued. "You might wonder how people with our gifts would end up slaughtered when we should have seen what was coming. While we have some blind spots in our Sight, it was also because we saw enough to know that the humans had been manipulated by the demonkin to fear and mistrust us. They were being used as weapons, while the real culprits hid themselves behind the scenes. Because of this, many of my people felt the humans were innocent, so they did not fight back.

"I would like to think we learned from our mistakes." Talwyn's voice gathered in strength as she continued. "My duty is to protect the keystone at Southgate above all else. Yet I've been having visions of your people for a long time, as have many others among my people. I cannot ignore these visions. They are why I am here. There is a dark sorcerer behind everything that happened to both of our peoples. Some theorize that we may be dealing with followers of Azedel, plotting through the centuries to fulfill his vision. We cannot be certain. Either way, the demonkin are now looking for you. I have foreseen that there will be a company of demonkin sent to find you and lay siege to you."

Again, there were murmurings. Some sounded concerned. Others sounded like they were looking forward to slaughtering a few demonkin.

She raised her voice again to be heard above the din. "There is more. Just last night, I had another dream-vision. My fellow guardians and I believe that the Dark Sorcerer is overextending himself, letting more of his plans slip through and into our visions.

I could catch more details last night. First, the attack will happen tomorrow night."

This time, when the voices spoke up, they were louder, angrier.

"That is not all." She held up her hand to stay them. "I couldn't see the reason behind it, but they are after your sorceress. You will need to keep her protected throughout the coming attack.

"We believe the events of the past four hundred years are all linked, and that they may also be linked to what happened three thousand years ago. We believe this because, in a little more than a month from now, the stars and planets will once again be aligned as they were when the Great Gate was last used."

Gasps of surprise sounded from all around. The voices once again grew louder and even more concerned. Talwyn knew this information would be a shock to them, so she gave them a few minutes to discuss this turn of events.

While she waited, however, she saw Airgan moving toward her and realized that the Elder Council had arrived during her speech. When Airgan was at the front of the room, just a few feet from her, he stuck his thumb and middle finger in his mouth and let out a loud, sharp whistle.

Talwyn watched Airgan carefully as the room fell silent. The Elder puffed out his chest, and Talwyn braced herself for whatever might come out of his mouth.

"We have been safe here, underneath these mountains, for four hundred years." Airgan's tone was arrogant and challenging. "Who is to say that the demonkin will find us if we stay hidden here? How could they know we were here to begin with? We should not risk exposing ourselves like this! We do not know this woman." He gestured to Talwyn. "Why should we trust her?"

"You should trust her because your dragon lord does." Dreyken spoke in a deep voice that carried for all gathered to hear and left the room silent. He looked around, meeting the gazes of many of his protectors.

Still, Airgan would not be swayed. "This is something you should have brought to the Elder Council before calling a meeting of the protectors."

"Have you not been listening?" Dreyken's expression was incredulous. He stood tall and pulled his shoulders back as he spoke. His stance and his fierce expression added to his presence, making it feel as though he had suddenly grown larger.

That's it. Be the leader you were meant to be.

Talwyn wanted to smile, but she held it back, certain that some, like Airgan, would think it was mocking and take offense.

"The demonkin are attacking tomorrow night! We need to use our time to plan and prepare, not to debate the issue in a meeting."

Dreyken looked around at his protectors once again. He exuded power and authority as he stood before them. "I trust Talwyn unequivocally. She has shown me things that she could have kept to herself. Things that will benefit our people. Things that can change our future for the better and bring back much of what we've lost."

"Give us some proof," Airgan demanded. "Tell us what she has shown you."

"It is not yet time."

"The Elder Council has a right to know."

"And *I* have the right to decide *when* it is best for you to know. I am the Dragon lord! It is time you remembered that, Airgan. It is time we *all* remembered that." Dreyken addressed the group confidently, looking very much the man he had just proclaimed himself to be.

Talwyn looked at the group of Elders, curious to see how they were responding to Dreyken. Airgan acted as though he was speaking for the entire Elder Council. However, the other members seemed pleased by Dreyken's proclamation, even proud of him. Andes and Skyran had huge smiles on their faces and were nodding approvingly. The protectors were standing at attention, instinctively responding to their leader's authority.

Talwyn decided it was time to get the meeting back on track. She stepped forward to address the crowd once again, looking at Dreyken as she did so. He nodded to her to go ahead.

"I came here to warn your people. I came to prepare you. To stand beside you in the coming attack. However, I admit I'm also hoping to gain your friendship and trust. Once the attack on your people is over and you are safe once again, I hope that some of you will come with me to Southgate. They will need help to defend against the attack that will shortly follow there. I also hope that there are warriors among you who will then willingly accompany us to the Great Gate, where we will need all the help we can get.

"Learn from the past mistakes of *my* people. Do not wait until your indifference to the others who dwell in our realm comes back to haunt you. Make the right choice now, while you still can. While all of Sterrenvar's people can work together. If you turn your backs on them now, there may be no going back."

"Are you threatening the Stone Dragons?" Airgan sneered.

"Nooo." Talwyn drew the word out as if she were explaining something to a small child. "I am merely informing you of the possible outcomes my people have foreseen."

"For now, however, we need to plan our defense," Dreyken said, and the protectors nodded their agreement.

"You need to have protectors with your sorceress at all times," Talwyn repeated. "I do not know why they want her, but I know they are determined to get to her. I suggest that you have warriors out on the mountain, trying to keep the demonkin from approaching too closely. You should also have sentries posted at each entrance. There will be demonkin who can change their appearance to look like anyone, and they will sneak in to grab your sorceress if they can."

Worried murmurs rose around them.

"How can we protect ourselves against such an enemy?" one protector asked.

"Right. How can we stop them if they look like our own people?" another asked. "How do we know who's who?"

"Their illusions are visual only," Talwyn explained. "If you can touch one, you can often tell that what you see and what you feel don't match. But I know it isn't always possible to get that close. So, watch for unusual behavior. Anything that seems out of the ordinary or contrary to what we've discussed here today."

"I will assign two of my best protectors to stay with Athnie," Dreyken said. "Since my warriors and I know our mountain best"—he suddenly looked doubtful of this statement and glanced at Talwyn before continuing—"we will plan the details."

Dreyken and his protectors gathered to discuss strategy. Talwyn looked around and noticed that the council members had dispersed to talk with the protectors. All except one.

Airgan now stood at the opposite side of the room, near an entryway. He was facing her, and he was speaking with a cloaked figure. She found this to be a little suspicious. Though she had seen a couple of Stone Dragons wearing cloaks within the mountain, it wasn't very common.

She slowly made her way over to Airgan. He glanced up and noticed her approaching. He then said something to his companion, who quickly sidestepped Airgan and left the room without turning around. She tried to glimpse the individual who was leaving, but to no avail. The mystery person was gone from her sight by the time she stood facing Airgan, her back to the gathered crowd.

Talwyn tilted her head and regarded him through narrowed eyes. "Why did your companion run off so soon, and..." she turned her head and looked around the room, "why were they wearing a cloak when no one else is? It isn't particularly cold here."

"You're an outsider. I do not have to explain anything to you."

"Oh?" She raised her eyebrows. "Given what we were just discussing, one might think it was suspicious. Like perhaps you are up to something. Is this something I should mention to your dragon lord and his protectors?"

Airgan glared at her, jaw clenched tight and his face reddening in what she could only assume was anger.

"Fine. I still do not think it is any of your concern, but just so you do not falsely accuse me of anything, that was my niece. And she was wearing a cloak because she wasn't formally invited."

Talwyn considered Airgan for a moment, watching for any signs of dishonesty. Seeing none, she could only assume he was speaking the truth.

Did he really sneak his niece up, hoping for an opportunity to get her close to Dreyken, then? Now, when there were events of so much more importance going on? Where were this man's priorities?

"Okay," she said. "Let's forget about your visitor for now and focus on you."

"Before you speak, I would like to remind you I am a member of the Elder Council, and you are merely a guest here."

She took a step forward and looked down at him, using their slight height difference to her advantage.

"You are poison to your people." She murmured, but she was unable to keep the disdain out of her voice. "You are trusted because you are a Dragon-folk, and Dragon-folk always make the best choices for the good of their people, right? No Stone Dragon wants to believe that one of their Elders is capable of deceit and manipulation, of being self-serving and power-hungry."

Airgan's face was once again turning red with anger and spite, but Talwyn continued.

"You may see yourself as powerful, as a puppet-master, guiding the strings from behind the scenes." She wiggled her fingers in demonstration, then paused thoughtfully for a moment. "Come to think of it, you are a lot like the Dark Sorcerer and his demonkin in that way."

Airgan jolted back, his eyes wide and mouth sputtering. "How dare you!"

Then she leaned closer and spoke directly into his ear. "Tell me, Airgan, what happens to the puppeteer once the strings have been cut? I pray for your people's sake that they are cut before you become the death of your race."

Airgan opened his mouth to speak, but Talwyn held up a hand to shush him. "Do not try to deny what I know is truth, Airgan. I am a seer, and I see through you."

With that, she walked away to listen and take part in the planning once again. She had a feeling that this wouldn't be the last time Airgan tried to manipulate things to his advantage. She would have to monitor him.

Tensions were high from the time of the meeting through the next afternoon as Talwyn helped the Dragon-folk prepare to defend their mountain home. Protectors and citizens held training sessions. Dreyken and his top protectors and advisors laid out and prepared defensive and offensive strategies. Healers and volunteers readied healing stations.

The upper areas—the holding cells and the throne room—made up the base of operations. These areas had the easiest access to the outside, were closest to the armory, and were far from their village under the mountain.

When most things were ready or underway, Talwyn made her way over to talk with Drarcio and Adrio. "I would ask you to invite anyone who will be defending the mountain down to the armory to choose weapons and armor. It is time to distribute Aleyn's gifts to your people."

Talwyn knew from visions, and from Aleyn himself, that he had fashioned special armor for the Dragon-folk. It was created in such a way that the inner layers would loosen and extend outward with a shift. However, even the best armorers could only do so much, and the Dragon-folks' physical forms were so different in both size and shape.

Talwyn accompanied the first group down. Once they reached the armory, she turned to face them. "The Stone Dragons, in dragon form, are much larger than in human form, to state the obvious. The armor has strategically placed links that release under the right amount of pressure, like when you are shifting from human to dragon form. So, the armor covers vital areas for your dragon form but leaves much exposed. When you shift back from dragon to human, however, the links will have to be reset. It will be more of a hindrance to you in that situation, and you'd be better off dumping it. So, this armor is better than what you had previously, but it has its weaknesses. I suggest you keep that in mind, especially if you want to shift from dragon to human form."

"We have natural armor in dragon form," stated one of the men.

"That is only an advantage if the enemy has not prepared measures that would be effective against your dragons," Talwyn countered. "If they have, then this armor gives you an advantage. Also, there are a couple of things you need to remember. The most important of these is that they are after your sorceress. Which leads me to another important point: as far as we can tell, the enemy does not know the extent of the seer involvement. They suspect we may be involved to some extent, as is clear because their sorcerer has blocked or blurred some of our visions. However, I don't believe they know that I'm here. They don't know that you've been warned and are preparing to defend yourselves."

"Our thanks to you for this advantage," said a female protector named Iniri, nodding her head to Talwyn. "We are in your debt."

"Don't offer your thanks yet," Talwyn said. "Save it for after our victory today."

Talwyn selected people from the first group of new weapons and armor to distribute the rest and show the others how the armor worked. Then she headed back up to the throne room.

Once there, Talwyn approached Dreyken, who was conversing with Adrio and Drarcio. They paused and gave her their attention as she approached.

"Everything is in place, Talwyn," Dreyken said. "There will be an archer at each entry point to watch for any approaching enemy and to defend against them."

"We are also going to have a couple of protectors hidden amid the rocks near each entrance," Drarcio added.

"You can take the highest access," Dreyken added.

"That's the way you brought me in the first night, right?" Talwyn asked.

"Yes." Dreyken looked at her with narrowed eyes, and she realized she'd just given him a pretty big hint that maybe she wasn't as unaware as he thought that first night. Luckily, he didn't pursue the topic . . . probably because they had more pressing concerns at the moment.

"Our thinking is that you are probably the only one among us who has seen an ainmith before. And probably less than half of us have seen a demonkin," Dreyken said. "You would know better what to look for and could likely give us the earliest warning possible."

Talwyn nodded. "Sounds like a good plan."

Before Talwyn could head off to her station, Iniri approached with one of the two females she had overheard in the throne room her first night here.

Iniri introduced her companion. "This is my sister, Sukia." Sukia bowed her head to the group. "We haven't had need of these in a few centuries, but Sukia is a bit of a historian. One of her hobbies is creating war horns from the horns of the beasts we hunt. I am hoping they can be useful now."

Iniri took a horn from her sister and held it up for the others to see. It was intricately carved and inlaid with gold and silver.

Talwyn took it from Iniri and examined it more closely. "This is exquisite."

"Thank you," Sukia replied.

Sukia glanced up at Dreyken, and Talwyn guessed from her expression that there was more than historical interest behind her war-horn hobby. It was also likely an excuse to get close to a certain hunter when he brought back prey.

I wonder how she'd react if she knew what Dreyken's hopes are for me.

Given that many women from his own clan had set their sights on him, she should be more flattered by his attention. Actually, she was flattered to an extent. She would just feel better about it—and less cautious, maybe—if she were sure his feelings for her were real. If she was certain they weren't because of a sense of mystery or the novelty of meeting someone new.

Sukia's eyes were still on Dreyken as she spoke. "I have enough to give to all the sentries, on the mountain and at the entry points. I thought this would make a quick way to signal one another if someone sees something."

Talwyn noticed that the way Sukia was regarding him was not lost on Dreyken, either. He cleared his throat and shifted on his feet uncomfortably. Glancing at Talwyn, he then said, "Thank you, Sukia. These will be very helpful." Sukia beamed at Dreyken, and Talwyn could not help but grin in amusement at his obvious discomfort. Dreyken despised being looked at with the type of hero-worship that Sukia obviously felt toward him. Even if Dreyken had not said so before, it would be obvious from his body language.

Talwyn cleared her throat and tried to stifle her grin. "If you will all excuse me, there is not much time left and I need to watch for signs of the enemy. Thank you again, Sukia, Iniri." Both females bowed their heads to Talwyn, then she turned and headed up to her chamber.

Once in her room, she made sure she had her best knives tucked into her boots. Her new daggers tucked into the holsters on her belt at the back of her waist, a short sword at her right side, and the horn on her left. Then she placed her favorite weapon, the bow, at her back, along with a quiver of metal arrows that were light but strong. She hoped she could find and collect any she had to use after the battle.

Talwyn turned to head out the door, only to find Dreyken standing there, looking at her with concern.

"I will go with you to keep watch."

"Don't be ridiculous, Dreyken." Talwyn stepped closer to him. "You are the Dragon lord, and today you made a great step forward in reclaiming your place in your people's hearts. As Dragon lord, you need to oversee preparations and make sure everything is in place."

Dreyken shifted his weight from foot to foot and rubbed the back of his neck. She knew he really wanted to be by her side, but she also knew he made significant progress today. He needed to continue that momentum by being the leader they hoped him to be.

She also didn't want to encourage his feelings toward her. Not while she was still unsure whether she could reciprocate fully. Yes, she was attracted to him, which was a very significant thing for a seer who had previously had a mate. But that still did not mean she was ready to lower her defenses and open herself up to the possibility of that kind of pain again.

"Very well," he said. "I will stay in the throne room to oversee everything for now." He pursed his lips together, almost as if the idea of that was making him ill. "But I will send Iniri to you for backup, and I will come to you again if I can."

He still stood there, shifting his weight and flexing his fingers repeatedly. She understood he was having a difficult time with the idea of not being by her side in this battle, and she knew what that meant. However, she was not yet ready to address what was happening between them, and she knew they needed to keep focused on the trials to come. So she pretended not to notice his struggle.

However, to make things a little easier for him, she said, "Fine. Send Iniri to me."

Dreyken still hesitated in the doorway until, finally, he closed the distance between them and cupped her face in his hands. His lips then met hers in a short but emotion-filled kiss. Talwyn braced herself to resist at first, but when she felt his soft yet firm lips on her own, her heart overruled her head, and she kissed him back. Then Dreyken pressed his forehead to hers and whispered, "Be careful. Stay safe."

"I will." She lifted her hands to cover his on her cheeks. "And you as well."

Dreyken nodded and took a step back. As he turned to leave, Talwyn called to him once again. "Dreyken." When he turned his attention back to her, she said, "You know that when they are done here, the demonkin will move on to Southgate."

He was quiet for a moment. Talwyn could see from his expression, and the stiff way he stood, that he understood what she was saying. She would have to leave to help protect Southgate, so the time was now short for him to decide if the Stone Dragons would aid in the fight. It may not be the ideal time to mention it to him, but no time would be ideal, and she wanted him to have time to mentally prepare.

"I understand," he replied. He looked at her with a serious expression for a moment, lips pressed together as if he were trying to hold something back. Then he gave a stiff nod. With that, he turned again and strode quickly back down the passageway to the throne room. Talwyn turned and headed up the tunnel that led outside.

CHAPTER NINE

Attack & Defend

Talwyn's senses were on high alert as she walked out to the edge of the wide stone ledge where Dreyken had gently placed her on her first night here. It seemed impossible that it had been only a few days ago.

It was dusk, and Talwyn knew from her visions that things would start happening once the half-moon was high.

The Dark Sorcerer and his henchmen likely wanted to use the cover of darkness as much as possible. Luckily, however, seers and

Folk all had excellent senses. On a clear night such as tonight, they'd still have enough visibility that they would not be taken completely by surprise. The enemy would have had more of a chance to do that if her visions hadn't given them forewarning and they didn't know what to keep an eye out for.

Still, she needed to be vigilant to make sure nothing sneaked through.

At times, Talwyn stood watching the northern horizon. At other times, she walked to the edge and peered down over the face of the mountain. As she stood watch, Iniri approached from the side.

"I have never seen a demonkin before. What should I expect?"

Talwyn continued to survey the skies and the mountainside while she spoke. "Well, since they are crossbreeds of demons and humans, they can vary somewhat. But there are some things that are the same. There were two different demon types brought across, and in limited numbers. So these days, they have very human-like features, but they are taller and broader. If you were tracking them, you would look for footprints that are wider than those of humans, especially at the heel.

"You can find demonkin who have pink-and-red-mottled skin. They look like they've been burned in a fire, almost. These demonkin have horns on their cheeks that continue up and around their temples. The other kind looks similar except their skin is variations of gray and black and tougher than human skin."

"Can both types disguise themselves?" Iniri's voice quavered a little.

Talwyn glanced at her at saw her brow was wrinkled and she was biting her lip. Her worry was to be expected. A few short days ago, the Dragon-folks' life in their mountain fortress was normal and calm. Then they get their first visitor in centuries, which would have been disconcerting enough without that visitor telling them they were about to be stormed by demonkin.

"No," Talwyn said, turning back to scan for signs of the enemy again. "Only the ones with the red-and-pink skin can, but not even all of those. From what my people have seen in visions over the years, this ability is rare these days. It started disappearing down through the generations."

"So, you said before that you can tell if someone is a disguised demonkin by touch, right?"

"Yes." She nodded. "If you know the person, you might see behaviors that are unusual for them. The only other way is by touch. They don't physically change like animal-folk. They have the power of illusion. It's like a mist that rises to cover their bodies, but if you touch them, you might notice that what you see and what you feel do not match. Especially if you touch their face or foreheads, because of the horns, of course."

Talwyn's description was interrupted when something caught her attention. "Look over there, Iniri." She pointed to a spot on the horizon.

Iniri looked in the direction Talwyn pointed. It took a moment or two before she said, "I see it. Are those the ainmith?"

"Yes." Luckily, the ainmith were white, so they were probably easier to see now that darkness was descending than they would have been earlier in the day.

"Wow." Although the ainmith were servants of their foes, Iniri's awe was clear when she spoke. "I have heard them described in stories, but I've never actually seen one before."

"There's about a dozen of them I can see so far. I estimate each one will carry three demonkin, so we are looking at around thirty-six demonkin attacking by air."

"Come here and look down." Talwyn pointed over the edge. Iniri stepped close and looked where Talwyn indicated. "That's probably another three or four-dozen scaling the mountain. Not even a hundred in total."

"That is good odds for us," noted Iniri.

"Yes, almost too good, given they are attacking a mountain where their enemy can see their approach . . ."

"Well, you yourself said they were not expecting us to be prepared."

"True, but they had to have expected at least one lookout."

"So, what are you thinking?" Iniri looked at Talwyn inquisitively.

"Well, it's either poor planning, they've spread their forces too thin, or they aren't really interested in conquering the Stone Dragon lair so much as capturing the sorceress."

"Which do you believe it is?" Iniri inquired.

"If you had asked me before my last vision, I would have said they've spread themselves too thin. This would account for us getting more of the visions that the Dark Sorcerer has been trying to hide."

"But . . ."

"But since I had that vision, I've wondered if maybe he has something else in mind."

"Something that involves our sorceress," Iniri stated.

"Exactly."

Talwyn looked around. There were three others stationed on the ledge with them that had arrived right after Iniri. Up above them, two of the best Stone Dragon archers hid behind some outcroppings of rocks. There would be more hidden along the mountaintop. They were ready.

Looking back out to the skies, Talwyn noticed the white forms getting closer. The demonkin scaling the mountainsides would be in range of their archers soon.

"Should we sound the warning?" Iniri seemed to read her mind.

"Yes." Talwyn nodded decisively. "It's time."

Iniri pulled her battle horn off her waist strap and gave one solid blow. Right away, they could hear the answering horns. Talwyn looked up to see the archers nocking their arrows. They readied themselves, then held, waiting for the enemy to move within range.

Talwyn nocked an arrow as well but held it low, aimed toward the ground. She hadn't yet had the opportunity to practice with the galanite arrows Aleyn had made for her, so she did not know their range or accuracy. She would guess, however, since they were crafted by a master, that both were good.

Talwyn took another glance down the slope of the mountain to check on the progress of the demonkin below. They were moving slowly, taking the time to shield themselves under outcroppings whenever they could. That was unfortunate. It would have been helpful if they were less intelligent.

Talwyn judged that the aerial assault would reach them before the climbers did, so she returned her attention ahead. The winged ainmith with their passengers were getting larger and larger as they approached.

She lifted her bow and arrow and pulled the string back close to her cheek. She waited. If she timed this correctly, she could use the ainmith's falling bulk as a weapon. Once she judged they were close enough, she took a deep breath. Then, breathing out, she let her arrow fly. It was like she had given a signal, as several other arrows were loosed all around her. She watched as her arrow flew straight at its intended target.

The ainmith Talwyn had aimed for pulled to its left, and Talwyn's arrow hit the right side of its neck. The beast screeched and faltered as it started losing blood profusely from its wound. At least she'd hit an artery.

The creature lost altitude but continued traveling toward the mountain as it did so. It crashed into the mountainside about a hundred paces below them. Talwyn watched the demonkin passengers jump free and grab any handhold they could find just before it hit. One of them grabbed hold of something, and two others went plummeting to their deaths on the rocks below.

The ainmith's now-lifeless form tumbled down over the mountain face as demonkin scrambled to move out of its path. The demonkin had already spread to the right and left, looking for alternate approaches, hoping to avoid their arrows. So the ainmith took a few demonkin down the mountain with it, but not as many as Talwyn had hoped.

A few feet away, Iniri and two other archers scrambled to safety as another ainmith crashed onto the ledge next to them. The beast had been killed, but now they had three demonkin on the ledge with them to deal with.

Talwyn held her bow in one hand as she unsheathed her sword with the other. Training with both hands and having hundreds of years to practice led to versatile champions, and she was grateful for that training now.

One demonkin lunged for her, and she sidestepped and brought her sword down on the side of its neck and over its collarbone. It was not a deep cut, but the demonkin dropped its sword and roared. Talwyn did not waste a moment; she used its distraction to bring her sword back and drive it through its chest. It was still skewered on her sword as she turned to put it between her and the outer side of the ledge. Then she brought her leg up and gave a powerful push-kick just below where her sword had struck, effectively clearing it off her blade and sending it over the edge at the same time.

"Take a few of your friends with you on your way down!"

Another ainmith was circling overhead, and Talwyn took a moment to assess its passengers. It looked like it was carrying two swordsmen and an archer. An archer who was now aiming at Iniri.

"Iniri, MOVE!" Talwyn lunged for her. However, before Talwyn had even finished the words, a male protector flew into Iniri from the right, knocking her out of the path of the arrow. The arrow struck the male instead of Iniri, and he dropped to the ground, taking Iniri with him.

Talwyn was not given the opportunity to check and see how they were, however. At that moment, she felt the strike of a blade across her back. She could feel the pressure of the strike, and it caused her to stagger forward a little. But she knew it hadn't pierced the galanite quiver and arrows, let alone the galanite chain mail armor she was wearing. Still, she was annoyed that she had allowed one of the enemy to get a strike in on her.

She turned to face the demonkin with her most sinister smile on her face. Stepping forward, she brought her sword diagonally down in front of herself. Her blade sliced through skin and bone easily as it struck. Hmm. The enemy must not supply all its soldiers with decent armor. How fortunate for her and her allies. She finished the creature off with her sword through its heart.

The Dragon-folk archers hidden in the rocks nearby had been busy while she fought, she now noticed as she looked around. The corpses of three other demonkin lay nearby, and a winged beast was taking its last breath as it lay across jagged rocks a dozen paces from the archers.

Knowing there were still more demonkin scaling the steep rock to try to penetrate the mountain, Talwyn had an idea. Inspecting the ainmith for the first time, she noted it was about the size of a horse. At least, it looked to be as tall as a large horse. However, it was thicker and shaped more like a dog, with ears that pointed up. Instead of fur, it was covered in white feathers. It had paws like a dog, but its claws were long and curved, reminding her of the talons of a bird of prey. Its mangled wings lay at odd angles over and around it. Its wing span was quite impressive. It was a magnificent creature. Too bad its master was an evil, dark sorcerer.

She slung her bow across her back, sheathed her sword, took a deep breath, and gave herself some words of encouragement. "You can do this." Then she braced her shoulder against the spine of the fallen beast, planted her feet firmly, and pushed with all her might.

"Merciful Universe! You need to stop eating rocks!"

The thing was very heavy, but Talwyn gave it another push, then another, then another, until it was just at the very edge. Then she peeked down again to make sure she was aiming correctly before giving it one last shove.

"Catch!"

The closest demonkin heard her yell and looked up—just as the winged beast came their way. On the way down, it knocked several of them off the mountainside to their demise, the impressive spread of its wings sweeping away any in its path.

Talwyn then turned and assessed the situation. She still had a few minutes before any surviving climbers reached them. So she took advantage of the brief pause to check on Iniri and the other protector. She hadn't even gotten to know his name.

Thankfully, both were alive and breathing. Iniri was groaning, trapped under the weight of her savior, who was unconscious. When Talwyn approached, Iniri looked up at her. "I'm okay. Just trapped."

"I'm going to check him over quickly before I move him." Talwyn said, sheathing her sword.

"Okay."

As Talwyn checked the protector for injuries, she could see none that explained why he had dropped like he had. "I don't understand. It looks like the arrow just grazed his biceps. Do you notice anything else, Iniri?"

Iniri looked over the man as far as her position allowed. "No, there's nothing I can see."

Talwyn moved the unconscious protector off of Iniri. As Iniri righted herself, she shifted and favored her left leg a little. "Are you injured?" Talwyn asked.

"My leg just got a little twisted. I'll be fine."

Talwyn looked more closely at the protector's wound. It looked tinged with green. "Do you see this?" Talwyn asked Iniri.

Iniri came closer to inspect the wound. Talwyn stood up and began searching for the arrow that struck him. She found it a couple of paces away, partially hidden in a small crevice. She picked it up and examined the arrowhead. It was coated in something that looked thick and sticky, almost like tree sap, except it was an unnatural green color. She'd never seen anything quite this shade before. It almost looked like it glowed.

"What did you find?" Iniri asked from behind her.

"It looks like some kind of poison."

"Poison? Is he going to die?"

"His breathing and heartbeat seem normal, but we should get him to a healer right away."

Talwyn took a strip of leather from her belt and wrapped the arrowhead, being careful not to touch it. Then she snapped the shaft an inch away from the arrowhead. She was just tucking it into a small pouch on her belt when the sound of metal scraping over stone could be heard from behind them. The demonkin who had not been knocked off the mountain by falling bodies had started to climb over the edge.

"Can you get him to safety?" Talwyn asked Iniri, who nodded in response. Iniri grabbed her downed savior's body by the shoulders and started dragging him toward the entrance.

Talwyn turned to face the demonkin. She quickly readied her bow, nocked an arrow, aimed, and fired before it even had a chance to react. It was only a few paces in front of her, so the force of the arrow striking knocked it backward. It fell into another demonkin that had just climbed up behind it, and they both went tumbling over the edge.

Talwyn followed and peered down. There were still two more demonkin that she could see climbing toward her ledge. She quickly dispatched of them with her bow and turned to take stock of the situation.

A few of the Stone Dragon archers had now moved toward the south slope and were firing arrows downward. She could not see what was happening from her position, so she ran to the edge, leaned out, and looked down. There were three ainmith circling around the southern entrance not far below.

Talwyn heard shouting and looked behind her. Stone Dragon archers were engaging three other beasts that had just arrived and were making loops above them. The demonkin archers were firing down at them from their higher vantage point, but the Stone Dragons used rocks and boulders as cover and fired back. A menacing screech made her turn again, only to see another ainmith heading straight for her with its front claws outstretched.

Already at the edge, she had nowhere to run, and there wasn't enough time to nock an arrow. So she pivoted to the side as it reached for her.

The creature's claws scratched her upper arm, but she avoided being gored. She grabbed on to its leg with one hand, her other still clutching her bow.

The ainmith flew into the open air, leaving her dangling precariously underneath it, far, far above the ground. Luckily, her awkward position under the beast shielded her from attack by the riders. However, she wouldn't be able to hold on long, especially since the ainmith was shaking his paw, trying to get her off.

Talwyn looked down again at the enemy attacking the entrance, and a crazy idea formed in her mind. But it wouldn't be safe while the riders were still on the back of the ainmith and could target her.

She awkwardly slung her bow over her shoulder with one hand. Once it was secure, she used both hands to pull herself up to wrap her legs around the forepaw as well. She reached out, grabbed the leg of the closest demonkin rider, and pulled sharply, yanking it off its mount.

She watched it fall : : : and fall, turning away just before it contacted the rocks below.

The ainmith lurched as the second rider, now having better access to her, swung at her with its sword every time the beast's wings went up. It wasn't the smartest decision.

On the third swing, Talwyn leaned her body to the inside, grabbing the ainmith's other front paw and releasing the one she'd been holding before the demonkin could make contact. What the sword did make contact with was the creature's leg. The clumsy strike didn't cut deep, but it was enough that the ainmith screeched and jerked. The attacker had leaned out precariously to reach her, so the ainmith's sudden movement sent the demonkin tumbling off to meet his friend far below . . . followed closely by the archer's bow.

That left only the archer who, without his weapon, wouldn't be able to target the Dragon-folk on the mountain, so she turned her attention to the greater threats.

She scanned below her, where the three ainmith still circled. Each winged foe was carrying an archer and a couple of swordsmen. The creatures were making passes in front of the entrance as the demonkin archers fired into it.

They were drawing fire, and the Dragon-folks' attention, away from another danger.

On the mountain face, and climbing down toward the entrance, were six demonkin who'd been dropped off above. This entrance opened onto a sheer drop, so the Dragon-folk stationed inside to defend this entry point would not see the climbers approaching.

"Oh no, you don't." She quickly formulated a plan. She watched their movements for a couple of moments as they circled below.

Looking up at the ainmith she was holding on to, she said, "I don't suppose you'd fly directly over those guys, would you? Didn't think so."

She shook her head. "How am I going to get you to go where I want you, big guy?" Deciding to tug on the feathers on one side of its neck to see if she could direct it that way, she reached up. It was then that she noticed a leather rope dangling from the ainmith's mouth. It looked like the demonkin used reins to direct the ainmith in much the same way that humans used them to lead their horses.

She reached out to grab the rope, but it moved away from her hand. The archer must have moved up to take control of the reins. She quickly snatched it before it could move again and gave a firm yank. The demonkin yelped and lurched to the side but stayed on.

Talwyn pulled on the reins while the demonkin was busy steadying himself, hoping this would get the ainmith to move in the right direction. Looking down, she waited until she thought they were on the correct path and released the reins.

"Universe, guide me," she muttered. She waited until the time was right, took a deep breath, then flung herself out into the air.

The air whistled as it blew by her in a rush, and for a tense moment, it looked as though her target might veer off to the right. Thankfully, the demonkin holding the reins steadied it.

The ainmith and their riders were focused on the entrance and were not expecting an attack from above, so her landing on one of the creatures' backs took them unawares. The winged beast faltered a little under her body weight as she landed with an *oof*, and the demonkin directly in front of her turned to her, wide-eyed.

"Surprise!" she said, quickly pulling herself upright. She brought her dagger up and sliced it across its throat. The demonkin grabbed at its gaping wound, but soon went limp and slid off the side of the beast. The next demonkin noticed something happening behind it. However, before it had fully turned to face her, she drove her dagger through the side of its neck and pushed it off the ainmith as well.

That left the demonkin archer. Thankfully, the creature's focus on its target and the cover provided by the blustering of the wind allowed her to creep up behind it unnoticed. As it was aiming an arrow at the entrance, she brought her dagger around and slit its throat as well. She then pushed the body off the ainmith and moved up into position to grab the reins.

CHAPTER TEN

Takedowns

"Hold your fire!" Dreyken shouted, just as his archers were preparing to fire a volley at the ainmith that was now preparing to make another pass.

"What is it?" Drarcio's voice sounded from beside him.

Dreyken was sure he had seen a streak of red fall toward the winged beast just a moment ago. This was confirmed when he watched one, then two, then three demonkin fall from the beast.

"Talwyn."

Drarcio followed Dreyken's line of sight to see what was happening. When he spotted her, his eyes went wide. "That is one fiery woman."

She aimed for the mountainside, which they couldn't see from their angle. They did, however, hear the screams as her arrows hit their marks, and saw demonkin fall to meet their end. Then they watched as she turned her bow downward to target the other beasts. The demonkin had apparently noticed the other, smaller entrance a couple of hundred paces below and had moved down to target that one.

Dreyken shook his head in disbelief. "She's crazy."

"I would use the word... fearless," Drarcio countered.

"Yes, well, a little fear is healthy now and then." Dreyken took a deep breath. "Time to test the new armor." He ran toward the exit and flung himself into the open expanse beyond, arms spread wide, shifting midair.

As his form expanded and his wings unfurled behind him, he felt the layers of the armor let go and spread out. Loops of the same fine mail as the armor had been created to fit around the middle fingers, and these now helped to pull the armor outward. As the lowest layers came free, a space was left to let the wings jut out and move freely.

The armor had felt thick and bulky on his human form, especially since he wasn't accustomed to wearing anything more than leather. However, on his dragon form it was light and hardly noticeable. Once he fully shifted, he flapped his powerful wings, feeling them catch the wind. He lifted into the air and made a pass over Talwyn, twisting and turning to ensure the armor did not restrict his movement before turning his attention back to the fiery seer.

Talwyn sent two arrows, one right after the other, into the heads of the ainmith circling some distance below. They plummeted to the earth, taking their riders with them.

Dreyken maneuvered his large, bulky frame beneath Talwyn's ainmith. He turned his head to the side to glance up at her. She was leaning to the side, watching him--hopefully, she'd understand his intentions. Sure enough, she jumped at just the right moment, landed on her stomach on his back, then pulled herself forward to sit over his shoulders.

She leaned over his neck so her head was just about next to his. "You missed me so much, you had to come find me, did you?" She spoke loudly enough that he could hear her voice above the wind that rushed by them. Dragon-Dreyken just shook his head at her and huffed a smoky breath. She ran her hand along the side of his neck in what was clearly an affectionate caress, and he shivered.

Dreyken now circled the winged beast Talwyn had just leaped from. Peripherally, he saw Talwyn lift her bow and aim, but the creature twisted to the side. Talwyn's bow moved from his sight and he heard her say, "It's just an animal that was following its master's commands." Dreyken pulled away from it and they watched as it flew up and over the mountain, back toward the north.

"There are more on the rock face." Talwyn used her bow in Dreyken's peripheral vision to point out the demonkin climbing toward the entrances. There were two approaching the higher entrance and four approaching the entrance below.

Dreyken circled around again, lining up with the demonkin along the higher path. He breathed out a blast of dragon-fire once he was in range, then quickly banked to avoid the flames. They wouldn't bother him, of course, but he didn't want to chance harming Talwyn.

The two now flaming demonkin lost their hold on the mountainside and plummeted to their deaths below.

As he moved through the air, Talwyn tightened her hold at the right moments and leaned with his movements as if flying on a dragon was natural to her. This gave him confidence that he could do what he needed to do without worrying about her falling.

Dreyken swept along the side of the mountain and once again circled back. This time, he reduced his altitude enough to target the demonkin that were lower on the rock face.

As they made their approach this time, Talwyn let an arrow fly. Dreyken watched it hit one of the demonkin. The creature didn't fall from the mountain, though. Instead, the arrow had gone straight through its body and wedged into a crevice in the rocks behind it, effectively pinning it in place.

Talwyn was an impeccable shot. He had assumed she would be good, but this was the first time he had seen her in action, and now the word *good* did not seem enough. She hit the demonkin in the heart on the first try, causing it to drop the bow and arrow it had trained on him. It amazed him she could make such a shot from this distance, especially considering they were moving and this was her first time riding on the back of a Dragon-folk.

Then they were in range of the other two demonkin, and Dreyken let go a blast of searing breath. He once again watched flaming demonkin plummet to the ground far below.

Dreyken turned and took another sweeping pass in front of the south face of the mountain. It seemed they had taken care of all the enemy on this side, so Dreyken approached the upper entrance and slowed down with big, slow, gusting flaps of his wings. His warriors moved out of the way so the bulk of his dragon could come inside. Once he landed, Talwyn dismounted and turned to watch him shift back to his human form.

His armor now hung on him loosely and dragged on the ground when he tried to move. He shrugged it off, then turned to Talwyn.

"You are absolutely insane!" Dreyken stalked toward her and she just grinned at him. He stepped closer. In a calmer tone, he asked, "How did you know I was the dragon? Was it a vision?"

"I didn't know."

He thought of the way she held on to him and the caress she'd given him, and he growled a low growl as jealousy flared in him.

She burst out laughing. "I'm kidding! I may have seen you shift one night when I went . . . exploring."

His brows lifted, and he huffed out a wry laugh. "Was there really any point in locking that door?" He shook his head as he moved forward to grasp her by the shoulders.

She shrugged. "Not really."

He ran his hands down over her upper arms and felt something wet under his right hand. Pulling it back, he saw blood.

"You're hurt." He looked at the long, deep scratch on her biceps.

"Oh, right. I forgot."

"You forgot?" Drarcio said from behind him. Dreyken was sure his friend's incredulous tone must match the expression on his own face.

"Just give me a moment." Talwyn closed her eyes and stood still. Dreyken watched her with furrowed brows. What in the Universe was she doing?

"Here's a bandage," Drarcio said, now coming to stand next to him and holding it out to Talwyn.

She opened her eyes and accepted the strip of fabric. "Thanks."

Instead of using the bandage to wrap her injury, she used it to wipe the blood away, leaving only a thin, pink scar.

"How . . ." Dreyken began.

"Inner-sight," she answered. She looked at him with furrowed brows and narrowed eyes. "Didn't I tell you about this before? About how seers can look inside our bodies and manipulate what we find there? To change our coloring and heal ourselves?"

"What, really?" Drarcio asked in a voice pitched higher than usual.

Talwyn looked at his friend and guard, quirked an eyebrow, and waved her opposite hand in front of what used to be a gash, but was now just a faint, jagged line. "Blocking pain is almost instinctual. I'm sure you can imagine why. But other illnesses and wounds take some concentration."

"You've told me many things. But hearing it would differ greatly from seeing it firsthand," Dreyken said.

Then he huffed and gently grabbed her upper arms again. "Do you know how worried I was? Do you understand how many things could have gone wrong with that stunt you pulled?"

"Didn't I just say that I try not to think of those things? In my line of work, it would be counterproductive. Maybe you should do the same."

He shook his head and chuckled. "I never would have guessed when I first brought you here that you'd make my heart beat faster in so many, not always pleasant, ways."

Unable to help himself and feeling no resistance from her, Dreyken pulled Talwyn to him and pressed his lips to hers in a passionate kiss. Her arms lifted around him and squeezed, causing him to growl again, for a different reason than before.

When they broke apart a moment later, Talwyn cleared her throat. "Ahem. Dreyken?"

"Yes?"

"You're, um, naked." She lifted her eyebrows and looked pointedly down between them.

"Yes, right." His cheeks heated as he realized that not only was he naked, but they were surrounded by his protectors. And the adrenaline and the kiss had left him in a state he'd prefer to only show Talwyn, preferably when they were alone.

"Can someone please bring me a robe?"

His people removed their clothing whenever they planned a shift. If they didn't get to disrobe first, their clothing ended up in shreds. So, they usually kept a couple of robes near each entrance, just in case. Dreyken was glad for that precaution now.

Drarcio approached and handed a robe to Dreyken, who stood facing Talwyn until he had pulled it on.

"You are one seriously fearless female," Drarcio said to Talwyn.

"I can guarantee you I am *not* fearless. I just do what has to be done and try not to think about what can go wrong while I'm doing it."

Drarcio grinned at his dragon lord and nodded toward the cave entrance. "Well then, my Liege, if you are throwing caution to the wind and shifting in front of the enemy, then I am going to send out a flight of warriors to sweep the mountain for any that remain."

"You may as well. I only agreed to the no-shifting to appease the Elder Council."

"You mean Airgan," Drarcio countered.

"Yes. Well, if the enemy wasn't sure of our existence before today, they will be soon, anyway. The entire realm will be."

Talwyn smiled at him with these words, and he could see the hope in her eyes.

Drarcio gave instructions to a couple of warriors. When he returned his attention to them, Talwyn looked between the two males. "Is your sorceress safe?"

Dreyken then realized they hadn't yet heard from the guards at the other positions. "I haven't been alerted to any problems, but let's go check in on her."

"How about we get you some proper clothing first?" Talwyn placed a hand on his forearm. "Drarcio can take a protector and go on ahead of us."

Talwyn and Dreyken took off running up the passageway. They entered the throne room, where healers were treating injured protectors, aided by several other citizens.

Talwyn looked around at those gathered there. "You go get dressed, Dreyken. I will wait for you here."

When Dreyken returned from his chambers, he paused at the entrance to his tunnel, just behind the throne. He watched as Talwyn slowly walked around the room to assess the severity of the warriors' injuries. Thankfully, very few had received serious wounds. Talwyn walked in his direction but stopped at a protector who was lying unconscious on some furs, Iniri by his side.

"Do you have any idea what poison was used?" Dreyken heard her ask the healer who was attending the male. Iniri looked up at the sound of her voice.

The healer shook her head, a baffled expression on her face. "No. I've seen nothing like it before. Other than being unconscious, he is doing fine. His breathing and heartbeat are strong."

"Are you okay, Talwyn?" Iniri asked. "I feel terrible that I had to leave you alone up there."

Talwyn placed her hand on Iniri's shoulder. "Don't worry. You got him to safety, and that is what matters."

Suddenly, an angry voice sounded from behind her.

"You!" Airgan hissed. "This is your doing! You led them to our mountain! We would still be living free of their notice if not for you!"

Dreyken quickly strode forward and stood in front of Talwyn.

"Mind your words, Airgan." His dragon's rumble was seeping through in his voice, clearly conveying his warning.

After the danger Talwyn had just put herself in protecting their people, he would not allow the elder's disrespect to go unchecked.

As usual, though, Talwyn responded before he could say anything more. She sounded frustrated and tired. "Airgan, you really need to get over this...distrust of me. There is clearly a sorcerer behind all of this, and sorcerers have ways of knowing things. Given that this scoundrel seems to be continuing Azedel's plans from three-thousand years ago, he may even lead a cult of followers. I think it's safe to assume there were also spies spread throughout the realm. My own people have seen proof of this."

"Rubbish!"

"And even if that were not the case, Sterrenvar is an island! A large island, yes, but an island, nonetheless. There are only so many places away from the other inhabitants where the Stone Dragons could hide unless they fled across the ocean. All someone would have to do is eliminate the possibilities. It's clear that this dark sorcerer's current plans have been centuries in the works, so he would have had time to figure it out."

As though he had not listened to a word Talwyn had said, Airgan stubbornly held on to his flawed reasoning.

"We have lived here for four-hundred years without being discovered. It is the only explanation. She exposed us!" He looked at Dreyken and pointed a finger toward Talwyn. "She led them right to us!"

Dreyken was losing his patience. "You are not all-seeing, Airgan. There are things I have seen from Talwyn that would prove what you are saying is just a story fabricated in your own mind."

"You are young and infatuated. Of course you would take her word."

"Again, I am telling you, it is not just taking her word! It is what I have seen with my own eyes."

Talwyn shook her head at the elder, disappointment clear on her face. "I may as well be speaking ancient elvish." She turned to Dreyken. "I'm sorry, but I don't have time for this. Your people are safe for the moment. However, now that the demonkin have failed here, they will regroup and head for Southgate, I'm sure. I am a Southgate guardian, and I need to be there to help them.

After I check on Athnie, I'm going to get some rest. I leave in the morning."

"You will not allow her anywhere near Athnie, are you? How can you trust an outsider with the first sorceress we've had in the clan in generations?"

Dreyken took a step toward Airgan and looked down to meet the older man's eyes. "Airgan, with your strange and paranoid behavior of late, I trust her much more than I trust you." Airgan's mouth dropped open.

He turned back to Talwyn. "Come. I'll show you the way."

CHAPTER ELEVEN

The Sorceress

A s the battle raged outside the mountain lair, Athnie remained in her chambers. Two protectors were stationed outside her doorway, and one protector watched over her from inside her room.

She had already been cooped up for hours in her small room, staring at the familiar stone walls she'd spent years looking at. Maybe she needed to change the decor to something less boring.

She couldn't even go chat with her parents in their adjacent room because they were in the upper levels taking part in the battle. And even if they weren't, the door that joined their rooms was locked up tight, supposedly for her safety, in case an intruder tried to gain access that way.

"How long do I have to stay a prisoner in my room?"

"You are not a prisoner, Sorceress," the protector replied. "You are here for your own protection."

"Do you really think a demonkin could get this far inside, Erdi?" she scoffed. "There's no way."

"Our Dragon lord doesn't want to take any chances."

"Who would want a sorceress who can't even do proper magic yet? *Why* would anyone want a sorceress who can't do magic yet?"

"We cannot know the enemy's—"

An unexpected noise from outside the doorway caught their attention. Erdi stopped and stood quietly, silently cautioning Athnie to do the same with a finger over his lips.

After a moment, he whispered, "That sounded like a scuffle."

Athnie stared at Erdi with wide eyes, suddenly taking the situation much more seriously. Erdi cracked the heavy wooden door and peeked outside. "Busio? What happened?"

"He passed out," Busio said, indicating his partner. "Help me get him inside." Athnie could hear the strain in Busio's voice as he held the weight of his associate.

"Here, put him on my bed." Athnie stood aside to make room, and the two males carried the limp form over and laid him down.

"Tell me exactly what happened," Erdi said. "Did you notice anything unusual before he collapsed?"

Erdi leaned over the unconscious male to check for any signs that would explain his current condition. Busio leaned over his shoulder, seemingly to watch as Erdi examined him.

Athnie was watching Erdi's examination as well when she caught a sudden movement out of the corner of her eye... just before Erdi collapsed to the ground. Athnie looked at Busio in shock. "Busio! What did you do? I saw you jab him in the neck with something."

"What I did is eliminate a potential complication."

"Busio!" Athnie's voice rose in alarm. "Why would you do such a thing? You are a Stone Dragon protector!"

"I am no Stone Dragon."

Athnie watched in horror as a mist seemed to uncoil from around Busio's form and retreat into his body. The beast that remained had reddish-colored skin. It also had small horns that started as little more than slight bumps on its cheekbones and gradually increased in size until they were a few inches long where they curled past its temples.

"You're not Busio." Her eyes were wide, and her body trembled.

"Very observant, young sorceress."

Athnie stepped back as the demonkin moved forward into her space. "How did you get this far?"

"Isn't it obvious?" The mist once again uncoiled and surrounded its body, leaving Busio's likeness in its wake. "It was rather easy, actually. You Dragon-folk have grown complacent during your centuries of solitude. I'm disappointed, really. I was hoping for more action." The demonkin heaved a dramatic sigh. "After a week of watching your mountain, bored to distraction, the least you people could do is provide some entertainment."

"What do you want?" She had hoped to seem calm, but she couldn't stop the tremor in her voice.

"That should be obvious too, young sorceress." The monster stepped toward her.

"But I can't even do magic yet! I'd be useless to you!"

"Ah, my dear, do not underestimate your own worth." It placed a finger under her chin and lifted so it was looking down at her frightened expression.

Another male appeared in the doorway. He looked like a Stone Dragon protector, but from false-Busio's lack of reaction, she suspected it might be demonkin as well. The male stepped inside and closed the door behind him.

The newcomer looked at Athnie, its eyes traveling over her from head to toe. Its intense gaze made her shiver.

Athnie looked from the one male to another. Her eyes were wide and her face pale. "If you take me from here, you won't get far. You'll be followed."

"Oh, we know we'll be followed—eventually," false-Busio said. "But you and I will be far from here by that time."

The other male seemed to take that as a cue. As mist swirled around its body, it changed its form from protector into an exact copy of Athnie, who sucked in her breath sharply.

"Remember, try to buy us at least a day, more if you can," false-Busio said to false-Athnie.

"I will give you as much time as I can. We know little about Dragon-folk, or how long the poison will keep them unconscious. The old man might buy us some time, but if they decide to do a physical examination, well . . ."

"Old man? What old man?" Athnie blurted without thinking.

"It's not your place to ask questions, young one." False-Busio's tone was one of warning.

"Why not? You plan to take me from here, so why does it matter?"

"It matters because you are wasting my time."

"I think you're lying, anyway. No one among my people would ever help beasts such as you. The Stone Dragons are good, honorable people!"

"Ah, so young and naïve," false-Athnie said. "You seriously underestimate the lure of the promise of wealth and power. We have yet to meet a species where we couldn't convince at least some of the population to help us. We are masters at manipulation, and we've had centuries to practice our skills."

"Are you actually *boasting* about such a deplorable, disgusting thing? Is this all your people want for themselves? To be known as master manipulators?"

"What we want," false-Busio said, "is to be respected enough that we can roam the land freely. To not be prisoners of the cold, dreary northern mountains. At least for your people, your exile is self-chosen."

Athnie scoffed. "Self-chosen? More like necessary to our survival after what your kind and the humans did to us. Besides, if you seriously don't see that what you are doing is going to get you the opposite of respect, then you are as stupid as your histories make you out to be!"

Her doppelgänger reached out and slapped her firmly across the face.

"Watch your mouth, young one. The sorcerer wants you alive, but he didn't say unharmed."

Athnie placed her hand on her stinging cheek. Her initial shock quickly turned to anger, and her skin began to heat and prickle.

False-Busio quickly stepped between Athnie and her demonkin twin.

"I can't believe you are letting a little girl get to you, Tenram." The monster tutted and shook its head. "Can't you see she is just trying to buy herself some time?" Under its breath, obviously intended for just its companion—though Athnie could hear it just fine—he said, "Remember what we were told."

Athnie's impersonator glanced at her, then to false-Busio. It gave a nod and took a step back.

False-Busio turned to Athnie. "No one is coming to help you, young sorceress. Our allies will see to that."

Then it turned back to false-Athnie, or Tenram, rather. "Just remember, you are the unconscious sorceress. Don't take any chances of someone catching you moving."

"Yes, I know."

False-Busio grabbed Athnie by the arm and dragged her toward the door. It paused just inside and turned to face her. "You might think yourself brave, but be careful not to confuse bravery with stupidity. Stupidity will only get people hurt.

"Now, Sorceress, you can make this easy or difficult. You can walk out with me calmly and quietly, trying not to arouse suspicions, or you can make a fuss. But, if you make a fuss, I will be forced to knock you out, as we did your friends there, and carry you. Anyone whose attention you got, I would have to kill.

"Personally, I hope you will come quietly. I would not appreciate having to carry your dead weight down the mountain." It gave her a sinister smile. "Plus, I don't think you'd want their blood on your hands, would you?"

Athnie' opened her eyes wide and pressed her lips together as she shook her head.

"Good. I'm glad we have an understanding."

The demonkin grabbed Athnie by the wrist and dragged her through the door, which it closed quietly behind it. The passageway was eerily silent, which was unusual, even here in the living quarters. There were usually the sounds of laughter, of children playing and people talking. Dragon-folk rarely closed their doors during waking hours, preferring to socialize.

Now, however, those who were not in the upper levels fighting off demonkin were locked away in their quarters in case trouble made its way down to them. At that thought, Athnie shook her head. Trouble *had* made its way down to her.

After a few minutes, Athnie could hear someone approaching up ahead. Her heart beat faster at the possibility of someone coming to her rescue. But then she remembered what the demonkin had said about blood being shed because of her choices, so she stayed quiet.

The demonkin shoved Athnie back roughly into a natural depression in the wall. Then, standing in front of her, it changed its illusion to match the cold, gray stone walls. It stayed there, completely still and shielding her from sight, as a protector passed not over two paces away. She could have reached out and touched him if the immovable wall of a beast was not standing right in front of her.

The demonkin waited until the sounds of the protector's feet had faded away before it again changed its illusion to look like Busio. It turned around and grabbed her once more. "Come on, young one."

When they were about to exit the tunnels where the living quarters were located, the demonkin grabbed a torch off the wall.

Athnie and her captor walked through the tunnels for some time. Athnie was surprised when, instead of heading up to where all the common entrances were, the demonkin led her to a tunnel that subtly slanted downward.

"You're going the wrong way."

"I don't think so."

Athnie let it continue without further advice. Let it get lost in the tunnels if it wanted. It would give her more time to escape.

It couldn't have been ten minutes later when the demonkin pushed her toward a narrow crevice in the wall. Not sure what it wanted from her, she paused.

"Move it," the demonkin growled.

"Move it where?"

"Through there." It pointed to the crevice. When she hesitated still, the beast gave her a shove. She started creeping forward. As she approached the crack in the wall, she could see it continued inward like a narrow passageway. A pale, filtered light illuminated the tunnel, so she figured it must lead outside. She moved into the space and was surprised when the demonkin squeezed its large frame through behind her.

Her captor placed a hand on Athnie's shoulder as they moved forward. After just a few moments, Athnie could see light up ahead. It was dull and pale, but brighter than the blackness of the caves and tunnels they were leaving behind.

Moonlight.

Athnie looked up to find they were in a deep crevasse that opened to the sky a hundred paces above. They squeezed through this narrow space, effectively hidden, and carefully made their way down toward the base of the mountain.

Apparently the demonkin were telling the truth. There's no way they would have found their way in and out so quickly without someone's help. Not to mention, how else would they have known about such an obscure entry point when she herself hadn't known about it?

She shook her head at herself. No, no! They must have disguised themselves and tricked someone into helping them. She would not believe another Stone Dragon would knowingly do this to his own people.

The demonkin led her at a quick pace, away from the mountain and along a path that headed directly into the cover of trees. Once off the rocky path where she did not have to use her hands for balance, the demonkin stopped and turned to her. It allowed another illusion to dissolve when it removed a small pack that Athnie could now see it carried on its back. It pulled a cloth out of this bag and unwrapped a pair of metal cuffs attached to a chain.

When it caught Athnie watching it intently, he lifted the cloth and said, "I didn't want them to make noise. Ruins the illusion."

"Right."

"Give me your hands."

"Why? You aren't going to put those on me, are you?" She took a step back.

Instead of answering, it roughly grabbed her by one wrist and attached a cuff to it. It repeated this on the other side. Athnie noticed the cuffs were attached to each other by a heavy chain that ran in between, then another chain ran out from them. The demonkin held this long chain in its hands and tugged on it in a silent demand that she follow.

Athnie looked up toward the mountain as the demonkin led her westward through the woods. Battle sounds faintly echoed above them—war horns, shouts, weapons clashing. The noise carried down to her even this far below. Though impossible to discern any details from this distance in the pale light of the moon, glimpses of the skirmish were sometimes visible through breaks in the foliage.

She was hit with a pang of despair—there was no way anyone would see her down here. Her people's sight was good enough to spot her in the woods on a good day, but there was no way they'd notice her at night when they were so fully involved in a fight overhead. Chances of rescue were slim, even if someone noticed the 'girl' in the bed was not her.

If only she'd started shifting already.

Wait. Does this mean the enemy knows I can't shift yet? Would they have risked only sending one henchman to escort me out if they thought I could shift?

She doubted it. One enemy wouldn't be enough to stop her if she had manifested her dragon already. If the demonkin came here looking for them, then surely they knew this.

But something didn't add up. There were not nearly as many demonkin attacking the mountain as she would have expected. That realization led her to a disturbing thought.

"Why are your people attacking our mountain?"

"Isn't it obvious?"

"Just tell me. Is this whole attack just a distraction so you could abduct me?"

The demonkin tapped the side of his head. "Ah, look at that. You do have a brain."

Athnie did not respond to his words. Instead, she muttered quietly, "I don't want anyone to die because of me."

"Don't worry. It looks like my side got the worst of it."

"Do you think that makes it any better?" Her voice was both hard and sad at the same time. "I don't want *anyone* to die because of me."

The demonkin glanced over at Athnie, and their gazes met. He seemed to look for something in her eyes. And whatever he found there caused his previously hard, icy gaze to soften a little.

They walked on for some time; Athnie wasn't sure how long, but the moonlit night turned to the gray light of pre-dawn, then the sun rose higher. She had never walked this distance outside before, and she was distracted by the sights, sounds, and activity in the surrounding forest, not to mention the smells. The fresh scent of the trees, flowers, and other plants was something she didn't get to experience often.

The young Stone Dragons who had not yet shifted could sometimes go walking in these woods in the company of an adult. After all, they couldn't be added to the schedule of nighttime flights to stretch their wings if they couldn't manifest wings yet.

But the walks in the woods were seldom and never in the light of day.

Every now and again, her pace slowed without her realizing it, and she would be jolted back to reality by a sharp tug on the chain. One of these times, when the demonkin gave a particularly hard yank, she looked up and saw that he had stopped. He was now standing in front of her, looking at her with a curious expression.

"What?"

"What are you doing? Are you trying to signal someone? What are you up to?" The questions came in quick succession.

"Nothing, no, and nothing." She sighed deeply. "Look, perhaps it means something is not quite right in my mind that I'm noticing these things while being kidnapped, but I can't help it. We don't get out much."

"What do you mean?"

"I've never been outside the mountain during the daylight before. Look at how the light plays as it filters down through the leaves. It's beautiful. Then there are all those sounds of small animals moving around us, in amid the trees." She tilted her head. "They're different from the nighttime sounds." She took a deep breath and let it out. "Smell that fresh, earthy scent? It's so different from the dank aroma under the mountain."

When she looked ahead again, he was still looking at her as though she were something strange.

"What?"

"Nothing." He shook his head. "I think you must be in shock. You are being abducted, and you are admiring the sights."

She shrugged. "Well, if today is my last day before heading back to the Universe, at least I've been able to admire the realm in all its splendor before I go."

"Are you sure you've never shifted before?" he asked. "Those are deep thoughts for someone so young."

She looked at him, trying to decide whether to say what was on her mind.

"Actually, I have started the manifestation period. I have yet to shift, but I can do simple magic. *Very* simple. Which is why I cannot fathom why you want me."

"The emperor has his reasons."

"Which are..."

The demonkin simply shrugged.

"Has he never shared these with you?" She gave him an incredulous look.

"He fears information getting into the wrong hands, so he tells us only what we need to know to get the job done."

"And you never worry that he might lead you astray?"

"It wouldn't matter if I did. We have no other options than the one he offers us."

"What does that mean, exactly?"

False-Busio glanced at her, then away. "Nothing. Now stop asking questions, or I will be forced to gag you."

She sniffed. "Wow, you could have just asked me nicely. No need for threats."

They walked on in silence for a little while before Athnie's curiosity got the better of her again.

"I don't see why you won't tell me things, anyway. I might be young, but I'm not stupid enough to think your leader will let me leave alive once he's done with me."

She looked at false-Busio, but he did not respond. Not verbally, anyway. But she did notice a slight tick in his jaw.

"He's going to kill me, isn't he?"

He kept walking, facing forward, and ignored her question. So Athnie gathered the chain until it was taut and gave it a tug. "Is he? I think I have a right to know."

False-Busio let out an incredulous laugh. "I'm abducting you right now. You think we're worried about your rights?"

Athnie dropped her gaze to the ground in front of her. Then she heard her captor let out a deep sigh.

"As far as I know, he needs you alive. I don't think he plans to kill you."

"As far as you know. But since he doesn't tell you everything, you can't say for certain, can you?"

He looked at her with an impassive expression on his face, though she noticed his jaw tick again.

Dusk was just upon them as they approached the western edge of the forest. False-Busio stopped and wrapped Athnie's chain around a tree branch. Then he shrugged off his pack.

"What's your name?" Athnie asked.

"Does it matter?"

"Yes. I keep thinking of you as 'the demonkin' or 'false-Busio' in my head. It would be nice to refer to you by a proper name."

"Fine. My name is Koromin."

"Well, Koromin, why have we stopped here?"

"We will be too visible if we cross that expanse ahead while it is still light. We are going to wait until it's dark before heading out to meet our ride."

"Our ride?"

"Yes. You didn't think we were going to walk all the way, did you?"

CHAPTER TWELVE

Surprises & Plans

"Dreyken!"

Talwyn and Dreyken had just started down the tunnel to the living quarters when Drarcio's voice called from up ahead. Talwyn looked up to see him jogging toward them.

"What's wrong? Is it the sorceress?" Dreyken asked. "Tell me she has not disappeared."

"She has not, my lord," Drarcio replied. "She is still in her chamber."

"Then what is it?"

"We need a healer to look her over. She is unconscious, as are Erdi and Bardrix."

"And Busio?"

"There is no sign of him, Lord Dragon."

"Unconscious?" Talwyn asked. "I don't suppose you noticed if there was a bright green substance anywhere on their bodies?

Drarcio shook his head. "No, we confirmed they were still breathing, then I ran up here to get help."

Talwyn shook her head. "I don't understand. My vision clearly showed her being abducted."

"Maybe they decided it would be too hard to sneak her out," Dreyken reasoned. "They have taken her out of the picture by rendering her unconscious."

"Well, let's worry about the why later. She is unconscious, and we don't know how or why."

Dreyken turned back toward the throne room. "Healer Lara!"

A dark-haired, middle-aged woman turned toward them while answering, "Yes, my lord?"

"Grab your best apprentice and follow us."

Talwyn, Dreyken, Drarcio, and the two healers made their way down to the sorceress' chambers.

When they had almost reached her quarters, Dreyken asked Drarcio, "Where are her parents?"

Dreyken turned to Talwyn and explained, "Her space is attached to that of her parents, as is customary for our adolescents."

"From what I was told by a neighbor," Drarcio said, "they headed off earlier to help with the battle. He says he figures they would be helping to clear the aftermath now."

"Has someone been sent to get them?"

"Yes, Lord Dragon."

"The room is not large," Lara said. "I suggest you all wait here while Eishlo and I check them over."

Talwyn reached out and touched Lara's forearm lightly. "Check for anything that might suggest they've been poisoned, like Mirzai." She had learned the name of the protector who'd pushed Iniri out of the line of fire, only to be hit himself when she was speaking with Iniri in the temporary healing room recently. "Their symptoms sound similar."

Healer Lara nodded and entered the room.

Talwyn, Dreyken and the protectors waited just outside the door as the healer and her younger apprentice checked over the unconscious Dragon-folk.

"Each of them has a small puncture wound to the neck," Lara called after a couple of minutes. "It is small enough that it would be missed by many at first glance. I believe they were poisoned, as you said, Talwyn."

Talwyn nodded and looked at Dreyken. She told him about what had happened on the ledge earlier that night. "I have never seen a substance like this before."

"I don't think it is fatal," Lara said. "Mirzai wasn't the only protector struck by an arrow with what looks like that same green substance. None of them show no other apparent reason for remaining unconscious."

"How can you be sure that it won't eventually kill them?"

Talwyn could hear the note of worry in Dreyken's voice when he asked the question.

"Actually, I can't be completely certain," Lara said. "I don't know what we are dealing with. However, their breathing and heart rates are steady. They seem to be recovering. Slowly, to be sure, but recovering nonetheless."

Dreyken let out a relieved sigh, and Talwyn reached over to squeeze his hand in support.

"I am going to give them a more thorough check to make sure they are in stable condition."

"Maybe we should just let them rest," a male voice said from behind them.

Talwyn turned to see Airgan and Herdrix walking toward them.

"It seems they will do that whether or not we want it," Dreyken replied. "In the meantime, Lara is going to look them over to see if there is anything we can do to speed up recovery."

Lara let out a sudden yelp from inside the room. Talwyn moved up to the doorway next to Dreyken and looked inside.

"What is it?" Dreyken asked.

Lara was slowly backing away from the sorceress and shaking her head.

Talwyn leaned to the side so she could see past the healer into the room. She gasped when she saw the first patient. Before she could give a warning, however, false-Athnie jumped off the bed, knocking Lara into her apprentice, Eishlo. They both flew into the wall. Then Athnie turned on Dreyken.

"Lara, what's going on here?" Dreyken attempted to fend Athnie off without harming her. "Has the poison made her lose her mind?"

"That's not Athnie!" Lara yelled.

"It's a demonkin," Talwyn added.

Dreyken momentarily froze at her words, but quickly refocused on his opponent, who was now attacking him with a dagger. This time, Dreyken fought back full-force.

Talwyn squeezed a little further into the room and looked at the other two patients. They didn't need any more surprises.

"The others are Dragon-folk," she let Dreyken know. She looked for a way to help Dreyken, but it was tight in the small room and Dreyken was doing fine on his own. So she moved to stand in front of Lara and Eishlo to keep them out of harm's way.

Dreyken smoothly sidestepped a strike and landed a solid punch to the demonkin's temple. His opponent dropped to the ground, truly unconscious this time, and its illusion dissolved like mist in the sunlight.

Just then, Drarcio burst through the door that joined Athnie's room to her parent's quarters. The other protector—Ucdi, if she remembered his name correctly—stood just behind him.

Drarcio looked down at the demonkin, who was lying at Dreyken's feet and no longer cloaked in illusion. It was now clearly visible for what it was.

It was a large, mottled-pink-and-red-skinned male with small horns along its cheekbones and larger ones at its temples.

"Looks like I missed all the fun," Drarcio said.

Talwyn chuckled and shook her head.

"How did it get in here?" asked Lara.

"That's an excellent question." Dreyken barely contained his anger. "Other than flying in, the only other way is to come up through the tunnels. Since they can look like anyone, they wouldn't have stood out, would they?"

"True." Drarcio nodded. "But most of the tunnels are very difficult to navigate, except for the higher, more visible ones." He paused thoughtfully for a moment. "Of course, there are some lesser-known tunnels."

"Regardless of how they got in, I suspect they may have had some help," Talwyn said

Suddenly remembering the two elders, she turned toward the doorway. They were nowhere in sight.

"Leave it to Airgan to leave when things get tough," Drarcio commented.

Talwyn suspected, though, that his sudden exit had more sinister motivations than cowardice.

Dreyken shared a look with Drarcio before locking his serious gaze with Talwyn's. They all knew what this meant.

"Looks like your vision was correct," Dreyken said. "Athnie has been abducted."

"Lara, Eishlo, there's not much you can do here at the moment. Mirzai can help you bring Erdi and Bardrix up to where the other injured are being treated."

"Yes, my lord."

Talwyn followed Dreyken into Athnie's parents' more spacious quarters, Drarcio moving back into the room as they passed. She could still hear Lara, Eishlo, and Mirzai out in the corridor. They were gathering people to help move the two unconscious protectors and the unconscious demonkin. She hoped they didn't put the beast in a cell too close to hers.

In the relative quiet of the parents' chambers, Talwyn turned her attention to Dreyken. He was looking at the floor and rubbing his chin. The worst had happened—they'd failed to keep the sorceress out of the enemy's hands.

Dreyken's brows were drawn close together, and he was frowning. Talwyn was concerned for him. He had never had to deal with such a situation before and, even though she only knew him for a short time, she knew he would blame himself. He would be beside himself with worry.

Talwyn glanced over to where Drarcio was standing quietly, a few paces from his friend and leader, and saw he was doing the same thing she was—watching Dreyken with concern-filled eyes.

She was tempted to jump in and start making decisions, both because that's what she was accustomed to and because she wanted to lighten Dreyken's burdens. But these were his people and he was the dragon lord. He needed to take the lead, but she would support him in any way she could.

"Busio is also missing," Dreyken said after a few moments of thoughtful silence. He looked up at her. "Do you think he's been abducted as well?"

Talwyn shook her head. "It's more likely he was knocked out," or worse, but she wouldn't voice that, "and moved some place where he wouldn't draw attention."

"Do you know what I'm thinking?"

"No. What are you thinking, Drarcio?" Dreyken asked.

"It seems awfully suspicious that Airgan has been so hostile toward Talwyn from the start. And that he is always sticking his nose in, even when it isn't needed. He seems to want to hold on to what power he has, resisting you at every turn. Then he shows up unannounced here tonight and takes off at the first sign of a fight. When we realized that there were demonkin in the mountain. He must have known we'd suspect they had help, someone on the inside."

"While all that is true, if Airgan is involved, he must have had help. Demonkin help," Talwyn said.

"How do we know he is not a demonkin in disguise, too?" Drarcio said.

"He's been face-to-face with Talwyn many times. She is a seer, don't forget. She would have known what he was."

"Yes, I would have," she agreed.

"So, how do we figure out who his accomplice is?"

"Well, as Talwyn has pointed out to me, my friend Airgan likes to feel important," Dreyken said. "To be involved in my decisions, even when he has no reason to be. We will need to watch him. We should also ask around to see if anyone has noticed who he's been spending time with recently."

"How do you know he hasn't already run off?" Drarcio asked.

"From what I've heard, he's been putting a lot of effort into positioning himself in the Elder Council," Talwyn said. "If he doesn't know we suspect him, or if he thinks we have no proof, then I doubt he would want to give up whatever power he has gained without a fight."

Dreyken suddenly started pacing in a circle. He stopped just as suddenly a moment later. He blew out a frustrated breath and put his hands on his hips. "All that fighting for nothing. They were just distracting us. Despite our planning and defense, they breached our mountain."

"I wouldn't have thought it possible." Drarcio shook his head.

"Let's focus on the immediate concern in all that," Talwyn said. "They've abducted your sorceress. And with the distraction they caused with the battle, they've gotten a head start."

"It's not much of a head start," Drarcio said. "They couldn't have had more than a couple of hours."

"A couple of hours would be plenty of time to throw off pursuers for those who are good at covering their tracks," Talwyn said. "We'll have to go slowly to track them, and they can hurry on ahead."

"I'm guessing you can help with that, though." Drarcio smiled at her.

Dreyken turned to her. "Do you think you can help me find her, Talwyn?" His voice was almost pleading, as was the way he looked at her with wide, imploring eyes.

"I'm sure I can," she said. "However, there remains the issue of protecting Southgate. I don't know for certain when the demonkin will attack. Since they have already been here, though, even farther south of the town, it would be safe to assume the attack will happen soon. I can't leave them unprotected. The keystone, and the people, are too important."

"So, we are left with three priorities here that all occur around the same time." Dreyken stroked his chin. "On the one hand, we need to find Athnie as soon as possible, before the trail is cold. Then there is Southgate and its keystone. We can only assume since the demonkin have just left us they will probably strike Southgate on their way back north."

His voice became strained. "But also, we cannot leave the Stone Dragons in the hands of the Elder Council, or anyone else whose loyalty we are not completely certain of. Not until we know how the demonkin found their way in here and if they had inside help."

Dreyken's words made Talwyn want to smile, and she would have if not for the dire situation. It seems the key to motivating Dreyken to reclaim his place was his own people. His worry for them finally had him stepping up, even willing to take on the Elder Council.

As for her, she'd have to quell the impulse to charge in loudly and aggressively when she was worked up. Dreyken didn't need her running roughshod when people angered her when he was just getting comfortable with his role as dragon lord.

"It's not really a question of 'if,' but of 'who' and 'how'," Talwyn said. "I don't see how they could have succeeded as far as they have without having someone on the inside." This had already been established, but she could understand why Dreyken was clinging on to the hope that it might not be true.

"And why," Drarcio added. "I want to know why one of our own would betray us like this."

Dreyken nodded. "Let's head back to the throne room. I have an idea, but we will need Adrio and Iniri to help as well."

Once in the throne room, they located Iniri and Adrio and headed to Dreyken's private chambers to discuss strategy. They quickly informed the two protectors of what had happened in Athnie's room.

Talwyn's eyes were always on Dreyken. She was simultaneously concerned for him and confident in his abilities. Her conflicting emotions made her feel a little unbalanced, and she knew they were caused by her growing feelings for him.

Dreyken stared down at the ground again, deep in thought. "So we have divided responsibilities, and we are unsure of who we can trust. In this situation, we will need to divide our forces if we're to avoid disaster. I have a plan, and I think it is our best option.

"You and I, Talwyn, will go look for Athnie—"

"Maybe it would be best if you stay here, Dreyken," Drarcio interrupted. "You are the dragon lord, after all."

"Exactly. I am the dragon lord. It was my place to make sure Athnie was protected, and I failed her." Dreyken's voice was firm and left no room for argument.

Drarcio nodded solemnly.

Talwyn was glad Dreyken had friends that understood and supported him so well. Knowing they were here for him made her feel a little better about having to leave soon.

"As I was saying, Talwyn and I will track Athnie. I will take a couple of trusted protectors in case we run into any trouble or need to fight to get her out.

"And Drarcio, since you are the most patient and level-headed of my trusted friends--"

"Hey!" Adrio objected. Dreyken ignored the outburst and carried on.

"I will leave you in charge of our mountain fortress. You will have the regular tasks of making the final decisions and watching over our citizens, of course. But you will also need to keep an eye out for anything suspicious that might lead us to whoever is in league with the demonkin. Check out anyone you choose to work closely with and do it regularly."

"Of course," Drarcio replied.

"I will send Adrio and Iniri to Southgate, along with a dozen of our strongest fighters."

"How will they know not to kill us, or that we can be trusted?" Adrio asked.

"I can help with that," Talwyn said. She crouched down and fished around in her left boot. When she stood again, she was holding an amulet.

Adrio looked at her with narrowed eyes, then looked down to study her footwear. "Just how many things do you carry hidden in your boots? Doesn't that feel uncomfortable?"

"I only carry a few essential items, nothing too bulky." She shrugged. "My boots have lined compartments inside. When I first started carrying things this way, it was a little uncomfortable. You get used to it."

"I will have to remember to remove or search the footwear of our visitors from now on." Dreyken said dryly.

"Even smelly footed demonkin?" Talwyn grinned at him.

"*Especially* smelly footed demonkin. But I'll order Adrio to do those for me."

Both Talwyn and Drarcio laughed at that. But the light moment was short-lived.

"So, tell us, Talwyn, how an amulet is going to help gain the trust of the citizens of Southgate," Adrio said.

"Most citizens will not recognize what this is, actually."

"Well, that's helpful." Adrio rolled his eyes. She grinned at him.

"You need to go to the castle gate and request an audience with the king. If you are denied, give them the amulet and tell them to take it to the king and let him decide. Once you meet with him, tell him I sent you and inform him of the situation. Let him know demonkin are in the area, and they should be prepared for an attack."

"And this amulet will make him believe me?" Adrio was clearly unconvinced.

Talwyn nodded. "Yes. It's a special amulet. The king will know what it is. I also paid him a visit not too long ago, so he's aware of what's coming."

"Good," Iniri said. "That's a start."

Dreyken walked to the doorway. "I need to make an announcement in front of the other protectors and citizens, so there is no question as to my instructions. Follow me."

There were still many Stone Dragons present in the throne room, either injured, helping the injured, or discussing the events of the day. Many paused in their conversations to watch Dreyken as he strode with purpose to his throne. He did not sit, but stood on the raised platform in front of the throne. Talwyn, Drarcio, stood to his right, and Adrio and Iniri stood to his right.

"My fellow Stone Dragons, you may have heard about what has transpired down below in the living quarters. So that everything is clear, I will confirm that Athnie has been taken by demonkin."

Gasps of disbelief and horror could be heard around the throne room. Dreyken quickly brought their attention back to him.

"We need to act fast before the trail gets cold. Talwyn and I will track them and bring Athnie back home. Talwyn is more experienced in tracking than anyone who's been hiding under a mountain for four hundred years, so we have a better chance with her help.

"However, for Talwyn to take the time to help us in this matter, Southgate would be left unprotected. Unless, of course, some of you would follow Adrio and Iniri there to help look out for the town and its keystone in her absence."

Voices rang out as many of the Stone Dragons offered their services. Dreyken held up a hand to quiet them.

"I truly appreciate your willingness to help our human neighbors. Thank you for that."

The strain in his voice showed his sincerity

"We will also need some protectors to stay here and watch over our people, and over those who fought so valiantly for us today. So some of you will be required to stay here and help Drarcio, who is my delegate, with the task. Drarcio and Adrio can settle the details with you.

"The sun is rising, so we will head out to track right away. The fresher the trail, the better." He addressed two male and one female protector. "Tolus, Norshan, and Helsi, you will accompany Talwyn and me."

Talwyn looked at the three Dreyken indicated. She'd seen them around, but she hadn't known their names before now. The protectors he'd addressed as Norshan and Helsi had spent much time here helping the injured. She'd seen them stand close, brush hands, and whisper to one another. When one of them needed something, the other always seemed to know. Seeing them together earlier today made her wonder if she should take a chance with Dreyken after all. Her longing for that closeness was almost as strong as her fear of it.

Dreyken's commanding voice had her refocusing back on him. "Let me repeat this so it is clear to everyone. Drarcio is my delegate. He acts on my behalf. He, above anyone else, is to lead in my absence. And I ask you all to respect that. There is more going on here than meets the eye."

The Stone Dragons thumped their fists once over their hearts in an expression of loyalty.

CHAPTER THIRTEEN

Tracking

Talwyn, Dreyken, and the three Dragon-folk protectors returned to Athnie's chambers to start their search from there. Now, they made their way slowly from Athnie's chambers and along the tunnel toward the throne room.

Talwyn led the others as she searched for signs of Athnie and her captors. She paused at a natural alcove in the stone wall, considering some small stones and scuff marks. Then she continued along the corridor again.

A short time later, they reached a divide in the passageway. One way led up toward the throne room. The other led to a rarely used tunnel that traveled slightly downward. This was the way Talwyn took now. She knew they were close to the outside wall of the mountain. Early morning sunlight peeked in through cracks here and there, and she could smell fresh air.

Talwyn kept walking close to the wall until she felt a slight breeze blowing through a crevice to her left. Moving closer to the wall of the tunnel, she noticed something. Like the one in Aleyn's hidden armory, the crevice looked too small to fit through until you saw it from a certain angle. She ran her eyes up and down along the jagged rock surrounding the opening until she noticed a tiny thread of fabric that had snagged on a jutting stone.

Talwyn tilted her head toward the crevice. "This way."

One protector, the huge brute named Tolus, looked at the opening, then back at Talwyn. "You're joking, right?"

Talwyn just raised her eyebrows at him before disappearing into the tunnel.

She could hear Dreyken encouraging Tolus behind her. "Oh, come on now. Don't be a coward. Talwyn knows what she's doing."

"One slight misjudgment and we could be stuck in there until we rot," Tolus said.

"I don't make miscalculations," Talwyn called from inside the passageway.

"Well, there you have it," Dreyken said, just before squeezing through the opening himself.

Tolus gave a huff behind them before squeezing his frame through the opening. Norshan and Helsi followed.

Before long, a crack opened in the ceiling above them.

Talwyn turned to Dreyken. "We're in a crevasse. Did you know this was here?"

"I did. Though, as far as I'm aware, very few know about it, and it hasn't been used in a long time."

"And you?" Talwyn looked at the three protectors. "Have you ever heard of this passageway?"

"Not that I can remember," Helsi said. The two males shook their heads.

"Well, this would seem to be more proof that the demonkin had inside help," Talwyn stated.

"Do you really believe that, Lord Dreyken?" Norshan asked. "Is that possible?"

"The evidence would seem to suggest so." Dreyken's expression showed his disappointment and anger.

"Unbelievable," Helsi said. She shook her head in disgust. "It goes against everything we stand for."

Talwyn understood their feelings, but she'd had more experience with the demonkin than they had over the past four hundred years. "Before you jump to the worst conclusions, don't forget that the demonkin have been manipulating others for centuries. It's how they turned the humans against your people, and then my own."

She pressed her lips together as she thought of Airgan and the dislike she had for him. She needed to remember the demonkin's treachery herself before thinking the worst.

"Still, our people should know better," Helsi said. "We are Dragon-folk. We are stronger than this."

"I understand how you feel, Helsi," Dreyken said, "but I'm inclined to agree with Talwyn here. We need to get the facts before we point fingers."

"The demonkin have been pitting the peoples of the realm against each other for hundreds of years now." Talwyn turned to glance at the others even as she continued forward. "It's time we stopped allowing them to tear us apart. It's time for us to come together."

They continued in silence for some time, not wanting to alert any demonkin if they were still in range to hear them.

"Why would they come this way, and not just jump on a winged ainmith and fly off?" Helsi asked a couple of hours later.

"To buy themselves time, I would assume," Talwyn answered.

"How does taking the longest route buy them time?"

"If they flew off, we would see them and take up the chase," Talwyn hypothesized. "If they went on foot on the northern side of the mountain, where there is less cover, your sentries would have spotted them and followed. This way provides the best cover."

"Also, I don't think they were counting on us discovering that Athnie had been replaced by a disguised demonkin as soon as we did," Dreyken said. "We have a good chance of catching up to them, I believe."

"I hope you are right," Tolus said. "If they harm her, even just a tiny scratch . . ."

"I know, Tolus." Dreyken placed his hand on the male's shoulder. "I know your families are close. We will find her."

The four shifters followed Talwyn as she tracked through the woods.

"Can't we go any faster?" Hours had passed since they started out, the sun moving from just over the horizon to high in the sky, and Tolus was clearly worried.

"We could, but I don't want to miss anything." Talwyn looked at the male and tried to reassure him. "So far, there have been no signs of a struggle. There are two sets of footprints, hers and the demonkin's. There is no waver to her stride, nothing that would show she's been harmed." The tracks were scuffed in a couple of places, as if Athnie had tripped or been pulled, but she left that part out for now.

"Good." Dreyken sounded cautiously optimistic. "Let's hope it stays that way."

It was a couple of hours before dusk when they finally neared the edge of the woods to the west of the mountains.

Talwyn peered across the open space ahead of them. "Let's move before we lose the light. Keep your eyes open. From here to the Sacred Forest, there is nothing but short vegetation and rock. It should be fairly easy to spot the signs."

"Norshan," Dreyken said, "you've spotted a wildern through the trees farther off than just about anyone else. Keep checking the distance. Let us know if you see anything suspicious."

"Yes, Lord Dragon."

They moved forward at a steady pace at first, since the trail was fairly easy to follow. As the light waned, however, they were forced to slow down. Talwyn had excellent night vision, and she knew the others in the party did as well. However, without the daylight, they saw more in black and gray, and it was harder to spot things that might stand out from everything around it.

When they were what Talwyn judged to be a little less than halfway between the southern woods and the Sacred Forest, she stopped. She walked in a circle for some time, then she cursed under her breath.

"What is it, Talwyn?" Dreyken asked.

Rather than answer right away, Talwyn said, "Norshan, scan the sky ahead of us. Do you see anything?"

Norshan lifted his gaze and scanned the dark sky ahead. "The moon is hidden behind heavy clouds tonight. I cannot see as far as I can on a clear night."

"Just tell me, do you see anything? Anything at all?"

Norshan studied the sky for another moment. "No."

Talwyn paced some more and cursed some more before Dreyken grabbed her by the shoulders. "Talwyn. Tell us."

Talwyn looked him in the eye for a moment before breaking away and gesturing to some marks on the ground.

"Do you see that? Those are the paw prints and claw marks of a huge beast."

"I see them," Dreyken said.

"Now, what do you see past this area?" She gestured to the ground just past where she paced.

The others looked carefully at the area she indicated.

"I don't see anything besides mossy earth," Tolus replied.

"Exactly. They must have had an ainmith pick them up far enough from the mountain to not be seen by the sentries."

Now it was Helsi's turn to curse. "Universe help us! What do we do now?"

Talwyn stood in thought for a moment, staring off toward the Sacred Forest. Then she looked at Dreyken and caught his gaze. "I need to sleep." She hoped he understood what she really meant—that she needed to See. She needed a dream-vision for guidance. There was no guarantee she'd get helpful information, but she wouldn't know if she didn't try.

"We should head to the cover of the forest since they seem to be headed that way, anyway. Then we can camp for a couple of hours, and I will attempt to sleep. With any luck, I'll see something that could help us."

Dreyken nodded and headed toward the forest. "Okay. Let's go." The others followed the Dragon lord. As they weren't tracking anymore, they could run, and they arrived at the first trees quickly.

As soon as they passed the edge of the forest, the four Dragon-folk began acting jumpy and paranoid. They startled at every little noise and looked around themselves suspiciously.

Talwyn smiled at them and put a hand on Dreyken's shoulder. "Don't worry if you are feeling apprehensive right now. It is one of the forest's magical protections. If you were evil, dark-souled beings, you would be frozen with fear right about now."

"Good to know," Helsi said.

"Why is it so much warmer in here?" Norshan flicked the collar of his shirt to fan himself. "It is nighttime, and it is early fall. It should not be this warm."

Indeed, Talwyn could feel the familiar warmth seep into her bones. She had not realized she had missed it until that moment. "This is the Sacred Forest. The magic keeps it forever summer in here."

Soon, they reached a small clearing. "You three set up camp here for the night," Dreyken said. "Talwyn and I will move a little farther off."

"Do you think that's a good idea?" Helsi asked.

"Don't worry. We will stay within shouting distance."

With that, Talwyn and Dreyken walked on until they found another small clearing not too far from the others. When they stopped, Talwyn turned to Dreyken. "Thank you."

"I didn't figure you'd want them to witness the nightmares that follow your visions."

"Well, you figured correctly. And I appreciate you thinking of it. I thought I might end up with a fight on my hands if I said I wanted to sleep separately from everyone."

"Well, it would have been a fight if you insisted on having no one with you. But as long as you let me stay by your side, we're good."

Talwyn nodded and then settled herself on a soft patch of grass.

"Would you like a cloak to cover yourself with?" Dreyken shifted to take his pack off his shoulders.

"No. Thank you. The temperature is just right here in the forest."

Dreyken stayed silent after that, allowing Talwyn to do what she needed to do.

She lay on her back, looking up at the sky through the shadowed foliage, and she took a deep breath. There were no stars to focus on tonight, so she went through the exercise of tensing and relaxing her muscles, one at a time, releasing any tension she had built up. Finally, she closed her eyes and let her mind drift out to touch the energy of the world and the Universe around her.

Seers could not choose what they wanted to see. Instead, the visions they received always seemed to lead them to wherever their help was needed most. As she drifted off to sleep, she hoped the Universe would decide that the place she was needed most right now was wherever Athnie was.

Talwyn startled awake sometime later the way she usually did: sweaty, breathing hard, and on the verge of panic. There was one thing that differed from all the other times, though. This time, when she startled awake, she could feel herself leaning back against a body that was at once soft and hard. The person holding her was stroking her hair soothingly as his reassuring warmth enveloped her.

"Dreyken," she breathed.

"I hope I didn't interrupt your vision," Dreyken said. "You were quiet and still for a long time, but then you started acting the same way you did back in the mountain when you had that nightmare."

"You didn't interrupt my vision." Her voice was barely more than a whisper.

"It didn't seem as bad this time."

"It wasn't." She knew he was referring to the nightmare. This time, it wasn't as clear or intense as it usually was, and she didn't feel that same sense of all-consuming despair at the end.

"Well, in that case," Dreyken said, his mouth close to her ear, "I would be happy to ease your dreams anytime you like."

Talwyn tensed up at his words, and he must have noticed, because he cleared his throat and moved to stand up.

"Let's have a bite to eat before we go find the others, so you can share what you've seen."

"Okay," Talwyn agreed. "You know, your people are very thoughtful. Well, except for Airgan. I don't know what his problem is, or how he can be so different from the rest of your people."

She thought back to just before they left to track Athnie. They had run off quickly to grab their packs, and even though only a short time had passed before they arrived back at the throne room, several citizens had gathered some provisions for them. Now, Dreyken was pulling dried meat from his pack. He offered Talwyn some before taking a piece for himself.

"Yes, my people are good people. They are kind and thoughtful. With Airgan, I think it's just, he has lived a long time. He watched us go from being a strong and proud people, respected by all, to being feared and doubted. From being able to live and fly freely to having to hide ourselves under a mountain. Now, he doubts and suspects everyone. At least, I hope that's all it is."

Talwyn nodded her understanding. They ate in silence for a short time before Talwyn spoke again.

"This may not be the best time and place—at all—to ask this question, but I've been wondering . . ."

"Yes?"

"Do Dragon-folk bond for life?"

Dreyken paused for a moment before answering. Given her reaction to his earlier comment, he likely hadn't expected this topic of discussion.

"It was more common when there were more of us, but it happens. It's one reason I've been reluctant to choose just any female who fits the job description."

"My kind bonds for life as well. So even though Elis's death occurred many years ago, it's still hard to let go."

"I understand." His voice was quiet and resigned.

"But it's also why I've been so confused."

Dreyken looked at her questioningly.

"After what happened to Elisedd, I had decided to never put myself in the position to be hurt like that again. There is only so much loss a being can endure, after all. It was an easy promise to make to myself under the circumstances."

"What do you mean?"

"Well, one interesting thing about my people is that we rarely even feel a physical attraction for another until we've found the one we are meant to be with. I figured I had already found my one, so I didn't expect . . ."

When the pause went on for some time, Dreyken asked, "Didn't expect what?"

"I didn't expect to ever feel that way about anyone again. I didn't expect . . . you." She looked at him uncertainly, almost shyly. Her heart was pounding.

Talwyn heard Dreyken's sharp gasp at her words. It was probably the last thing he expected to hear at a time like this, but she needed to tell him. When he reached out and cupped her face in his hand, tracing her cheek with his thumb, she knew she'd been right to let him know.

Then she let out a chuckle. "Something else I don't understand is why you feel anything for me. I'm loud, sarcastic, argumentative and, inside, I feel like I'm broken in so many ways." She tapped her chest with her fingers.

"Broken?" He let out a little laugh. "Surely you jest. You have more bravery, wisdom, and spirit than anyone I have ever met. You make me feel alive. I've woken from a sleep I didn't even realize I was in, and you make me want to be a better male. You are fiery . . ."

"Fiery? Ha! If you didn't find me attractive, you'd be calling me an arse, I'm sure."

Dreyken shook his head and laughed. "You really are something else."

"Yes. An arse. You can say it, you know. It's not like I don't already know." She'd been informed of it a few times before.

His smile was warm and cherishing as he looked at her. "Tell me, Talwyn, how is it you can be so charming and such an arse at the same time?"

Talwyn let out a laugh of surprise at his words, but it was quickly silenced when he brought his lips to hers for a gentle, reverent kiss.

Dreyken then pulled back reluctantly and cleared his throat. "Would you prefer to discuss your vision with me privately, or with the others as well?"

Talwyn weighed that decision for a moment. "Let's talk with the others. There is nothing I don't want them to know about, and we can save time by not having to repeat it."

Dreyken then stood and held his hand out to her. "Come, then. Let's go."

Talwyn took his offered hand, and he easily pulled her to her feet.

As they walked to where the others were camped, Talwyn tried to shake off the vulnerable feeling that her nightmare and her talk with Dreyken had left her with. She stood taller, pushed her shoulders back, and cleared her expression. It wasn't too difficult to pull the aloof, sarcastic cloak over her again. She'd been doing it for years, after all.

They found Tolus, Norshan, and Helsi sitting around a small fire, eating meat of some kind. It didn't look like the provisions they were given, so Talwyn figured they must have hunted while she was sleeping. The three protectors lifted their attention from their food at the sound of their approach and looked at Talwyn expectantly.

"Did you see anything that could help us?" Helsi asked softly.

"I believe so." Talwyn took a seat on a fallen log across from the others, and Dreyken sat down next to her. When she looked up, she noticed Helsi smiling at her warmly, and knowingly.

"Keep in mind, we don't get to choose what we See, and I can't always tell if it's the past, present, or future."

"It's okay." Helsi spoke in a soft and encouraging tone. "If you can give us anything at all to go on, it's a start."

"The place I saw is here in the Sacred Forest. If I'm right, and I believe I am, it's north-northeast of my village."

"What was it, exactly?" Dreyken shifted to face her on the log.

"I saw a group of demonkin gathered around some kind of contraption. The dark sorcerer was there, but, as usual, his cloak hid his face. They were talking about getting the thing ready for the sorceress."

"What was this contraption?" Norshan asked.

"I couldn't tell. I've seen nothing like it before."

"What did it look like?"

She looked at Dreyken as she answered his question. "Well, if I didn't know better, I'd say it was a large, rectangular block of ice. But there's no way they could have a block of ice in the Sacred Forest for any length of time. It's too warm here. And where would they get one this time of year? Maybe it was glass."

"Glass?" Norshan said. "That would be just as hard to get as ice, if not harder."

"Well, you said the dark sorcerer was there. Maybe there's magic involved," Tolus suggested.

"Oh, there's magic involved for more than whatever that thing is." Talwyn was certain of that. "For example, how did they get past the protective spells to enter the forest in the first place?"

"Good question." Dreyken's expression betrayed his worry.

"Yes, and it's a major cause for concern. We see examples repeatedly of how powerful the Dark Sorcerer is. Blocking our visions, enabling his demonkin to enter the forest." Talwyn said.

"If he is there when we get there, none of you is to confront him alone," Dreyken added. "Do you understand?"

Dreyken looked at each of his people with a stern expression before turning to give it to her as well. Talwyn lifted her eyebrows and held up her hands in surrender.

"How can we expect to defeat a being that powerful?" Tolus asked.

"Well, that's why myself and my fellow champions are searching for allies. We can't do it alone. Our best chance is to have as many of the realm's people come together as possible. We will also need the Sorcerers of the Light. And the Ternias."

"What is the Ternias?" Helsi asked, at the same time as Norshan asked, "There are still Sorcerers of the Light?"

"One question at a time," Dreyken admonished.

"To answer your questions, of course there are still Sorcerers of the Light. Any sorcerer or sorceress who is on the side of good and will help protect our realm is a Sorcerer of the Light. They still meet from time to time, as far as I know."

"And the Ternias?" Helsi asked.

Talwyn gazed into the fire and thought of how to explain. "Many, many years ago, there was a powerful seer sorceress named Dimia. She had visions that our realm would be threatened by a powerful magical being. We believe it is this time we are in now that she foresaw. She also foresaw that we would come into possession of an...artifact that could stop this sorcerer."

"Where is this artifact now?" Dreyken asked.

"It's on the way to the Great Gate." She paused. "Well, technically, it's on its way to Eastgate, and then from there to the Great Gate. My friend Maelona is bringing it."

"And what about the keystones?" Dreyken asked. "You said the seer champions were protecting them, and that they can stop the Great Gate from being used again."

"True, but since the four guardians, including myself, have headed off in different directions with no actual way of knowing with any certainty if the others are successful, we decided it was best to have a backup plan. Plus, the Dark Sorcerer has already figured out how to get past the magical protections of the Sacred Forest. So it seems to me that it would be best not to assume anything."

Dreyken nodded. "I agree with you on that."

"Not to mention," Norshan added, "an evil creature that powerful should not be left unchecked. So even if the keystones were effective, he should be hunted down, anyway."

"True. But I agree with Dreyken. Do not take him on yourself. Wait for magical backup." Talwyn met everyone's eyes to emphasize this point. Norshan pressed his lips together but didn't say anything. She knew what that suggested.

"I mean it, Norshan."

"Okay, I get it. But how are we going to rescue Athnie if the dark sorcerer is there?"

"The same way we seers accomplish most tasks—with patience. This sorcerer has rarely been seen, even in our visions. This would suggest that he stays hidden as much as possible. So, we just have to wait until he leaves, then we'll only have his demonkin lackeys to worry about."

"Let's hope you're right," Norshan said.

"How far away is this place, anyway?" Helsi asked.

"Far-enough away that we will need to fly there. If you are willing. It would probably take me a week to travel there on foot."

"Well, it's a good thing we just ate." Tolus patted his stomach.

Talwyn spoke as she worked things through in her mind. "We know they were picked up by an ainmith and that they were likely almost a day ahead of us. I just spent . . . how long, sleeping?" She looked at Dreyken.

"It wasn't more than a couple of hours."

"Good. How fast can you fly in your dragon forms? Would you say you are faster than the ainmith?"

Norshan sat up straighter and puffed out his chest. "Without doubt."

"They will undoubtedly be there before us, but we still have a couple of hours of darkness, which will make it harder for anyone to spot us. However, I suggest we stay low, close to the treetops, and we should land before we get too close. Then we'll go the rest of the way on foot. I will give a low whistle when it's time to land."

"Who will you be riding with?" Tolus raised a brow at her.

"She rides with me." Dreyken's tone brooked no argument.

"Of course, Lord Dragon." Tolus bowed to Dreyken. Talwyn couldn't help but roll her eyes a little.

"Let's get moving."

Dreyken, Tolus, Norshan, and Helsi stripped off their armor and the light clothing they were wearing underneath. They then put their armor back on and put their clothing in their packs.

Talwyn couldn't help but be awed a little as she watched the four of them transform. As they shifted, the layers of the armor that Aleyn had constructed for them pulled loose to fit their dragon forms. There were exposed areas, of course, because of the size difference, but the new armor covered most of their vital areas.

Dreyken's beautiful dragon almost blended into the surrounding night. Every now and again, she could see light from the moon, which was now trying to peek through the clouds, reflect off his dark, smooth scales. He moved close to her and bowed low so she could climb on easily. She sat herself on his back with her legs dangling just behind his wings, in much the same manner as the first time she had ridden his dragon.

The only other time she had ridden before now, there had been a battle going on. So she hadn't had the time to truly appreciate it. But now, as Dreyken spread his great wings, flapping them in large, slow strokes to lift them into the air, she felt a thrill of exhilaration that only increased as they rose higher and left the ground below.

CHAPTER FOURTEEN

The Dark Sorcerer

Talwyn watched the sky as the sun rose to its highest and then began to lower again.

As she traveled with the four Dragon-folk, Talwyn scanned ahead for any signs of trouble. She couldn't resist looking down now and then. She took in the trees and the landscape of her beloved forest from a dragon's-eye view for the very first time. Even when it was only lit by pale moonlight, she found it to be magnificent and captivating.

Turning her attention back to the task at hand, she watched the landscape for the area she knew they would need to land in. It took her a moment to orient herself to the forest below, as she had never seen it from this point of view before, and they were flying close to the treetops. Once she saw a couple of landmarks, however, she knew exactly where they were and where to go.

Once they passed the dips and shadows of her home, the Valley of Sight, she knew they were getting close. Talwyn took out her bow and nocked an arrow. She observed the forest as they flew. Even with the excellent eyesight of the seers, archers hidden in the trees would be hard to spot.

A little farther on, they reached the place Talwyn was watching for. She gave her low whistle and brought her bow forward, into Dreyken's line of sight, to point out where she wanted them to land.

The Dragon-folk circled the area twice to orient themselves before descending into the small clearing that Talwyn had indicated.

"Not bad." Talwyn dismounted and stretched her cramped muscles. "A week or more's travel on foot done in less than a day by dragon." She smiled at Dreyken, then watched his form shimmer, shrink, and reshape back to human.

"That's nothing." Norshan grinned. "We could have done it in even less time if we had flown higher. There are currents up there that help us move through the air much more quickly and easily."

"Yes." Tolus smirked in Talwyn's direction. "And that's not to mention that Dreyken was carrying an inexperienced rider. It wouldn't do to have our guide lose her hold and plummet to her death."

Talwyn smiled back at him. "You underestimate my skills, my friend. Once this is all over, we will go flying up there in those air currents you speak of. Then I challenge you to fly your fastest and see how well I hold my place."

"Did you not hear it when I said she rides with me? I didn't just mean this time. I meant every time." Dreyken's voice was firm, and Tolus's eyes widened with worry. His expression relaxed again, however, when he looked at Dreyken and saw that he was smiling.

A few feet away, Norshan let out a great guffaw of laughter. Talwyn wasn't sure if it was because of Dreyken's statement or Tolus's reaction, but she couldn't help but grin at the sound.

The dragons shrugged out of their now-too-large armor and retrieved their clothes from their packs, which they had carried in their great claws as they flew. As they dressed, Talwyn began re-clipping the links of Dreyken's armor back into layers so he could don it again in his human form. Once the others had finished dressing, they reset their armor and put it back on, as well.

"It would be in your best interest to not shift from dragon back to human during battle. Or if you do, don't expect to put your armor back on. This armor is ingenious in many ways, but resetting it from larger to smaller form takes too long to make it convenient to do in battle."

The others grunted their agreement as they finished up with the armor. Then they pulled dried meat from their packs before returning them to their backs. Once they were done, Dreyken stood and looked at Talwyn. "Where to next?"

"Follow me." Talwyn motioned ahead with a lift of her chin. "Be as quiet as possible."

Dreyken, Norshan, Tolus, and Helsi followed Talwyn, as she had instructed. They chewed on their meat and looked all around as they walked, the unfamiliar sights constantly catching their attention. Because of this, they weren't always mindful of where they stepped, and not as quiet as Talwyn. But she knew they had very little experience traveling through wooded areas. In fact, they had very little experience traveling anywhere that wasn't the inside of a mountain.

After some time, the party heard sounds up ahead, and then voices. Shortly after that, Talwyn heard Athnie's frightened voice. At about the same time, Athnie and their enemies became visible through the trees. Talwyn and the others positioned themselves in a crouch just inside the forested area that surrounded the clearing.

"Are you going to kill me?" Athnie spoke to a tall, cloaked figure.

A deep voice responded. "Kill you? Interesting thought. It all depends on you, my dear. On how willing you are to cooperate."

Talwyn's eyes widened at the realization that the Dark Sorcerer was here now, speaking with Athnie. This was not something she had foreseen. Something must have changed. She was glad now that she had taken the time to warn the others not to take him on themselves.

His presence complicated their rescue plan.

She looked at Dreyken and the others, signaling to get their attention. Once they were looking her way, she pointed to the hooded figure and mouthed the word *sorcerer*.

"Are you going to beg me for your life, little one?" The sorcerer's drawl was somewhere in between menacing and indifferent.

"No." Athnie held her chin high even though her voice wavered.

"So brave." There was a hint of condescension in the sorcerer's voice.

"No, it's not brave. Just, why should I beg you for something that's not yours to give or take?"

"Hmm." The Dark Sorcerer turned to give Athnie his full attention. "Such a mature sentiment from one so very young."

Talwyn agreed with him, though she doubted they'd agree on much more.

Athnie did not respond to that comment. She stood silently, but looked directly at the sorcerer. She held her chin high, even though her bottom lip trembled and her body shook.

Athnie was wrong when she said she wasn't brave. She was, indeed, very brave.

After a brief pause, the evil sorcerer continued. "Do not fret, my dear. What I have planned for you will not even hurt much. Who knows, once this is all over with, maybe we will have a chance to sit and talk. I can tell you all about my plans, and why I am doing what I'm doing. Maybe you will even choose to stand by my side."

Talwyn got the feeling that the words were meant to be reassuring. However, his voice and tone were anything but.

Peripherally, Talwyn noticed two demonkin who were out of the sorcerer's line of sight give each other a look. Interesting. At least the sorcerer's words gave some reassurance that he did not intend to harm Athnie. Not yet anyway.

"I doubt that." Athnie's voice was soft, but assertive.

"Do not judge so soon. There are others skilled in using magic who have joined me of their own accord."

"I can't even do magic yet. I don't understand why you want me here."

"You do not need to understand, young one. And certainly not before you've allied with me of your own free will. But I will say this: it is not your skill so much as your magical potential that I need."

"Please, just let me go." Athnie's low voice was shaking now, and it sounded like she was struggling to hold back tears.

Norshan lurched forward, but Talwyn grabbed his arm and held firmly. He looked at her, and then at Dreyken, who shook his head at him before he reluctantly relaxed his position again.

She understood how Norshan felt. She really did. Seeing this crack in the girl's defiant demeanor broke Talwyn's heart. She wanted to rush in there and grab her as well. However, that was tantamount to suicide. They didn't know enough about the Dark

Sorcerer's power to counter him effectively. All they really knew was that he was extremely powerful.

From where Talwyn's group was standing, their view was partially obscured by trees, bushes, and demonkin. However, when the sorcerer turned to address one of his lackeys, the lowering sun momentarily illuminated his face within his cowl.

Talwyn sucked in a breath. This was possibly the first time any seer had seen his face, since he always kept it hidden in their visions. It was just a flash and then it was gone, but she had seen it.

For the first time in a long time, Talwyn felt thankful for her excellent memory. She would never forget that face.

It was a remarkably ordinary face. If he were a human, she'd think he was in his thirties. Brown hair and a scruff of a brown beard. She couldn't tell the color of his eyes from here and with such a brief glimpse. There was nothing that hinted at the evil inside. If she passed him on a street, she probably wouldn't even have noticed him. That could be more dangerous than if it stood out, since it meant he could wander the realm at will, pretending to be just like anyone else, and no one would notice.

The sorcerer spoke to his follower. "There's been a change of plans. I am taking this one back to the east."

"Has something happened, emperor?" the demonkin asked.

"Yes, but you do not need to know the details."

"What can we do to help?" the demonkin asked.

"Take Skydancer. Go to Southgate. Tell Torradan that this chamber," he placed his hand on the icy-looking box, "is reserved just for him if he should fail in his task."

Without another word, the Dark Sorcerer turned and stalked off toward the northwest, accompanied by another demonkin who dragged Athnie along with them.

The three dragon protectors fidgeted in their hiding spot, and Dreyken signaled them to hold. Talwyn was glad to see they agreed on this. The last thing she wanted was to start a fight when the Dark Sorcerer was still close enough to hear and retaliate.

She leaned in toward the others, whispering, "We will watch and listen. Maybe we'll learn something that can help us get her back."

A few minutes passed before the demonkin guards spoke. Talwyn suspected they were also waiting for the sorcerer to be too far away to hear them. She held her position, hoping they would say something that could be of use to them.

"I don't understand why there's so much bleedin' secrecy," said one of the demonkin. "Why can't the emperor tell his own soldiers what his plans are? Doesn't he trust his own followers? Or is it just us lowly ones he doesn't trust?"

"Don't take it personally, Kydoch," his companion replied. "He's only been telling those who need to know and, even then, only enough to get the job done."

"Doesn't that seem a little paranoid to you?"

"Look at it this way, Kydoch. If the emperor's plans were to fail now, it would be another three-thousand years before anyone could try again. His own goals aside, think of what that would mean for us. Without demon blood to add to our lines, we'd probably be extinct by then."

"It's too bad our females can't bear young." Kydoch's lips twisted as if he were tasting something sour. "If we weren't forced to use human females, our bloodlines wouldn't have become so weak."

What? Talwyn's eyes widened in surprise. Well, wasn't this some very interesting information? And not only was the information interesting, but so was the grimace on Kydoch's face when he spoke of being forced to use human females. Was it the fact that they were human or the fact that they were being used as incubators, possibly against their will, that bothered the male?

"Do you think there might be more of 'em?" Kydoch asked.

"More of who?" the demonkin closest to him asked.

"You know, more like the one he has watch things for him?"

"I doubt it. I think they were killed off a few hundred years ago. But you never know."

Talwyn had been crouching behind some bushes, but she fell back into a sitting position when she heard what they were saying.

Could it be? Could there be a seer working with the Dark Sorcerer?

She was so caught up in a whirlwind of thoughts that she didn't hear footsteps approaching. The first sign that got through to her was when she heard her name, whispered in a familiar voice.

"Talwyn Survalor."

Dreyken and his three protectors jumped and spun around, searching this way and that for the source of the voice.

Talwyn held her hand up to the shifters to signal them to hold. "Berinon Sagespirit." She nodded her head with respect as the older male appeared from around a tree, followed by two young protectors. She recognized her Elder's companions as two of the four current apprentice champions.

"I am afraid we will have to wait until later for introductions." Berinon bowed his head to the others. "I'm sure the demonkin must have heard us by now."

Sure enough, when they turned to look back toward the clearing, the demonkin guards were approaching the tree line with swords drawn.

Talwyn looked at the others. "Let's go."

They were just entering the clearing when Talwyn caught movement above the trees to the north. She signaled to the others, and they watched as a large, white ainmith lifted into the air, carrying four passengers, including Athnie.

Without warning, Norshan charged full-speed into the clearing. The demonkin whirled toward him, swords raised. However, before they could attack, Norshan shifted into his dragon, beat his great wings, and took flight. Talwyn looked on in horror as one of the demonkin took a bow from its back and aimed at Norshan, who was now flying directly for the ainmith carrying Athnie and the sorcerer.

Talwyn, Dreyken, Tolus, and Helsi quickly engaged the demonkin, trying to draw attention away from Norshan. The Dragon-folk had their swords drawn, and Talwyn quickly grabbed her bow and nocked an arrow.

When the older demonkin male saw they were outnumbered, it shouted out for help. Talwyn quickly silenced it with an arrow through its throat, but it had gotten the attention of its party, anyway. Soon, half a dozen more demonkin ran over the hill from the north.

Talwyn let two more arrows fly in quick succession. The first one hit its mark, and the demonkin who had just crested the hill fell to the ground, lifeless. Her second arrow was blocked by her other target's small wooden shield. The arrow was galanite, so it pierced the shield but didn't do any damage to the wielder.

"No!" Helsi's scream sounded from across the clearing. She looked in Helsi's direction, then followed her gaze to where Norshan was now engaging with the enemy in the air.

Norshan let out a great stream of fire. His aim was true, and the ainmith and its riders should have been little more than ash. All but Athnie, of course, who, since she was a dragon shifter, would not be damaged by the fire.

However, when the flames dissipated, Norshan's targets remained aloft and untouched. A blue glow surrounded them, protecting them from the heat of the dragon's fire.

"I told him we couldn't take the sorcerer on ourselves." Talwyn muttered the words to herself. Then her eyes were drawn back down by sound and movement as a demonkin ran, yelling, toward Helsi as she was distracted by the spectacle above. Talwyn nocked an arrow and let it fly, striking the demonkin under the arm it had raised to strike at Helsi, who had still not pulled her attention from the sky. The demonkin stumbled a little, a look of shock and pain on its face, before it fell to the ground, dead.

An unexpected sharp pain hit Talwyn across her lower back as she was struck with an impact that caused her to stumble ahead a couple of steps. That's twice now that she'd allowed that to happen. Luckily, she was still wearing her armor, so the sword did not cut her. She quickly used her inner-sight to deaden the pain. She would deal with the bruising later. The demonkin that had attacked her while her back was turned stood there as if it wasn't expecting her to still be standing, and she took the opportunity to grab her dagger from her belt, spin around, and slit its throat in one swift, smooth movement.

With her own allies moving all around while they fought the demonkin, Talwyn put her bow away and grabbed a short sword from a fallen opponent. She ran toward a demonkin approaching Dreyken from behind while his attention was diverted by another that attacked from the front.

To draw the demonkin away from Dreyken, she gave a wordless battle cry as she approached. The demonkin looked in her direction and took a couple of steps toward her as it brought its sword around to defend.

The sounds of swords clashing rang throughout the clearing. These demonkin were well trained, holding their own against the protectors. The skill of her opponent surprised her—demonkin lived shorter lives than shifters and seers and, thus, were usually less experienced.

Soon, however, Talwyn saw her opening. Her adversary swung its sword overhead, and instead of using her sword to block, she quickly did a spinning jump, moving toward and diagonally out from its body. As its arms dropped, she was in the air behind it. She brought her sword around with a backhanded strike, and the demonkin's head rolled to the ground just as she landed.

She heard a male cry out in pain and curse behind her and turned to see that a demonkin had skewered Tolus through the thigh. The female seer warrior who had come with Berinon stood between her and Tolus, so she called out to her, "Alastrina, down!"

Alastrina immediately dropped into a low crouch and braced her hands on the ground in front of her, clearly understanding what Talwyn wanted.

Talwyn ran toward her, jumped onto her back, and used her as a springboard so she could leap high into the air. As she came down, she angled her sword straight down in front of her, impaling the demonkin with her sword and pinning it to the ground.

As she landed and moved to pull the sword free of the demonkin, Tolus complained grumpily next to her. "I had it."

She turned to him and nodded. "I know."

"Talwyn has always been a little . . . enthusiastic, shall we say, in her physical pursuits," Berinon said as he approached them from behind.

"That's good news for you." Tolus looked at Dreyken and waggled his brows.

She could feel her face flush in embarrassment. "He meant physical training and battle."

"Still, I'm sure that's transferable to other . . . areas." Tolus waggled his brows at her.

"What is it with you Dragon-folk males?" Talwyn asked in an exasperated voice. "That's no way to speak in front of my Elder."

Tolus chuckled from where he sat on the ground, pressing his hand to his wound.

"Aren't you supposed to be in pain or something?"

He stopped chuckling, but it was still clear that he was holding laughter back.

She looked around, making sure there were no other demonkin left standing, or lying in wait to attack.

A moment later, there was a screeching cry, and they all turned to watch another ainmith taking off from just beyond the rise to the north. It looked to be carrying a single passenger, and it headed south, toward the gate town.

As it flew into the distance, Tolus let out a string of loud curses in its direction.

CHAPTER FIFTEEN

Love, Loss, & Berinon Sagespirit

With the immediate danger taken care of, Talwyn and Dreyken jogged to where Helsi kneeled, sobbing, on the ground. The others followed close behind.

"What happened to Norshan?" Dreyken asked Helsi in a soft voice.

Helsi was shaking her head and taking deep breaths in an obvious effort to get her emotions under control.

"T-the s-s-sorcerer. He s-shot something at him." She stammered the words out between sobs. "It was like a ball of blue light or energy or something." She sobbed again, and again sucked in a few calming breaths before she continued. "H-he f-f-fell."

"Where did he fall, Helsi?" Dreyken was kneeling in front of her, looking her in the eyes.

She pointed to the northwest. "That way. I cannot bear to look."

Talwyn watched Helsi intently as Dreyken reached down to squeeze her shoulder.

"Tolus, stay here with her." Dreyken turned and strode in the direction Helsi had indicated. "Talwyn." He signaled with a tilt of his head that he wanted her to accompany him.

Talwyn looked at her Elder. Berinon nodded to her, and the three of them jogged off to locate Norshan.

Dreyken introduced himself to Berinon as they started off. "I am Dreyken, Lord of the Stone Dragons." He respectfully bowed his head to Berinon.

"It has been quite some time since I've been in the presence of a Stone Dragon. I am honored." He bowed his head to Dreyken. "My name is Berinon Sagespirit, Elder of the seer people."

Talwyn was still looking back at the protectors. "I know that pain."

"What's that?"

Talwyn turned to meet Dreyken's eyes. "Helsi and Norshan are mates, aren't they?"

Dreyken looked at her, lips pressed together, concern etched clearly on his face. Talwyn wondered if he was going to answer, but after a moment, he nodded.

"Why didn't I know that sooner?" She spoke more to herself than to the others. She should have realized it from the way they interacted with each other back in the mountain. As a seer, she should have noticed their connection. She must have unconsciously ignored the signs. The idea was disconcerting. How many other things had she missed because she still held on to past traumas?

Dreyken looked at her in silence for a moment before speaking in a soft voice. "Dragons are private about such things. And besides that, you met them when they were on a quest to find Athnie."

Talwyn looked forward once more as they continued to jog quickly to where Helsi had pointed.

"There he is," she said, picking up speed. She had expected to see his dragon form, but he lay lifeless on the ground, looking like a fragile human in a sea of too-large mail armor.

She ran over and kneeled next to him. Berinon and Dreyken quickly followed, and Berinon kneeled at his other side. Dreyken hung back a couple of feet as she and Berinon examined his protector.

"Is he . . ." Dreyken began, but he was too choked up to finish the sentence. Talwyn looked at him, compassion, sorrow, and guilt twisting her gut into a knot.

Talwyn stood and walked a few feet away, her back turned to the others. "By the Universe! I never should have gotten you involved in this. I should have let Airgan have his way." She turned and saw Dreyken looking at her, his eyes wide with surprise.

"Yes, I know how that sounds, given how hard I worked to get you to agree to help." She took a breath and looked up at the sky. "I just . . . it's just—this is not right."

Berinon moved to her side and placed a hand on her shoulder. "War and senseless killing never are, my dear." He studied her for a moment. "You are comparing her to yourself, what you have lived, are you not?"

"Of course I am. How could I not? Helsi's loss is my fault. She will face so many demons because of my interference."

"The demonkin still would have gone for the sorceress, even if you had not gone to the mountain. The Stone Dragons would have been pulled into the fight either way." Berinon's voice was soft and reasonable, but she wanted to reject his words.

"Talwyn." Dreyken moved close to her and took her hand. His eyes glistened with sadness and sympathy. "Norshan, Helsi, and all the others knew what they were signing up for." He looked down at his fallen friend. "Norshan was one of the first to come to me to voice his opinion. He thought—he believed—we should be involved. He insisted that this was our fight too, that we could not keep pretending like the realm outside our mountain doesn't exist. Helsi agreed with him. That is why they were both here with us today. I chose them not only for their skill, but because of how strongly they felt about this. You cannot place the blame upon yourself.

"None of us want war. Unfortunately, this sorcerer and his army are forcing our hand. If we want peace, if we want our freedom, we are going to have to fight for it. You were right about that, Talwyn. You were right."

Talwyn looked at Dreyken, then down at the ground. She did not respond to his words. She understood what he was trying to say, but this situation was bringing back old fears. Helsi was undoubtedly going through soul-rending pain right now. Dreyken was right. It was the Dark Sorcerer who was forcing these dangerous times upon them. But who was to blame didn't really matter. It didn't change the fact that she felt that old familiar anxiety, that old familiar fear. She did not know if she was strong enough to survive that kind of loss again.

"Shall we build a pyre for him?" Berinon's words broke her from her thoughts. She turned to look at Dreyken.

"No." Dreyken shook his head. "We are impervious to flame."

"Yes, of course." Berinon chuckled, but it was a sad sound. "So silly of me."

"Our way is to place our dead in the throne room for people to say their last goodbyes. Then, after two days, we take them out to the cliffs on the south coast and we give them to the ocean. I will have Helsi and Tolus take him back to the mountain to begin his preparations." Dreyken bent and lifted his protector's lifeless form, and they headed back to find the others.

Once they reached the clearing again, Dreyken carefully laid Norshan's body at the feet of his mate. He kneeled before her with his head bowed for a moment before speaking.

"Norshan will be remembered for his bravery and his fearlessness, but most of all, for his loyalty to his people and to the realm."

Helsi nodded. She was still stifling her sobs.

After a moment, Dreyken stood again and addressed Tolus and Helsi. "This is Berinon Sagespirit. He is a seer Elder." Then he turned to Berinon. "These are two of my protectors, Helsi and Tolus." Tolus was kneeling next to Helsi with his arms around her in comfort. "The protector who fell is Norshan."

"My companions are Alastrina and Nechtan." Berinon waved a hand toward the young warriors who stood a few feet behind Helsi. "They are two of our apprentice champions." They all nodded to each other.

"Helsi." Dreyken's voice was soft and cracked a little. He paused and cleared his throat before continuing. "You and Tolus can take him back to the mountain for preparations."

"No." Helsi's tone was abrupt but was softer when she spoke again. "No, Tolus should stay with you and help. I will take him home."

"You shouldn't be by yourself at a time like this."

"You shouldn't be without all the warriors you can get at a time like this." Her voice was emotional, yet firm. "Norshan would not want that."

Dreyken considered her for a moment before nodding.

Helsi leaned forward and placed Norshan's arms across his chest. Tolus passed her a short length of rope, which she used to secure his wrists together. When she stood, Dreyken and Tolus took a few steps back, and the seers followed suit.

Without undressing, Helsi shifted. Her clothing shredded and her armor expanded outward until she stood in her dragon form before them. Gently, very gently, she wrapped her great front claws around her mate's body. She unfolded her wings, and they watched as she lifted into the sky.

The others drifted away one by one, but Talwyn stayed, watching the sky, until they disappeared from sight.

No one spoke as Dreyken and Tolus gathered wood and stone to build a fire. Alastrina and Nechtan had headed off into the woods to hunt, and Berinon was examining the icy, rectangular box. At first, Talwyn sat on a large boulder, lost in her thoughts and emotions that fluctuated from numb to painful. But then she shook herself. She was just sitting there while the others were being productive. She headed over to help Berinon and stood at the opposite side of the contraption from her Elder.

"He was here, Berinon. The Dark Sorcerer was here."

Berinon shook his head worriedly, but only seemed slightly taken aback. "This is worse than we thought. It was concerning enough when we found out that demonkin had breached the borders of the forest. Now to find out they are this deep inside the forest, along with the sorcerer himself. Obviously, they have found a way to counteract the protective spells."

Just then, the two seer apprentices returned with a small deer, and the others gathered near the firepit, which was now ready to go. They all took part in preparing the meal. Talwyn was a little surprised, in a good way, at how well they all worked together. She felt her first brief twinge of optimism since Norshan had fallen. A short time later, the meal was ready.

Talwyn looked around the clearing thoughtfully as she ate. "It's too bad no one left a demonkin alive."

"Well, I would have if you hadn't jumped in." Tolus sat across the fire from her. He had bandaged his leg wound while they were off retrieving Norshan's body. "That's how it got a strike in on me. I was trying to subdue it without killing it, but it wasn't cooperating."

"Imagine that." She looked at the lifeless forms on the ground. "I have some questions that need answering."

"That's why I was trying to keep it alive. I was hoping we'd be able to learn something from it that might help us free Athnie."

"Well, from what we overheard, it's doubtful that any of the demonkin here knew much, but I figured it was worth a try."

"You never know. Maybe one of the higher-ranking henchmen might have known something it wasn't telling the others. Maybe they just need a little convincing to talk." Tolus's tone was menacing, which was a little ridiculous. Talwyn doubted the Dragon-folk ever tortured anyone. But, then again, who knew? Maybe they would if they were pushed far enough.

"For now, maybe we can concentrate on trying to find a way to free Athnie ourselves." Dreyken sounded sad, almost guilty, when he spoke.

Berinon looked at Talwyn questioningly. "Would you like to fill us in on what we missed before our arrival?"

"Athnie is the Stone Dragons' sorceress. She was captured by demonkin and brought here."

"We think the sorcerer had planned to put her in that contraption." Dreyken pointed toward the clear, rectangular chamber. "But it seems he changed his mind."

"So, we only need to figure out what that is, why the sorcerer changed his mind about putting her in there, where they took your sorceress, and how they could enter the Sacred Forest in the first place." Alastrina's words were laced with frustration.

"Should be simple enough, right?" Talwyn gave her a wry smile.

"Well, since we have no live demonkin to interrogate, let's question the dead ones," Dreyken said. He stood up suddenly and walked from body to body between the lifeless demonkin. The others moved to help him, but Dreyken held up a hand. "No. I want to look for similarities or inconsistencies, so it is best if only one of us does it."

He made his way from body to body, crouching low to look them over and search them. After he made his way around to all of them, he plucked something from around a demonkin's neck and walked back over to where Talwyn and Berinon stood.

"Every one of those beasts was wearing one of these." Dreyken held up a chain. Dangling from it was an amulet with white powder encased in glass and metal.

Talwyn took it from him and examined it. Then she handed it to Berinon. "What do you think it is?"

Berinon placed the amulet on a boulder, then picked up a smaller rock from the ground. He smashed the rock against the amulet once, then twice, then again, until the glass shattered. He looked at the contents carefully, sniffed it, then dipped his finger in and touched it to his tongue.

"Bone dust."

Tolus looked from the amulet to Berinon. "How can you be sure from that small amount? Are you saying you are familiar enough with the taste of bone to be certain?"

"No, young dragon. It has little to do with taste. But once a substance is inside a seer's body, we can use our inner-sight to examine it."

"But you barely touched it to your tongue."

"What can I say? I am old and very practiced."

Talwyn nodded. "True. It probably would have taken me a few minutes." She looked at Berinon. "Did you sense anything special about it? Something that would allow them to enter the forest?"

Berinon dipped his finger into the small sample and placed it on his tongue once again. This time he took a moment or two as he considered.

"There is magic in this bone dust. Old magic. Unfortunately, I am not a sorcerer myself, so I cannot tell you more than that."

Tolus shook his head in disbelief. "Wow. It doesn't seem fair that you seers have so many advantages."

Talwyn looked at him with a serious expression. "Let's just hope our advantages, combined with those of our allies, will be enough to defeat the Dark Sorcerer and his horde." Then she spoke to Berinon again.

"Do you think those amulets allowed them to enter the Sacred Forest?"

"It is likely." He took an undamaged one off another demonkin and examined it. "It wouldn't be the first time magical amulets were used to access the forest." He gave Talwyn a knowing look. Giving amulets to allies so they could enter the forest undeterred was a custom that the seers had used for centuries.

"I can't find a seal on this." Dreyken's voice sounded from a few feet away. Talwyn and Berinon turned their attention to where he was now trying to open the chamber the sorcerer had planned to put Athnie in. "How was he going to get her in there?"

Talwyn walked over and carefully studied the box. She could see that the interior was hollow but could not see any evidence that would show how to place a person inside. "I can't see a seam either.

It looks like it could be a solid block of ice with a big air bubble inside."

She ran her hand along the surface, paying close attention around the edges. "I can't feel any seams either." She stood back and looked it over. "It looks like ice, and it's cold like ice, but it isn't melting. What do you think it is, Berinon?"

"I'm not sure. I've seen nothing like it before."

"So, what do we do now?" Dreyken addressed his question to Berinon.

"I think . . ." Berinon began slowly. "I think we will need Maelona to help us figure out how to free your sorceress if she has indeed been encased in a chamber such as this one by the time we find her."

"Do you think she could do it?" Talwyn asked.

"I'm sure she can do many things that she hasn't yet allowed herself to do."

"Who is Maelona, and how can she help us?" Tolus asked.

Talwyn and Berinon exchanged a look of worry, which then shifted to a look of agreement.

Talwyn took a breath. "Maelona is a friend. And a fellow seer champion."

"And she is also a sorceress," Berinon added.

"A sorceress?" Dreyken's brows rose in surprise, and his expression turned hopeful. "Is she powerful?"

Talwyn nodded. "Rumor has it. But it's hard to say for sure since she has always refused to use her magic. Well, that's not exactly true. I saw her use it in some limited ways when she was very young, but not since she returned to us as a post-adolescent."

Tolus huffed. "Well, that's not really helpful."

"I think it's safe to say she is coming to terms with her need to embrace that side of herself." Berinon looked at Talwyn again, and she nodded her agreement.

"Okay," Tolus said. "But what could she do to help?"

"Her father was a powerful sorcerer as well." The Dragon-folk's eyes widened at Berinon's revelation. Usually, each species saw a sorcerer once every few generations. They were very rare.

"I don't know how much you know about seers," Berinon continued, "but aside from our ability to see the past, present, and future, we also have what we call inner-sight. It's what I just did to identify the bone dust. But I will tell you more so you can understand.

"This ability allows us to see inside our own bodies and to manipulate elements there. We can use it to change hair, eye, and skin color, for example, by repressing some elements or pushing elements to the surface."

"Really?" Tolus's eyes were wide, and he stared at Talwyn in wonder. In answer, Talwyn changed her wild, red hair to straight and black, changed her green eyes to blue, and darkened her fair skin.

"Wow." Talwyn chuckled at Tolus's awed tone. "If I hadn't seen the shift for myself, I wouldn't recognize you right now."

"I really don't know how you can be impressed. I can change my hair and eye color. You can turn into a dragon and breathe fire. My talents are nothing compared to that." She changed back to her normal coloring.

"Yes, but we can't hide ourselves in plain sight or see the future," Dreyken countered.

"I didn't realize you were shifters too," Tolus commented, almost absentmindedly.

Berinon looked at him. "Well, most do not consider us to be true shifters, as we don't really change our form, except in the most basic of manners. We manipulate elements that already exist in our bodies. We can also use this ability to heal ourselves when we are ill or injured, if it isn't too severe."

Talwyn shifted uncomfortably, not wanting to think about a time when an injury was too severe. Luckily, Berinon continued his explanation, drawing her mind away from her painful memories.

"Maelona's father, Eluard, could use his magic as a bridge to see inside others. Mostly, he used this ability to heal. In our village, he was well respected. He was a sorcerer, an Elder, and a healer. Our people greatly felt the loss when he passed back into the Universe."

Talwyn realized what he was getting at. "If Maelona could use her magic in this same way, then she could potentially use it to see inside. Make sure Athnie is okay. See what kind of magic is at play here and how we can free her."

"So, where do we find her?" Dreyken seemed ready to jump up and go to her right now.

Berinon looked up to the sky, which was now dark and dotted with stars. He studied the moon for a moment before looking back at Dreyken.

"If my calculations are correct, and they usually are, the Great Gate is about two days' hard march, directly to the north."

"Directly to the north?" Talwyn felt a flicker of alarm inside her chest.

"Indeed." Berinon pressed his lips together.

"So, we're on a ley line right now?"

"We are."

"I don't think this is a coincidence." Talwyn couldn't believe it, but in hindsight, she should have known.

"Nor do I," Berinon agreed. He frowned deeply, and his eyes were serious and unfocused. His expression gave Talwyn a foreboding feeling.

"What are you talking about?" Tolus asked.

"I will explain it all to you, but not right now." Berinon pointed to the moon. "There is no time.

"According to what I have seen, Talwyn and Dreyken need to be back at Southgate as soon as possible. Our best chance for Southgate and the Stone Dragons to come together meaningfully is if the Dragon lord himself is there to consult, strategize, and work closely with the King of Southgate and his men. We will meet Maelona about two hours' march south of the Great Gate sixteen days hence, and the battle will begin five days after that."

Tolus looked at Talwyn with narrowed eyes. "Have you been holding out on us?"

"No." She huffed a short, sarcastic laugh. "It just so happens that Berinon is many centuries older than I am. He has had much more practice in deciphering visions than I have, and he knows what to look for to give him more clues."

"It's true." Alastrina spoke from the rock where she and Nechtan had sat to listen to the conversation. "He's better at it than anyone else in our village. That's why we all go to him for help when we don't understand something we've seen."

Nechtan nodded his agreement beside her.

"And Athnie?" Dreyken shook his head. "I cannot just abandon her to an unknown fate. She is my responsibility."

"With respect, all the Stone Dragons are your responsibility, Lord Dragon," Tolus said.

"But Athnie is just a child, and she is the first Stone Dragon sorcerer in centuries."

"Then I suggest you leave Tolus with me when you and Talwyn head back to Southgate," Berinon said. "He, Alastrina, Nechtan, and I will search for Athnie. But remember, we are not powerful enough alone to face the sorcerer and his demonkin. You will both need to do what you can to finish up at Southgate quickly and head out to meet us again.

"We know that Maelona and any allies she has gathered will head to the Great Gate from the east, and that the Dark Sorcerer said he is taking your sorceress in that direction. Once we have reached the meeting place, Tolus can scout ahead to find Maelona. We will explain what we've seen here and see if she can release your sorceress. For now, though, we all need to get some rest. There are only a couple of hours before Talwyn and Dreyken will need to leave."

A while later, the group of seers and dragon protectors sat together around a crackling fire after having a brief rest. Talwyn barely noticed the conversations going on around her. She was silent, contemplating what they had seen and heard earlier.

Berinon's voice interrupted her thoughts. "Talwyn, my dear, you look as though you have much on your mind. Is there something you would like to share?"

"There is, actually." Talwyn looked across at him. "We were listening to the demonkin talking just before you arrived, and I heard some concerning information. I would like to run it by you and get your opinion."

"By all means.

"Where to start?" The others around the fire stopped their conversations and turned their attention to Talwyn and Berinon. She took a deep breath. "Well, first, the demonkin mentioned needing demon blood to strengthen their bloodlines. One male said that their females are sterile, and so they are forced to use human females."

"That is very disturbing news. That means the demonkin are motivated by more than just greed or fear of the Dark Sorcerer. Their future is on the line. This will make them even more determined."

"It also means there are human females in need of rescuing." Alastrina and Nechtan looked at Dreyken with wide eyes after he spoke. When he saw their expressions, he shook his head sadly. "We may never forget what the humans did to us, but since they were being manipulated four hundred years ago, I guess we can grant them forgiveness."

Talwyn couldn't help but smile warmly at his candor. "Not to mention it wasn't these exact humans who took part in what happened. For us, it wasn't that long ago. For them, it was generations ago."

"Also, it is clearly wrong for any female to be held against her will and forced to breed." Dreyken shook his head. "It is unbelievable. Don't these creatures have any sense of decency?"

"Unfortunately, many of them do not," Berinon said.

"And that's not all." Talwyn turned to Berinon again. "They said there was someone helping the sorcerer. Someone who helps him see things."

Berinon looked up at the sky and nodded thoughtfully, but he did not respond right away.

"Do you think it could be a..."

"A seer?" Dreyken interrupted. His voice betrayed his concern.

Berinon looked at Dreyken, then back to Talwyn. "I do not believe there are, or have been, any among our people who would willingly help a dark sorcerer."

"But you don't know for sure, do you?" Tolus asked.

"What I know is that three hundred years ago, when our kind were hunted, there were those who could not be accounted for among the dead. Some of our people seem to have just disappeared. I also suspect that a sorcerer as powerful as the one we now face might have ways of getting others to give him information, willingly or not."

It was silent for a few moments as they considered the implications of this possibility. The seers in their group were now very tense and worried about what this might all mean.

After some time, Talwyn picked up the story from where she left off, but she looked at Dreyken as she spoke. "That's why we retreated deep into the Sacred Forest and protected our home with spells to make it hard to find. Turns out, sorcerers aren't the only beings that others will try to capture and use for their own purposes."

"That just . . . infuriates me!" Tolus stood up and began pacing. Or limping, rather. "How can any being think he has the right to claim someone else's life like that? Whether it be to kill a people off, or to capture them for their own purposes, or to keep them as breeding stock, the result is the same. That person's life is forfeit. It is not right!"

"And it will only get worse if the Dark Sorcerer succeeds in his plans. He wishes to subjugate all who will follow him and enslave those who resist." Talwyn looked at Tolus's bandage as he paced, afraid he might cause the wound to bleed again.

"And now we know why the demonkin follow him so unquestioningly, I suspect," said Berinon.

"Because they are evil bastards?" Tolus supplied.

"To some degree, maybe. But believe it or not, not all demonkin are evil. Just like not all humans or shifters are good."

Tolus scoffed, but Berinon ignored it and continued.

"However, we now know that the Dark Sorcerer, their self-proclaimed emperor, has something they want. Something they need. He holds the key to their race's survival."

Everyone was silent for a moment until a curse burst out from Tolus.

"Universe help us! How are we supposed to defeat the most powerful dark wizard our realm has seen and his demonkin army that is fighting against their people's extinction?"

"You're a dragon, Tolus!" Talwyn stood up in front of him, forcing him to stop his pacing.

"And I'm also a bloody realist!"

"Would it really be so bad if the demonkin went extinct?" Alastrina's voice was low, but her question caught everyone's attention just as well as Tolus's shouting had.

Dreyken stood quickly, and everyone turned to look at him. "Enough! We are dragons, and you are seers. Talwyn came looking for our help because she knew this war would be brutal, and your people cannot take on this evil alone. So we will help, because we are strong, and we should not be hiding under a mountain while the rest of the realm is destroyed around us." He glanced at Alastrina. "But we will not be condoning the extinction of any species in the realm."

"Why not?" Tolus spoke in a challenging tone, so different from when he apologized to his Dragon Lord earlier that day. "They exterminated the dragons. They almost exterminated us. And then they did the same to the seers."

"Exactly, Tolus." Dreyken jabbed a finger in the male's direction. "And we know it was wrong of them. We know it was evil. We feel that to the very depth of our beings. Every day, we live with the repercussions of their actions. So if we accept that for another species in the realm, then we are wrong, we are evil. It would go against everything we stand for. We would be no better than our enemies."

Talwyn smiled proudly at Dreyken, then stood and moved to his side. The others were quiet as they took in Dreyken's words of wisdom. Talwyn was glad he was finally accepting and embracing the role he was born to—the role he was born for. She knew he had it in him, buried underneath the complacency she had seen when she first met him. He just needed to bring it to the surface.

Then, quietly, as he was a naturally quiet being, Nechtan spoke. "We may not have a choice, anyway. We cannot stand by and watch them destroy the realm."

Dreyken looked at him. "That is true. But let us be clear that we fight to protect the realm, not to destroy a species."

"How about we also not forget that they are evil demon spawn," Tolus said.

"Again, you are labeling the entire group as evil, young dragon," Berinon said. "It is unlikely that this is true. I have yet to meet any species whose population is entirely good or evil. All we really know is that they are highly motivated by what the Dark Sorcerer is offering them."

A thought occurred to Talwyn, and she sighed wistfully. "If they are loyal to the Dark Sorcerer because he can offer them a future, then it's too bad we can't offer them the same in a different manner."

"How could we possibly do that when it would mean allowing more demons to cross over into Sterrenvar?" Tolus asked.

"That's why I said it's too bad we *can't*." Talwyn's reply was sarcastic but lacking her usual bite. She sighed. "Anyway, this is all based on a snippet of an overheard conversation. We don't know the complete story, I'm sure. But it gives us something to think about."

"Well said, my child." Berinon nodded approvingly.

"Well, it's time for Dreyken and me to head out." She turned to Berinon and grasped his forearm. "You stay safe, old man."

"Don't worry about me, child. There is still a lot of fight in this old body yet."

Talwyn looked at him. In physical appearance, if you compared him to a human male, he would look perhaps to be in his late fifties. However, he had been alive for close to seven hundred years. His hair was still dark in places, but was mostly gray and white now.

"There'd better be," Talwyn said. "I'm not ready to lose anyone else just yet."

CHAPTER SIXTEEN

Magic & Science

"Oh, by the Universe! Universe, save me!" Athnie said as she watched Norshan fall to the ground far below. "He's dead. He's dead! Oh, Universe, help me! What do I do? What do I do?"

She spoke quietly, muttering to herself. She would have never thought the others could hear her, especially over the sounds of the wind whipping by. So she jumped with a start when Koromin, who was seated directly behind her on the ainmith, leaned into her and whispered in her ear.

"Calm yourself, Sorceress."

It was then that she realized she was rocking back and forth and shuddering. She felt flushed and hot. Very hot. Like her skin was about to burst into flames.

"Take some deep breaths," Koromin said. "You need to get your panic under control, or you will force me to do it for you."

If he was trying to make her feel better with his words, he was failing by strides. In fact, his words made her feel more panicked. If a strong, seasoned warrior like Norshan could be killed so easily, what chance did she have? "He killed him! He's dead!"

Her breaths were coming faster now, and her heart raced. She felt something like electricity in the air, sparking in her hair and between her fingertips.

"Fine," Koromin said from behind her. "When you wake up, just remember that you forced me to do this."

She felt a sudden jab to the side of her neck. Everything went black.

Athnie awoke slowly, sliding in and out of consciousness for what seemed like a long time. During her more aware moments, she thought she heard snippets of conversation. However, she couldn't be sure they weren't just dreams.

"If it weren't for that idiot dragon, she would be awake right now, and we could move forward . . ."

". . . certain it's safe to put her in there?"

"It has never been tested with a subject under the influence of the drug. We cannot afford to lose her, so we will wait . . ."

After several episodes like this, she had a period where she was lucid long enough to open her eyes.

"Ah, awake at last."

"Koromin?" she croaked.

"Yes, it's me. None other than your personal guard."

"What happened?"

"You were panicking. I had to put you to sleep."

"But why?"

Instead of answering, Koromin posed a question of his own. "Were you aware of how close you were to being able to shift?"

"Manifestation."

"What?"

"My people call it manifestation."

"Yes, well, what it is called is not the important point here. Did you know that powerful emotions such as fear and panic can cause the sudden onset of your 'manifestation'?"

"What?" She echoed Koromin's earlier question.

"The emperor thought that might be the case, so he told me to be prepared. Fortunately, I had these on me." He held up a vial that contained a green substance and a needle.

"What is it?" Athnie asked weakly.

"This is the same substance that rendered your protectors unconscious back in your room under the mountain," Koromin responded. "Don't worry, it doesn't leave any permanent effects. As far as we know, anyway."

"Come now, Koromin," said another familiar voice from a few feet away. This voice caused her to shiver with discomfort. She turned her head to the side and saw the same cloaked male from back at the weird glass box approaching from a doorway. He moved briskly, shoulders back and head high. He wasn't overly tall. In fact, he was shorter than the demonkin she'd seen by around a pace or so. But his confident bearing made him seem larger than life.

He was the sorcerer, she now remembered. She had seen the evidence of that firsthand.

"You would not want to cause more panic, would you?"

"Of course not," Koromin responded with a bow. Her demonkin guard was so much stiffer, more well-behaved, so to speak, around the sorcerer. The change in demeanor made her uncomfortable.

Athnie noticed the look the sorcerer gave to Koromin. He narrowed his eyes and glanced sideways at him, and Athnie guessed he was either suspicious of him or disappointed in him. Her mind was still not clear enough to grasp what that might mean, though. Her eyelids were closing of their own accord. She shook her head and bit the inside of her cheek, not wanting to sleep again amid her enemies.

"Don't fight it, young one," the sorcerer said. "Allow yourself to rest some more. We will speak again once you are awake and clear-headed."

She didn't know if the male had put a spell on her or if it was the lingering effect of whatever she'd been drugged with, but her consciousness once again floated away from her.

The next time Athnie awoke, she felt much more aware of her surroundings. She took a deep breath and caught the scent of fresh air and ainmith. The wild, earthy smell of that animal was going to stick with her for a while. Strange. She would have thought that extreme fear would cause events to pass in a blur. But that's not what happened to her. She could remember insignificant little details from her ride here, and she figured they would stay with her for some time to come.

Athnie did not get up from where she lay, but she turned her head to look around her. She was in a tall tent of some sort, from the look of the fabric all around that billowed in the wind.

"She's awake."

Athnie looked in the direction the voice had come from and noticed Koromin standing in the doorway, looking out at someone. He then turned back to face in her direction but did not speak to her.

A short time later, she heard footsteps approaching. Then the same tall, cloaked male who had brought her here, who kept his face hidden in a cowl, appeared in the doorway.

"Ah, good," the sorcerer's voice drawled as he came into view. "You have awoken. How are you feeling?"

Athnie did not answer the question, which she thought was a pretty stupid one, given the circumstances. She just looked at him with an angry expression. She didn't think she'd really fooled him, though. He had already seen evidence of her fear and panic.

"Now, now. No need to begin our association on such hostile terms."

She figured he meant his words to be soothing, but his friendliness seemed fake to her. And a little creepy. She knew he was just warming her up so he could get whatever it was he wanted from her. "You killed him. You killed him, and you kidnapped me. I don't know how you can think that was *not* starting out on hostile terms."

"Those were both regrettable, but necessary, actions. I hope you will come to understand that."

The male was definitely crazy. She decided she would say nothing more for the time being. She did not know how easily he could become volatile, but she knew what he was capable of.

By the Universe! What if what he had done to Norshan was just a sampling of the kinds of things he could do?

"I wasn't going to offer you this," the sorcerer continued, interrupting her thoughts, "but from what I have seen of you, I think a friendship between us would be beneficial."

Athnie let out a huff of disbelief through her nose.

"Do not be so hasty in making your decision. You do not yet know what I can offer you. I am afraid you will be required to go into the Chamber of Life," he continued with a sinister grin. He really should stop with his attempts to seem friendly and approachable. It just made him seem more creepy.

"That cannot be helped. However, if you do so willingly, and you agree to stay and work with me afterward, I might try to spare as many of your people as possible."

She wondered what, exactly, he considered as *possible*? Out loud, she asked, "How long? How long would I have to stay and work with you?"

"That's something we can decide later."

"And what do you need me to do for you? It's not like I'm capable of much."

"Yet, my dear," he said in a smooth voice. "You are not capable *yet*. But if I were to instruct you, you could become powerful as well. You would not continue doubting your worth this way. But for now, what I need from you will be passive on your part. All you need to do is to rest within one of my chambers until after the passing of the alignment."

"Alignment?" Athnie asked.

"Yes. I am sure your histories have spoken of it. It is the period when the planets Aragus and Chephus align with the moon. It has a stabilizing effect on the magical hub. The source of magic. Only during this time can I use it to open the Great Gate."

Athnie looked at him with narrowed eyes. She didn't know whether he was trying to trick her with fancy words or if he was telling the truth.

"How can planets and stars affect the magic here in the realm?" she asked.

The sorcerer laughed. "Oh, dear girl, don't look so skeptical. It is a matter of science. You see, I'm not just a sorcerer; I am a man who studies the world and all its mysteries. Have you ever noticed how the tides ebb and flow in harmony with the phases of the moon?"

"Of course not. We don't get out very much these days. Certainly not enough to notice patterns in things that happen outside. And from what I hear, that's your fault."

"How silly of me to forget, even for a moment. Of course, you wouldn't have noticed."

What Athnie noticed was how he ignored her accusation. Though it didn't matter if he responded to it or not. It wouldn't alter the truth.

"Well," the sorcerer went on, "the tidesdo ebb and flow with the moon's phases. This is scientific, not magical. There are many, many other effects the moon, sun, and stars have on our world. Many of these are unknown to most people in our realm. But I have been studying these things for a very, very long time."

"And you want what from me, exactly? To sit in your box until the stars and planets do their thing so you can open the Great Gate and let the demons in?"

"In essence, yes."

"And you are asking me instead of just shoving me in there because . . .?"

"You are young. You do not yet realize your potential. Once I am emperor of the realm, I will need powerful friends to keep things running smoothly. You could be one of those friends."

"And you say if I do this for you, that you will spare my people?" She did not forget what he had promised earlier in the conversation.

"As much as is possible, yes," he answered. "I will do what I can to minimize casualties for your people. However, do not forget, if they ally with the others to stand against me, there will only be so much I can do."

She thought about this for a moment. "How do I know I can trust you? I mean, you won't even show your face. To anyone, as far as I can see. That doesn't exactly inspire feelings of trust."

"Believe me, it has nothing to do with trust. It is so information is not seen and passed on to those who could use it against me."

"Like the seers?"

He paused and stood perfectly still for a moment. "And what do you know of the seers?" he asked, a note of suspicion in his tone.

She realized her mistake in mentioning this, so she tried to come up with something that wasn't exactly a lie, but wouldn't give him too much information.

"Well, everyone knows about the seers. They are a tribe of beings who can see things they shouldn't. That's why the humans killed them, right? But there are no seers left, are there? So why would you worry about that so much?"

He was quiet for a moment. Athnie wondered if he could see right through her lie. But then he changed the subject.

"So, will you help me?" he asked in a gentle voice.

"How will me going into that thing help you? What's the purpose of it?"

"Let me be honest," the sorcerer said. "You are here, in this place, because we encountered more resistance at Eastgate than we expected. We have thus far been unable to secure the keystone there. You do not need to know all the boring details," he said with a wave of his hand. "I will just say that someone like you being inside one of my chambers—well, it's something to fall back on should we fail to neutralize the keystones."

She thought about the large, rectangular box that seemed to radiate the cold it resembled. "Will it hurt?"

"Only if you try to fight it," he said.

"Can I think about it?"

"Of course. It is not quite time yet to bring the chambers into play, so you have some time to decide."

"Thank you," she said. He nodded to her, then turned to head back out of the tent.

Athnie spent the rest of the day trying to figure out what to make of everything the sorcerer had said. He was leaving out a lot of important information, so it was hard to make sense of the bits she knew. And among the most significant of the things she knew was that these chambers of his would make the defense of Southgate and its keystone almost pointless. If only she could warn them. Or if only she could think of a way to sabotage the contraption on her way in, or once she was inside.

She was still trying to think of solutions when she fell asleep that evening, a couple of hours after dark.

In the middle of the night, Athnie was startled awake by the feeling of a hand covering her mouth. She fought back at first but stopped abruptly when a voice close to her ear whispered, "Shh. It's me, Koromin. I just want to talk."

Athnie nodded, and Koromin removed his hand from her mouth slowly, as if he were worried she might change her mind and start screaming at any moment. But what would be the point of that? She was surrounded by more of his people.

"Sure, you want to talk now," she whispered once his hand was no longer silencing her. "You didn't seem to want to talk to me much on the way here."

"Listen, I can't stay inside here for long. Someone might notice I'm not at my post outside."

She regarded him for a moment. With her shifter senses, she could see him well enough in the dark, though his features were dulled. He looked even more like a human—or a Folk in human form—with the color of his skin mostly hidden by the lack of light. Only his horns, which were so much smaller than those on the other demonkin she'd seen, set him apart. His brow was furrowed and he was frowning. He looked worried.

"So talk," she said.

"Right. Look, I just wanted to tell you . . . to suggest to you that you cooperate with the emperor. He's going to put you in that chamber whether or not you agree, so why make it harder on yourself than it needs to be?"

"I know that. I'm not as naïve or as gullible as your emperor seems to believe I am. But I need time to think."

"Think about what? A way to escape? Because if that's your plan, it will be even harder on you when he captures you again. He may have been giving you some pretty words to win your loyalty, but I've seen him do many not-so-pretty things."

"You mean like murder one of my people in front of me?" she asked bitterly. A tear escaped and made its way down her cheek, and she trembled. Maybe he wouldn't notice in the dark. When he didn't respond, she took a breath to calm herself and said, "What do you care, anyway? You're the one who brought me here."

When he didn't respond after a few moments, she tried a different approach.

"Why are you trying to warn me against your own leader? If you disagree with the way he does things, why do you follow him?"

Koromin puffed out a breath and moved to lie on his back beside her, looking up at the ceiling of the tent.

"I guess you can say that he was the lesser of two evils. Don't get me wrong; he has many loyal followers who do his bidding without question, without wavering. There are also many who follow him out of fear. I'm sure you've noticed how powerful he is, and you haven't even seen everything he can do. Then there are those who, like me, follow him because he is offering a solution to our problem. And it's the only solution we have found so far."

"What is this problem? Have you tried to find anyone else who could help?"

He chuffed bitterly. "Like the other species in the realm would help us. There are too many of my kind who have caused havoc throughout the realm in the past, and those who still thrive on causing chaos."

"So," she pushed, "what is it?"

He turned to consider her in the darkness. Athnie got the impression he was trying to decide how much to tell her.

"Our species is in danger of extinction. Most of my kind believe that this problem can be solved, and our people strengthened, if we help the sorcerer open the gate. We will then have fresh, full-demon blood to add to our lines.

"Ironic, isn't it, that my people are in danger of extinction for purely genetic reasons when we have caused the near-extinction of others? I'm sure you probably consider it a kind of poetic justice."

Athnie thought about this for a moment. "You know, our dragon lord has been under pressure for some time to choose a mate. He has been using the argument that we should look outside of our kind for mates so that we can strengthen our own lines.

So, my people might be more understanding of this than you imagine."

"Maybe. But how is your moral support going to help us, really? We aren't like the Dragon-folk. Your genetics are the dominant ones in almost every match you could imagine. For us, we end up with more and more human traits the more we breed with them. And . . ."

He hesitated, and Athnie was worried he was going to stop talking. Finally, he went on.

"Well, demonkin females are born sterile. Something about the combinations of our particular genes, according to the emperor. This means that male demonkin have only been able to produce offspring with humans. So our stock has been getting weaker and weaker. We've been becoming more and more human. We're losing our demon abilities."

Athnie turned her head to look at him in the darkness. "Well, that explains a lot. You don't seem much like the descriptions of demonkin I've read about or heard of over the years. Your features are much more human than I expected."

"I am one of the lucky ones, favored among our kind. I have just enough of the physical traits of the demonkin to be allowed to join the emperor's legions. And, as you've seen, I have the power of illusion. If I return successfully from the fight, I might even be permitted to mate and conceive offspring—not that I want to do that, really. But you are right. The demonkin are not what we once were."

Athnie smiled at him. "Well, if that means more demonkin like you, then I don't think that's such a bad thing."

He gasped—a short, quick sound—and looked away. If there was enough light to see it, would his cheeks be flushing even redder?

She lay quietly for a moment, thinking over what he'd told her. "Maybe your people are thinking about this the wrong way, though. What if you considered it the natural evolution of your people and just accepted your fate?"

"There are actually a few of us who do. Who are happy with becoming more human, in fact. But the sorcerer is very . . . charismatic, let's just say. Very persuasive. He loves magic and thinks of humans as lesser because they are not magical. All shifters, even those who cannot channel magic to do their bidding, are magical. As are the long-lived species like the elves. The emperor believes that non-magical beings like the humans are not fit for more than being slaves."

"That's horrible!"

"Keep in mind that all demonkin alive now are born of human mothers. So many of my kind think more of them. But the sorcerer has demonkin fathers remove their children with strong enough demon traits from their mother's care as early as possible. He wants to minimize. They...*we* are trained from an early age to be the emperor's loyal soldiers.

"The biggest obstacle to finding peace in the realm is the fact that most demonkin are desperate for our kind to hold on to what little magic we can. Many are power hungry, lured by the possibility of the strength we will gain if we pair with demons again."

"And yet, you are telling me all this. Why?"

Athnie felt Koromin's shoulder shrug against her own. Considering what he was and who he worked for, she was surprised at how comfortable she felt about being this close to him.

"I'm not sure. Maybe I hope that those of my kind who wish it can one day live in the realm freely, without disdain and mistrust. That has to start somewhere."

"But why me?"

"I can't explain it, but I trust you, even though you are young. It has been clear from the beginning that you care about all living creatures in the realm, including my kind. Unbelievable as that is. And I know that one day you will be a powerful sorceress. Maybe you will be able to help the demonkin who feel as I do."

Athnie looked at him, trying to gauge his sincerity. After all, demonkin were believed to be crafty and deceptive, known master manipulators. Then, deciding it may not matter anyway, she shrugged and said, "That's if either of us is even still alive after this."

"Yes, there is that worry. Speaking of which, don't let on to any of the others that I've been talking to you. It would be the end of me."

With that, Koromin got up and, stopping to peek out of the tent doorway first, crept quietly back outside.

CHAPTER SEVENTEEN

To Southgate

As Talwyn and Dreyken were preparing to head back to Southgate, Talwyn decided this would be the best time to discuss strategy. If the wind whipping past on the way here was any sign, it would be difficult to talk and be heard when they were in flight.

"I would like us to fly back the way we came and land just outside the forest. That will take us almost directly to the west of Southgate. From there, we can creep in through the forest. If there are any demonkin lying in wait, we may be able to surprise them, or gain more information from them."

"You are quite sneaky, aren't you?" Dreyken smirked at her. "Of course, I've known this since shortly after we met. "

She turned to face him fully and took a deep breath to steel her courage. "Now that we're on the topic, I have a confession to make."

"A confession?" He looked at her with narrowed eyes.

Talwyn nodded. "Remember when you first picked me up and brought me to the mountain? Well, I wasn't unconscious then. I wasn't sick or injured at all."

"But I checked you over. Your skin was hot and dry to the touch. Those are signs of heat illnesses."

"Inner-sight."

He put his hand on his hips, looked up at the sky, and chuckled wryly. "Right. Inner-sight."

"Are you angry at me?"

He looked at her. "Strangely, no. I can see why you did what you did. And if you hadn't tricked me, chances are you wouldn't have gotten inside and I would not have met you. I would have preferred a more honest method, but . . ." He shrugged.

"What can I say? This is how my people have been forced to deal with problems in the realm for the past three hundred years. Sneaking around and staying hidden in the background is how we've come to operate."

"So your people have been in hiding, much as the Stone Dragons have."

"Yes. Except we have also been very much part of the realm. But the humans, or anyone else for that matter, didn't know it."

"Are you afraid the humans will discover this and find it to be deceitful?"

"There is always that possibility. However, back when we started down this road, we knew the humans were being manipulated and used. But at that time, we didn't know by whom, or what their goal was. Of course, we knew the demonkin were involved, but who was behind it all? Who was directing the demonkin? We couldn't leave the realm unprotected, but we also needed to keep the peace. Keeping an eye out while staying hidden seemed to be the best solution."

Dreyken slowly shook his head. "It amazes me, this capacity your people have to care for and protect those who almost destroyed you. Take you, for example. They killed your entire family."

"That was mostly the demonkin. The humans were just along for the ride."

"Still, they knew what was happening and did nothing to stop it. In fact, they supported it."

"Well, this is what my family believed in. What they would have wanted." Her throat felt tight with emotion, so she took a deep breath and let it out. "I could have been bitter and angry and gone on a killing spree, or I could honor their memories by following their beliefs. Given they were also my beliefs, the choice was pretty clear."

"You are amazing." Dreyken stepped close to her and took her by the hands. "So amazing." He stared into her eyes. Then he leaned forward to meet her lips in a searing kiss.

Talwyn couldn't help but be swept up in his embrace. She wrapped her arms around his neck and pulled him close, pressing her body against his. However, a flash of the memory of Helsi, sitting heartbroken on the ground with her dead mate at her feet, quickly cooled her heated emotions. She slowly pulled back.

"We need to go."

Dreyken sighed. "I know."

"But let me just make one thing clear before we leave." Talwyn's voice was suddenly firm. "If we are doing this," she said, gesturing between them, "you are not allowed to die. Do you understand?"

Dreyken's smile was both sad and warm as he gazed at her. "I understand. And the same goes for you."

Talwyn nodded. "Good. Now that we have that settled, shift so we can leave. Don't forget, land outside the forest to the west of Southgate."

"I won't forget."

Dreyken had already taken off his clothes, put them in his pack, and put his armor back on while they had been talking. So, in one swift moment, he was no longer standing in front of her as a man, but as a dragon.

He bowed low and Talwyn climbed on, seating herself as she had on the trip here. She firmly gripped his armor to prepare for taking off.

Dreyken's muscles tensed and relaxed underneath her as he flapped his mighty wings. The wind pushed down around her as he lifted from the ground. Then they were flying above the trees once again.

It was a dark and cloudy night, and Talwyn got a bit of a fright when Dreyken suddenly climbed sharply upward. She held on tightly with her hands and thighs, and soon they were hidden in the clouds. Talwyn didn't know how Dreyken knew where to go with so little visibility. Maybe Dragon-folk had a sense about these things.

Soon, Dreyken slowed the beating of his wings, yet they seemed to fly faster than before. That was when she realized they were riding one of those wind currents the others had spoken about when they had landed in the clearing earlier.

Talwyn was a little nervous to be flying so high and so fast, but she also felt elated. It was an amazing feeling. She laid her torso out along Dreyken's neck and yelled out, "This is incredible! If I were a dragon shifter, I'd want to fly all the time."

Once the words were out of her mouth, she worried they would upset Dreyken. His people had been hiding out in the mountains these past four hundred years, without the freedom to fly free like this. She didn't want him to feel like she was judging their decisions. Maybe he didn't hear her past the wind in his ears.

When Dreyken turned his head to look at her, she saw his eyes sparkle and a little puff of smoke rise from his nostrils, and she knew he had heard. But instead of being offended, he looked amused.

Time passed slowly as they made their way back south. Talwyn enjoyed flying but couldn't help but worry about what was happening at Southgate, worry that they were taking too long to get there. Southgate was her responsibility, but Athnie was Dreyken's. She was glad they had met up with Berinon and the others. She knew Dreyken would not be returning to Southgate with her now otherwise.

They approached Southgate from the northwest. Even in the dim light of early morning, she could see the gate town some distance away. There were no signs of fire or smoke or anything else that would indicate fighting or destruction. She allowed herself a sigh of relief.

The sky was just barely beginning to brighten as Talwyn and Dreyken landed in the area Talwyn had described to him.

"How long have you been guardian of Southgate?" Dreyken asked after he shifted back and was taking off his armor.

"About fifty-five years," Talwyn replied. "I was an apprentice for nearly a century before that."

"And I assume you have visited Southgate many times during that period?"

"I wouldn't say many. Just a few, really. We monitor things from the outside as much as possible, especially after what happened three hundred years ago."

"How is it that no one, especially among the older humans, has recognized you and realized you were aging much more slowly than they were? Surely someone would have noticed you weren't human."

"As you've already seen, my people are talented at blending in and at disguising ourselves. I can even add wrinkles and make myself look older if I want to. Though I admit, I do that as little as possible. Usually, it's enough to change hair and eye color. Also, I often use a secret way into the castle. Usually, only the king sees me."

"Do they know about us? The Stone Dragons, I mean."

"I'm sure they've heard the legends, but I doubt many believed them."

"Lovely." He sounded disappointed.

"I sent Adrio with the amulet. If he did as instructed, he would have met with the king soon after he arrived. The gate kings are also guardians, so are much better informed than the population at large. The king will decide how and when to introduce the Stone Dragons to the people."

Talwyn looked at Dreyken and noticed his expression was worried. "What is it?"

"I am just trying to not envision being shot out of the sky by a volley of arrows from our own 'allies' the first time they see us shift."

"Well, then it's lucky you have this fine new armor." Talwyn grinned at him. "At least you know your vital organs will be protected."

"Yes, but if they get our wings, the fall would certainly be painful."

"Depends on how far you're falling. Don't forget to tuck and roll."

Dreyken chuckled. He was now clothed and armored. "I'm ready."

Talwyn could have skirted the tree line to reach the gate town. However, she was eager to get back under the familiar comfort of the cover of trees and bushes. "Follow me and be careful how you step. We need to go in quietly, keeping an ear and an eye out for any demonkin."

"Do you think they will be here already?"

"They left your mountain not too long ago. If they haven't regrouped near here already, they will soon."

Now and then Talwyn listened, or sniffed the air, or looked at the ground or bushes.

"The Stone Dragons were once skilled trackers," Dreyken stated in a low, wistful voice behind her. "It's hard to practice tracking skills when you're surrounded by rock, though."

Soon, Talwyn spotted some signs of activity in the area. She moved left, deeper into the forest. After a short time, she signaled for Dreyken to stop. She cautiously crept forward to peek through the foliage into a small clearing beyond. She touched her finger to her lips to signal Dreyken to be quiet, then she waved him forward.

When Dreyken neared where Talwyn was crouched, she pointed forward. In a small clearing, a group of demonkin sat around the dying embers of a fire. There were six of them that Talwyn could see, and they were quietly chatting among themselves.

Talwyn and Dreyken watched and listened for a time. Eventually, the demonkin spoke about their plan of attack.

"Well, best start cleaning and sharpening my sword," one of the two demonkin closest to them said. Its voice was gravelly and rough, as was common for demonkin. Talwyn did not know how they ever got away with impersonating humans with voices like that. Maybe they pretended to have sore throats.

"Just relax a bit and have some more spirits," the other responded. "There's time yet before morning."

"The sun's already rising. You just don't want to be made to feel you should do some work. Don't forget, we need our rest as well if we are to be successful."

"How hard can it be to defeat a bunch of humans? We could probably do that sloshed out of our minds."

"Don't underestimate the humans. The emperor himself warned us against that. Besides, we don't know if they'll have backup or not. The emperor's last message said it is a possibility and to stay alert."

"We should just charge on in there and end 'em all right now. The longer we stay here, lurking about, the more chances they'll have to spot us. What are we waiting for, anyway?"

"Not sure," the first demonkin said. "The emperor has always been the secretive kind. Cialur said he thinks it has to do with waiting for some more soldiers and beasts to make it here."

"Well, why ain't they here already?"

"Probably tied up in a battle somewhere. It ain't easy to fight a war in a bunch of different places at the same time."

Talwyn felt reassured by the conversation that the demonkin would not be making a move this morning. So she quietly led Dreyken back to the spot where they had veered left. From there, they continued to the east, and slightly north, once more.

Soon, they approached a small hill with some rocky outcroppings dotted around it. Talwyn led Dreyken to one of these outcroppings and moved aside a few large rocks. This uncovered an opening that was only slightly larger than was necessary to accommodate Dreyken's large frame if he entered on hands and knees.

Dreyken groaned. "Why are you always leading us through these narrow spaces?"

"And here I thought it was Drarcio who was a baby about climbing and crawling through tight spots."

They moved through the tunnel, which descended at a steep decline. Luckily, it widened a few feet inside, so that by the time they had reached the bottom, it was tall enough to stand in and wide enough for two people side-by-side.

Talwyn now stood facing a barred metal door, which reminded her of the door to her mountain cell.

Dreyken reached out and tried the door. "It's locked."

"Not for long." Talwyn crouched to retrieve a long metal key from inside her boot. She then quickly unlocked the door, relocking it once again when they were through.

"Is that how you got out of your cell back in the mountain?"

Talwyn gave him a sly smirk and a wink. "I can't tell you all my secrets."

Turning to move down the tunnel again, Talwyn commented, "But, I will say that I've about had my fill of being surrounded by rock."

She had mostly gotten over her claustrophobia in the years since her family's deaths. But she was feeling it again with the many cave interiors she had been exposed to recently. "I don't know how your people do it. How can you not miss the freedom of being underneath the open sky?" She hoped he wouldn't notice the tightness that had snuck into her voice.

Talwyn took some calming breaths and tried to push aside the blooming, anxious feeling of being trapped. She tried to focus on their current mission instead.

Dreyken sighed. "More than half of us were born under that mountain. It's hard to miss something you've never known. The rest are grumpy old dragons who remember nothing but war and destruction." Then he asked, "Where does this tunnel go, anyway?"

"To the castle."

"The castle? Couldn't the enemy sneak in unannounced this way?"

"I'm sure they could. Assuming they could find the entrance and then get past the locked doorways along the way."

She paused for a moment and explained more fully. "All the gate castles have a tunnel like this. It serves as a means of escape from the castle should it fall to an enemy, and it allows the seer guardians such as myself to enter undetected. Honestly, though, we don't use these tunnels very often. Seers tend to just change their coloring, and maybe their clothes, to disguise themselves and then walk in like anyone else. Not that we visit often, anyway. It's only in dangerous times, when no one can move freely in and out of the castle, that we would use the tunnels."

They kept moving forward until they came across a second barred, locked door. Talwyn quickly opened that one and locked it again when they moved through, as she had done with the previous one. After another short distance, they entered a space that seemed to open into a storage room of some sort. To the untrained eye, it looked like a previously plundered storage room, since there were empty wooden crates strewn recklessly about. But Talwyn knew better.

"This looks like a dead end," Dreyken commented. "But I am going to assume it's not, after seeing some of the other places you've taken us through."

"Good assumption." Talwyn moved to the far wall and ran her hand along its surface. Then she pressed in on a small, jutting stone. A section of the wall pulled back and to the side.

"Was this designed by the same builder who made the tunnel in the storage room?" Dreyken asked.

"Same species, different builder." Talwyn tried not to think too much about who that was. She was feeling emotional at being back here, but she knew she needed to focus on the now, and not the past. There was too much at stake for anything else. So she pushed those feelings down and promised herself she would deal with them once this was all over. She moved to the hidden door but, before she could enter, Dreyken grabbed her hand.

"Are you okay, Talwyn? You seem tense. Agitated. Is there something wrong?"

She glanced back at him, then looked around at anything but him. "Yes. I'm fine."

He tugged her hand gently, and she looked at him, meeting his gaze. He was frowning at her, his expression a mask of concern. She closed her eyes and took a deep breath, then she turned to fully face him.

"It's just, you remember the nightmare you woke me up from that night back in the mountain?"

He nodded solemnly.

"Well, what happened in that nightmare originally occurred close to here."

His eyebrows rose in realization, and he pulled her to him. He enveloped her in a tight, warm hug and stroked her hair.

"I'm so sorry. It must be hard for you to be back here."

She wrapped her arms around him and buried her face in the crook of his neck. "This helps. Thanks."

She let his embrace warm her for a moment before pulling back. "I may have needed that more than I realized."

"I'm here, anytime you need me."

She smiled at him. "I know. Thank you." She took a step back. "Come on. Let's go."

They moved through the hidden door, then listened to it scrape shut behind them. Immediately in front of them, a set of stairs led upward.

Talwyn turned to look at Dreyken. "Are you ready to meet the King of Southgate?" She didn't really need to ask, though. Dreyken seemed agitated and nervous, yet his mouth was set and his stance firm. It was like she could physically see his determination.

"These stairs will lead us through a hidden passage that travels up through the castle walls themselves, so make as little noise as possible. At the end, it will take us to the king's private receiving room. It's an outer room of his chambers, so it would be best if we listened for a while before going through, just to make sure the coast is clear."

Dreyken nodded his understanding.

Talwyn started up the stone steps and was pleasantly surprised at how silently Dreyken followed behind her. She would have expected him to have made more noise with such a large frame to carry around.

They sometimes climbed narrow stairs set at a steep angle, and sometimes they crept through level passageways. Now and then, as they moved silently along, sounds of voices or movement could be heard from the other side of the walls. There had been silence on the other side for some time, however, when Talwyn finally stopped.

They now stood in front of what looked—in the darkened space and to anyone who didn't know better—to be a solid wall. Talwyn pressed her ear to the stones to listen for movement or voices. Her head was turned toward Dreyken, and when she saw his questioning look, she pointed to a seam in the wall where a faint sliver of light was peeking through. Dreyken's eyes widened a little, and he nodded in understanding.

After a short time, Talwyn leaned back and brushed her palm along the smooth surface until she found what she was looking for. She pressed in on the circular carving in the wall until a click sounded and a section of the wall swung inward like a door. She stepped through to the other side, waving Dreyken behind her.

Once they were through, she pressed a similar carving in the stone next to the door, and it swung shut once again.

Chapter Eighteen

The Royals of Southgate

alwyn hadn't been in the king's receiving room for years. Not since the previous king had occupied the throne.

When she had met the current king for the very first time, he was a prince, just coming of age. He was visiting the seer village with his father. Few people visited their hidden valley, so it was a source of some excitement. That was a little over fifty years ago, and the most interaction she'd had with him since was when she had checked in with him on her way to see the Stone Dragons. That time, she had met with him in his throne room. It was hard to believe that was just a couple of weeks ago. It felt like so much more time had passed.

Talwyn looked around the receiving room now and noticed how different it was from when the previous king had occupied the space. The furnishings were updated in a more modern style, yet were still of a high-quality, hand-carved wood. It was much richer than she was accustomed to, but agreeable. The high level of craftsmanship was clear in each piece she laid her eyes upon. Her gaze continued to sweep the area until it paused on a familiar tapestry. It was older and a little more threadbare than when she had last seen it, of course. But there before her, the family tree of the royal house of Southgate stood represented in some of the most precious materials to be had.

She stepped forward to get a better look, reacquainting herself with the piece. Her eyes traveled the lines all the way back to when the kingdom of Southgate was first established. That was almost three thousand years ago. Only three generations for her people, but many more for the humans. Enough time for castles to crumble and fall and have to be rebuilt. She knew the castle at Southgate had been repaired and remodeled as needed over the millennia. There were even images depicting this tireless work on the tapestry.

"Impressive," Dreyken said from over her shoulder.

"My father commissioned that shortly after I was born," a rough, much older, masculine voice said from a doorway off to their left.

They both turned to look at the King of Southgate, who had about sixty-five years behind him. His hair and beard were neat and white. His face was wizened, yet his eyes were clear and intelligent.

"It isn't the original, of course, and this one will not be the last."

"Your highness." Talwyn bowed deeply to the king. Dreyken followed her lead and bowed as well. When they straightened again, Talwyn introduced her companion.

"King Caratacos, this is Dreyken, Lord of the Stone Dragons."

King Caratacos practically beamed with excitement. He moved forward a few steps so he could grasp Dreyken by the forearm. Dreyken jumped a little at the sudden contact and his eyes were wide. Talwyn couldn't help but smile at his bewilderment. He hadn't met many new people in the past four-hundred years, and he seemed a little taken aback by the king's enthusiastic welcome.

"When your protectors arrived here, I said to myself, 'I never thought I would see the day.' Dragon-folk at Southgate. And now, here I am, meeting Lord Dreyken himself. I am honored this is happening in my lifetime and thankful to learn that your people will be with us in the battles to come."

Dreyken cleared his throat and stood up straighter. "It is our honor. I hope our peoples will become great friends."

"Your tapestry is amazing." Talwyn brushed her fingers gently along the soft fabric. "This is actually not the first time I've seen it, but I'm as impressed by it now as I was the first time. Your family history displayed here before us in all its glory."

"Yes, and I particularly like the depiction of the battle there at the top." Dreyken pointed to a group of figures on the tapestry. "I assume that represents the Sorcerers of the Light's defeat of Azedel."

"Yes, you are correct." King Caratacos smiled at Dreyken. Talwyn was happy to see them get along from their first meeting. It gave her hope for the future. "We also have a room filled with art that depicts the realm's history in more detail. Each Southgate king gets the pieces repainted by an artist in their lifetime, so that we do not lose our history to the ravages of time. New pieces are added whenever significant events occur. There is a portrait of Azedel himself in there, originally painted by an artist who knew him personally."

Dreyken's brow shot up. "That is impressive! I would love to see it."

"I would love to see that, too. We haven't been able to see him in visions and, I have to admit, I'm curious. But how about if we wait until after the end of Sterrenvar as we know it?" Talwyn said with a smile.

She turned to face the king. "Your highness, on our way in we came upon some demonkin camped in the forest just outside your borders. They did not see us, and we listened long enough to discover that they plan to attack soon. They are waiting for something. Reinforcements, maybe."

The king did not seem surprised by this information. "Yes, our own scouts spotted a pair of demonkin sniffing around two days ago. Having an idea of when they plan to attack, however—that is helpful indeed."

He walked to the door of his outer chamber and swung it wide. The king's personal guard turned to look their way. Obviously surprised to see unexpected visitors behind his sovereign, he pulled his sword from its sheath.

"Stay your hand, Brice. They are friends. I will make formal introductions once you call the captains to my war room."

"Yes, your majesty."

"Send someone to escort our other guests there and call for my children on the way as well."

"Of course, sire." With that, Brice bowed, then marched off quickly to do the king's bidding.

King Caratacos turned around and went back through the door to his inner chamber. A moment later, he returned with a regal, white-haired woman who looked to be about his age. "I present to you my wife, Queen Boudicca."

"It's an honor to meet you, your highness." Talwyn bowed low.

"My love, these are Talwyn, seer guardian of Southgate, and Lord Dreyken of the Stone Dragons."

The queen smiled big and bowed in return. "I am honored to meet you as well."

"Let's head down to the war room." King Caratacos gestured to the door.

The king led them down the hallway and stopped before a massive oak door. "You find that at Southgate, protecting the keystone, and the realm, is very much a family affair." He pushed the door open and ushered them inside, where several others were already assembled.

They gathered around a large, oval table that was also made of oak. The king looked around. "It seems we are just waiting for Keeva and our other guests."

Almost immediately after he spoke, Adrio and Iniri were ushered into the room. They greeted the king and queen, then moved to sit with Talwyn and Dreyken. Talwyn was pleased to see them safe and well and obviously accepted by the king and his family.

Talwyn was sitting with her back to the door, and Dreyken, Iniri, and Adrio were to her left, in that order. Adrio was at the top curve of the oval table, so he was looking toward the door when they heard it open. Talwyn watched as his eyes grew wide and his mouth gaped, and she turned to see what had caught his attention.

A human woman who looked to have about thirty years walked in through the door. She had brown hair so dark that it was almost black. It was pulled back neatly into a high ponytail. As she got closer, Talwyn noticed that her hazel eyes were flecked with brown and gold. Her facial features were striking and well-defined. Her expression and carriage were stern and regal.

This all seemed to contrast with her clothing. Instead of the fine dresses that would be expected wear for female royalty in Southgate in the past, she was dressed in soldiers' leathers. Talwyn was glad to see that Southgate had changed with the times.

Taking her gaze away from the woman, she looked to the king and queen. Just as she suspected, the woman's eyes were the same as the queen's. She was the princess of Southgate.

"There you are, finally." Turning to Talwyn and her companions, the king said, "This is my daughter, Keeva. She has just returned from a scouting trip."

"It's a pleasure to meet one of such beauty and grace," Adrio blurted as he stood and bowed. Talwyn looked at him, one brow raised. As she turned, she caught Iniri's eye roll from just beside him.

King Caratacos ignored the comment and continued introductions around the table. Gesturing to the right side of the queen, he said, "Our son, Lugus."

Lugus had almost the same hair and eye color as Keeva, except his hair was a shade lighter. He also looked, to Talwyn's eyes, to be close in age to his sister.

"Seated to my son's right are my four captains."

King Caratacos stood and addressed the room. "I would like to introduce you all to Lord Dreyken of the Stone Dragons."

There were murmurings from around the table as the king's men stood and bowed to Dreyken. Dreyken bowed his head in return.

He was standing tall with his shoulders back, but he also wore a small, warm smile.

Regal, but approachable, Talwyn thought.

"Next to him is Talwyn Survalor, seer champion and a guardian of Southgate."

There were more whispered words of awe and more bows.

"Their two companions, whom some of you have already met, are Adrio and Iniri, two of Lord Dreyken's elite warriors from the Dragonburn Mountains." More bows and nods.

"Let's get started. It seems we have no time to lose. We have been preparing for an attack since you passed through a few weeks ago, Talwyn, and we've been on high alert since we first spotted the demonkin two days ago."

"Excellent." Talwyn was pleased that the king had taken her word about what was coming their way and begun preparing.

The king then turned to Keeva. "What news do you have from your scouting trip, my daughter?"

"From what I could see, there are only a few demonkin inside the Sacred Forest—"

"Well, that's good news," Lugus interrupted.

"But," Keeva continued, shooting an irritated look at her brother, "there is a group of them gathering just outside the forest edge to the northeast."

"How many?" asked King Caratacos.

"I would guess about three dozen. Maybe another dozen in the forest."

"That's not as many as I would have expected."

Talwyn cleared her throat and added the information she had. "Well, we know they are attacking all the gate towns at around the same time, trying to take out as many keystones as they can. Their numbers are spread out, and I don't suppose there are all that many demonkin left, if what we overheard just last night is any indication."

"Well, that's an advantage to us then," Lugus said.

"Don't underestimate them based on their numbers." Talwyn did not want them to be caught unawares or defeated because they were overconfident. "They have also used snowbeasts and ainmith in their battles."

"What are snowbeasts and ainmith?" Keeva asked.

Talwyn started with the easiest one to explain first. "The ainmith are large, white, winged creatures that look like an enormous dog with feathers and wings. Except their claws are long, curved, and very sharp, like those of a bird of prey. They can carry three or four demonkin, who can then attack from the sky. The demonkin used these during their attack on the Stone Dragons.

"Snowbeasts are a similar shape, size, and color—so close, in fact, that the ainmith are referred to by some as 'winged snowbeasts.' Snowbeasts are dangerous not only because of their size, but also because of their icy breath. They can freeze a person solid in seconds. Supposedly, they will often stomp their victims after freezing them, thereby shattering them."

"That's disturbing," Lugus said.

"Very," Talwyn agreed. "So I suggest you stay out of their line of fire if they are used in the battle and let all your soldiers know to do the same."

"We most certainly will," the king said, eyes wide.

"We also don't know where the Dark Sorcerer will be. If he comes here, we probably won't stand much of a chance. Lucky for us, he can't be everywhere at once, and it appears he has been staying out of sight as much as possible. We suspect it's one of his tactics to keep my people from seeing too much in our visions. He can block his own mind, but he can't block what everyone else is seeing."

"Well, let's hope he will stay out of sight for the coming battle," Adrio said.

"Our new guests have brought us some updated information as well," the king explained to his assembled people. "On the way in not too long ago, they passed a group of demonkin camping in the forest just outside of town. According to what they overheard, the demonkin plan to attack soon, possibly within the next day or two."

"We are ready, my lord," one of the Southgate captains said.

"Thank you for your efficiency and vigilance, Delling," King Caratacos responded.

"Were they in the Sacred Forest when you saw them?" Delling asked Talwyn.

Talwyn nodded. "Yes, they were. They were hiding close enough to spy on Southgate."

"But I thought only good magical creatures could enter the Sacred Forest," Delling said. "So how is it that these evil creatures could enter?"

"Honestly, we didn't know how, not for a long time. We suspected there was magic involved but weren't sure. However, we have recently found a clue that reinforced this idea."

"How can you have not been sure? I thought seers could foresee the future, as well as see the present and the past," Lugus said. "So why are these things a mystery?"

Talwyn was irritated at having to explain this repeatedly, all because of the rumors spread by demonkin three centuries ago. But that wasn't Lugus's fault. So she took a deep breath so she could respond calmly. "Well, first, my people cannot see anything, anywhere, at any time, regardless of what past rumors have stated. We see only what the Universe gifts us with.

"Second, when we have seen relevant information, anything that is directly related to the Dark Sorcerer has been blocked by him, as I just explained."

"So," Lugus said, "this dark sorcerer has been blocking visions from all the seers?"

"I'm afraid so."

"But how is that possible?"

"All I can tell you is that this sorcerer is powerful. Probably more powerful than Azedel himself."

"Powerful enough to block your visions and neutralize the protective spells on the Sacred Forest," the king stated.

"Unfortunately, yes."

"Do we even stand a chance against such a force?" one of the king's captains asked.

"According to our visions, there are many scenarios that might play out, depending on decisions that are made along the way. But several show us being victorious. So yes, we stand a chance." Talwyn left out the part where less than a quarter of the scenarios showed them to be successful. She could carry that worry on her own.

"He may be a powerful sorcerer," Dreyken said, "but he is only one man. You will have the seers and the Stone Dragons on your side, both of whom are powerful in themselves."

"I also don't think that the Dark Sorcerer expects seers to be working with you." This was the part that gave Talwyn the best hope. She loved having the element of surprise on their side. "Or the Stone Dragons. Even if Dragon-folk and humans hadn't been avoiding contact with one another for the past few centuries, he would probably expect the Dragon-folk to be preoccupied with finding their sorceress. So, the Dark Sorcerer probably didn't see the need to send a lot of soldiers to attack the town.

"Our other three seer champions will recruit allies as they go as well, hoping to protect the other gate towns and building up our forces before we make our way to the Great Gate. Other shifter species and anyone else who will join with us."

"What about a sorcerer?" Keeva asked. "Do we have one of those?"

Talwyn gave her a smile. "Actually, we do. But she won't be with us until the Great Gate."

"And is this sorcerer as powerful as the Dark Sorcerer?" Lugus asked.

"Well, it's difficult to say for sure, since she has been ignoring her powers for most of the time that I've known her. But I suspect she is a lot more powerful than even she herself realizes."

"Suspect?" Lugus asked. "Well, I hope your suspicions are correct."

Talwyn hoped so as well. "Also, I know for certain of at least one other Sorcerer of the Light in existence and it's likely she will be there with us for this second Battle of the Gate as well."

"May the second Battle of the Gate go our way, just as the first did," Lugus said. There were sounds of agreement from all around the table.

King Caratacos slapped his hand on the table, bringing everyone's attention to him. "Well, let's get down to planning. There is not much time left before the attack. Captain Delling, would you like to inform our guests of what we've come up with so far?"

"Yes, my king." Delling stood and addressed all assembled. "We are hoping our plan would let the enemy spies believe we are complacent and unprepared, drawing them in to attack us on our own terms. But I believe the plan will work even better now that we have more precise information on when they might attack." He gave a nod to Talwyn, who returned it.

"The night before the attack, we will have a large celebration in our outer bailey, and all the town's citizens will be invited to attend. A celebration of the coming harvests, if you will. At the end of a long night of festivities, the townsfolk will return to their cottages. Or so the spies will think.

"In reality, when all the people are gathered in the bailey for the celebration, we will have our soldiers switch places with the townsfolk, donning their outer robes. They will wander back to the cottages randomly toward the end of the evening. We are hoping this will entice them to attack when they think we are drunken and unawares."

"And if they don't?" Adrio asked.

"Then our soldiers will have comfortable cottages to wait in until they do attack," Delling explained. "And when they do, we will allow them to enter through the town and close in on the castle walls. When the time is right, the soldiers will exit the cottages and surround the enemy."

"What do you think, Talwyn?" the king asked.

Talwyn nodded. "It could work. This fits with some of what I have seen. It also means that if they decide to raze the town on the way in, the citizens will be safe inside and those better prepared for an attack will be there to fight back. I like it." Then another thought occurred to her.

"I would suggest, though, that the dragons fight in human form until the demonkin show their hand. Once their reinforcements show up with snowbeasts and ainmith, we can surprise them with a show of force. Catching them off guard like this could be the difference between defeat and victory.

"But I need to warn you all. This sorcerer is one of the most powerful in the history of Sterrenvar. He is the reason my people have been searching the land in all directions for allies. We will need all the help we can get to stop him from opening the Great Gate.

"For the here and now, though, for the Battle of Southgate, we do not have enough allies to stand against the Dark Sorcerer should he attack with his demonkin. We have no sorcerer to help us at the moment. If he shows up here personally while we are also trying to defend against his army, it is likely Southgate will fall. You need to have a plan to evacuate the civilians if this man they call their emperor shows up here. If that happens, the only thing to keep the keystone safe will be if they cannot find or get into the keep to destroy it. We will just have to hope it is enough."

They now discussed in more detail what the Dragon-folk' roles would be. When they had settled the details and had tweaked any for problems they could foresee, King Caratacos addressed the group once more. "It is almost time for our midday meal. I suggest we all head down to the great hall to get some food and a little rest. We need to be alert. Our sentries will watch for movement from the enemy, and we have to be ready to move when they do."

<h1 style="text-align: center;">CHAPTER NINETEEN</h1>

<h1 style="text-align: center;">The Keystone</h1>

Most of the king's people filed out of the room, but Talwyn stayed behind to speak with the king. Dreyken remained behind with her. "Your majesty, I wanted to ask you about the keystone and the plans for its protection."

"I am hoping we will be victorious, and they will not make it inside the castle walls," the king replied.

"Will anyone be posted near the stone in case any demonkin get through?"

"Do you think that is likely?" Concern etched his brow.

"Lord Dreyken, could you please tell the king what happened when you went to check on your sorceress after the battle at the mountain?"

"Of course." He turned to the king. "We thought our mountain was near impenetrable by outsiders. The demonkin attacked our fortress, but it turned out to be a distraction. Some demonkin snuck inside and kidnapped our sorceress during the battle. They'd left one of their own to impersonate her using their power of illusion to buy themselves time."

The king's brows shot up.

Talwyn had been listening thoughtfully as Dreyken spoke. His retelling of the story gave her an idea. "During the coming battle, we should attempt to capture a high-ranking demonkin and try to find out if it knows where she is. And how to free her if she has been put in that contraption by the time we get there. It's a long shot, given the Dark Sorcerer's need for privacy, but it's worth a try."

Dreyken nodded, then they were silent for a moment before the king spoke again.

"So, it's true then, what they say about the demonkin and their ability to disguise themselves as others?" His worry was clear in his facial expression and in his tone of voice.

Talwyn nodded. "It is. My people can see through their illusions, but there aren't that many of us left. And let's not forget about what happened here, within these very walls, fifty-five years ago."

Her voice cracked on the last words as a memory flashed through her mind of Elisedd lying in a pool of his own blood on the floor.

The king nodded solemnly as he remembered. "I was young then. I believe I was outside in archery training. My father told me about it later. You were here, were you not?" he asked Talwyn.

"I was."

"Was he your mentor?" She could hear the concern in his voice.

Talwyn nodded. She cleared her throat, which strained against a tide of sudden emotion. "And my mate."

She felt Dreyken lay his hand against her back and lean into her. She appreciated his strength and his warmth at that moment. It grounded her and kept her from drowning in the memory.

"And you think it possible that some demonkin may sneak by and make it to the keystone?" the king continued.

"I wouldn't have believed it possible for demonkin to make it as far under the mountain as they did," Dreyken said. "So I wouldn't take anything for granted."

Talwyn took a calming breath and spoke again. "Perhaps we should go check on the keystone, just to be certain everything is fine. Then we can decide on a course of action."

"That's a good idea," the king said. "Meet me in the throne room in ten minutes. I will go collect my children and then meet you there."

Talwyn and Dreyken bowed to the king, who then hurried out of the room. However, they lingered behind.

Once the door closed behind the king, Dreyken turned to Talwyn and took her hands in his own.

"Are you okay?" he asked.

Talwyn nodded her head and cleared her throat again. "It's just, being back here, the threat of demonkin looming over us—I didn't expect it to affect me so much."

Dreyken wrapped his arms around her and rubbed his hands soothingly up and down her back. "Let what happened to Elis, to your whole family, serve as a reminder of why they need to be stopped. Let it spur you on in the difficult moments."

"I'm sorry you have to witness this. It's not really fair to you."

"Nonsense." Dreyken pulled back a little to look in her eyes. "Keep your tough, sarcastic façade for those who don't know you well. Think of me as your safe place, where you can bare your soul and rest your head and receive some of the comfort you deserve."

Talwyn lifted her hand to touch Dreyken's cheek. "Thank you." Then she placed a soft kiss to his lips.

She pulled away but took Dreyken by the hand. "Come. We shouldn't keep the king waiting."

Talwyn and Dreyken entered the throne room just moments before the king and his children appeared through a door opposite them. The king waved them over as he moved behind the throne.

"It's through here," he said, and he pushed on a stone that looked like any of the others around it.

The sound of something metal squealing as it released echoed as an area of stone the size of a small door appeared and swung slightly inward.

"Are the Stone Dragons the only people in the realm who don't have secret doorways and passages?" Dreyken let out an amused huff. "Well, that we knew of, anyway."

Talwyn had actually thought about this some. "It's not that surprising, if you think about it. The Stone Dragons have a reputation for being the most honest and straightforward of us all. And that's a good thing. I'm not surprised to find that you are less suspicious and secretive than others. Though I am sure you are more so now than you were four hundred years ago or so."

Prince Lugus stepped inside, grabbed a torch from a wall sconce, and lit it using a flint and steel. The king immediately entered after him, followed by Talwyn and Dreyken, and Princess Keeva took up the rear. Once they were all inside and the king had lit a second torch, Keeva pushed the stone door shut behind them.

The passageway immediately turned to the left and led down a set of stairs that continued downward in a wide spiral.

"Do these stairs go around something?" Dreyken questioned.

"Yes," Talwyn answered as they descended. "All the gate castles are built in this manner. In the very center is a keep. It is wide and cylindrical and continues underground for some distance. This staircase encircles it."

Down and down they went for some time until, finally, an opening appeared before them. Prince Lugus went through first, his torch illuminating the ground before him, which had now leveled.

Once they had all entered, Talwyn explained, "If an intruder found the hidden doorway and made it down this far, they would then have to figure out which of these three doors is the correct door. Then they would have to unlock it."

"What if someone had a metal thing like the one you used on the cell door and the doors in the tunnel on the way here?" Dreyken asked.

Talwyn shook her head. "That wouldn't work here. There is a hidden way to open each of these doors, much like the door above."

They were now all standing in a line in front of the third door. Keeva, however, still stood at the bottom of the stairs. The king looked over at her, and she reached above her head. As far as Talwyn could see, she was pulling down on a small ledge in the rock. Whatever she did, though, unlocked the door in front of them, and Lugus pushed it open.

At that moment, the king lowered his torch a little, illuminating the patch of packed soil around his feet. He was about three feet back from the door.

"Wait," Talwyn commanded, her heart suddenly picking up speed. The others froze in place and turned to look at her.

"What is it?" Lugus asked.

Talwyn walked over next to the king and pointed to the ground. "Look at that."

The others sucked in sharp breaths as they realized what she was indicating.

"Footprints," the king said.

Talwyn noted the enormous size, and how they were unusually wide at the heel. "Demonkin."

Keeva gasped. "How is this possible?"

"May I borrow your torch, your majesty?" Talwyn reached out.

"Yes, of course," he said. He handed it to her.

She shined the light from the torch on the ground as she moved around the area.

"There are demonkin footprints all around the doors." Then she moved to the wall opposite and walked from one end of the short tunnel to the other. "It looks like only one set, though. It seems they were looking for a way to get in and paced back and forth here a bit. But there are few footprints on the opposite side, so it doesn't look like they discovered how to open the doors." She sighed in relief and looked up at the others. "Still, let's be cautious as we move ahead, just in case."

The others nodded, then Lugus moved farther in through the doorway. They all followed.

"If someone could figure out how to open the door," Talwyn explained to Dreyken, "they would then have this to contend with."

Lugus lifted his torch, illuminating the surrounding area. After a moment, Dreyken spoke. "What is this place?"

"It's a labyrinth." It was Keeva who answered this time. "Anyone smart enough to get this far would still have to figure out which entryway to take. If they managed to choose the right one, they'd then have to decide which paths to take to get them to the center, where the keystone is."

"Incredible," Dreyken said.

Prince Lugus led them around the circumference of the circling passageway. They passed more than half a dozen entryways before he stopped in front of one. Talwyn looked at it and compared it to the ones she could see on either side. There was nothing that made it stand out from the others.

"Through here." Prince Lugus gestured ahead of him. They followed him inside.

Lugus led the others through stone passageways that twisted this way and that. Occasionally, Talwyn could see the torchlight flickering on the water that trickled between and down over the stones. The flames cast eerie shadows on the walls around them. The air smelled earthy and dank down here, and it was cooler than it had been on the main floors of the castle. When they reached the end of the tunnel, they faced nothing but another stone wall.

"Did we take a wrong turn?" Dreyken sounded confused.

"No." Lugus pushed on several stones surrounding the door in a pattern. As in the throne room above, there was a clicking and a creaking sound as the wall unlocked and swung away from them, just wide enough to allow them to pass through.

Dreyken shook his head. "It would be impossible for anyone who had not been here before, or who wasn't shown the way, to get down here, or through there. You are very thorough, your highness." Dreyken smiled appreciatively at King Caratacos.

"Well, I can't take the credit," the king replied. "It was my ancestors, aided by the Sorcerers of the Light, who built this keep and this castle to protect the keystone. Of course, that was three thousand years ago, so it's been rebuilt and fortified many times since, but the original idea remains the same."

"Let's go," Keeva said, walking ahead of her brother, who followed on her heels.

They entered a circular chamber. Lugus placed his torch in a wall sconce, then walked to the large, square stone in the middle of the room.

"Is that the keystone?" Dreyken asked.

"It is the stone box that contains the keystone." Talwyn pointed out a barely visible seam that ran near the top, where the cover-stone met the box.

"Let's check to ensure the keystone is still whole and undamaged," King Caratacos said. Lugus, Keeva, and Talwyn all moved to one side of the box, placed their hands along the edge, and pushed.

The stone lid didn't seem to budge at first, but soon the sound of stone against stone could be heard as it slid toward the back. They pushed it a little less than halfway off, then stopped.

Talwyn leaned over the box and placed her hand inside. She ran her palm along the stone and felt nothing out of the ordinary. It was smooth and warm to the touch, as it should be.

When Talwyn stepped back, Dreyken stepped up to look.

"Wow." He peered at the opaque purple stone the size of a small boulder that lay inside. It was sleek and somewhat rounded and seemed to have an internal radiance.

Talwyn watched Dreyken as he studied it; the awe and reverence he felt was clear in his facial expression. He reached out and brushed his fingers along it.

"It's warm," he said.

Talwyn nodded. "It's the magic that flows through it. The magic that's in it. It acts kind of like the narrowing of a channel, holding the magic back and letting it through slowly. Imagine a river flowing along, then narrowing. The water will pool just before the flow becomes restricted. There is more magic that stays held within it than what lies at any one point along the ley lines beyond it. At least, that's how it was explained to me. I don't fully understand all the mechanics involved, but I understood that much. So, you can see why the keystone is heavily protected."

"I can indeed. The keystones are essentially small pools of magic."

"And that is why we are here." King Caratacos gestured to the stone. "We need to make sure it is safe and has not been compromised before the demonkin arrive. We thought it near impossible for any demonkin to breach the keep, but the footprints in the outer passageway confirm you were right to be cautious. With a powerful sorcerer involved, we cannot leave anything to chance."

"No one would have believed the demonkin could enter the Sacred Forest either," Lugus said, "yet there have been sightings for close to a week now."

"And let's not forget how they got to my sorceress," Dreyken added.

Talwyn turned to the royal family. "So, what's the plan, your majesties? As seer guardian of Southgate and the keystone, I would suggest that King Caratacos stay close to the stone, maybe even here in this chamber. I am accustomed to working from the outside, and the king's place has always been to protect from within.

"Our Elder and our champions discussed this before I left the Valley of Sight. It was agreed that it would be best to keep it that way, with the seers on the outside and the kings on the inside. But you are the rulers here, so if you have any other suggestions, I will be open to them."

"I think that's a brilliant plan," Keeva said quickly. Talwyn suspected she was thinking more of keeping her father off the battlefield and out of the line of fire.

"Someone should also keep watch in the outer passageway of the keep, near the bottom of the stairs," Talwyn said.

"I think you should take that honor, Keeva," Lugus suggested.

Keeva pressed her lips together in an unhappy expression, but after a minute, she responded, "Fine."

"And I will lead our men on the battlefield," Lugus said.

"Okay, that's settled then." Talwyn clapped her hands together. "Now, let's head back up to make final preparations for the battle."

CHAPTER TWENTY

News From the Mountain

Talwyn stood on the allure of the castle wall at midmorning, looking out over the expanse between the castle, its surrounding town, and the edge of the forest. Then she turned and gazed to the northeast. She was certain the demonkin horde would attack from that direction. She continued gazing out absently, deep in thought, until a voice interrupted her musings.

"Do you think they will attack today?" Dreyken asked.

"No. My visions showed the attack happening at first light. I think it will happen tomorrow. I don't believe they will wait any longer than that."

"Well then, let's take a few moments to ourselves." Dreyken held out his hand to her. "I found something that I want to show you. Take a walk with me?"

Talwyn wasn't sure that was a good idea, but she was agitated and needed a distraction. Maybe taking in some of the scenery would help clear her mind. So she turned to Dreyken and nodded. "Okay, let's go."

Talwyn and Dreyken descended from the allure and then walked side-by-side. Instead of venturing outside, as she expected, Dreyken led her inside to a walled area. He opened a door and gestured for her to enter. When she looked around, she could see they were in a walled garden, a courtyard.

Flowers of varying colors and sweet scents covered the ground, except on the stone pathway that wound its way through. They followed the path until it led to a stone bench near the very center of the area.

"How did you know about this place?" Talwyn asked as she continued looking all around.

"I passed by the doorway earlier as someone was exiting and I noticed the flowers. Then I asked Keeva about it.

"Let's sit," Dreyken said, waving his hand toward a bench. It didn't escape Talwyn's notice that he allowed her to sit first, then sat as close to her as he could get. His side was pressed up to hers, and then he lifted his arm to put around her. She was going to protest, but he spoke before she could.

"I just want you to be comfortable. Allow yourself to relax."

So Talwyn did just that. Taking a deep breath, she leaned against Dreyken in what turned out to be a very restful position. She took another deep breath and suddenly she was no longer just smelling the fragrant flowers. She also smelled Dreyken. It was a pleasant odor, both earthy and spicy. She'd smelled nothing quite like it. It was very alluring.

"It seems kind of strange to have a private garden right in the middle of the inner bailey like this," Talwyn commented, trying to distract herself from those thoughts. She needed to clear her mind.

"Apparently, the queen has always loved flowers of all sorts, so she would bring them home and plant them here whenever she found a new one."

Dreyken moved his arm around her waist and absently rubbed his thumb back and forth along her exposed skin where her vest had lifted away from her pants a little.

Well, that was distracting. That small motion would definitely help clear her mind of her vision. He was barely touching her, but the light, caressing contact was sending jolts of awareness through her and thoroughly heating her skin.

Talwyn cleared her throat and said in a husky voice, "You should probably stop doing that."

"Doing what?"

"That thing you are doing with your thumb."

Dreyken turned his attention fully toward her, and then a slow smile spread across his face. She was sure he was noticing the flush his touch was causing.

"Why? Does it bother you?"

"Yes."

"In a good way or a bad way?"

She paused for a moment, trying to rein in her physical reaction before she responded. "I haven't decided yet."

"Let me help you decide, then." He cupped her jaw, turned her head toward him, and kissed her.

It started out soft and slow, but soon he became more demanding, claiming rather than kissing. She melted against him, powerless to the feelings he aroused in her. His hands again found their way to her bare skin as they pushed up just underneath the hem of her vest. And though his kiss was firm and demanding, his touch was still light, almost magical in the way it sent thrills of awareness through her.

Talwyn pulled back and lifted herself just enough to turn and swing her leg across his until she was straddling his lap. She pressed her body as close to his as she could, feeling the hardness of his powerful form against her through their clothes. He wrapped his arms around her in a tight embrace, then relaxed it so he could explore.

Dreyken's hands made their way up farther along her back. He moved them forward, skimming his fingertips along her rib cage. She moaned.

The sound surprised her, and a moment of reason flickered through her mind. If she didn't stop this now, it would soon get to where she could not. Talwyn finally pulled back, panting, and pressed her forehead against his.

They sat, catching their breaths for a few moments, before Talwyn spoke. "You make me feel insane. It doesn't seem to matter what I logically decide. The moment you touch me, it's no longer my mind that's making the decisions."

"Sometimes it's good to let go." Dreyken placed a short, sweet kiss on her mouth. "To not think. To just feel. And in matters such as these, it should be our hearts that rule us, not our heads."

"That idea is . . . terrifying to me."

They were still sitting like that, Talwyn in Dreyken's lap, forehead to forehead, trying to get their breathing and their erratic hearts back under control, when the door opened.

"There you are," came Adrio's booming, amused voice. "Sorry to interrupt." Talwyn turned her head to look at him over her shoulder. He was wearing a mischievous grin that suggested he wasn't sorry at all.

"What is it?" Dreyken asked.

"I just wanted to let you know Helsi has returned."

"Helsi has returned?" Talwyn grew concerned, finally standing from Dreyken's lap.

"I have," said Helsi as she came around Adrio.

Talwyn walked over to her and took her hand. "Are you sure you're okay to be here? Norshan—"

"Norshan would have wanted to be here." Helsi's voice was firm. "And since he can't be, I will be here in his place."

Talwyn nodded in understanding.

"Besides," Helsi added, "killing a few demonkin will help me reap my vengeance on the one who killed him."

Talwyn gave Helsi's hand a squeeze.

Then Helsi turned and gave her attention to Dreyken. "Lord Dragon, I also wanted to let you know Drarcio was attacked as he slept last night."

"What?" Talwyn said, at the same moment that Dreyken said, "Attacked?"

"Don't worry, he's okay. The male is very alert, even while sleeping. He awoke to an assailant standing over him with a knife. He moved just in time. The knife was aimed for his heart but barely grazed his ribs."

"Who was his attacker?" Dreyken asked.

"We don't know. He was hooded, but Drarcio believes it was a male. There was a struggle, but the assailant got away. Drarcio pursued him out into the tunnel, but it was as if he just vanished."

"Hmm." Talwyn knew what that signified. "Unless the Stone Dragons have suddenly learned how to conceal themselves, it seems likely there was yet another demonkin under your mountain."

"Under our noses, you mean." Dreyken let out a curse, then addressed Talwyn. "If I'd been smarter about it, I should have had you go on a tour of the living quarters to look for anyone who wasn't what they seem."

Talwyn shook her head. "I don't think Airgan would have been too keen on that idea. He would likely have tried to put a stop to it." Then she remembered something.

"Actually, you know that meeting when we were talking to the protectors about what I had seen, and the Elder Council arrived? I went over to confront Airgan when you began planning with your warriors. There was someone with him at first. I couldn't see who it was. When I approached, the person took off without turning around. I remember thinking at the time that it seemed very suspicious. But Airgan said it was his niece, and she took off because she shouldn't have been there. I didn't think much more of it at the time, since we know he wanted you to choose her as a mate. I may be overthinking it, but it seems like it has to be more than a coincidence that she was wearing a cloak with the hood up and I never got to see her face."

"That's another thing," Helsi said. "After the attack, Drarcio called all the protectors and Elders together to inform them of what happened. Airgan didn't show up. We searched for him, but he was nowhere to be found.

"I don't trust that male," she added. "I'm sorry if I'm overstepping, Lord Dreyken. He's an Elder, I know. But his behavior has been strange ever since Talwyn showed up at the mountain. The way he has treated Talwyn and the way he's been slinking around—this is not our way."

"I couldn't agree more," said Adrio.

"He also asked me many questions when I returned," Helsi continued. "I think he was prodding to see how willing I would be to share information with him."

"And that right there is a demonstration of the male's character," Adrio said. "Questioning a female who is in mourning, trying to gain an advantage by exploiting a person's moment of weakness."

"Drarcio wanted to send someone to warn you in case Airgan shows up here," Helsi said. "I volunteered. I wanted to be here for the battle, and I know that's what Norshan wanted as well."

"Speaking of Airgan's motives, why does Drarcio think he would come here?" Adrio asked. "He's an Elder, not a young warrior."

Talwyn thought about that for a moment. "His main motivation would likely be to undermine Dreyken's leadership, like he was trying to do back in the mountain. Or worse. It doesn't seem likely that it was Airgan who attacked Drarcio, either. I don't see how an Elder would have escaped Drarcio. So he probably has an accomplice. I would say we all need to watch your dragon lord's back."

"Surely you don't think Airgan would do anything to harm Lord Dreyken?" Helsi said. "I mean, trying to bolster his own importance to the Dragon lord I could see, but it is not the dragon way to be so underhanded and evil."

"We don't know what he's thinking. We still don't know how the demonkin got to Athnie unless they had help from the inside. They may have gotten to Airgan as well. History shows us that demonkin are sneaky, underhanded, and the ultimate manipulators. I, for one, am not willing to bet Dreyken's safety on what the usual dragon behavior would be. After all, this is not a normal situation. There are beings, like the demonkin, who would do anything to gain the upper hand in war."

"Yes," Dreyken said, "that's a good point. We must remember that we are at war. Doubt everything. Stay vigilant. Not just about Airgan. Keep alert to anything going on around you that might seem suspicious. After all, it is better to be overcautious than dead."

Dreyken looked at Helsi with a worried expression. Talwyn was sure he was concerned about Helsi coming to help at Southgate so soon after losing her mate. She was as well. It made her wonder if Helsi was going into battle to seek vengeance, not caring whether she herself came out of it alive or dead. After all, that's how she'd felt after she lost Elisedd.

She was going to have to keep an eye on Helsi as well.

And with that reminder, Talwyn was back to worrying that she might not figure out how all the pieces of everything she'd seen went together in time to make any difference.

"I am going to deal with this situation the way we seers do best," Talwyn announced. "I'm going to blend in and check things out from behind the scenes."

CHAPTER TWENTY-ONE

Disguises

Talwyn walked through the castle town, alert to anything that may seem suspicious. She had changed into the simple cotton clothing of a Southgate farmer, and her hair and eyes were now both a medium-brown color. She doubted anyone outside the castle itself would recognize her or know who she was, but she was still cautious. In times such as these, with demonkin once again implicated in the realm's troubles, it was best not to take chances.

She kept out of sight as much as possible and tried to blend into the crowd as the townspeople bustled about in their daily routines. It was kind of nice, actually, just wandering around the market, looking at the food and wares people offered for sale. But in just a short time from now, this town would be a much different place. In the meantime, she would watch for any demonkin in disguise or any sign of Airgan, and listen for any suspicious interactions.

She was a couple of hours into her surveillance when she noticed a figure walking across the market square with short but hurried footsteps. He wore a cloak with a cowl over his head and walked with his shoulders hunched forward. He cast glances all around him every few seconds, as if he was looking for someone, or hiding from someone.

Well, that behavior certainly seemed suspicious.

It was kind of funny, really, how people tried to hide by wearing hooded cloaks, but hooded cloaks always made her more suspicious of the wearer.

She followed this figure, who seemed jumpy and always on the lookout. Now and then, Talwyn would duck behind a building, a cart—whatever was around, really—to change her physical traits without being seen. She even changed her gait and the way she carried herself. If the paranoid man glimpsed her, she did not want him to realize he was being followed.

She was almost certain it was Airgan from the way he moved. His gait differed slightly from the one she had noticed back in the mountain, but he was an Elder and had been around long enough to know some tricks. This knowledge, added to the familiarity of some movements, increased her certainty.

It still seemed impossible to her that someone of Airgan's age could fight off a younger, trained protector such as Drarcio. She was certain he had help, or there was something she was missing. So, rather than capture him right away, she followed him to see what she could discover. She wanted to figure out what he was so nervous about and what he was watching for. If he was being followed by someone other than her, she wanted to find out who it was. So she stayed back far enough, she hoped, to not be spotted.

At first, he seemed to wander around aimlessly. It soon became apparent, however, that he was making a progressive sweep of the town while trying not to be obvious about it. What, or who, was he looking for? Drarcio had been attacked. Had it been Airgan who did it? Would he now go for his dragon lord?

Talwyn continued to follow him at a distance as he made his way through the town. She had to give it to the Elder—he was sharp. He glanced around regularly, and now and then he would stop to look at something. He kept his cowl on and his head down, which gave him the opportunity to check behind him more carefully. Because of this, she had to stay farther back than she was comfortable with to ensure she didn't get seen.

Airgan was now slowly making his way to the castle gate. The townspeople were moving things into the outer and inner baileys to prepare for tonight and tomorrow's plans. This was in the guise of preparing for a big party, however. They did not want to tip off the demonkin that they knew they were being watched.

Airgan took advantage of the crowds and waited for a large group of Southgate citizens to pass. He slipped in among them unnoticed.

Talwyn followed him through the gate, but lost sight of him in the crowd. She kept an eye out as the crowd dispersed on the other side of the open portcullis. She had gone about twenty paces in from the gate, but still did not see him, so she stopped where she was and turned to look all around her.

Clever old man. Managed to give a seer the slip. It should have been embarrassing, but for some reason, she found it amusing. She chuckled and shook her head. She'd been doing this for so long, she'd gotten overly-confident, it seemed.

She would feel worse if he didn't have over twice her years. Apparently, the doubt and mistrust he had displayed toward her back in the mountain was not only directed at her. She doubted he would be this good at stealth if he wasn't spurred by paranoia and suspicion.

Talwyn wandered through the outer bailey, trying to spot him. Once she finished her circuit, she moved into the inner bailey. She had just begun her surveillance when there was a commotion over by the entrance that led to the throne room. She moved closer, listening while monitoring the entrance.

A guard was standing between two men, who were shouting at each other.

"He stole the necklace I just purchased for my wife!"

"I did not! Check your information before you go flinging wild accusations!"

"Then why is the chain hanging out of your pocket?"

The first man looked down at his pocket and saw that there was, indeed, a chain hanging there.

"What in the . . . I did not put that there!" He pulled it out and held it up.

Talwyn stopped listening, because she had just spotted a cloaked figure moving swiftly through the entrance behind the men. The guard who was supposed to watch the entrance was currently occupied with preventing a brawl.

Being careful not to be spotted, she followed the cloaked figure into the castle. Carefully peeking around the entryway, she made sure it was clear before stepping through. She did not see the male at first and wasn't sure where he had gone. But she figured it would be best to head toward the throne room.

Talwyn did not enter right away but stood outside looking in, trying to stay out of sight as much as possible. The king and Dreyken stood a few feet in front of the throne, facing each other. One of the king's guards stood in the back corner, far enough away to give them privacy but still keep watch. A dark-haired guard was facing away from her, addressing King Caratacos. Dreyken stood next to the king.

There was something strange about that guard.

"My Lord," said the guard, "I have been asked to inform you that the dragon Elder Airgan has been spotted in Southgate."

"What?" said the king and Dreyken at the same time.

At that moment, a cloaked figure moved out from behind a statue close to where the males stood. He ran at them, a dagger in his hand. Caught up in the news they'd just received, King Caratacos and Dreyken did not notice the attacker right away. Talwyn wasn't sure if he was going for the king or the dragon lord, but either would be disastrous. She was across the room by the door, too far away to do anything but yell, "Look out!"

Then, several things happened in quick succession, almost too fast for Talwyn to take it all in.

As the attacker closed in on the men, one of the king's guards, who had been standing just a few feet away, ran for the assailant. Instead of going for either the king or Dreyken, the cloaked figure headed toward the guard who had just delivered the news of Airgan. But the king's guard got to the attacker before he reached his goal, tackling him to the ground. As he fell, his hood dropped back. Just as she had suspected, it was Airgan.

Airgan struggled frantically and yelled hysterically.

"Where is she, you evil demon spawn? Where is my Neri?" Then he bellowed at the guard, "Let me go! Let me go! He did something to her. I know it! Where is she? What did you do with her?"

The guard, unable to calm Airgan down, hit him on the head with the hilt of the dagger he had taken from him just seconds before.

This only caught part of Talwyn's attention, though. She was still halfway between them and the door and so had a view of the entire scene. The dark-haired guard moved behind Dreyken. Only, as he moved, he turned his profile to her.

It wasn't a guard at all! It was a demonkin in disguise. From this perspective, she could see both his true face and the fine mist of his illusion that covered it. Dreyken and the others did not know this danger was among them. They could not see through the demonkin's illusions as seers could.

Suddenly, she noticed a glint of a weapon in the demonkin's hand. She bent down and grabbed a throwing knife out of her boot, then ran as fast as she could toward them. She was still running when she threw her knife full-force. It hit the demonkin in the temple, and the creature fell sideways onto the ground from the force of it.

Dreyken and the king looked from her running toward them, to the now-lifeless form of the demonkin on the ground beside them.

"What in the Universe—?" King Caratacos said.

"What is going on here?" Dreyken echoed.

"Well, I guess you shouldn't have hit Airgan on the head," she said to the guard as she stopped beside them. "I'm sure he could answer that question much better than I can." She turned to Dreyken and King Caratacos. "All I can really tell you was that I spotted Airgan and started following him. He ended up here, where I first thought he was after one of you, or both. Now, it appears he may have been following someone as well. We'll have to wait until Airgan wakes to get more information than that." Addressing the guard again, she said, "It's a good thing you only knocked him out. He might finally shed some light on what's been going on in the mountain."

She looked up from Airgan's motionless form to notice that King Caratacos and the guard were looking at her with strange expressions on their faces.

"What?"

"Talwyn?" The king's tone was questioning.

"Oh." She suddenly realized she was still blond-haired and blue-eyed. She quickly switched back to her normal coloring.

"Amazing," the king said. "I almost didn't recognize you."

"Well, that's what I was going for—not being recognized."

"And doing an excellent job of it."

Dreyken moved beside Talwyn and took her by the hand. Then, addressing the king, he asked, "Is there somewhere we can take Airgan? Somewhere safe where he can heal, and we can question him when he awakens?"

"Yes, follow me," King Caratacos responded.

Talwyn and Dreyken were sitting in the room monitoring Airgan when he stirred about a half hour later. Talwyn got up, went to the door, and opened it just enough to tell the guard that Airgan was waking up so that he could inform the king.

Airgan came to slowly, blinking his eyes against the late-afternoon sun that was pouring in through the window. He seemed confused at first, but when he spotted Dreyken, it seemed to jog his memory, and he sat bolt upright in the bed.

"By the Universe!" he gasped, clutching his bruised head. He quickly shook it off and looked at Dreyken.

"Lord Dragon! It was a demonkin! The guard was a demonkin. It was Neri, too! I mean, it was impersonating Neri. Where is it? I need to find out where Neri is."

"It is dead, I'm afraid," Dreyken said.

"It was about to run your dragon lord through," added Talwyn. "There was no choice."

"Many apologies, Lord Dragon! I didn't know! I didn't mean for any of this to happen. All the years I have behind me and I failed to see the signs."

"Slow down, Airgan." Dreyken placed a hand on the old man's shoulder. "Take a deep breath. Start from the beginning."

"Right." Airgan took a breath. "Right. I assume you know by now that Drarcio was attacked?"

"We do," Dreyken confirmed.

"Well, after the attack, protectors were sent to gather the Elders to inform us of what had happened. I immediately went to find Neri to discuss the incident."

"Who is Neri?" Talwyn asked.

"One of Airgan's nieces."

"My youngest niece," Airgan added. "She is the youngest daughter of my younger brother. Or she was. I don't know if she's alive or dead. How am I going to find her now?"

Talwyn thought of her own people. Her own family. How some of them had disappeared, and her people never knew what had happened to them. Her people assumed they were taken or killed. Three hundred years later, and they still did not know for certain. She didn't think this was a good time to mention this to Airgan, though. He seemed upset enough right now.

"Go on, Airgan," Dreyken urged.

"After I learned of the attack, I went to find her. She was not in her quarters. It was the middle of the night, and after what had just happened, and what had happened to the sorceress, I was uneasy. So, I went to look for her.

"I caught up with her in a tunnel leading to a lower entrance to the mountain. She was holding the bloody knife still. I confronted her, and she started speaking some nonsense about how she failed, but it didn't matter. He was just an arm, and it was the head she needed to chop off to render the body useless. Then she said something about loose ends, and she attacked me.

"I got the knife from her—" Talwyn raised her eyebrows and he added, "Do not look so surprised. I may be old, but there's a reason I survived the attacks four hundred years ago. Anyway, in the ensuing struggle, I realized the physical form I was feeling did not match what I was seeing. It probably took me longer to figure that out than it should have, but I was caught up in the struggle.

The form I felt was taller and broader than the one I was looking at. The one I had thought was my niece.

"Then I thought back to what had happened when Athnie was taken, and to what you told us before the battle of the mountain, Talwyn. You were right. And you were right to trust her, Dreyken. Me, I was just an old fool, too blinded by my arrogance to even notice the differences in my niece."

"The demonkin are skilled manipulators, Airgan," Talwyn said in a soft tone. "It's likely they were watching for a while before they took her place. They would have gotten to know her mannerisms, her manner of speech. It's what they do."

"There is no excuse, really. I've been thinking about it, trying to remember if I saw a change in her. I believe the demonkin may have been in her place for months. Months! She had always been a smart girl, one who never held back her thoughts, even when they were a little blunter than one might have liked."

Airgan stood up, then wavered a little, as if he might fall over. Dreyken gripped his elbow to steady him.

"Then something changed?" Dreyken asked.

Airgan nodded and began pacing back and forth.

"Thinking back, a few months ago, she started flattering me more. Saying things that suggested I should have more power and importance than I did. She would talk of how complacent you were, Dreyken. How lost you seemed. How you needed the leadership of someone strong and sure to help guide you. It started slowly and was subtle at first. She became more insistent, more convincing as time went on.

"It was she who urged me to push you to find a mate. She convinced me that your refusal to do so was evidence that you did not put our people first. That you needed someone to guide you in the right direction. She suggested we try to influence you to choose a female we knew and trusted. She argued it meant that we would be sure that someone who put the future of Stone Dragons first would have your ear. Now, I think she was just trying to place someone we could manipulate into a position close to you. She mentioned it to Ninhré, who, of course, agreed with her and was keen to put that plan into motion."

Talwyn instinctively stepped closer to Dreyken. Immediately, she realized what she'd done and shook her head at herself. Apparently, she was subconsciously afraid one of his admirers would show up out of nowhere and snatch him.

Stupid, illogical heart.

"Looking back, I can see the manipulation in it all," Airgan added. "In everything she—it—has said and done. I fell for it all and enabled this demonkin to influence me and, through me, our people. Me, when I've been vehemently denying the need of our people to become part of the realm once again. How could I have been so stupid?"

"There have been many people over the years who have asked themselves that same question," Talwyn assured him. "It has nothing to do with your intelligence and everything to do with the demonkin's skills at manipulation and chaos."

"Still, I am ashamed, and I can never apologize enough for my part in these schemes. Perhaps, in the future, we can ensure we have some seer friends visit us regularly and check the clan for things the rest of us cannot see."

"Perhaps," Dreyken said, glancing over at Talwyn. One side of his mouth lifted slightly, as if he was trying to fight a smile. "For now, though, what is done cannot be undone, and we need to plan how to beat them in the future."

"How did you know this guard was the demonkin you were looking for?" Talwyn asked.

"It wasn't too difficult. I may be old, but I am a Stone Dragon, after all. The demonkin had a head start, but I just shifted and surveyed the land from above until I caught sight of it running toward town. It was more difficult inside the gate town, of course. But given what it had said about cutting off the head to render the body useless, I figured it would be a safe bet to head to wherever the king and the dragon lord were."

He paused for a moment, then asked, "Do you think Neri might still be alive? Do you think we can find her?"

Talwyn looked at Dreyken, and they shared a look of sadness and doubt. Airgan mentioned he noticed changes months ago. The chances of finding her alive and well after all that time were low.

"It is not likely, but nothing is impossible." Dreyken said in a soft voice. "For right now, we need to focus on the coming battle.

Talwyn's visions have shown that it will happen tomorrow. The demonkin will attack in the morning."

"Of course, Lord Dragon. What can I do to help?"

CHAPTER TWENTY-TWO

The Battle at Southgate

It was early morning, the day Talwyn had foreseen as the day of the battle. She was sure of it now. The grayish color of the sky blended into the red-orange light of the sun as it fought to make itself seen above the horizon. This and the landscape, the birds dancing on the winds—these all were familiar to her, as she had seen them before in dream-visions.

The townspeople and the soldiers had switched places the previous evening, as planned. Now, they just had to wait.

The sky was brightening, but a heavy mist still covered the patches of marshland that lay just beyond the ring of cottages that made up this part of the castle town, obscuring what lay beyond from their sight.

Talwyn knew from dream-visions that the demonkin were most likely to attack from this direction. It was an area of family cottages and not much else. The demonkin scoping out the area likely thought this would be the easiest way to approach.

If it was indeed magic amulets that allowed the demonkin to enter the forest, chances were good that there would not be enough for an entire company of demonkin. Not to mention their ainmith. So, chances were also good that some would skim along just outside the tree line between here and Eastgate to the northeast.

In this section of the castle town of Southgate, there were no soldiers, no obstacles, no barriers. Nothing but the homes of the simple farmers who tended the fields to the east, who were currently still sleeping.

Or so the demonkin had been led to believe.

The king had sent out runners to inform the farmers that they and their families were invited to attend a gathering in the outer bailey the previous evening. While they were there, the soldiers had disguised themselves in farmers' clothes or cloaks so as not to rouse suspicion among demonkin watching from outside the town's borders. The people had a lot of fun making sure merrymaking could be heard far into the woods. Later, once darkness had settled in, the soldiers disguised as farmers made their way out to the cottages.

Now they were waiting and watching.

"Any sign yet?" Iniri asked as she approached Talwyn from behind.

"Not yet. But if they stick to the plan they had in my latest vision, it will be soon."

"What are we watching for?" Iniri asked.

"Keep your eyes trained on the area where the forest meets the marshland. With the mist, it will be a little harder to see, but the first signs of movement should be just there." Talwyn pointed to an area a few hundred yards ahead.

"Well, ladies, we are about to get into position," Adrio said from behind them as he came up the stairway to the allure. "Are you sure you don't want to join us down there, Talwyn?"

"Maybe later. For now, my arrows will do their best work from up here."

"We will see you after the fight, then," Iniri said as she turned to join Adrio.

"Maybe sooner, if I am needed on the ground," Talwyn said. "You two take care of yourselves."

"We will," Iniri assured her, then reached to clasp Talwyn's forearm.

Adrio moved in next, but as he clutched Talwyn's arm, he pulled her to him in an embrace. "You take care of yourself as well. Our

Lord Dragon would be distraught if anything were to happen to you."

And she would be distraught if anything were to happen to him. But the thought of what they'd come to feel for one another and what that meant made her sweat.

Iniri and Adrio then turned and made their way down the stairs.

Talwyn turned her attention ahead once more. She watched the tree line through the mist, which was dissipating as the sun rose.

"Stay sharp," she said, just loud enough for the archers a few feet to either side of her to hear. "They will not let the advantage of reduced visibility pass by them."

The archers moved into position. They stood mostly hidden behind the merlons, ready to move at a moment's notice to fire their arrows through the arrow slits.

Just as she predicted, not more than a few moments later, she spotted movement.

"North-northeast," she said.

She pulled the leather wraps from around her belt and began looping them around her hands until they were fully protected. Then she bent down to check the rope at her feet to make sure it was securely attached—just in case she needed it. Then she stood back up and nocked an arrow loosely in her bow, which she held pointed down for the time being. Her senses were on high alert as she watched for any familiar, or unfamiliar, signs.

"Let them come in through the cottages. We will allow the soldiers to catch them by surprise, and we will target anyone making it in from behind."

"Got it," the archer to her left said.

They watched as the enemy demonkin began sneaking in between and around the cottages. They were trying to move silently, hoping to take the town by surprise.

The demonkin at the front line passed beyond the circle of cottages headed toward the outer castle walls. The Southgate soldiers burst forth from inside the small homes, yelling wordless battle cries as they came.

The humans faced the demonkin head on at the outer perimeter. The sounds of metal clashing on metal, battle cries, and cries of agony when someone was injured floated up from down below.

Wanting to be down there helping, but knowing it would be best if she stayed up here for now, Talwyn fidgeted and bounced on the balls of her feet. She watched and waited for the demonkin to be in the right position—surrounded by the humans, but not mixed with them. They didn't want to take the chance of injuring their own.

The Southgate archers began firing arrows at any demonkin that were clear targets. Talwyn was aiming at the back, knowing her bow could fire farther than any of the others here. She took out as many demonkin archers as she could. Since they had distance weapons, they had stayed back and were firing at the Southgate soldiers.

The demonkin archers tried to fire back at her, but they had the disadvantage of being in the lower position, and their arrows fell short.

It wasn't long before the demonkin and Southgate were so mixed, engaged in battle, that arrows were no longer very effective.

"I'm going down there." Talwyn slung her bow back into its place, grabbed the rope she'd left by her feet, wrapped it underneath her thighs, and jumped backward through the crenel. She lowered herself quickly. She had left the rope short to make it harder for the demonkin to grab it and climb. So, at the bottom, she let herself drop the rest of the way to the ground. She immediately turned, unsheathed her short sword, and ran into the melee.

Ally and enemy were fighting with swords, pikes, knives—any weapon they could think of seemed—all around her. She jumped in to help where needed, but the Southgate soldiers were holding their own.

Talwyn glanced around and spotted Lugus fifty or sixty paces away from her. He was dressed as any other soldier, yet he was surrounded by several demonkin. Either they had figured out he was someone of importance, or he turned out to be such a powerful fighter that they needed to join forces to defeat him. Talwyn jumped in to help him.

She ran toward Lugus and his assailants, yelling loudly. One of the demonkin who'd been attacking Lugus turned and focused its attention on her. It raised its sword in expectation of defending against hers. However, as soon as she was in range, Talwyn dropped to one knee, spun backward, and swung her sword around, hard and fast. It struck the side of the demonkin's knee, and the force of her blow was so strong that its leg was almost severed. It looked as though it was barely hanging on by some ligaments and sinew.

She looked up again to see a second demonkin bringing its sword down on her from above. The beast apparently intended to split her in two. She brought her own sword up just in time to block the blow. But she kept her sword moving up, then sideways, so that it pushed the demonkin's own sword out, causing it to lose its balance. She then delivered a powerful push-kick straight to the sternum. The demonkin flew into the air and landed a few feet away.

Lugus then appeared from her left. He jumped in and drove his sword down through the demonkin's chest.

He looked at her and grinned.

"Don't forget, we need to take one alive. Preferably one of some importance who might tell us where the sorcerer has taken Athnie."

"I promise you; I will not forget." Then he ran back into the battle.

The demonkin hoard now gave every sign that they were being overwhelmed, and it wasn't long before Talwyn heard a demonkin captain sound their retreat. The Southgate army did not cheer at this, however. They had already learned from Talwyn that there was more to come.

"Get ready for the second wave!" Then she ran back, grabbed her rope, and climbed up to the allure once again. Once there, she sheathed her sword, coiled the rope up, and took out her bow again.

Suddenly, she noticed a thick mist approaching. It was almost like a wall of cloud moving in their direction.

Talwyn swore under her breath, then yelled out a warning. "The sorcerer is with them! Keep sharp!" There were more muttered curses from all around, and she could hear her warning being passed along to the others all along the wall and down to those below.

This was something she had not foreseen. It was either a last-minute decision or something he had kept from the others. She had realized this was a possibility, of course. But since he was flying off toward the east the last time she had seen him, she'd figured it was unlikely he would come here. Either way, it was an unexpected complication.

One that significantly lowered their chance of being the victors here today.

The demonkin were pulling back, and the fog was rolling forward. It was a magical fog, so, though Talwyn could see it, she could also mostly see through it because of her true-sight. Her human and dragon shifter allies could not, though. They would be blind targets for the demonkin army and their snowbeasts and ainmith.

What she wouldn't give to have a few more seers here with her right now. How could one being keep watch over an entire field of battle? Something would surely slip by.

No! She wouldn't allow that to happen.

She could now hear the thundering footfalls of approaching snowbeasts. The ground shook, and she could feel the tremors even here by the castle wall. She had warned the others about them, but none here, other than herself, had ever seen one. She hoped they all remembered what she told them.

"Remember to keep moving! Don't make yourselves targets!"

Snowbeasts were nasty, vile creatures. She and her allies had plans for the beasts, but the fog complicated matters. Of course, the enemy would have hindered vision as well, so that was something, at least. Unless they were made magically immune to it.

Talwyn grimaced and swore under her breath at this thought. She felt frustrated that she didn't know more about the sorcerer and his capabilities. Frustrated and useless.

She tried to shake off the negative thoughts. This was just like the time she jumped onto an ainmith mid-flight. She just needed to stop thinking about it and take things as they came.

Talwyn nocked an arrow and lifted her bow. She aimed at the closest ainmith in the sky ahead, which seemed to lead a flight of a half-dozen. They stopped and circled at a distance they must have thought was out of range.

But they hadn't yet met her fancy new bow.

She let her arrow fly. It struck her intended target perfectly, hitting the front of the beast's chest. Assuming ainmith had organs in the same general area as other animals, the arrow should have penetrated its heart.

Sure enough, the animal dropped a few feet, tried a brave but feeble attempt at a flap or two, and then plummeted to the ground. Two demonkin directly below it noticed and jumped out of the way in time. A few others weren't so lucky.

Her attack on the ainmith spurred the enemy into action. Where they had been approaching calmly and in formation before, they now charged ahead. The snowbeasts charged forward from the rear, overtaking the demonkin and heading straight for the Southgate soldiers.

It was at this point that Talwyn unhooked her battle horn—the same one Sukia had given her back in the mountain—and blew into it.

Her signal spurred the dragons into action. She did not look behind her, but she could feel the currents of wind being pushed against her, caused by the flapping of great wings. The dragons arose, two at a time, from within the inner and outer baileys. These half-dozen dragons were the fiercest and strongest among the Stone Dragon protectors and warriors. Helsi was with them. And in the front, larger and more commanding than the rest, was Dreyken himself.

The dragons targeted the snowbeasts on the ground, attempting to stop them before they froze any of the Southgate soldiers.

Above them, archers rode the ainmith, and they now took aim at the dragons. Before they could get more than a couple of shots in, however, flames shot down on them from above. Another half-dozen Stone Dragon-folk, led by Adrio and Iniri, had hidden up high above the clouds. They were lucky there were clouds today, and that Talwyn had a dream-vision two nights before, letting her know the ainmith would travel below them.

Talwyn looked around. Her allies were holding their own against their enemies. But she had a niggling suspicion that tried to push its way forward from the back of her mind. Something wasn't quite right.

Then it hit her.

The fog was clearly magical, something produced by a sorcerer. If it was indeed the sorcerer, where was he now? Why was he not retaliating? And then she thought back to the battle at the mountain, and how it had all been a diversionary tactic. She suddenly had a thought that made her a little sick to her stomach.

She turned slowly, surveying the fog-covered field below. When she saw nothing suspicious, she turned more to her right, surveying the outer bailey below and behind her. Then she spotted it. There was a hooded figure flanked by two other large males heading straight through the gate into the inner bailey. They weren't looking up at the battle, but they were taking advantage of the peoples' distraction. One of the large males turned his head in profile to her, giving her a better view. She knew without a doubt—two disguised demonkin were escorting a sorcerer through the gates.

She made to take off in that direction, but hesitated and looked back to where Dreyken was now sending jets of fire down upon a snowbeast. As soon as it seemed he wasn't in immediate danger, she called to him.

"Dreyken!"

She did not know if he could hear her from this distance, but she had to try.

"Dreyken!" She yelled louder this time. Dreyken turned his head slightly and looked at her from the corner of his eye.

She pointed to herself, then into the bailey. It wouldn't be a very clear message, but she hoped he could figure out that she wanted him to find her inside as soon as he could.

His attention was then pulled away from her by an ainmith that was attacking from his far side.

Talwyn paused for just a moment, looking at him and wanting to help. She knew he could handle himself, though. He could take that ainmith without her. She hoped.

She warred with herself for only a moment before nocking an arrow and firing at the ainmith. The arrow headed straight at its target, but she did not wait to see it hit. She put her bow back in its place on her back, then took her coil of rope and dropped it down, on the inside this time. She quickly made her way down and took off at a run toward the main castle and, specifically, the throne room.

When Talwyn arrived at the secret door behind the throne, it was slightly ajar. She pushed it open the rest of the way and ducked inside. Wanting to take the demonkin by surprise, she did not light any torches. She crept quickly and quietly down the stairs to the tunnel, but slowed at the bottom. Moving stealthily, she peered out of the stairwell into the dark corridor beyond.

She spotted a form lying unmoving on the floor just a few feet from the bottom of the stairs. "Keeva!" She ran over to her side. There was no blood and no visible injuries, but she was unconscious. Kneeling next to the princess, Talwyn checked to see if the girl was still breathing. She was. "Thank the Universe!"

Talwyn saw no one else and sensed no movement, so she made her way into the corridor, looking toward the doors.

A large hole had been blasted into the second door, undoubtedly caused by the sorcerer who was with the demonkin.

Moving quietly, she made her way inside. The stone walls were thick and magically reinforced, yet the sorcerer had blasted holes through them any time he came to a dead end. She figured that, as a magical being, the sorcerer must be able to sense the magic of the keystone, because they were traveling unerringly toward it.

As she approached the inner circle where the keystone was housed, she heard sounds of fighting that got louder the closer she got. She reached the sorcerer-made entry to the chamber and carefully peeked around toward the sound.

The two demonkin were engaging the king in a sword fight. The old king was handling himself surprisingly well against his two large attackers. He parried and spun and thrust, moving faster than she would have expected for a human man his age. So Talwyn turned her attention to the sorcerer.

"Don't kill him," the sorcerer yelled to the demonkin. "We can use him for leverage at the Great Gate." Then he turned and walked toward the keystone.

Talwyn sprinted out, placing herself between the cloaked sorcerer and the keystone. As she ran forward, she nocked an arrow in her bow and pointed it at him.

The sorcerer showed surprise for only a moment. He stopped in place and looked at Talwyn with a smirk on his face.

Talwyn looked him over. "You are a sorcerer, but not the sorcerer they call their emperor."

"Very observant. I'm not sure how you know that, but it is quite impressive that you do."

"I'm afraid I cannot let you destroy the keystone."

The sorcerer shook his head and looked at Talwyn with an apologetic expression. "I have no choice, I'm afraid. It's either the keystone or me."

"That sounds like a choice to me."

"Come now, would you place a stone above your own life?"

"If it meant saving the realm, then yes, without question."

"Well, you are much more self-sacrificing than I am, it would seem." He gestured with his hand as if he were brushing dirt off an object. "You will have to move from there or be moved."

There were no longer any sounds of fighting, which worried Talwyn. She glanced to her right and noticed the king lying on the floor and the two demonkin now quietly approaching her.

"Stop where you are, or I will let my arrow fly."

Glancing back at the sorcerer, she saw him give the demonkin a subtle nod. From her peripheral vision, she saw one of the demonkin load a bow of its own and raise it in her direction. She loosed her arrow just before she dodged the demonkin's arrow and jumped behind the stone box that held the keystone.

The demonkin's arrow had missed her, but hers was true to target. Unfortunately, she could see now that the sorcerer had shielded himself magically. The arrow lay on the ground a couple of feet in front of him and she could see the shimmer of magic.

The demonkin spread out to either side and moved in toward her, trying to box her in. She quickly formulated a plan.

Sorcerers expended physical energy when using magic. This was common knowledge. She was outnumbered and was facing two demonkin and a sorcerer. She didn't know how powerful this sorcerer was, but given they were on a ley line and so close to a keystone, she knew whatever power he had would be amplified.

If they were going to end up taking her out, then her best bet was to cause the sorcerer to expend too much energy to magically destroy the keystone before they killed her.

She leaped out from behind the keystone and ran toward the sorcerer, firing arrows at him as she went. She kept moving and tried to keep the sorcerer between her and the demonkin as much as possible.

The sorcerer's shield flickered repeatedly as she hit it with her arrows. The demonkin were having a hard time aiming at her without hitting the sorcerer. Eventually, however, the demonkin with the bow stopped firing at her, and the two of them went in opposite directions to trap her. When the demonkin archer saw an opening, he fired at her again. She tried to move out of the way, but she was not quite fast enough.

The effects of the toxin hit her right away. She used her inner-sight to slow its spread through her body, but she felt groggy and sluggish. Unconsciousness would hit her before she could stop the poison completely. Her enemies were nothing but blurs, but she stayed on her feet and kept moving. She knew she would only have a short time before she lost consciousness, so she needed to change tactics.

"She's strong," a demonkin said. "I've seen no one withstand even the slightest amount . . ."

"Then stop trying to knock her out and kill her!" shouted the sorcerer.

The archer nocked another arrow. Talwyn dropped her own bow and ran at the sorcerer, who opened his eyes wide in surprise. He lifted his hands, and a ball of flame formed between his palms.

Just as he pulled back to throw it at her, she veered to the side, ducked, and swept his legs from under him with one of her own.

The sorcerer fell hard, his head impacting the ground. She pulled out a knife from her boot and raised it, but before she could strike, a sharp, intense pain hit the back of her shoulder and radiated out. She glanced down and saw an arrow head jutting from the front of her shoulder, just underneath her collarbone.

The demonkin were now moving toward her and the sorcerer. With her last bit of strength, she brought the knife up again and used both hands to stab the sorcerer in the chest.

Then she succumbed to the darkness.

CHAPTER TWENTY-THREE

Casualties in the Keep

Dreyken ran down into the keep, out of his mind with worry. At the bottom of the stairs, Keeva's still form lay on the ground. The familiar tingle and heat that happened before a shift rose under his skin, but he fought it back. His dragon was too large to be useful in here, and he needed his human hands to help. He paused just long enough to check that she was still alive, then he set off for the doors.

He did not slow down until he saw torchlight through the makeshift doorway that was blasted into the central chamber. Creeping into the room, he spotted two demonkin holding up the sorcerer ahead. The sorcerer placed his hands on the keystone.

"Can't—too weak," he heard the sorcerer say. But it barely registered in his mind. He had just noticed the king lying on the ground over to his left. There was blood trickling from his ear. His eyes then swept to the right, and his heart rate raced when he spotted Talwyn's limp and bloodied form lying on the floor.

Dreyken shook his head as pain ignited something feral in his chest. He was blinded by rage and sorrow, his emotions fanning the flames inside him. He could feel himself getting hotter and hotter, his insides blazing until he could hold it in no longer. The fire could not hurt him, but it could scorch his enemies until nothing was left but embers and ash.

Without shifting, he let out a great roar, and with it came a tremendous blast of flame, an inferno aimed directly at the sorcerer and his companions.

His enemies screamed in agony but managed to duck behind the keystone. He kept his flame going for a minute as they stayed crouched out of sight. He did not know if his dragon-fire did much damage, and he didn't bother to check. His fury had burned out alongside his flame, and now his mind and heart were consumed with worry for Talwyn. He needed to check on her, but he needed to calm down first. She could not withstand the heat radiating from him at this moment.

He walked over to her and kneeled about a foot away. "Talwyn! Talwyn, wake up." His voice was rough and unsteady. He was shaking with fear, choked with his anguish. He knew he needed to get her to a healer, but he couldn't touch her yet.

Closing his eyes, he breathed in deeply, then blew it out slowly, trying to calm himself down. He needed to calm down, for Talwyn's sake. He could breathe fire without shifting, but without his dragon-hide, there was no protective layer between the heat of his body and anything he touched.

After a couple of minutes, he felt himself cooling. As soon as he thought it was safe, he carefully broke off the arrow shaft close to her body. He left the rest where it was for now, figuring it would help stem the bleeding. Then he picked her up and carried her upstairs.

He ran out through the throne room, cradling her in his arms. As soon as he saw some Southgate citizens, he yelled out to them.

"You there! The king and the princess are down in the keep. They're injured. They need help!"

The citizens looked at him holding the bloodied and unconscious Talwyn and gaped at them for a moment. Luckily, one of them came to his senses. "Right away," he said, and he grabbed a couple of others to head down to the keep.

Dreyken then turned to another human, a female. "I need a healer. Where can I find one?"

"Follow me." She ran off and Dreyken followed her, speaking softly and earnestly to Talwyn the entire way.

"You'll be okay. I've got you. I need you to be okay. Fight, Talwyn. Stay with me. Stay with me."

Dreyken stood in the healers' area along with Queen Boudicca and Prince Lugus. There were several beds occupied with fallen soldiers, but they were interested in three in particular.

On a bed to the left, one healer was examining Keeva. Thankfully, she was now conscious.

"How are you feeling, Princess?" the healer asked.

"Ugh. Like my head was used as a combat target. And everything is spinning."

"You were hit on the head pretty hard. It may take a week to heal if you rest and follow my instructions."

"Don't worry, I will see that she does," Queen Boudicca assured the healer.

"But what of the Great Gate? I need to be there." She attempted to sit up, but then pressed a hand to her head and lay back down again.

"Do not worry, Princess Keeva," Dreyken said. "There is time. If you are not well enough to march with the others, I will have one of mine stay behind to carry you there."

"That would be much appreciated, Lord Dreyken." She glanced over to where her father and Talwyn lay at the far end of the room.

"The healers wouldn't let us go over there while they were working on them," Lugus said. "Apparently, soldiers fresh from the battlefield can contaminate open wounds." He gave his sister a little smirk.

Keeva then turned her attention to the ten soldiers lying in beds lined along the opposite wall. Dreyken turned his attention there as well. One man was covered over with a sheet so he couldn't be seen. The other fighters were in various states, from sleeping to sitting up.

"What happened out there? Since we're here, I assume we won?"

"Yes, we were very lucky," Lugus told his sister. "The dragons gave us the element of surprise. Thanks to them, what you see in this room is the worst of the injuries." He looked at Dreyken and gave him a nod. Dreyken nodded in return.

Dreyken then looked over to where Talwyn lay. She looked to be just sleeping peacefully. The healer who had been working on her had left her side to go help with King Caratacos.

Dreyken waited tensely along with the queen and her children while the healers worked on the king. After a short while, though, a healer lifted the sheet up to cover his head.

He heard Queen Boudicca's sharp intake of breath next to him. Then she sobbed. Lugus went to her, wrapped an arm around her, and led her to Keeva's bed, where they held each other and mourned together.

There was a knot in Dreyken's stomach, and a sharp pain stabbed at his chest. He had not known the old king for long, but it was long enough to know he was a good, honorable man. His loss would be felt by all of Southgate, he was sure.

Dreyken moved away to give the royal family some privacy. He approached the healer who had worked on Talwyn. "Is she going to be okay?"

"I believe so. I bandaged her arrow wound. It did some damage but is not life-threatening. It will heal with time. Now we just have to wait for the poison to wear off."

"Thank you. Thank you for your help."

"Thank you as well for telling us about the poison they used." The healer glanced at the sleeping warriors on the bed and back at Talwyn. "It's good to know it is not fatal. I just wish we had some way to neutralize it."

"Can I go see her now?"

"Yes, go ahead."

Dreyken approached Talwyn's bed and took her hand. He'd feared the worst when he'd entered that chamber and saw her lying on the ground, motionless. But she was strong—his fierce and fiery warrior. He should have known she would not have given up that easily.

For a moment there, however, he had been afraid. He had felt pain such as he had never experienced before, and he'd thought his world was ending. In that moment, he gained a perfect understanding of Talwyn's fear of losing those she loved.

CHAPTER TWENTY-FOUR

Awakening

Talwyn's return to consciousness was slow. She wandered back and forth between consciousness and oblivion many times without fully waking. But each time she gained some awareness, she could heal herself some. It started with her sensing a foreign substance in her body. It wasn't natural, so her body couldn't break it down. Instead, she sent it back along the path it had entered from. It took her a couple of tries to get it out completely, as the process would be paused when she was pulled back down into unconsciousness. Once it was all out, she focused on healing her wound.

Talwyn finally woke up. The first thing she registered was the comforting sound and smell of a wood fire that crackled nearby. Next, she heard chair legs scraping against the floor. Her eyelids fluttered against the light in the room. "Dreyken?"

"He'll be back soon." It was a female voice. Not Dreyken. Talwyn opened her eyes and turned toward the voice.

"He's okay?"

"Yes. He's good."

"Helsi?" Her voice was rough and gravelly. "How long . ."

"About a day and a half."

"A day and a half? What happened? The battle . . ."

Helsi held up a hand. "We won, don't worry. You just need to relax and heal right now. I'm sure Dreyken will fill you in on all the details soon."

The sadness was clear in Helsi's voice, even as muddle-headed as Talwyn felt at that moment.

Talwyn's mind was still a little fuzzy. There was something else she needed to ask about, but she couldn't remember what.

Helsi stood and went to a nearby table, where she poured some water and brought it over to Talwyn. She placed her hand behind Talwyn's head and lifted her enough to take a sip.

"You've healed amazingly fast. Your wounds are already almost completely healed."

"Inner-sight." Her voice was still rough, but the water had soothed her throat some.

"What?" Helsi asked.

"Inner-sight. My people can see and manipulate the elements inside our bodies. It's what allows us to change hair and eye color. It also allows us to heal ourselves, if we have enough awareness to do it. I could have healed much faster if the demonkin hadn't used their cursed poison on me."

"Well, that's a valuable ability. I wish my kind could do that."

Talwyn touched the bandage below her collarbone. "That poison slowed me down enough that I'm probably going to have a scar, though." She looked at Helsi carefully. "Why are you—"

"Why am I here?" Helsi finished for her. "Because Lord Dreyken would not leave your side unless he knew someone he trusted was with you. He wouldn't leave at all until he knew for sure that you would recover." She paused before continuing.

"He loves you, you know."

"I know." Talwyn's voice was wistful, even to her own ears.

"And you love him." It was a statement, not a question, so Talwyn didn't respond. She didn't need to.

"And yet, you resist. Why?"

Talwyn took a deep breath. She was about to make up some excuse, but then she thought, if someone was going to understand, it would be Helsi.

"I've suffered a lot of loss in my life, Helsi. My parents, my sister, and, later, my mate."

Helsi looked at her in surprise.

"Yes. I was mated before, and he was killed by demonkin in this very castle."

"I'm so sorry." The sadness in Helsi's voice mirrored her own. Talwyn reached out and grabbed her hand.

"After that, I kept others at a distance as much as possible. I just don't think I'm strong enough to open myself up again and then end up losing someone else. I don't think I'd survive it."

"But you don't know that you'd end up losing them. You could end up going first, you know. Just look at where you are right now. You came awfully close this time around. Besides, I thought seers believed that all living energy goes back into the Universe and, thus, never really leaves us."

"We do. *I* do. But it doesn't keep me from missing them. It doesn't keep it from hurting. I'm sure you understand."

Helsi sat back in her chair and looked at Talwyn thoughtfully for a moment before speaking again.

"If someone came to you, Talwyn, and told you they could take away all your pain but, in exchange, they would have to erase your loved ones from your past, as if they had never even been there, what would you do? Would you give up the time you spent with them to not feel the sorrow and heartache from their loss?"

Memories flickered through Talwyn's mind, one after the other, in quick succession. Running through the woods, playing hunter and prey with her sister. Her parents teaching her how to hunt and fish. Elisedd teaching her how to fight and wield a bow. Those special, private moments she shared with Elisedd. Would she give all of that up to lessen her own pain? There was a time she might have said yes, but now . . .

"No."

"Good." Helsi nodded her approval. "I know I wouldn't give up a single, fleeting moment with Norshan, not even a second, even if it meant taking away this pain. The pain shows us that what we had was real and true. That it was worth fighting and suffering for. I don't believe the pain will ever go away, and I'm good with that, because it shows me he's still with me. But I know I will grow accustomed to living with the pain, and that I will go on to live the rest of my life still carrying his love inside me."

Talwyn was silent for a moment, absorbing Helsi's words. Then she looked at her friend. "Why are you here, Helsi, instead of back at the mountain?"

"I'm heading back after the feast tomorrow night. I just wanted to make sure you were okay, and to help as much as I can before I leave. Norshan was never one to leave friends in need, so I'm sure he'd understand." She smiled a sad, nostalgic smile at this.

"Well, thank you for everything, Helsi." Her voice was earnest and sincere, and she hoped Helsi could hear in it how much she appreciated all her help and support.

Then, to lighten the mood, Talwyn changed the subject. "So, tell me about this feast."

Before Helsi could respond, the door opened behind her, and Dreyken walked in. Talwyn watched as he stopped in his tracks and his face lit up with happiness. She could not help but smile back at him.

Helsi cleared her throat and stood up. "Well, I'll head out now. I'll see you two later."

As soon as the door shut, Dreyken sat on the bed next to Talwyn and pulled her into a tight hug.

"Ow, ow, ow!" Talwyn said.

Dreyken pulled back with alarm and looked her over. "I'm so sorry! Is it your shoulder? Are you okay?"

"Relax, I'm just kidding. I'm fine."

"Don't do that to me! You've given me enough of a scare already."

Before she could even apologize, he pulled her to him again and covered her mouth with his own. His kiss was soft and cherishing, full of emotion. If she hadn't already known how he felt about her, that kiss would have left no doubt.

"You gave me such a fright, Talwyn." He stroked her hair softly as he spoke. "When I walked into the keep and saw you lying on the floor, I thought I was too late. I was out of my mind with..." His voice broke.

At his comment about finding her lying on the floor, some of the fogginess cleared from her mind, and it hit her that there were many things she had missed out on. Many things she didn't know.

"Dreyken! Keeva and the king, how are they?"

"Keeva is fine. They snuck up on her and knocked her out with something heavy. Probably the hilt of a weapon. She had quite the headache when she woke up, but she seems to be doing fine now. Or she will be in a week or so, according to the healer."

"And King Caratacos?"

Dreyken looked down at the floor for a moment, then back up to Talwyn. "He didn't make it."

She trembled, and Dreyken wrapped his arms around her tightly once again and continued to stroke her hair.

"There will be a feast tomorrow night in his honor. A celebration of his life and his legacy. Do you feel up to attending?"

"Of course. Of course I'll attend. It's the least I can do."

She continued to shiver in his arms. After a moment, she whispered, "I could have saved him, Dreyken. If I had just gone to help him first. But I went for the sorcerer. I could have saved him."

"You can't blame yourself, my love. You made a choice. There's no way to know what would have happened if you had gone to the king first. He might have perished anyway. The sorcerer might have blown you both away and then destroyed the keystone, and then where would we all be?"

"What about the demonkin and the sorcerer? What happened to them?"

"When I arrived at the keep, the demonkin were holding up the sorcerer. Apparently, you had done a lot of damage before I got there." He smiled at her. "When I saw you lying on the ground, not knowing if you were alive or dead . . ." He paused and swallowed. "I just lost my mind. I let out a blast of fire at them—"

"You shifted in there? How was there room?"

"No, I didn't shift."

It took a couple of seconds for his meaning to dawn on her. "I didn't think you could breathe fire in human form."

"Normally we can't. Our histories talk of only one other who could do that: the very first dragon lord. My ancestor. It's one reason he was chosen to be Lord of the Stone Dragons. But that's a story for another time." Dreyken's eyes were wide as he spoke, but there was a slight grin on his lips.

"That's amazing."

Dreyken nodded. "I've often wondered if I was really the right person to lead the Stone Dragons, but knowing this, I feel like it's a sign."

"I've believed you have what it takes from the moment I met you. I don't need a sigh to tell me that."

He smiled and hugged her again, pulling her close and putting his chin on her head. She stayed like that, just absorbing his warmth and strength for a few minutes before leaning back.

"So, the demonkin and the sorcerer?"

"Right. Well, after the blast of fire, I focused my attention on you. I brought you up to the healers and sent others for Princess Keeva and King Caratacos. Later, when the fighting was over, Lugus came to see his sister and father. I told him what happened. He sent protectors down to sweep the keep and the rest of the castle. They found one dead demonkin, badly burned, still behind the keystone. The other demonkin and the sorcerer had disappeared in the chaos."

Talwyn thought for a moment. "I stabbed the sorcerer in the chest before I passed out. There should have been blood. Wasn't there a trail that could be followed?"

"There was," Dreyken replied. "But once they got outside—well, there was a lot of blood out there, and it was lost."

"A lot of blood? What happened out there?"

"Don't worry, most of the casualties were the enemy. It was like you said. They weren't expecting the Dragon-folk. I doubt they thought we would help after what the humans did to our kind. They were overwhelmed before long. It took us a little while to figure out how to kill the snowbeasts, but once we did, they didn't stand a chance."

"*Most* of the casualties, you said?"

"One Southgate soldier was killed and there were several injuries, but we were very fortunate compared to the other side."

Talwyn looked down at the floor and nodded.

"Are you okay?" Dreyken asked.

"I'm fine. I just hate that there has to be any killing or death, or any battle. It's necessary sometimes, I know. The Dark Sorcerer isn't the type to discuss problems nicely over tea. For example. "

"Most of us do, I think. And yet, here we are. But you were right, Talwyn. We needed to take a stand. The Dark Sorcerer is intent on his goals, and he forced our hand. Our only other option would have been to sit back and allow him to make subjects and slaves of us all, and you know we couldn't allow that."

"That wasn't *the* sorcerer down in the keep." Talwyn suddenly remembered she hadn't told anyone yet.

"What? What do you mean?"

"It was a sorcerer, but not the one they call their emperor."

Dreyken's eyes betrayed a hint of shock. "Just how many other sorcerers are working with him?"

"I got the feeling this sorcerer wasn't necessarily a willing participant in the Dark Sorcerer's schemes."

"Why do you say that?"

"He mentioned something about not having a choice. How it was the keystone or him."

"Huh. I wonder how many others are working for him by force, and if we can use that to our advantage?"

It was quiet for a couple of minutes as they both mulled this over. Then Dreyken cleared his throat.

"There is something else I wish to discuss with you."

"Okay, go ahead."

"I want you to know that I had already decided to come to Southgate before I knew the sorceress was missing. I figured I just had to stay long enough to ensure that our mountain was secure and to recruit a few warriors to accompany me."

"Why are you telling me this now?"

"Because I want you to know that I had already made my decision about the male I wanted to be." He met her gaze and held it as he continued. "You were right about me, you know. I was just sleepwalking through my life, letting things happen, playing the part, but never really living, never really appreciating those around me.

"Until you, Talwyn. You woke me up. You opened my eyes to who I am and who I want to be. With you, I finally found my passion—for life, for my people, for you. And I want you to know that I can be the kind of man who is deserving of you. That I *want* to be that male. That I will strive to be that male for the rest of my life."

Talwyn returned his gaze with watery eyes. When she responded, her voice betrayed feelings of both affection and sadness.

"The question was never if you were deserving of me, Dreyken. I could see who you were, and I knew you would figure it out eventually."

"Then what was it? What *is* it?"

"The question is whether I am in a place where I can open myself up to that kind of risk again. Whether I can truly and wholeheartedly be a partner to someone again, or if my past has damaged me and hardened me too much to give another man what he truly needs and deserves. To give you what you truly need and deserve. I don't know if I can let go of the past enough to do that."

"Well, that's just it, Talwyn. Maybe you shouldn't try to let go. Maybe you should just accept that you were lucky enough to have had such a great man as part of your life. He was your past, yes, and he is still part of you. But,"—his tone was hesitant, yet hopeful—"maybe you can also come to accept that you are fortunate enough to have had two good men in your life, to have found a deep, abiding love again after such tragic loss. It is what you deserve."

Talwyn looked up and met Dreyken's eyes as he finished speaking and was awed by what she saw there. What he had just described—it was a confession, a description of how he felt for her. This was what he was offering her: a deep, abiding love. She just had to be brave enough to accept it.

Dreyken took her hand in his, brought it to his mouth, and placed a soft kiss above her knuckles. "You have told me that seers believe the Universe sends you visions for a reason. Well, maybe *you* were sent to *me* for a reason. And I do not just mean to solve my problem of being forced to mate with someone I don't love. I mean, you were sent to me so we could find each other, so we could find that abiding love. Because I do, Talwyn. I love you more than any words could express, and I want to be your mate, for as long as the Universe wills it."

Taking her hand and placing it over his heart, he asked, "Will you accept me as your mate, Talwyn?"

Talwyn looked up to the ceiling and let out a big breath, as if she was thinking it over. "I don't know," she teased. "What would that entail, exactly?"

She met his eyes and was surprised to see the intensity burning in them. She swatted him. "I meant, since you are Lord Dreyken of the Stone Dragons, would there be more than just the standard declarations between the two mates?"

He smiled at her, the fire in his eyes dimming but not disappearing. "Well, yes. There are a few words of promise that need to be said to each other and to our people. As I see it, though, this is just a formality. You have done so much for me and my people that, as far as I am concerned, you are already a part of us."

He shook his head a little and let out a chuckle before meeting her eyes with what she could only describe as an expression of awe. "My friends always teased me for my romantic notions of finding a mate. Yet, before you, I would never have believed that someone could come to mean so much to me in such a short time. That I could feel so much passion and protectiveness at the same time. That I could love another so fiercely.

"And I know that what I feel for you is pure and true. Despite our different backgrounds and our different experiences, we fit. We belong together, Talwyn. You are a part of me, and my heart is forever yours."

Talwyn looked up into his eyes as tears spilled from the corners of her own. She placed her palm on his cheek, and whispered, "In that case, I would be honored to be your mate." Then she pulled him to her for a passionate kiss.

CHAPTER TWENTY-FIVE

Dream-Vision of the Past

That night, Talwyn lay in bed in the guest room that had been set up for her, staring up at the ceiling. She should have been sleeping, trying to heal and opening her mind to visions. Her mind was currently too distracted to allow sleep to drift in, however.

She was thinking about the Dark Sorcerer. She wondered why he wasn't present at the battle. Was he busy with whatever he had planned for Athnie?

She was bothered by the kidnapping of the Stone Dragons' sorceress. Athnie was too young to know magic well or to have become proficient at it. So why kidnap her? And why put her in that box?

She turned it over and over in her mind, but she couldn't figure out the motive. She figured the Dark Sorcerer would have a backup plan should he fail to destroy the keystones, and it likely had to do with that. Yet she did not know how a young, unproven sorceress could be part of that.

What if the sorcerer sacrificed her young life before she ever really lived it? What if they couldn't find a way to free her? What if even Maelona couldn't free her?

What if, what if, what if? There were too many unanswered questions. As a seer, she was completely unaccustomed to having so little information. She did not like it one bit. What was his motivation for the kidnapping? How was it part of his end game?

After lying there in the dark mulling this over for what felt like hours, Talwyn's eyes finally got heavy. Her eyelids drifted shut and her breathing evened out as sleep overtook her at last.

A mountain lioness wandered in the trees near the foot of a mountain, stalking prey. She was tracking the scent of a wildern as it traveled toward the sound of a babbling brook and the accompanying scent of fresh, clean water.

The lioness crouched low, preparing to pounce, as an arrow came flying by, hitting the wildern at the exact spot in its chest to penetrate through and pierce its heart. The mountain lioness froze, not daring to move for fear of alerting the hunter to her location. She did not want to become the hunter's second successful prey of the day.

She watched, mesmerized, as a human male appeared a few feet from the wildern and made his way over to it. He cleaned and dressed the carcass, leaving what wasn't needed for any animal that might wish to partake of it. Then he dragged the carcass away on a wooden sled.

Ashiri, the lioness, waited for some time to make sure the human had left the area. Then she headed out to the remains left behind and ate. Once she was satiated, she sniffed around. She picked up the human male's scent. It was fresh and clean, but with a hint of something she couldn't identify. It was intoxicating.

Ashiri had been without a mate for some time, so this alluring male scent called to her. She decided to follow it. She would be cautious, of course, until she learned more. If she spotted any signs of trouble, she could always turn around and head the other way.

Ashiri had followed the male to a small human village and had watched him from the shadows for three days now. He seemed to be proficient at hunting and otherwise caring for himself, but he also seemed private. He spent a lot of time alone in his dwelling, which was on the outskirts of the village, with no close neighbors. At least this was a good sign that he did not have a mate.

She wanted to approach him, but she noticed that he, and the humans he interacted with, all wore clothing. She hated clothing. Uncomfortable stuff. But she supposed it made sense for humans to wear it since they had no fur to cover them and protect them from the elements.

So she waited until dark to sniff around until she found some female clothing hanging to dry outside a dwelling. She quickly shifted to human form to grab it, since she did not want to tear it or dirty it. Then she ran off into the woods next to the village to put the clothing on and wait until morning.

The male had been visiting her in the woods every day for a month now. Ashiri felt they were becoming close. He always brought her little gifts. Sometimes it would be food made by bakers in his village. Sometimes it was new human clothing, which was good since she had none of her own. And sometimes, it was little wooden figures he had carved himself.

She did not have a house, of course, so she kept his gifts in a den she used when she needed shelter.

She had been quick to learn the human language, which was typical of her kind. Learning a language was always easy if it was that of a form she could shift to.

"Ashiri, my dear, come here," said the man, whose name, she had learned, was Morcant.

She walked over to him, a bright smile on her face. He reached out to cup her cheek. His thumb stroked her cheekbone. "So beautiful," he whispered.

"I know you are a shifter, my love. I always find you here, in the woods, and the only clothes you wear are the ones I've brought for you. Do you not trust me enough to tell me what your animal is yet?"

"I will not tell you." Ashiri saw a flicker of disappointment, and something else she couldn't quite identify, cross his face before he quickly cleared his expression.

"If you really want to know, I will show you." She was still smiling, but inside her stomach was fluttering with nerves. She knew this was the best way to test him, to see if it really mattered to him or not that she was not human. So, she took a deep breath and shifted.

"You are a mountain lion," Morcant said in an awed voice. He was smiling, and he had not so much as flinched when she shifted.

Then Ashiri shifted again, but not to her human form.

"And a wolf?" he asked. His voice now betrayed some confusion. She shifted again.

"And a bear," he said. Ashiri watched as his expression changed from confusion to realization. A huge smile spread across his face.

"You are an all-shifter," he said, his excitement clear. Then, under his breath, as if he were talking to himself, he added, "This is even better than I thought."

His words were confusing, but she could not question him about it since she was not in human form. She did not want to shift back right now because the only clothes she had brought here today now lay in shreds on the ground. She did not really care about nudity, but she knew humans did, and did not want to offend Morcant.

And anyway, she was just happy that he seemed to be pleased and not frightened or disapproving.

Ashiri was so blissfully happy. Morcant had asked her to be his wife, and she had agreed. He also asked her to move to his dwelling near the human village. He explained it was only right since she was to be his bride. Today was the day she would see his home for the first time. Today, his home would become hers as well.

They walked hand-in-hand through the doorway of his large stone cottage. She walked to the center of the room and slowly spun around. It was a large room that had a cooking area and hearth on one wall and shelves lined with books on the opposite wall. On the third wall, there were two doors.

There was a small round table with two chairs close to the hearth, and two long wooden tables covered with glass bottles and vials just in front of the bookshelves. A smaller table stood between them with books, both opened and closed, strewn across it.

Ashiri had explored villages and towns in human form before, so she recognized most of the things in the room. However, she had been raised in the woods and the mountains and had lived there all her life. Morcant's home was immensely different from the caves and dens she had known, but she found it appealing nonetheless.

"You like books?" she asked Morcant. He nodded to her without speaking.

"I never learned to read," she said. "Not much need for books and reading in the wilds."

"I will read to you," Morcant said. "Perhaps you will learn."

She looked at him, and when she saw his sincere expression, she nodded and smiled.

"Come," he said, holding his hand out to her. "Let's have a drink to celebrate your first day in your new home." He led her over to the small table and pulled the chair out for her. She wasn't sure what he was doing at first until he gestured at her to sit. Then he went to a small cupboard and took out two cups and a bottle of some liquid. He sat across from her and poured a small amount into each cup before handing her one.

"To your new home, and to the future," Morcant said, and he lifted his drink to his lips.

Ashiri did the same, lifting her cup and drinking deeply of the delicious draught. When she finished, she noticed Morcant had lowered his cup without drinking.

Ashiri blinked slowly. Her eyelids suddenly felt very heavy. She looked across to Morcant and realized her vision was blurring.

"Morcant," she said, "there is something wro—"

Everything went black.

Ashiri awoke slowly. The first thing she noticed was that she was cold. How odd. Usually, her fur kept her warm enough.

She was also lying on a hard, uncomfortable surface. Her eyes fluttered open, and she took in unfamiliar surroundings. This was not the forest, nor was it her den. It was a small room with stone walls. Where was she?

She tried to get up to look around, and she felt a peculiar heaviness weighing her down. She lowered her gaze to look at herself and *noticed two things: she was in human form, and there were heavy metal cuffs around her neck, wrists, and ankles. What was going on? Where was she? She tried to think back to the last thing she could recall before waking here, and suddenly it hit her.*

Morcant. He must have put something in her drink.

As the full weight of that betrayal sank in, Ashiri's heart broke. She clutched her two hands to her chest and wailed mournfully. She had never known pain such as this. Had never realized that the humans were capable of such deceit. She did not want to believe that the man she loved was capable of such duplicity. However, all the evidence suggested he was.

Morcant must have been close enough to hear the sounds of her sorrow because, suddenly, he was at the door.

Filled with pain and heartache so heavy that she found it hard to breathe, Ashiri looked up at him from where she sat on the cold ground and asked, "Why? You said that you loved me. That you needed me."

"Oh, but I do need you, my dear. In fact, I need you so badly that I was not willing to risk you refusing to cooperate, then shifting and running off."

Ashiri shook her head as she continued to clutch at her chest. She was now rocking back and forth.

"This is not right. Not right," she muttered. "What could be important enough to take another's freedom?"

Even though she wasn't really expecting an answer to her question, Morcant pulled up a chair that was near the door and sat himself in front of her.

"I am so glad you asked, my pet," he said. "Tell me, do you know what I am?"

"A treacherous man with a soul as black as midnight on a cloud-filled night?"

"Oh come, come. Don't be so dramatic," he said. "I am a human, yes, but I am also a sorcerer."

Ashiri looked up at him sharply and pinned him with a questioning gaze.

"All those books and bottles upstairs? Research," he said.

"Research for what?" Ashiri asked.

He regarded her for a moment before answering. "Tell me, Ashiri, do you know why shifters, seers, and elves live so much longer than humans?"

Ashiri shook her head in the negative.

"It's because of the magic of the realm. My theory is that, in the very beginning, we all started out the same. Then, whether the humans lost our magic, or the other species gained theirs, the result is that those who live close to the edges of our realm, on the island's coastlines, have no magic, while those who remained close to our source of magic are made from more. The ability to shift, the extra-long lives—these are all because of the magic of our realm.

"Yet here I am, a rare human sorcerer, and a powerful one at that, if I say so myself. And even though I can wield magic, draw in

magical energy, and bend it to my will, I am condemned to a short human lifespan."

"But how do you know this? You cannot be certain how long you will live."

"You're right, to a degree. I cannot be completely certain. Yet, for the most part, I age at almost the same rate as other humans. A little slower, it seems, but from my observations, I estimate I will gain a couple of decades at the most. Why should the other magical species, who are little more than wild animals, get to live for centuries, sometimes close to a millennium, when I, a human *sorcerer, get only a century or two?"*

"I do not question the will of the Universe."

"Well, I do!" he snapped. Ashiri jumped at his sudden anger. "I do," he repeated more calmly. He leaned forward as he spoke, his eyes wild and fierce.

Ashiri cringed back at the vehemence in his voice. He was obviously mad. She needed to be careful of her words.

"I challenge the will of the Universe," Morcant continued. "I will bend the rules to my will, just as I bend magical energy to do my bidding."

The table behind him lifted into the air in a demonstration of his words.

"And you, my dear"—he gave her a wicked smirk— "you are going to help me." The table dropped with a thud behind him.

"Imagine my delight when you showed me you are an all-shifter. An all-shifter! The rarest of all shifter species and, I am willing to

wager, the most magical of them all. You are going to help me with my experiments, and we will not stop until I find a way to extend my life.

"So, you can see why your cooperation was too important to leave to your will. I may never find another all-shifter in my human lifetime, and this is too important to leave to chance."

Ashiri did not respond. She just stared at him with disdain, her mind already thinking of ways to escape. Then, almost as if he had read her mind, he stood and spoke again.

"Do not bother trying to escape. Your manacles and collar are magically enhanced. They are incredibly strong, with no visible locks to pick. And I guarantee you, they are strong enough that, if you try to shift, you will be strangled long before they break."

Talwyn woke briefly, heart pounding, as the dream-vision drifted away. She had the thought that the human man in her vision was vaguely familiar just before she was quickly pulled under again.

CHAPTER TWENTY-SIX

Puzzles & Celebrations

"You look troubled, Talwyn," Dreyken said from right beside her. She hadn't even noticed him arriving. "Are you okay?"

"Not really, no."

"Did you not sleep well? Did something happen?"

"Well, I slept, though I wouldn't say well."

"Nightmares again?" Dreyken asked.

"No. Visions, actually."

"You saw something concerning?"

"I don't know. I don't know how everything fits." Frustration laced her voice. "That's the problem. As a seer, I am not used to operating in the dark like this. And those rare times I have been confused in the past, I've had Berinon to confer with. He's very good at clarifying things. Too bad I didn't have this vision before we saw him in the forest."

"Why don't you share your thoughts with me?" Dreyken suggested. "Maybe I can help you figure things out."

Talwyn considered him for a moment, then nodded. "In my dream-vision last night, I saw a female shifter. An all-shifter."

Dreyken's brow lifted in surprise. "An all-shifter? So your vision was of the past, then."

"It must have been. According to our histories, no one has seen an all-shifter for, what? About fifteen hundred years?"

"That matches what our histories say as well."

"So now the question is, what does this vision from the past have to do with what's happening in the realm now?"

"Could it be completely unrelated?"

"It's possible, of course, but not likely. Most of the time, when we have visions, they turn out to be significant to what is happening in the realm. Even when they're of past or future events."

Dreyken was quiet for a moment before asking, "What else did this vision show?"

"The all-shifter woman had been captured by a human sorcerer. He was talking to her about using her for experiments to extend his life."

There was more thoughtful silence from Dreyken.

"Well," he said after a few minutes, "there is one link at least. There was a sorcerer involved."

"Yes, but what does a long-dead sorcerer's experiments have to do with what is happening now?"

"Could this be the same sorcerer who is behind what is going on currently? Is it possible his experiments succeeded, and he found a way to extend his life?"

"What I have seen would have happened fifteen hundred years ago, probably more. It doesn't seem possible. Then again, I certainly don't know everything there is to know about the use of magic, and I have no idea what his experiment was. So I guess anything is possible."

"What if the histories were wrong?" Dreyken said. "Maybe there were all-shifters around after the last recorded ones. If that's the case, then what you saw might not have been that long ago."

Talwyn huffed out a frustrated breath. "Right now, we have many questions and few answers."

"Maybe what you have seen will become clearer as time goes on and events come to pass."

"Let's hope it's not too late by then."

That evening, Dreyken stood in front of the window of his room at Southgate castle. From here, he could look out over the expanse of land that sat between Southgate and the Dragonburn Mountains. The sky was darkening. It had been less than a week since he had last seen his mountain fortress, yet with everything that had happened in between, it felt like a lifetime. He hoped all was well there, and that Drarcio had not run into any more trouble.

Southgate was too far away from the mountains for him to see anything that would hint at the state of things, of course. Yet he could not help but to look in that direction. Of course, it was also important that he himself, as dragon lord, be here at Southgate, as it would show respect and care to the fallen king and his family. He hoped it would help to build positive relations with the humans here.

His people were on the cusp of a significant change. The entire realm of Sterrenvar was. He needed to be strong enough to lead his people through it. If things went well, the Stone Dragons and the people of Southgate would become allies. Maybe there could even be free travel and interaction between the two communities. It could help solve many issues. Maybe some of his people could even find mates here at Southgate.

Which led to another, more personal reason for staying. He would not leave here unless Talwyn was leaving with him.

Strange how it was mere weeks ago that he and his people didn't give a second thought to Southgate and its fate. Or the fate of anywhere else in the realm, for that matter. All they thought about, all they cared about, was their own people. The only time his mind turned outward to the realm was when he thought about the advantages of finding a mate outside of the Stone Dragons. Even then, it was for selfish reasons: to strengthen the bloodlines of his people, and because he could not find a female particularly suited to him within the mountain.

Talwyn was right. He had lived his life in a daze, just going through the motions. Like she said, his people deserved better. And the realm deserved better from his people. From the time he carried her into his mountain, he had felt a change in himself. It was like he had awoken from a hazy dream, and he saw his people, his realm, and himself fully, for the first time.

He owed so much to her.

His thoughts were interrupted by the sound of soft footfalls approaching behind him. His Talwyn.

"I'm ready."

He turned to her and smiled when he saw her. The healers had changed her out of her bloody clothes after he had brought her to them, and Iniri had taken the clothes to clean and repair. This was what she was wearing now—her clean leathers. The major difference was that her hair was left loose to fall down her back. Whenever she hunted, traveled, or fought, she kept it tied back in a braid. He liked it best like this—the way it was the first time he'd seen her.

"You look beautiful."

"Yes, well, all I did was clean up and put my old clothes back on. I know that many of the females here dress up for special occasions, but I don't really feel comfortable in their style of clothing. Of course, as a seer, I can blend into any culture when I have to but—"

He interrupted her with a kiss. "You are perfect just the way you are." He reached out to take her hand. "Come. Let's go down."

When they entered the great hall, Dreyken stopped and looked around. A huge smile formed on his face as he took in the sight before him. The Southgate humans and the Stone Dragons who supported them in battle were all intermingled. Talking with each other, laughing, enjoying each other's company. There was a large, rectangular, wooden table that could seat probably two dozen people in the center of the room. Many other tables were also set up throughout the large space.

"Talwyn," he heard a voice calling from his right, and he turned to see Lugus approaching them.

"I am so glad to see you up and about." Lugus grasped Talwyn's forearm in greeting.

"I'm so very sorry about your father, Lugus." Talwyn's voice shook when she spoke. Dreyken squeezed her hand.

"Thank you." Lugus gave her a smile tinged with a hint of sadness. "Here in Southgate, it is the custom to celebrate the life of the one who has passed. Come, you will sit at the main table with my family." As he led them to their places, the other guests made their way to their seats as well.

Lugus, who was now King of Southgate, sat at the head of the table. To his right was Queen Boudicca, and to his left sat Princess Keeva.

Lugus sat Dreyken next to the queen, and Talwyn next to him. Across from them, Adrio sat next to Keeva, and Iniri next to him. The rest of the guests at the main table were composed of the other Dragon-folk who had taken part in the battle and the king's captains.

Since Talwyn had been unconscious and missed some happenings, Dreyken leaned in to explain the biggest news to her. "The role of leader could have been passed down to Queen Boudicca, of course, but with her age, she let it pass to Lugus. His father had already been grooming him for some time, apparently."

The table was laden with many kinds of food—roast pig and various other meats, breads, fruits and vegetables. Anything one could ask for. Guests passed the dishes around and each person loaded their plates with the foods that interested them. As Lugus had said, this was really a celebration of the life of the king, and of the Southgate soldier who had fallen. Dreyken learned his name was Peadar. He was a young but valiant soldier who had given his life protecting a Stone Dragon from attack by a snowbeast.

Friends, family, and acquaintances of the king and his fallen soldier told stories about them. Sometimes the stories told of their fierceness and bravery. Other times, they told of odd predicaments they got themselves into. Whatever the story was, it was clear that they were well-known, loved, and appreciated.

There were many tears and much laughter this night. Dreyken thought that this was a lovely way to celebrate loved ones who had passed back into the Universe. Looking around, he noticed that Talwyn and his own people seemed to enjoy the evening as much as he did.

About an hour into the festivities, Helsi came to speak with them.

She first addressed the royal family. "Thank you, King Lugus, Queen Boudicca, and Princess Keeva, for your generosity during my stay here, but it is time I return to the Dragonburn Mountains."

"We understand," Lugus responded. "I thank you for coming to stand with us when your fallen mate awaits his own parting ceremony back in the mountain. It must not have been easy for you to be here while we celebrate the lives of our own fallen."

"I am glad I was here for this, your majesty. It gives me a different, quite positive, point of view to consider."

Dreyken stood and clasped Helsi by the forearm. "Safe travels back to the mountain, Helsi. I am not sure I will be back for Norshan's ceremony. If I don't make it, I will celebrate with you when I return."

"Thank you, Lord Dreyken."

Talwyn now stood and embraced Helsi. "Thank you for everything, Helsi," Dreyken heard her say. "I will remember your words of wisdom. Take care of yourself."

"You as well, my friend." With that, Helsi turned and headed out.

Dreyken looked at Talwyn with his eyebrows raised. "Words of wisdom?"

She just smiled at him and shrugged, then sat down once again.

CHAPTER TWENTY-SEVEN

Links

It was hours later when the festivities finally wound down. Once it was quiet and most people had left, Lugus addressed Dreyken and Talwyn.

"I realize it is late, but my family would like to show you something while we are all here together." He stood, and Keeva stood with him.

"Of course." Dreyken rose from his chair and Talwyn followed suit.

Lugus turned to Adrio and Iniri. "You are welcome to join us as well." They looked to Dreyken, and he nodded his approval.

"Are you coming, Mother?" Keeva asked Queen Boudicca.

"I think I will head back to my chambers. I am old, and all this activity has me worn out. Besides, I think I am ready for some time alone right now."

"Of course, Mother." Keeva embraced her. "Be well, and we will see you in the morning."

Lugus and Keeva walked out of the great hall into the corridor. Dreyken, Talwyn, Adrio and Iniri followed.

Lugus spoke to them as they walked. "War is never a good thing, my friends. Yet even in the darkest times, good can be found. I think the good in this battle is the opportunity it gives us for our people to come together.

"My family and I have discussed it, and we would like to extend an open invitation to the Stone Dragons to come and go as they please here in Southgate. We would like to work out trade between our peoples, and you can have a safe place to visit where you wouldn't have to hide who you are. You would be welcome to shift freely here with us."

"I am honored, King Lugus." Dreyken was truly touched by this gesture. "I would very much like it if our peoples interacted freely with one another."

He glanced down at Talwyn and she beamed back at him.

"Good." Lugus nodded. "We can work out all the details later. Right now, I want to show you something, so you can see for yourself the sincerity of my offer. Plus, it is good for allies to know something of one another, don't you think?"

Dreyken didn't get to answer this question for, as he asked it, Lugus pushed open an enormous door to a magnificent room. It was more than a room, though. That word wasn't nearly adequate. It was more like a very large gallery. As they walked inside, the three Stone Dragons, and even Talwyn, stared around them in awe. The room was very long, wide, and tall. Paintings covered the walls from floor to ceiling and corner to corner.

Most of these were framed canvases of various sizes, but there were also several tapestries. Dreyken looked up and noticed that, high above him, the ceiling was painted in relief. There were images of great battles and feats of heroism, with golden accents and curving arches.

"Your father mentioned this room when we first arrived." Wonder colored the tone of his voice. "These paintings are your histories, aren't they?"

"They are," Keeva answered.

Dreyken stepped forward to look closer and noticed that they seemed to be in chronological order from left to right, top to bottom. He turned in a slow circle and noticed there was still space left on the wall behind them.

"How far back do they go?" Iniri asked.

"The paintings in this room depict events as far back as the Battle of the Gate, three thousand years ago," Keeva said. "To the very beginning of Southgate. To the reason the gate towns were created."

"Of course, none of the paintings in here is that old in reality," Lugus explained. "The best artists of each age repaint them as close to the original as possible every generation. That way, our history is never lost."

"And these pictures give you enough information?" Adrio asked. "Do you not worry that they can be misread or misunderstood?"

"Even the most wordy and descriptive book can be misread," Keeva answered. "The artwork in here is actually very detailed and precise. Our artists are very talented and conscientious. Whenever we add something new, they interview many witnesses to each event, so they have more than one point of view. A very observant eye could discern all the significant details. It is not just the bigger picture you see when you stand back. Come, take a closer look."

Keeva and Lugus led them to an easel set up in a corner of the room. On it, there sat what looked to be a recently completed painting.

"Our current artist paints outside most of the time," Lugus said. "He talks about how sunlight is the best light to paint by. He finished this painting just this morning. It's amazing he had time to gather accounts and complete the image. The paint isn't completely dry yet, which is why it is sitting here. But once it is dry, I will find a place of honor for it on the wall."

Dreyken moved closer so he could inspect the artwork. It took him a moment to register what he was seeing. Once he did, his mouth dropped open. He heard Talwyn gasp beside him and knew that she saw it, too.

The painting was both terrible and wonderful at the same time.

It was terrible because it depicted a bloody and violent battle. Dragons and ainmith battled it out in the sky. Humans and demonkin fought below. Demonkin bodies lay broken and lifeless on the ground. There was a Dragon-folk blasting fire into the open maw of a snowbeast. There were archers on the castle wall firing arrows at the demonkin entering at the back of the fray. Dreyken let his eyes drift over the painting. There were even individual battles depicted in what one might consider the background. He had a feeling that there was a lot of accuracy in these representations of individual melees.

The painting was wonderful because it depicted humans and Dragon-folk fighting together, side by side, against a common enemy. It showed a dragon taking the blast of ice breath from a snowbeast while protecting a human. It showed a human archer firing an arrow at an ainmith when it was trying to attack a dragon from behind.

The painting was wonderful because it showed a newfound respect, understanding, and camaraderie between two very different peoples who, once upon a time, were enemies but were now clearly friends.

Once Talwyn had had a good look at the painting of the battle they'd recently endured, she moved aside so the others could get a better look. Then she wandered off to the left, looking at the paintings in reverse-chronological order. When she was almost back at the beginning, her eyes caught on one specific portrait. She looked at it more carefully. It took her a moment to realize that there was something familiar about the seemingly human male depicted there. She walked toward it slowly, taking in his features.

Thoughts and memories drifted through her mind as recognition came about like puzzle pieces clicking together.

Her dream-vision. *Click.*

The evil sorcerer at the chamber. *Click.*

"What is it, Talwyn?" Dreyken asked from behind her. She jumped at the sound of his voice. She hadn't realized he was so near. He moved closer to her. So close that they were almost touching, and she could feel his warmth.

She, however, was feeling quite chilled, with gooseflesh rising all over her skin and the tiny hairs on her forearms standing on end.

"Lugus," she called, her gaze never leaving the portrait.

Lugus turned from where he was standing with the others and made his way over to Talwyn and Dreyken.

"Yes?"

"Who is this in this painting?"

"That is a painting of Azedel, the sorcerer who first attempted to open the Great Gate three thousand years ago, so he could set a demon army loose upon the realm."

Of course, Talwyn knew who Azedel was, but she was too distracted to point it out.

"It is said that this is a very close likeness. The original artist knew him personally and each artist who has repainted it since has done so painstakingly, taking care to get it as close to the original as possible."

"What's wrong, Talwyn?" Dreyken reached out and ran his palm along her arm.

"Do you remember what I told you about my dream-vision? The one with the human sorcerer who captured the all-shifter?"

"Of course."

"Well, the male in this painting looks similar to the human sorcerer in that vision. Very similar. Close enough to be related."

"Are you sure?" Despite his words, his voice showed alarm, not doubt.

"Definitely. The hair and eye color, the shape of the eyes, nose, and jaw." Her hand shook as she pointed out the features. "They are definitely related." If not the same person.

Then Talwyn spun around to face Dreyken and Lugus. "And that's not all. I glimpsed the Dark Sorcerer, the one the demonkin call their emperor, back in the clearing we tracked Athnie to. I only saw him for a moment when the sunlight hit him as he turned.

This only clicked to me when I saw this painting. What I recall of the Dark Sorcerer's features matches this painting completely."

"How is that possible?" asked Lugus.

"Are you saying there's an evil plot to take over the realm that's been passed down from generation to generation within the same family for three thousand years or more?" Dreyken did not sound disbelieving. Rather, he sounded shocked and more than a little concerned. "Could our evil sorcerer today be the great-great-great-great-great-grandson of Azedel?"

Talwyn thought about this. For shifters and seers, three thousand years would only be three or four generations. For humans, however, it would be closer to thirty-eight generations.

She and Dreyken had discussed the possibility that the Dark Sorcerer and the sorcerer in her dream might be the same person. That he somehow figured out how to extend his life. But here was proof of someone who looked like him thousands of years ago. Could he have lived this long? Or was the Dark Sorcerer a descendant who just looked remarkably similar to his ancestor? Was this even possible?

Talwyn turned back to the painting once more and let her gaze travel the lines of the man's features. Then she finally answered Dreyken's question.

"Maybe."

But she feared it might be worse than that.

Glossary of Terminology

Aragus: One of the two planets that line up with the moon at intervals to cause The Great Alignment

Azedel: An evil and powerful sorcerer who discovered how to use the power at the hub of the ley lines to create a magical gate that would allow demons from another realm to pass over into the realm of Sterrenvar

Axes: Points where two ley lines join, resulting in increased magical power

Chephus: One of the two planets that line up with the moon at intervals to cause The Great Alignment

Crimsonleaf leaf: Healing leaf

Crimsonleaf tree: A very tall tree with green leaves over most of the foliage and capped with dark red leaves at the top. All its leaves have healing properties, but the red ones are more potent.

Dragonburn Mountains: A mountain range to the south of the Sacred Forest and outside of the magical ley lines

Demonkin: Descendants of demons that bred with humans who lived to the north of the realm

Demons: Evil beings originally from another realm that were brought through the Great Gate by Azedel to help form his army and subjugate the land

Dream-visions: True visions of the past or present, and true or possible visions of the future that the seers receive as they sleep, when their minds are most open to the messages of the universe

Sacred Forest: A large, dense forest range found within the magical ley lines at the center of the realm of Sterrenvar, and home to most of the magical races of Sterrenvar.

Galanite: A very strong and light metal found beneath the Dragonburn Mountains; very useful for fabricating armor and weaponry

Gates (Gate Towns): Eastgate, Westgate, Southgate, Northgate were fortresses built atop the keystones to protect them. They eventually developed into castle towns.

Great Gate: The gate formed from magically imbued, large, rectangular, and upright stones placed in a circular pattern (similar to Stonehenge) on top of the hub of the ley lines. This gate stabilizes the power at the hub, allowing a portal to be opened between realms, but can only be used during the Great Alignment. Azedel created the Great Gate with the intention of freeing demons to cross over and form his army, which he would then use to subjugate the realm of Sterrenvar and all its people.

Guardians: Those assigned the responsibility of protecting the realm and/or the keystones

Hub: The center of the diamond shape of the ley lines at which point more lines from the four axes join to result in markedly increased magical power (see also, The Source)

Inner-sight: The ability to see into one's physical self and manipulate the elements present there in order to heal or change appearance

Keystone: One of four stones imbued with magical properties meant to act as a deterrent and obstacle to anyone hoping to misuse the power of the ley lines. The keystones are intended to have a dampening effect on the amount of magical power flowing to the hub and, therefore, the Great Gate.

Ley lines: Invisible lines of magic that join at four points (axes), forming roughly the shape of a diamond. More of these lines travel from the axes to the center (the hub).

Protectors: Those assigned the responsibility of protecting their villages, towns, and people

Seers: A race of people of the realm of Sterrenvar who have the gift of Sight, with images of the past, present, and future coming to them in dream-visions. They are also capable of seeing into their own physical selves, an ability referred to as inner-sight.

Sight: (capitalized) The ability to receive images of the past, present, or future during dream-visions

Seer champions: Seer warriors trained with the possibility of eventually becoming guardians of the four Gates and their keystones. Until that time, the provide support for the guardians when needed.

Folk: Beings that can shift between human and animal form at will. More human than animal, their spirits and physical forms contain elements of both. They share a strong kinship with the true animal they share form with.

Snowbeast: A large animal that lives mostly in the northern mountain range of Sterrenvar called the Pilcier Peaks. It has matted white fur, and is similar in shape to a hyena, with its front legs slightly longer than the back, thus making the shoulders taller than the rump. On an average snowbeast, its body is as broad as a human male laying horizontal and it is twice as tall as the average human male. The snowbeast has an icy breath that can freeze a man solid in seconds. Rumor has it that they have been known to stomp their victims after freezing them, thereby shattering them.

Sterrenvar: The name of the realm in which this story is set

Thanks for Reading!

I hope you enjoyed
A Realm of Seers and Shifters.

If you would be kind enough to leave a review
on Amazon or wherever you purchased the book,
it would help make a big difference to how this
book is represented in the algorithms. The better
represented it is, the easier it will be for other readers
to find it.

A huge thank you in advance!

Your Free Book is Waiting

— ·— —·—

The Guardians of Sterrenvar is a companion short story collection to the *A Trial of Kingdoms* series. The short stories can be enjoyed as stand alones, or they can be read to deepen readers' understanding of the main characters and how they are connected to one another.

Read about Talwyn Survalor's "ghost," learn about how the friendship between King Nele and Maelona Mistreaver began, and see the hints of the threats faced in the main series stirring many years ago!

If you like mythical shifters, courageous heroes, and dark prophecies, then you'll love these spellbinding adventures.

Get a free copy of the short story collection here:

Also By Sherry Leclerc

<u>A Trial of Kingdoms:</u>

A Realm of Seers and Shifters (Book 1)

Demons and Damsels (Book 1.5 - *A Trial of Kingdoms* novelette)

A Tribe of Dragons and Dreamers (Book 2) July 2023

Book 3 TBA

Book 4 TBA

The Guardians of Sterrenvar (*A Trial of Kingdoms* short story collection) - **FREE to newsletter subscribers**

<u>Dragon Flightmasters:</u>

Shendahli (Book 1)September 2023

Ori (Book 2)TBA

Rixtan (Book 3)TBA

Rafe (Book 4)TBA

About the Author

Sherry Leclerc is a Fictionary certified StoryCoach editor, Fictionary content creator, certified copyeditor, educator, and independent author of fantasy and sci-fi books. She also writes sci-fi romance under a pen name and has planned a series of nonfiction books with helpful information on writing and editing.

She is the owner/operator of Ternias Publishing & Editorial Services, through which she offers various editorial services and writing and publishing advice. She also has a YouTube vlog focused on providing information on writing, editing, and author tools and resources to new and aspiring writers.

Sherry happily resides in a chaotic household in Sydney, Nova Scotia with her husband, two sons, dog, cat, and two birds.

If you wish to keep up to date on new releases, promotions, and giveaways, please subscribe to my newsletter by checking out the sign-up form on my website.

You Can Reach the Author at:

Website: https://sherryleclerc.com/

Facebook: https://www.facebook.com/SherryLeclercAuthor/

Twitter:
https://twitter.com/sleclercauthor

Instagram:
https://www.instagram.com/sherryleclercauthor/

TikTok: https://www.tiktok.com/@sherryleclercauthor

www.ingramcontent.com/pod-product-compliance
Lightning Source LLC
Chambersburg PA
CBHW061210190726
48288CB00001B/128